Realms of Darkover

Darkover® Anthology 16

Edited by

Deborah J. Ross

The Marion Zimmer Bradley Literary Works Trust
PO Box 193473
San Francisco, CA 94119
www.mzbworks.com

Contents

INTRODUCTION

by Deborah J. Ross

As I began work on this, the third Darkover anthology I have been privileged to edit (the first two being *Stars of Darkover* and *Gifts of Darkover*), I reflected on the title and its various meanings. The title came first, in the contrary custom of publishing, and so needed to be both flexible and evocative. As has often been observed, the more narrowly defined the theme of an anthology, the lesser the likelihood of receiving enough creative, insightful, beautifully executed—in short, brilliant—stories. At the same time, an utterly bland title fails to arouse the reader's interest. I liked the idea of inviting talented authors to play in the "realms" of Darkover because that could mean so many things. One source defines a realm as an area of responsibility or rule, deriving from the Old French *reaume*, probably from the Latin *regalimen*, from *regalis*, of or belonging to a *rex* or king. Another refers to a community or territory over which a sovereign rules; it is commonly used to describe a kingdom or other monarchical or dynastic state. The word is also used for a sphere of activity or influence. So much for definitions; writers are notoriously adept at coming up with their own story ideas, performing a bit of ritualistic and arcane hand-waving in the general direction of the definition, and proceeding according to their own creative guides.

Which is just fine with me.

In fact, I much prefer that submissions *not* be twisted into five-dimensional pretzel shapes trying to fit a theme or title. Sometimes, of course, the consequence of an author haring off after a story that has the bit between its teeth and is not answering at all to direction is that it no longer fits within even the broad and somewhat elastic bounds of what I am looking for.

In that case, the result is still to be preferred because the story is true to *itself.*

"Realms" lends itself easily to Darkovan Domains or the Hundred Kingdoms that preceded them, and also to the various historical eras—realms of time as well as geography and politics. It also suggests fields of imagination—realms of *laran*, for instance, both those described by Marion Zimmer Bradley and those newly imagined or interpreted by the authors. As in the previous two Darkover anthologies, I have looked for stories that do not necessarily adhere with scholarly meticulousness to the letter of established canon—an impossibility given the inconsistencies of Marion's own novels—but are faithful to the *spirit* of this marvelous world.

Author and contributor Rosemary Edghill writes, "Each generation gets the Darkover it needs." She points out that the books written by Marion in the 1960s "were all about equalizing and liberalizing sex roles, and the whole Cleindori/Sharra arc was an exploration of whether or not you should throw out the baby with the bathwater: the Tower customs were strangling and stagnating and needed to change—but who decides that? And what do you change, and what do you just give up? And then there's the exploration of colonialism (from both sides!) as the Darkovans fight to retain their heritage and their unique identity at the same time that Terran paternalism wants to solve all of Darkover's problems for it in their traditional cookie-cutter way. So Darkover is, in the end, a kind of Harry Potter mirror of the *zeitgeist*, reflecting not just our beliefs, but our hopes as well."

Needless to say, I was pleased to receive stories that touch on and explore "realms of whatever issue defines our times." Often the stories complement and reflect one another, in the way of "great minds thinking alike." In this vein, Diana L. Paxson continues the story of a transgender woman who joins the Renunciates in "Housebound," and Robin Wayne Bailey tackles drug addiction in "Sea of Dreams." Shariann Lewitt ("Tainted Meat") involves a shape-shifter, but also the bond between a *laran*-Gifted swordsman and an owl, reminiscent of the woman-hawk relationship in *Hawkmistress!* In "The Fifth Moon," Ty

Nolan's shape-shifters are quite a different sort, shedding new light on one of Darkover's intelligent, nonhuman races, as does Leslie Fish's "Old Purity." Other, sometimes unusual forms of *laran* play pivotal roles in "Sudden Tempest," by Deborah Millitello and "The Snowflake Fallacy," by Michael Spence.

This anthology contains a number of stories in which the climate of Darkover—in particular its heavy snowfalls—is to be reckoned with. "Realms" expands to include seasons! While rescuers battle inclement winter conditions in "A Walk in the Mountains" by Margaret L. Carter and Leslie Roy Carter, Jane M. H. Bigelow offers a surprising solution to such travel in "Snow Dancing."

In a beautiful example of story mirroring, "Stormcrow" by Rosemary Edghill and Rebecca Fox, and "Impossible Tasks" by Marella Sands each delve deeply and compassionately into the resilience of the human spirit in the face of horrific odds. The heroine of Barb Caffrey's "Fiona, Court Clerk in Training" also faces daunting obstacles, but does so with the determination typical of so many Darkovan characters and with a sense of humor.

Whether new twists on old themes or the reflection of contemporary concerns, I hope you will find these stories as delightful and thought-provoking as I did. Darkover is indeed alive and well in such capable hands!

Deborah J. Ross
Boulder Creek CA

TAINTED MEAT

by Shariann Lewitt

The ability to telepathically link with a bird—natural or mechanical—and thereby experience the exhilaration of flight and the capacity to "spy" at distance, has long enchanted readers of fantasy. Such creatures played a pivotal role in one of Marion Zimmer Bradley's early explorations of a Darkover-like world, *The Falcons of Narabedla*. Later she developed the idea more fully in *Hawkmistress*. Usually the bird serves as eyes and wings for its human master. Here Shariann Lewitt offers a different interpretation, however, one in which the personality and instincts of the bird influence the man as well, and the resolution of the story hinges on mutual respect between two different species.

Shariann Lewitt has published seventeen books and over forty short stories, including "Wedding Embroidery" in Stars of Darkover and "Memory" in Gifts of Darkover. When not writing she teaches at MIT, studies flamenco dance, and is accounted reasonably accomplished at embroidery. Her expertise with birds arises in part from being the devoted servant of two parrots.

Gerell MacAran had been shocked to be summoned to Danilo Syrtis's quarters in Comyn Castle, next to King Regis's own. Syrtis, the King's paxman and acknowledged partner, was a powerful man in his prime. He moved with a swordsman's grace, but years of administration and burdens had left their marks on his face. And he, Gerell, only five years out of the cadets and newly departed from his training at Hali Tower, could not imagine what his kinsman wanted of him. He had not thought that he'd disgraced his family when he finished his advanced healer training at Hali. He had the talent for it and so had

8

continued after most young Comyn left. He had thought of becoming a healer; it would suit him. And he spent extra effort to learn a great deal about sword wounds and poisons, for the thought of being a healer attached to an Academy of Arms appealed to him. In the future. Maybe.

He wasn't quite sure what he wanted just now, but he would do almost any honorable work to avoid returning to his mother and three older brothers. He had no future at Hawkenvale, with Dyan and Everard both married with children already. He was the youngest, he cared little for farming, and his mother wanted to marry him off to some healthy farm girl who wanted babies. The notion of what faced him at home made him want to live in a small attic room alone and sell his sword for a living. Or maybe learn enough more to become a truly skilled healer. Or a kept boy. Anything but Hawkenvale.

Gerell found the small sitting room relaxed and comfortable, like a private office in the nice country house where he had grown up. It was rumored that the royal pair preferred these rooms, so much less formal and impersonal than the official Kings' Chambers. Wine, nuts and slices of cake sat on a tray in front of them, but neither touched the snacks. Gerell found that all hunger had fled at the summons from his very important distant cousin.

He had though he had been sent for because his mother had been distressed by his decision to stay in Thendara and find work for the Council. She could have called on Danilo Syrtis; their relationship was not close but she had been kind to him when they had been young. But instead, the King's paxman had begun with a discussion of the *Terranan* invitation to a demonstration of swordsmanship.

"Would you be interested, for the good of all of us?" Danilo Syrtis asked. "They have made the overture and we must respond in good faith, though many of our best will refuse."

Gerell nodded. "I would be happy to."

"Many people say we should not consider this exhibition since the Terranan use distance weapons. They do not understand honor," Syrtis continued. "But I think it is more complex than that, and that if we attempt to interact with them we will discover more about them."

"I agree, cousin," Gerell answered immediately. "Besides, I would like to learn more of their fighting styles, and no better way to do that than to actually fight."

"Without edged weapons," the King's closest companion stipulated. "Several of them have studied the sword and the request came not from their administration but from a group of the fighters themselves."

Gerell tried to keep his face neutral. No edged weapons, even if it was a demonstration, showed a distinct lack of understanding. "How many are there?"

Danilo smiled. "We need to find two more men and two women. I have already made a request at Thendara House for the women. For the men—I thought of you and hoped you would help me recruit the others. I was thinking of Orain Jadaine, but I wanted to ask you about him first."

Gerell had seen Orain only in passing since their relationship during their time as cadets had ended, and so far as he was concerned he had been a mere child at the time. "I think we should be fine. Whatever was between us is long over. I have the greatest respect for his skills with a sword, and I think he would be interested enough in Terran fighting styles to be willing to compete."

Danilo nodded. "I am very glad he would not be a problem for you. I hope he will agree. One of the Terran men is very tall. We should have someone to match his height. I was thinking of Allart Storn or Cisco Aillard."

Gerell considered them. Both were elegant stylists with their blades, and both were very tall. In fact, they were matched against each other so frequently that both had begun to refuse bouts. Everyone understood that they were bored fighting each other and would likely be intrigued to be matched with someone new. "I would ask Allart first, since he is easier to track down and I know he's in Thendara. Aillard could well be in the mountains now, and don't want to waste time if we don't need to."

"Excellent," Syrtis agreed. Now that the simple business was finished Danilo would finally approach the real subject of the meeting. After all, he really didn't need Gerell's advice about who to recruit. And while it was kind of him to ask about how things stood with Orain, he also knew that Gerell and Orain both would do as requested and manage their feelings if any remained. So there had to be some more important reason the King's paxman had specifically requested his presence.

"Bruno Sovenias has returned to Thendara," Danilo said. "You understand what that means?"

Gerell swallowed hard. "We need to find him."

"And kill him. And yesterday would not be soon enough," Danilo said. "But we need to do it discreetly."

"And you want me…" Gerell's voice trailed off, knowing the only possible conclusion.

"I am truly sorry to ask, kinsman. But very few have the skills to confront Sovenias, and fewer who could even possibly find him. Some say he's a shape shifter…"

"There are no shape shifters," Gerell said, more to reassure himself. "The very few with that Gift died out, and the rest of the Comyn made certain that particular ability had been thoroughly purged."

Danilo looked at the window, with its sweetly scented flowering vines scenting the intimate space. "So the history says. But. Still. It is possible that a Gift that appears to be eradicated can return. We have lost so much knowledge of genetics. But you know more than most, and you have some of the old strength as well."

Gerell knew he had no choice. Other swordsmen might have the skills to fight if Sovenias were only one of the greatest swordsmen of his generation. A very few of those had enough *laran* to track him. No other great fighter had spent as much time in a Tower as Gerell, not to mention the MacAran Gift.

There were no shape shifters. They had not existed for hundreds of years. But if there were, the animals were more sensitive than men to that particular deception. He would know from them if something that deeply wrong were around, and he would be able to spot it more quickly than anyone else.

Speed would be essential because Bruno Sovenias was a paid assassin with an unmatched record. He had already made an attempt on King Regis, which had only been thwarted by Danilo's quick thinking and quicker sword. But Sovenias never failed, or so he said, and he would not let this commission end in failure either.

"You are very young, cousin, and much of your time here has been at Hali. But it is nearly time for that to end in any case."

Gerell often felt—not quite stifled in the Tower, but he certainly was not fulfilled by his work there. The MacAran Gift was not only rare, but not suited to Tower training. Nor had he ever stopped working with the sword every day, and twice a tenday he attended Masters lessons and practices at the Academy of the Sword in Thendara, for that gift was as deep as his Gift for rapport with animals.

"Above all, we need to stop Sovenias. Are you willing take up this task? You know I have tried to do this myself, but Sovenias knows me. If not, will you at least lead me to him?"

Gerell looked the older man in the face and rose. "You had my agreement the moment you asked. I shall do anything I can to stop him. I assume that the *Terranan* competition is an excuse for me stay in Thendara."

"We will prepare quarters for you here," Syrtis said, but Gerell shook his head. "I will do better out in the city. If I were to stay here it would be obvious."

"You are right," Danilo agreed. "As you wish, then. Let me know where you are, and an aide will give you enough to cover your expenses."

"I can cover…" Gerell started to say, but Danilo put his hand up, cutting the younger man off. "If you want to consider yourself a hired sword, consider this a commission."

Gerell smiled for the first time that afternoon, which brought out his dimples and the cheerful sparkle in his eyes, for the truth was that he was most often of a cheerful and optimistic frame of mind. And while he knew finding Bruno Sovenias would be both difficult and dangerous, he was excited by the challenge.

Gerell MacAran lay on the bed in the attic he had settled in and had paid two tendays' rent, cash in advance. He had taken only two changes of clothes and his sword with him, so he had little to deposit in the one trunk under the window. But the bed had been clean, and the second room had a sturdy table where he could bring food or write, two good lamps, and two comfortable chairs. If the blanket was a little worn and the fabric on the chairs faded, that only made the place feel comfortable and homey. He had not grown up accustomed to riches and in the Tower his quarters were plain.

But he had the attic to himself and privacy was paramount. No one would walk in on him here while he searched. He hadn't seen any other place where he would be half so secluded from interruption. He considered his plan before he went to hunt Sovenias. He knew he couldn't use the MacAran Gift the way his ancestors could. Few people in recent time even had it in enough measure to do more than make them better trainers and riders, or hunters. What he had learned had been on his own, outside the Tower.

A bird would be best, he thought, a raptor that he could entice with an easy meal. That meant that he would have to find that meal himself. He went to the local market and looked over the meats available. Small rodents would be preferred food for the kind of hawk he thought to link to, and so he bought a small rabbit-horn that had already been skinned. Excited to begin the experiment, he returned to his attic room, threw the rabbit-horn onto a plate on the table, and pulled off his boots. Then he lay on the bed and pulled his starstone out of the small sack around his neck. This he took in his hands as he cast out to touch a bird in the vicinity.

Having a monitor would be better. Gerell admitted to a bit of unease, going out of his body without someone to monitor him and call him back if he went too long, if the silver thread attaching him to his physical form started to grow pale. There was no help for it though, and Danilo had spent enough Tower time to know what he had asked. But he agreed it was vital that

no one know that Bruno had returned. And so he cast himself
out, first seeing his own form on the bed, and then moved over
the streets to touch a winged consciousness. It was hard to work
through an unfamiliar animal. If he were to really develop the
MacAran Gift fully, he should bond deeply with a single
creature, a horse or hawk, one that was long lived. But the
MacAran Gift was not one meant for a Tower, and so he had
little opportunity at Hali. He felt for a mind compatible to his
own, one that would carry him willingly. He caressed the small
ones, calming them, letting them know of his kindly attentions.

If you come with me on this flight you will get much food, he
projected in images and feelings that birds would understand. He
sent out again and again as he sought a receptive mind, and then
he found a curious one who wanted to know more. He slid into
her mind so softly she could barely feel him. She was beautiful
and strong, and her mind was fixed on hunting. There were
babies in the nest to feed, or his offer of food would not tempt
her. Her feathers were ghostly pale and she could glide almost
soundlessly. Her hearing was so acute that she could identify the
heartbeat of a single tiny mouse running under his own height in
snow. Her great eyes saw through the dark clearly, so that full
daylight burned with its brightness.

They flew. He had flown with a raptor before, but never one
so silent, so vigilant. He saw as he had never seen, and he set her
a quest, a deep desire like the desire to feed her chicks. He did
not see Sovenias as an image, but more as a feeling of the man.
Birds have little sense of smell, so he sent the sound of Sovenias'
gait, his run and his walk and the rhythm of his sword and the
sound of it in the air. The great white bird perched on a branch
and turned her magnificent ears to one side and then the other.
Listening.

She had heard these sounds before, and recently. Gerell
carefully made them sound like food, and she understood the
hunt all too well. She had babies to feed, always hungry. She was
not particularly intelligent, but she had a fine memory for the
sound of prey. She listened, and amazed Gerell with what she
heard.

Through her he could hear a horse settling uneasily in a stable he could identify as a hostelry near the Renunciates' House. The bird dismissed that as of no interest (meaning she could not eat it) along with the pacing of a woman (he could tell a woman by the swish of her skirts) and the rustle of a breeze through the tops of trees throughout the city. Layer upon layer of sound changed his usual, quiet perception of the night. So much alive, so much moving, so much making sounds that he had never heard.

She flew the first night over the neighborhood but did not want to venture too far from her nest.

Gerell had wanted much more, but he knew the Sech owl had already tired and felt anxious about her chicks. Carefully he led her back to the window outside his room. She stood on the branch of a tree just in view as he followed the silver thread back to his body. The great bird flapped her wings impatiently. He opened the window and brought the skinned rabbit-horn to the sill. She swooped down and took her payment. He still had enough rapport with her to assure her that she would receive the same if she returned.

Then he settled down to eat his own meal, a thick slice of chervine pie and a large measure of nuts that had been roasted with honey, and went to sleep. During the next tenday he spent daylight in the Academy of the Sword with Master Paolo and the two local women who were also taking part in the Terran demonstration. On the eleventh day Allart arrived at the Academy. Gerell knew him well enough, though they had never been matched, nor had they ever become friends. Two more days until the competition and he had yet to find Sovenias. Not that he would stop after the demonstration, but he had a feeling that Sovenias would be there. No sword master would miss watching what the Terranan did with their weapons, even if they refused to fight with decent edges. So he refused dinner with Allart after practice, pleading a need for sleep justified by the dark rings under his eyes.

He bought the usual rabbit-horn on his way back and climbed the four flights to his rooms. The bird waited outside on the branch, and he slid into her mind as easily as he slid into his trousers or his fighting consciousness. She recognized him and welcomed him (or at least the rabbit-horn she knew awaited her) and then they flew together. This night, desperate, he delved deep into his memory for anything he could recall about Sovenias. Not just his looks and his hair, but his stance, his voice, his habit of playing with the four rings on his fingers when he was deep in thought. To all of these he attached the meaning *prey* and *need!* so that the bird shared his own sense of urgency and might be able to discern more characteristics to observe.

They flew together high above Thendara in circles, listening. Then, very faintly and far away he heard a voice he remembered, asking politely for drink and a dinner at a public house near the Terran Base gate. *That*, he pointed out to the raptor. Without any question she honed in on the sound.

Bruno Sovenias spoke politely to the server, and softly to everyone else. Through the great Sech owl could make out much of what the assassin said she also heard and identified his heartbeat, as one identified prey. "Thank you, the tripe stew would be fine. I have come a very long way these past two days. Might you have a bed available as well?"

The bird began to flow with the night air out to the tavern but Gerell pulled her back. They had been out longer than ever before, though he was aware that while he was connected to the predator he had her sense of time and there was only now and anxiety (*babies, hungry babies!*) But he knew was tired, at the edge of his resources.

Changing direction confused her; the prey was in this direction and the prey was food. Gently Gerell showed her the rabbit-horn waiting for her close by. Enough for all the chicks. He guided her back to the window outside his quarters, and made sure she could see the rabbit-horn on the table. Then, slowly, he withdrew from her consciousness as she fell on the meal.

He followed the silver cord back down into his body, which felt cramped and silent after the wonders of the bird's night. He came back to full consciousness freezing and starving. He had made provisions for his host in the air, but none for himself. He grimaced as he realized that he had become too used to the normality of Hali, where rich food was served in the early dawn for the matrix workers. Heavy sweets laced with honey and dried fruits, rich cuts of meat dripping in gravy and sweet sauces, and honey everywhere. Except after work, he found honey too sweet, but now he craved it. Anything, anything at all. He had managed to provide every other evening, but he had not first needed to spend time with Allart and then the desperate urgency that drove him to forget his own larder.

He had to drag himself from his bed and descend the four flights of stairs before he stood in the street. The bakery was closed. So was the cook shop. No surprises there—it was late. Idriel had set and Mormallor had sunk low on the horizon. He had to find food, and nearby. He heard muffled voices a little way off and hoped that there would be a tavern or an inn. He found the place and they were starting to clear the clientele for the night.

"You've had enough for the moment and drunk up more than we've got. Come back tomorrow when there's more," a hearty, cheerful woman with a scarf around her short, graying hair called after the disgruntled drinkers.

Gerell ran up to her quickly. "Please, *mestra* I know it's late but could you spare a few minutes for a hungry man to eat?. I can pay, and well, and will take anything you have."

She appraised him carefully, noting the glints of copper in his brown hair, the quality of his clothes and the sword at his side. "We have some bits left over and you're welcome to them, but do not keep us from our work. And you will leave when we do, once the place is clean and put away."

Gerell nodded quickly and darted inside. He took a place at the table nearest the kitchen door. When the woman appeared again she had a large platter loaded with less appetizing cuts of meat, noodles, and crumbling cakes, no doubt going stale. Like the owl, he needed sustenance, and so it devoured it all uncaring. He finished before the owner and her crew had completed wiping down the tables and sweeping the floor. He had paid what she asked when he was served, and left a few *sekals* under the empty plate in gratitude.

He had planned to wake early and get to the house where he was certain Sovenias had stayed before the assassin had eaten breakfast. Instead, after the night's work and insufficient fuel, he woke close to noon and needed provisions from the bakery before he could continue hunting his quarry. There he bought seven different pastries, a short loaf, and a small jar of honey. Once he finished his breakfast and stored the leftovers for later, he realized he smelled rank and needed to go to the public bathhouse he had frequented in the neighborhood. The bathhouse was certainly adequate—plenty of hot water, soap and a large towel—but nothing near the facilities at Hali. He was used to bathing with fine scented soaps, and a different one for his hair, and two thick towels that absorbed the water off his skin and hair quickly. Most of all, it was private and the water had always been crystal clear.

The sun had lowered considerably and it was near enough time for him to report to the Academy of the Sword to meet with the others who had come to demonstrate with the Terranan. He would have to get to Sovenias a little later, which frustrated him terribly. He would prefer to simply the miss the meeting just to come, but he could not avoid it. He had pledged to participate and that pledge bound him as deeply as any other.

Orain Jadaine had already arrived when Gerell slipped into the ring. The group of competitors already had begun talking about Terranan fighting styles when Gerell joined them. Orain studied him for a moment and then turned to the others. It made Gerell quiver. Surely Orain was every bit as beautiful as he remembered, *chieri* pale with near silver hair that fell past his shoulders and ice blue eyes. He moved with the compact grace of a highly skilled swordsman, and Gerell found himself remembering the best of times with Orain, and not the worst.

Maybe he had misled Danilo, and himself as well. Maybe Orain was not so deeply in his distant past as he would like. One thing he did know was that he wanted, badly, to be at his best for his former lover. He wanted to show his ability, his speed, his elegance with the sword.

Master Paolo entered and spoke a little about the demonstration the next day. "We know very little of Terranan fighting styles. In fact, we were uncertain that they had their own traditions whereby they could remain within the Compact, so this will be a fact-finding experience for us. You are among the best swordsmen and women in Thendara. By fighting with the *Terranan* in the exhibition, for so they say this will be, you will learn about their forms of swordsmanship. And by watching, you and I shall learn more. So let us get to work here and see what we each need to polish."

"Excuse me, but why do you think that they have suggested this?" asked one of the Renunciates, who Gerell thought might be Cassilda n'ha Karis, the most famed of the Free Amazon fighters.

Master Paolo looked directly at each of them in turn. "We have spent the past days trying to figure out the answer to that very question, *Mestra* Cassilda. We think they might wish to gather information as we intend to do. Beyond that, the organization comes from their Cultural Office, so we think this may be a way interacting between us. The truth is, I do not know. They have not said."

Cassilda shrugged and they got down to work. At the end of the hours of practice, Gerell was sweaty and tired but felt good. Mostly good. He had not been paired with Orain more than once, and he had managed to stay focused on the pattern Paolo was trying to teach them. Mostly.

Something in their bout felt profoundly more intimate than it should, Gerell thought. The way they moved together with the sword shared a deeper knowledge of each other's bodies. He saw that Orain still favored his left eye too strongly and wanted to warn him about it, but it was no longer his place. And he led with the wrist so that an opponent who knew where to look would know where to anticipate his next blow. The memory of Orain's body was too immediate, as if they were lovers still, as if the past six years had evaporated and they were still the cadets who would go off after practice to explore their bodies without swords.

But after practice things changed. Orain turned away from him and declined an invitation to dinner, mumbling something about a previous engagement. Gerell felt as if he had been slapped across the face, and he realized that his cheeks must have been burning. Maybe Orain had found someone else. Or maybe it was best not to think about the past, about what they had shared. And now Gerell remembered what had pulled them apart: Orain pulling away from him, dwelling on his gifts and his desire to train in the Tower. About his being Comyn (extremely minor) and about his (very distant) kinship with Danilo Syrtis. In the beginning it had not mattered, but as Gerell concentrated on his work at Hali, training his *laran*, Orain had become closed and withdrawn. And finally they had split, Orain furious and stalking away while Gerell refused to run after him for the hundredth time.

Gerell reminded himself that he had better things to do. He had located Sovenias. All he had to do was find the inn and kill the man. So much easier than thinking about what had gone wrong with Orain and how things could have been different.

So he returned to his quarters with the rabbit-horn that his Sech owl would expect (he realized he could not disappoint her and he very much looked forward to meeting her chicks when she deemed them ready to leave the nest) and three slices of chervine pie (the local cook shop spiced it just to his taste) along with his usual honeyed nuts and returned to his rooms. He ate one of the pieces of pie, and then took the rabbit-horn carcass to his bedroom where the owl waited outside his window. He gave her the food and assured her they were not flying together this evening, which she found very strange. Still, she did not hesitate to take the meat and fly off to feed her young.

Gerell buckled on his sword belt and brushed off his clothes and he went out into the sunset to hunt Bruno Sovenias.

Six inns near the Terran Base were possible candidates, Gerell thought. He visited each of them and asked after a guest with the description of Sovenias. *Shape shifter* echoed in his mind, but he ignored the thought though it made him shiver slightly. He knew it was only story, but he couldn't help remembering his friends telling frightening tales when they camped out in the mountains, and the worst were always about the shape shifters. Davil had told one where the shape shifter had to kill, and then took on the likeness of the newly dead. Gerell had not been able to get that out of his mind for weeks, and whenever he found a newly killed bird he wondered if there were a shape shifter flying overhead.

Of course he knew now that this was only a myth for children, but the image had haunted him. Even now he found the thought disturbing though he knew it was untrue.

Six inquiries and nearly three hours of walking and he could not track the man down. He knew he had heard Sovenias's voice clearly. He knew that the inn had served tripe stew the night before. As it turned out, three of them had served tripe stew. And he could not identify the hostess he had clearly heard the night before.

Angry and frustrated, he returned to his attic to find the owl waiting on her usual branch. He had no second rabbit-horn for her and he let her know, and know that he was sorry.

She was a simple creature, but she had fed her babies until they were stuffed, and she had eaten her fill and still there was something left. She was a creature of habit and she went hunting with him. That had become her pattern and she saw no reason to change it.

Gerell was grateful. He lay back on his bed and took out his starstone and slipped again into her consciousness. And he rose up in the night, full of the bird's strength and desire. There was prey. She had found it and now she wished to find it again. It felt good to find prey, to kill it and eat it. Gerell, riding her mind, agreed.

And so they searched again, gently swooping over the inns where tripe stew had recently been on the menu. He listened through her ears and heard stable boys brushing horses and chervines, serving men and women taking orders and delivering dinners, guests at all three inns talking about business or the food or dice. Or about the *Terranan* demonstration. Some had even come to town to see that among whatever other errands demanded their attention.

He heard everything, and owl listened even more intently, but he heard no trace of Bruno Sovenias's voice. Had he really heard it so clearly the night before? Or had he been so desperate he had imagined some other similar voice to be the one he sought?

Owl was certain she had heard correctly. Owl trusted her ears absolutely and as Gerell rode in her mind he understood, as she did, that she was never wrong. Not about a sound. The Gerell part of his mind had to agree. Her hearing and her sight were beyond any senses he could have imagined.

Sleeping? She considered when they could find no trace of Sovenias's speech or gait anywhere in the vicinity.

Or maybe some other place. Gerell agreed that must be the case. Only small children and the very old would be asleep now.

So they flew on silent wings through one street full of taverns and then another. Through one area that seemed quiet to another group of taverns. They listened and listened but heard nothing like the voice they had encountered the night before.

Then she started to listen for the heartbeat. Every creature had a unique signature—this was how she could find and follow Gerell, and she would find the prey as well.

Finally the bird felt the call of her nest too strongly and Gerell guided her back to the window so he could return to his body. Then he opened the window wide enough so that she could enter his room, but he had no other food for her. He took out his own slices of pie and dug chunks of meat out of them. She tasted delicately and then threw them on the floor, the table, away from her. Cooked meat with gravy was not food. She wanted her flesh raw.

Gerell reached out to her to apologize (and remind her that he had given her a nice fat rabbit-horn earlier.) He found the telepathic link easier each time he touched her, as if their nightly bond when he merged with her consciousness made her open to more typical communication.

She let him know that she expected extra meat on the morrow. Her babies were growing quickly and needed more food. Then she launched silently out of the window and into the night.

They met at the Academy as usual, but today stands that would hold hundreds of spectators had been built around the sides. Master Paolo's many assistants had been up since dawn to arrange the space and rake the center. Two long benches had been arranged for the competitors on one side of the ring; a dais had been built on the other with a table and three high chairs. For the judges, Gerell assumed.

He had not brought a weapon, as he would be horrified to have even his practice sword blunted. Master Paolo had taken care of that detail and settled on blades that each had found adequate, but not so fine that they could not be sacrificed. Gerell picked his from the rack and loosened up with his usual routine. Allart and the two women were doing their exercises. Orain, as usual, was late. Gerell tried not to pay attention until the *Terranan* delegation arrived.

He had never met a Terran before. They looked rather ordinary. One was very tall and his skin was so dark that it appeared he had been painted or burned. One of the men could have been local, with his dark gold hair and blue eyes. But the third man took his breath away. As dark as Orain was fair, this man moved like a fighter, fluidly with a deep calm at the center. His eyes were as dark as a night with one moon, and he wore his black hair long and tied behind like a Darkovan.

"Hello" Gerell said to him, trying to remember to speak slowly. "I am Gerell. What is your name?"

The dark man gave him a beautiful smile. "I am called Miguel at home, but if it is easier you can call me Mikhail. They are the same." And then the man held out his hand. Gerell shook it and felt that both of them waited longer than necessary to let go.

The judges were just starting to separate them on their benches when Orain finally flew in the door. "I apologize..." he said, but let it drop as he took a seat on the far end of the bench from Gerell.

With the rest of the team between them, Gerell could not study Orain as he wished. Not because he felt compelled by the bond they had once shared, but because something about Orain struck him as wrong. His expression seemed not quite what Gerell would expect from Orain. Yes, Orain was arrogant, but Gerell would expect Orain to study the *Terranan* both on the opposing team and in the stands. Orain had always been curious about people from different circumstances, and especially about the Terrans. "Are they people like we are, do you think? Their bodies are much the same, but do they think like we do?" he would ask as they passed the gates and walls of the Terran enclosure during their time at cadets. But this Orain barely glanced at the visitors. He didn't even linger on the dark beauty, and Orain had never been disinterested in a beautiful man.

And then there was little time to pay attention to anything but the bouts.

Two of the women were up first, Casilda against a tiny woman who held her sword in as style Gerell had never seen before. Neither had Casilda. Great fighter that she was, she adapted as best she could, but the alien style appeared to confuse her. Casilda's style appeared to confuse the Terran woman as well. They danced around each other carefully, but it seemed that the Terran missed several of her blows by hair's breadth. Used to a full-length sword, Gerell decided. Casilda had watched carefully for an opening and suddenly came in under the small woman's guard with three ferocious hits.

After the women, Allart had his match with the very tall man, who in fact was not only quite good but also used more familiar technique. They appeared evenly matched, and Gerell thought that Allart was drawing out the bout to learn more about the variations this man tried.

Then he himself was called to the arena. He didn't know if he was disappointed or relieved that he was not fighting the very beautiful man who was a clear distraction. The opponent who faced him really did look Darkovan but as soon as he drew his sword his alien training became evident. Gerell had to concentrate to watch how he moved and where he thrust. Unlike a Darkovan, he wove very little and attempted little distraction as he relied on speed and strength to make up for strategy.

Drawing him out was easy. Gerell feinted to the left and drew him across the sand as he evaluated the man's technique. Which was certainly sound but not particularly imaginative, and Gerell could have ended the bout at several points. He even let the Terran get a touch on his leg as he studied the attack as well as the defense. Finally he decided that he had evaluated as much as he needed, and he spun quickly and delivered the three required blows and it was over.

The next match were the remaining women, the Terran clearly older and very sharp. She seemed familiar with the women's fighting knife and wielded it effectively, though with the same direct focus as Gerell's opponent. She won her round, which Gerell decided was a sacrifice for the sake of education, as Fiona was not even breathing hard and had employed none of the distracting moves he had anticipated.

And then Orain and Miguel. Gerell wondered if they had been paired because Orain was so very pale and Miguel dark. Both so very beautiful that Gerell wanted to watch them move forever, but worried about being overt in the nature of his interest. Orain was no longer interested in him and the Terran was—a Terran. Still.

As he watched he saw that Orain fought differently than he had before. He danced on the sand beautifully, but he seemed to favor his right eye just a bit when even yesterday at practice he had favored his left. And there was something to the way he moved his wrist, something a little more smug than Orain had ever been. But it had been years, he argued to himself. Orain could have changed—he had changed himself. Maybe he would appear different too. But yesterday Orain had been himself. Now he seemed—

The fighters danced around each other and exchanged the first two parries, clearly testing each other. Where had Orain picked up that neat little feint, Gerell wondered. He hadn't seen it yesterday in practice and it was a nice trick, one he would like to master himself. And then Orain dropped, rolled toward the Terran, and came up close enough to grasp him with bare hands, which clearly shocked Miguel but the dark man had the presence of mind to jump suddenly towards his assailant.

Gerell thrilled at the audacity of the move, the sheer invention of it. Orain's fighting style had indeed changed, but Miguel…

Gerell watched Miguel for a few moments instead. He had to admit that Miguel fought beautifully, with more poetry than any of his teammates. Something about Miguel's ease in the ring, the looseness in his arms, the way he shifted weight rapidly, made him even more glorious in movement than stillness.

Fighters reveal a great deal about themselves in a bout. Miguel was as generous and honorable as he was original and intuitive. Gerell nearly choked on desire when Miguel hooked Orain's weapon from him, and then took it and tossed it back with a smile.

But Orain, Orain had shown only contempt for the gesture. That was not Orain. The Orain Gerell knew would have…

Orain turned quickly and thrust at Miguel from behind. Gerell nearly choked at the affront as he rose, cursing the blunted instrument at his side. Then he, and the rest of the audience, saw the sun-red drops on the sand. The Terran was bleeding. His hand wavered and then the sword slipped from it as he grabbed his sword arm and sank to the arena floor.

Orain turned and ran. And then he was not there at all.

Shape shifter.

Gerell whipped around trying to spot—Bruno Sovenias. No wonder he hadn't fought as well as anyone expected. He couldn't while holding Orain's shape. And if he had held Orain's shape and taken his place—Gerell felt as if he had become an ice storm in the Hellers. If that stupid story that frightened him as a boy were true, then it had been easier to take Orain's shape as he died. He pushed his panic firmly down. That was a myth, a story, nothing more than his own childhood fears.

And yet—shape shifters did not exist. He had known that until this moment when he had seen differently..

He could hardly see the people around him through eyes that had suddenly filled. Much as Orain had hurt him, he had never expected this final hurt to be so deep—or so soon.

Gerell turned back slowly to the arena, where Miguel lay bleeding, his hand mottled with specks of dark reddish purple and his arm twitching. At least here Gerell could do something. He had far more training as a monitor than the usual Comyn who had spent a single season in a Tower. And after a moment of concentration on the drops of blood on the sand his training, he knew what poison this was. It was one he had studied carefully, a medicine and a poison both at different concentrations and slightly different formulations.

Immediately he joined the few monitor-trained spectators around the fallen *Terranan*. He touched the man's shivering, feverish arm and told the others to take Miguel to the small chamber to the side of Master Paolo's office, where the trainers and massage specialists and someone with some monitor skills cared for those who were injured during lessons and practice.

The Terran contingent protested vigorously. "Our medicine…" the tall man start to say, but Gerell cut him off. "This is a poison well known to us, and we may be able to cure him. But let us treat him quickly. By the time you get him to your base he will be past saving." Then he ignored the *Terranan* and paid attention only to Miguel.

When Miguel had been gently laid on the pallet, Gerell ordered the others out. Gerell cut away Miguel's sleeve and laid one bare hand on the swiftly mottling arm. In the other hand he held his matrix, out of its pouch and with direct contact with his skin. Here his training took over, and his mind automatically calmed as he sank deeply into the body of the poisoned man. Down, deep, he descended step by step, from seeing all the circuits of energy glowing though Miguel's body. Some of them were already dark and the shadow was expanding quickly. Gerell tried to force it back, to bring the healthy brilliant light circulating through the blocked channels, but he was not fast enough.

Hemmia was like that, he remembered. It thinned the blood rapidly to hemorrhage and bleeding burst through the body. As a medicine healers used it carefully in very tiny doses for those whose blood had clotted and blocked their arteries.

Further. Down to the blockages themselves, individual grains eating the blood cells and making them flow too rapidly, bleeding out of their assigned paths.. He saw each grain as glowing dark purplish green, and there were too many of them. Calm. Further down. He could enter one of the dark chambers that was the evil and draw it into himself, but his energy was strong. One by one he absorbed the energy of the poison and carefully discharged it into a glass of water that had been set for him to drink. One by one. His mind jabbered at him that he was going too slowly; his training told him that he had to focus only on the task at hand. One channel freed, he went to the next.

He pulled farther back to see how the blood circulated and felt great relief that many of the grains of poison were gone. But there were many left to go and so many of the artery walls had been weakened by the poison, and he was so very tired.

And he felt an energy and focus pour into him. Tightly aimed at each of the grains of poison, he knew they were prey and he was the hunter. He could not fail, he hunted to live. Each one was so fast, so easy, in the small mind that enveloped him, and the conquest of each delighted that mind again and again. And so they worked though dusk to clean each bit of drain from the man's circulatory system.

Then it was done, clear and clean and properly, as it should be. The other mind registered great hunger and desire, and Gerell agreed. Two rabbit-horns tonight for the Sech owl who had come to his aid.

Yes, clean meat, Owl agreed. "That was tainted meat, yes? We must not eat tainted meat, even if we are hungry and it tastes good." He could feel her maternal instinct to teach him even as he reassured her of a good meal to come.

But first he had to rise, to find food for himself. He staggered out of the treatment room to find that only the Terrans and Master Paolo had remained. And that Danilo Syrtis waited with Paolo in the Master's office while the Terranan remained on the benches outside.

"Here, eat," his kinsman said, handing him a large pastry rich with nuts and honey. "I have heard a number of very strange stories from a number of people."

Gerell wolfed down the food. Utterly depleted, he needed to

return to his patient, and also to hunt Sovenias with the owl. Who had come to him without his calling when he most needed help.

"It's true," Gerell said without preamble. "Sovenias is a shape shifter. He took on Orain's likeness but I felt something was wrong. And then when I went to give chase, he disappeared into the crowd. Completely and utterly disappeared. I could not find him as Bruno Sovenias either. But I decided that I was better equipped to aid the Terran than to chase shadows. Our honor, our shame—this was supposed to be friendly and now—"

"And now it is much better than the Terran will live," Master Paolo said firmly. "That at least you have done. He will rest here for the night, and perhaps for tomorrow as well. You need to sleep."

Gerell nodded and stood. Syrtis held his arm gently. "We have already explained the situation with Sovenias to the Terrans. They have been quite decent about it. Now go home. We have a full shift of Guards searching for him. I have a litter for you outside, you should not walk in this condition."

"I can ride," Gerell protested. "With another pastry or two I will be fine, I promise you."

Danilo looked as if he were going to protest, but Master Paolo stepped in. "There is food in my office and you are welcome to it. Eat up and see if how you feel. You can spend the night here if you're too exhausted."

But Gerell shook his head. He could not stay at the Academy, no matter how appealing the idea. He had to provide for Owl. He owed her.

And after a bowl of barely warm tripe stew, Gerrell was definitely able to ride. He went by the market for two rabbit-horn carcasses, big fat ones. The owl certainly deserved her reward tonight. She would need to eat well, too, because he was not yet finished. Guards could search all they liked, but Gerell was going to kill the murderer, for Orain. For Orain's death. And maybe for Miguel as well.

He could feel Owl's presence close by as he rode back to his humble rooms. She waited, as always, on the branch outside his bedroom window. He opened the panes and she swooped in, took both rabbit-horns, one in each foot, and swept away. She would return, and so he settled down to sleep with the window open. She would wake him for the night's hunt when she returned.

He awoke in the dark to a sharp beak biting his neck. Not so deeply that she broke skin, but enough to rouse him instantly with his hand under the pillow clutching his knife. He ruffled her feathers and thanked her for her return, and the resonance that flowed between them was more clear and natural than it had ever been. She was very pleased with herself. She had stuffed her chicks and then herself, and she had flown over the city. She had flown, strong and glorious and silent in the night, and she had seen the Guard discover the body of Orain Jadaine in an alley close to the Academy.

Before Gerell could give himself to grief once again, Owl interrupted. They need not fly again tonight. She had located the prey. Now he must come along to help her kill him. And eat him. Gerell was sunk deeply enough into her consciousness that he did not find the idea appalling.

Where? He thought to her. And then images flashed through his mind, a tavern sign, the sound of Sovenias's voice and gait, a vision of the speaker, again in Sovenias's form, sitting at a table alone. And his heartbeat, unlike any other. She remembered clearly from the night they had identified him eating tripe stew. And then the view from above with the streets laid out so that Gerell thought he could find the place. He came down the four flights of stairs, and she waited for him on the lintel of the building across. Then she launched herself into her slow, silent flight, guiding him through the dark. He had the eyes of a man but was linked to her in a light rapport so he had some sense of her vision as well. Not so clearly as when they were fully bonded, but he could see by Liriel and Idriel as clearly as if the great Bloody Sun hung overhead.

The tavern was not so very far, and Gerell felt as strong as if he had rested and eaten for a week. Then he saw the sign and let the owl know that she had done her part and more for the night.

Gerell entered the tavern cautiously. After today there was no doubt that Sovenias could recognize him on sight. And he had to believe that the assassin still carried a poisoned blade. Inside, he scanned the patrons quickly to see if he could recognize Sovenias, but he could not, not without a better view.

Silly fly-mate. That *one.* Owl knew very well which one she had tracked. She heard not only his voice, but his heartbeat, and each heartbeat was unique. She could see him through any disguise, if this in fact were one. Or if it was his true face.

Gerell tapped him lightly on the shoulder. "Bruno Sovenias? I believe we have a matter to settle, if you would be so good as to come outside."

The man turned slowly and took a long look at Gerell as if he hadn't noticed him before. "We do?"

"Orain Jadaine, for one. And using an edged blade in a demonstration that specifically forbade them. And poison for another."

Sovenias shrugged. "Go home, little Comyn. Go home and get pampered and treated like you're some kind of princeling and leave real fighting alone." He spat, then turned back to his meal.

"Come now," Gerell replied firmly.

"I don't really need to kill you, boy," Sovenias said. "No one is paying me. I don't like to kill if I'm not paid."

"Who paid you to kill Orain? And the Terran?"

The assassin shrugged. "Not your business, and I never betray a client."

The landlord came over, and Gerell realized that everyone in the inn was watching them. Perhaps their voices could have been softer. "Gentlemen, you are disturbing my other guests. Please either take it outside, or stop. Immediately."

"I will continue until you accompany me to the stable yard," Gerell announced loudly.

Sovenias shrugged. "It's your death, boy. I strongly recommend that you leave alone, and quickly…"

"I will not."

"In which case I will dispatch you and return to finish my meal. It is quite tasty, actually, and I will return before it cools." With that, Sovenias rose and followed Gerell out to the yard.

They both drew their swords and studied each other before committing to movement. A white shadow flickered at the edge of Gerell's vision, but he dared not think of anything other than his opponent. Sovenias's lazy stance radiated confidence, and then he feinted quickly to the left before pressing the attack. He was fast and strong, and Gerell knew two things—Sovenias had held back in his bout with Miguel, and he had watched Gerell fight and learned something of his preferences.

Gerell danced back under the onslaught, maneuvering the assassin around to the cobbles. Sovenias laughed unpleasantly and moved quickly away from the paving, attacking Gerell from the side. Gerell spun, a little too slowly, though he was able to parry the killer's blade. This time.

Yes, boy, fear. I would have left you alone. It was your choice to die tonight.

The words pressed into his thoughts, and Gerell grew even angrier, which pleased Sovenias even more. Gerell pressed the attack again, but this time Sovenias danced to the left and thrust to Gerell's sword hand. The blade did not touch but it was far too close, and Gerell started to fear.

Then, silently, the white shadow detached itself from the roof of the barn. *No!* Gerell screamed telepathically to Owl, but she was a great killer herself and she swooped out of the sky with her talons out before her and grabbed Sovenias by the back of his neck. She flapped her soft white wings around his face so he could not see and plunged her beak into his scalp.

He screamed and Gerell thrust directly to his heart. Gerell felt him die, swiftly and surprised. That was all Sovenias had in the end, utter disbelief that he could have been bested, let alone killed. Gerell stood over him and withdrew his sword as Owl showered him with approval, as she would do when her chicks made their first kills.

Now we eat, she announced happily.

For a moment, just a moment, his rapport with her was so strong that biting into the warm raw flesh seemed the most natural, reasonable thing to do.

And then he was struck with the horror of it. She would eat a person, and him with her! Disgust flooded him and his gorge rose.

No, his mind screamed into hers. *Stop!*

She lifted her beak for a moment. We hunt and we eat, she explained simply. You are silly fledgling and you are hungry. Come here and eat fresh meat.

No! he replied, mind to mind. And then his mind was blank. Why should she not eat fresh meat she had killed? What would make sense to her? She was pure predator and he had emphasized that Sovenias was prey.

Tainted. That is tainted meat. We must not eat tainted meat. He pushed the thought, the image into her fiercely focused mind as strongly as he could. He gave her the image of how they had healed Miguel, of the poison that thinned both his blood and the artery walls that surrounded it. How the dark grains had flowed through him.

Tainted! he repeated.

Owl cocked her head as if listening to something very difficult to hear or understand. *Good meat, how is it bad?*

He understood that she needed to know how he knew. Tainted. I can smell it. I can taste it in your taste.

She fought him, her ever-present hunger and her desire to hunt pushing back at his mind with the ferocity only a raptor could feel. He struggled against her knowledge and her need.

I cannot eat this. It will make me sick. If it makes me sick, it will make you sick.

Logic. With a raptor. He was turning crazy. Birds did not understand any logic. What was wrong with him?

Then he felt her turn, tear away from the tempting feast before her. She knew how his body reacted to her eating the corpse, and in her world there was only one thing that would make a fresh kill sicken any being. Taint. She could not risk bringing tainted meat to her chicks.

Slowly she raised her beak and stepped away from the cooling remains of Bruno Sovenias. *I must hunt fresh meat*, she told him.

Then she took to the sky and he withdrew from her mind as she killed several mice around the tavern, and two small songbirds to take back to her nest.

Gerell stayed beside Sovenias' corpse until several Guard came, called by the landlord. "Tell Danilo Syrtis that Bruno Sovenias is dead," he said.

He was kept under guard until Danilo himself arrived. His elder kinsman looked exhausted and had obviously dressed in haste, but he surveyed the scene carefully. "Thank you. I had hoped that you would be able to find him. I had not expected you to kill him, and I am grateful for that. I am even more grateful that you are still alive. You will return to Comyn Castle with me and rest."

Gerell shook his head. "With your permission, I would prefer to go home."

Danilo studied him for a moment. "Granted. On the condition that you ride out with the Guards here as if you were a prisoner. We don't need the landlord and the rest of the guests asking too many questions or making up stories. This way, all they will think is that it was a grudge match and you were properly apprehended."

Gerell nodded. He had never been so tired, and being apprehended didn't sound so bad but the Castle was farther than his own attic, and all he wanted was sleep.

Gerell arrived at the gate of the *Terranan* base alone. He was escorted to a white room and asked to sit, and someone brought a tray of what he took to be snacks, but he was not hungry. The stern older woman who had competed in the demonstration came in to greet him. "Yes?" she asked.

"I am here to apologize for our team, for the dishonor of the fighter who fought with an edged blade and poison. He is dead."

"Yes, yes, you people have apologized a dozen times. We have agreed that it was an isolated incident and there was no intention on the part of your government or the team. You did not need to come to tell me that."

Her Darkovan was excellent, fast, and with only a touch of an accent.

He bowed slightly. "*Vai domna*, I would like to see the man

Miguel who was injured by this person. I should like to tell him directly that we have avenged his honor."

She studied him for a moment, then shrugged. "As you like. He appears to have completely recovered and is back to work. I will have him brought here. I know our medical people would like to know how you discovered your antidote to this poison. We should communicate more clearly on healing matters. You were, I believe, the one who saved him."

Gerell held his empty hands apart. "I have some small training in caring for sword wounds. I can tell you no more than that."

"Miguel Ortiz will be summoned. Please make yourself comfortable." With that she left. But Gerell was not comfortable. He was anxious and hopeful and too many emotions mixed at once.

It is very simple. You wish a mate. You need a nest. Show your nest and some lovely delicious food and it will be done.

Gerell laughed. Owl, get out of my head. I'll do this on my own, thank you.

She screeched once and settled her feathers, but the bond between them had become something Gerell could not dismiss. Owl was part of him as he was part of her, and he appreciated her for herself, and not simply what she could show him.

He might have thought more about it, but Miguel arrived and Gerell was struck by his delicate features and warm sincerity.

"Thank you for saving me," Miguel said, his voice soft and his eyes meeting Gerell's and not letting him go.

"It should not have been necessary," Gerell answered. "We are dishonored, all of us, by your suffering. This was never meant."

And then Miguel laughed. "I am glad it happened. Truly. Because I know no other way that I would have seen you again, and I very much wanted to."

The desire Gerell felt was mirrored in Miguel's eyes, and suddenly he found himself in the Terran's embrace. "Would you like to join me for dinner?" Gerell asked, and his voice had gone low and husky with yearning.

"Oh yes."

Far away an owl hooted her approval. Maybe the human was learning something. Maybe, like her other chicks, he would soon be ready to hunt on his own.

SNOW DANCING

by Jane M. H. Bigelow

Early in the creation of this anthology, I received a note from author Jane M. H. Bigelow, whose story, "Healing Pain" appeared in *Gifts of Darkover*. She wrote, "I keep thinking about skis and Darkover. They'd be so useful for winter travel on a planet where a snowless night is a sure sign of summer! Critical things like medicine or information can't always wait until the snow's decreased enough for a horse to make its way. Yet so far as I know, Darkover doesn't have skis or anything like them. Old fashioned cross country skis, like the ones that used to be called Norwegian snowshoes, would be easily within Darkovan technology." I have been on (cross-country) skis only a handful of times in my life, and as far as I know Marion was not a skier, either, but Bigelow's query made perfect sense. Although there may have been a perfectly good reason why Darkovans did not use skis in the past, I was quite convinced they would take to the sport, perhaps not as ducks take to water but some more frozen analogy. In Bigelow's creative hands, this story element is woven seamlessly into a dramatic and uniquely Darkovan story.

Jane M. H. Bigelow had her first professional publication in *Free Amazons of Darkover*. Since then, she has published a fantasy novel, *Talisman*, as well as short stories and short nonfiction on such topics as gardening in Ancient Egypt. Her short story, "The Golden Ruse," appeared in *Luxor: Gods, Grit and Glory*. She is currently in the throes of revising her second novel, *Children's Knives*.

Jane is a retired reference librarian, a job which encouraged her to go on being curious about everything and exposed her to a rich variety of people. She lives in Denver, CO with her husband and two spoiled cats.

Snow glittered on the high peaks above Margali, shining too brightly for her to look at it for long. She rested her eyes on the near view, where trees grew in the shelter of the ridge line. Last night's winds had blown the narrow horse path nearly free of snow up here.

It felt so good to take long strides, to look farther ahead than the walls of a room. A breeze shook snow loose from the branches above her and she dodged hastily, laughing. One clump caught in her hair. She shook it out of her braid, but didn't put up the hood of her cloak. The view and the freedom were worth a little snow. The air smelled of snow and pine trees. All she heard was the wind—and someone laughing?

Margali rubbed her eyes and peered down into the treeless valley below. A Terranan—he must be a Terranan; no Darkovan dressed in such odd tight clothing—was dancing in the snow.

She'd seen Terranan only on her rare visits to the Trade City, and then they were usually inside a shop or a jaco seller's booth. Here on the outskirts of Caer Donn, they were rare indeed.

It looked as if he was on the snow, walking across it with a strange yet oddly graceful gait. She stepped cautiously to the edge of the path and crouched down so that she didn't cast shadows past the trees that bordered it. Bad enough to be nosy without getting caught. Besides, everyone knew the Terrans were mad. This one looked more so than most. She had to see more, though.

Usually her mid-day walk did nothing more than clear her thoughts and get her away from the noise of the crowded house. Small wonder that her sister Camilla had accepted marriage to a farmer living a day and a half walk from Caer Donn to get out of it. Estevan was nice enough, Margali thought, if hardly the most exciting man she'd ever met. Now Camilla's own house was nearly as noisy, filled with her four children's arguments and laughter. Hah. There's one thing the so-clever little sister didn't foresee.

It was a pity that Camilla's early marriage had left Margali with the rest of the household to manage. Yes, and more of a pity that the fever eight years back had taken so many young men and women. Some said the Terranan had brought it with them. Margali wasn't sure about that, but she knew many families had suffered losses, some worse than theirs. Being Comyn had been no protection from the disease.

She pushed the thought away. Now the man glided off across the snow in swooping turns, then walked back uphill to his companion across the snow. Margali rubbed her eyes. Had she really seen that?

He thumped his companion on the back; she thought he spoke. Was he actually speaking cahuenga?

Margali drew her starstone up by its silk cord and cradled it in one hand. She reached out with her mind to hear better. No proper teacher would condone such a frivolous use of a gift, would she? Margali grinned. She'd only had a proper teacher for a few weeks when her *laran* finally wakened. Some of the lessons just hadn't stuck.

The Terranan's voice came clearly to her. "Come, friend, try!" He had a horrible flat accent, but yes, that was cahuenga. Another unusual thing for a Terranan.

He stepped sideways towards a boulder left by the rock slide that had cleared the valley. "You are nearly my tallness—"

Margali grimaced in frustration. Now she couldn't see what was happening. She crept out another two steps.

The edge gave way under her feet. Margali felt herself slide forward. She clutched at bushes as she went past; the winter-killed branches broke off in her hands. *I wish I'd changed into proper boots*, she thought. It had seemed like too much trouble, too likely to give one of the servants time to trap her with a question. She'd been sure that the wind would have blown the horse path clear enough for ordinary shoes.

She stumbled, tripped, half-fell as she ran downhill. That ripping sound was her underskirt, she hoped, and not the outer dress. Her feet shot ahead of her as she reached the edge of the snow.

Oh, no, no, she was not going to slide into two strange men on her back with her legs sprawled out. No. Raise her body up, forward. Oh, no! Too far to one side. Arms windmilling, she got more-or-less upright. She hadn't felt so clumsy since her first dance lesson with boys. Learned that. Pretend this is dancing. I can. Do. This. Wind-packed snow blurred past her.

The one thing she couldn't do was stop. Evanda and Avarra, was she going to slide all the way down to the valley's end?

An arm across her ribs brought her to an abrupt halt; air whooshed out of her lungs. "Good for no skis," the mad Terranan said cheerfully.

Margali could only gasp for breath. He frowned down at her. "Here, I will take you to a sitting place." He slid one of his arms under hers as he sidestepped over to the flat boulder.

Margali felt herself blushing. To be held by a stranger like this! She hoped the Darkovan with him didn't know who she was. She didn't recognize him. Yet she could hardly object. The drifts were deep here in mid-valley; even her big feet would sink straight in now that she wasn't sliding past.

The Terranan looked more confused and anxious to her than threatening. He let go of her as soon as he'd settled her on the boulder.

"Nodisrespectintend," the Terran said.

"What?" That hadn't been cahuenga, had it?

He spoke again, more slowly. "Nodis resp ect intended."

Not cahuenga. Casta this time, though the accent was even worse and he'd gabbled it off as if he had no idea what the words actually were.

His eyes slid sideways, and Margali saw that the other man, the Darkovan, stood nearby. He clutched a walking cane in one hand. He looked ready to use it on the Terranan's head.

The Terranan grinned. Was he crazy, or just amazingly brave? "My boss made me memorize that before she—"

Wait, she?

"Let me go out of the Terran Zone alone. I hope I got it right. I know I'm not supposed to touch, but..." he shrugged.

"No offense is taken," Margali said slowly.

"Domna," murmured the Darkovan, "He's harmless, really. A bit mad, but then, what Terranan isn't?"

"I heard that," said the Terranan. He didn't sound offended. "Domna, I am Alan Kirkwall, of the Terran Base Environment department. My helpful companion is Martin. He's a genius with wood."

She nodded to him from her perch on the rock. "I am Margali Lanart. How do you do that?"

"The skis really help." At her baffled look, he leaned on one of the sticks and lifted his left foot up off the snow. He had a long board attached to it, curved up at the toe end.

So that's how he danced across the drifts.

"Would it please you learn?"

Where did he learn his casta, old plays? It's charming, though. Do I want to learn? It looks like so much fun! Though how I'm going to keep my family out of it... "Yes, thank you, it would please me."

Once, Margali's family home had stood surrounded by fields. A small orchard had grown just to the south of the house; a few twisted trees still remained. Gambling, poor politics, too many sons or none at all; this sept of the Lanarts had known all the catastrophes. Most of the land had been sold to men eager to have new homes, with *Terranan* luxuries, still close to Caer Donn's crowded center. Sometimes, when the wind came down from the Hellers and drove fireplace smoke right back down the chimneys, Margali envied them their boxy, inelegant houses.

The worst of both worlds, Margali's youngest sister Elorie complained. They had neighbors too close for her liking, and a long walk into the part of town where most of the shops still stood.

Margali's household included her great-uncle and great-aunt, with Great-Uncle being in uncertain health; five cousins; one remaining sister, Elorie; three full-time servants, and Margali. She was only able to steal time enough for a proper ski lesson a couple of times a week, less as the winter deepened and the household errands took longer to run over snowy streets.

She scraped up the money to buy the first trial pair of skis that Martin had made, not quite right for her, but close. Trying to learn an outlandish Terranan trick was pure self-indulgence, as bad as the year she'd studied formal botany. Worse; botany at least improved her skills at preparing medicines. She never injured herself memorizing botanical classifications, either. Margali rubbed ruefully at her left shoulder, still sore from a fall.

Also, botany never left her alone with a man not remotely related to her. Never mind that he was completely well-behaved. Strange, how quickly it had come to seem normal to be alone with him.

"Sorry," he said when he touched her left knee through her kilted-up skirts. She wore a pair of boy's breeches, unearthed from one of the attics, beneath the skirt. She could barely feel his touch enough to know whether she needed to move the knee forward or back. "A little, umm, wider," he said, and blushed like a girl in her early teens.

Teens—Elorie turns twelve this winter. Better check and be sure the tiny bottle of kirian hasn't changed color—it should still be good, Grandmother got it fresh when my *laran* finally wakened—but—ouch! Margali caught a ski tip and nearly went over. She put her thoughts on the present.

That afternoon was the first time she got it right. Kick, glide, kick, don't cut the glide short, find the rhythm. Then she did, and it was like running in a dream, the kind where she could run with giant steps and never tire. She stopped thinking about just how to place her feet, just when to move each pole. She was dancing with the snow.

She finally came to a stop at the bottom of the hill nearest the city, laughing. "Oh, this is wonderful!" She sneezed, and pushed some sweaty wisps of hair off her face.

Alan cheered. "Yes! You have a gift for this!"

Margali kept her skis in an empty herdsman's bothy, along with a too-short old skirt with a cracked leather hem and a pair of boy's breeches. She had to bring the ski waxes each time; she'd found out the hard way that some small animal found them tasty. The bothy sat just a few feet from the horse path; Margali had chosen it for that, and because wind kept the entrance scoured clean of all but a skin of polished snow. She and Alan often sat on the narrow bench outside it to talk after skiing.

On a rare sunny afternoon she stood there instead, shaking snow out of her skirts. She'd fallen hard going uphill. *Anyone can fall going down. I have a real talent, yes indeed.* Some of the snow had gone past her scarves and high neckline to melt slowly in her bodice. *No doing anything about it here.*

Alan helped to brush snow from her right shoulder and side with more vigor than Margali felt was really needed. "Ouch! That's right where I landed," she complained as he knocked snow off one shoulder.

"You need better skis. You know those things are too stiff. You can't," he waved his hands in frustration, looking for the word, "you can't hold, that's not it, stick? Not like you need to do."

Margali shrugged, and wished she hadn't as her shoulder twinged. "They're good enough to learn on."

Alan waved at her skis. "I don't believe in 'good enough to learn on'. You'll learn bad habits, trying to make up for a ski that's too stiff and too short." His accent still made her ears hurt, but his grammar was better, less painfully formal. "You need something more...bouncy?"

"These will do well enough." She'd tried to explain to him that being part of an obscure branch of a minor noble family didn't mean that she had money just lying around in heaps. Time, money, there was never enough of either.

She turned to haul the skis inside the bothy, shrugging her shoulders irritably at the feeling of wet clothes. The cord and bag that held her starstone clung stickily to her skin. With her hands full of skis and poles, she couldn't get it unstuck.

Alan called after her, "You're making mistakes because you're tired. With the right skis you would spend more power traveling and less fighting your equipment. And you would not have fallen just now." He added, "You will have bruises tomorrow. You are lucky that it was not worse."

Margali thumped that equipment down in a corner of the bothy and came back into the sunlight. "What's the point, Alan? I don't have time for more than short runs, any more than I have money enough to buy another pair of skis."

The rising wind half-covered his sigh. "They're well enough for short runs. But, Margali," he hesitated and then went on, speaking fast, "Don't you ever get a day off?" *Can't this precious damn family of hers manage on their own for one day? She ought to tell them they'll just have to learn.*

Margali stared at him. How dared he think that way about her family, and about her? She could perfectly well stand up for herself when she thought it necessary. Her cousins and sister were learning more all the time, and they filled the house with laughter. She should look again into training for Elorie when her *laran* wakened; Margali had a feeling the girl had a trace of the old weather foretelling gift. Her great-uncle and great-aunt were a source of knowledge; right in her own house she had the best advice on herbalism, cookery, and mending a roof, as well answers to questions on history and music. If she'd missed out on a few parties, well, no one had everything. She didn't mind about the parties. Not being allowed a little more time to study using her *laran*—

Then it hit her. She'd heard his thoughts as clearly as if he were kin. "Alan," she murmured. "I heard what you thought about my family. You must not curse them."

"Oh hell, did I say that out loud? Look, I'm sorry, I didn't mean any insult." His eyebrows nearly met.

"Alan. Listen to me. You didn't say it. I heard you, as I might hear one of us."

He tilted his head to one side and the other, much like a puzzled dog. *I hope he can't hear my thoughts!*

He stared at her with his mouth open. Then, "You can read my mind?" His voice quavered.

"No, no. it isn't the same thing at all. I heard what you thought right then, because you thought..." Margali tried to think how to put it. "You thought as though you were speaking. I'm amazed that I can hear you at all, mind to mind." Everyone said *Terranan* were head-blind. Well, it wouldn't be the first time in her life that she'd found what everyone said to be wrong.

Alan spoke cheerfully, with just a hint of gritted teeth. "Maybe I did say it, just very quietly? That must be it. Look, Margali, I've heard the reports that some of you have psychic powers. Haven't seen it myself—"

"Yes, you have."

"Sorry, but hearing you say it happened isn't the same as experiencing it myself."

"You just did." Why couldn't he accept it? The proof was right there.

"I'm not saying it's impossible," he raised one hand, "I'm just not convinced. Not yet."

It took no telepathy to know that this was the best she was going to get right now. Margali tried, and failed, to imagine a world where no one knew what anyone else was thinking, ever.

"Look, why don't I come up to your house? You've got *some* land around it, right?"

She stared at him in dismay.

He nodded briskly. "Then we could do some practice and save you the, the... *commute*." He'd used a *Terranan* word. "You must have a word! The time it takes to get from your house to your work and back again, I mean."

"I don't think so," said Margali. "Why would we need to talk about walking downstairs, or outdoors to the farm?" She managed to keep her voice calm, but her heart raced. No, no, no, he mustn't come to the house. No. These two worlds must not touch. She'd worked so hard to keep them apart, each safely in its own box.

There was already too much to explain. Her sneaking away to spend time alone with a *Terranan* would shock the entire household, except possibly Elorie, who'd see it as a Doomed Love. Great-Uncle might very well think he needed to defend her honor somehow. The thought of Great-Aunt Clotilde questioning Alan about his family made her cringe. And the younger children... Margali flinched from even considering their reactions.

She seized the chance to turn the conversation. "And you, don't you ever have a *work* day? I'm sure the Empire didn't send you here to teach me how to ski." *Or to try to tell me what to do.*

He bristled. "I work! I work my shift and more, every week. I keep the systems running smooth all night long, the hours nobody else wants. I do it so well they can't even see it. Heat and light are just a gift from the fairies, I guess! And I'd better go get some sleep before tonight's shift." He turned, and added over his shoulder, "I am not telling you what to do! I know more about skiing than you do, right?"

Margali gasped. "Alan, I didn't say that."

He leaned on his ski poles a moment before he answered. "Yes, you did. I mean, I *heard* it, Margali. Maybe you didn't mean to, but you did. I haven't got time for this." He kick-glided across and up the valley at a speed Margali could only envy.

I would've apologized if you hadn't stomped off. Margali shook her head. It was just as well that he had.

It was pure luck that she hadn't had to answer questions yet. Her household and friends were used to her odd habit of going for unnecessary walks, so they didn't question that. Cattle and sheep had been moved to their winter pastures weeks ago; the herders had gone, too. A few late travelers had seen Margali and Alan; what they made of the sight Margali neither knew nor cared. They hadn't recognized her and gone to her great-uncle to express concern.

She also didn't want to hear Alan's reactions to what he'd doubtless consider her primitive living conditions. *How does one man keep the entire* Terranan *city warm and lighted? Wonder if I'll get a chance to ask?* She groaned at the thought of the trudge home. All that arguing had given her muscles time to cool, even if her temper hadn't.

When she woke the next morning, she knew she wouldn't be asking Alan anything soon. The world beyond her window was solid white. For most of the next four days, she was housebound. It snowed nearly all the time, sometimes sideways. Even Castle Aldaran's high towers disappeared from sight. The younger children whined. The older ones sulked. Elorie had to be ordered to stop playing the long, sad Ballad of the Two Brothers. That brought tears.

Margali wished she could simply doze through the long days as the elders did. There was much too much time to remember that stupid quarrel with Alan, and to wish that she had a way to reach him. A letter? Who would carry it for her? And sending a message to "Alan Kirkwall, somewhere in the Terran Zone", might not work too well.

Sometimes she almost felt him thinking of her. That was nonsense. One chance mental touch when they were both distressed, and she was dreaming like a romantic girl! The man was Terran, for pity's sake. Even if he wanted to speak to her mind to mind, and after the way he'd left she had no reason to think he did, he wouldn't know how. Certainly no *leronis* would help him. He probably didn't believe in them, either. She went and counted the sacks of dried apples again. There were still fifteen.

When she wasn't brooding about the state of her friendship with Alan (it was only a friendship, she told herself firmly) she worried about Camilla. Her sister and her household were in worse shape in their windswept valley than Margali. Snow had come down so hard and fast at the farm that it had blocked two of the chimneys. Clearing those would be dangerous work, and until it was done they'd be miserably cold.

On the afternoon of the fourth day the storm finally broke. There was even some sunshine. The children burst from the house like a river in the spring; Margali did the same. She hoped it had quit at Camilla's home, also, but right now she couldn't bring herself to worry about anything.

All around her Margali heard the scrape of shovels and the wild whoops of children. She felt like whooping herself. She did allow herself a giggle at the reaction that would get.

Drifts still clogged the street in front of many houses in spite of all the shoveling. Her skirt hems, crusted with snow, dragged at her legs by the time she'd reached the street that led to the horse path. *I wish I had my skis.* Could she make it to the bothy and have strength left to ski? *Is Alan out there right now?*

Even the horse path had snow piled ankle-deep on all but its windward edge. Beyond it, the snow of the valley glittered unmarked in the lowering sun. No Alan, not even his ski-tracks. Margali touched where her starstone lay, feeling the tiny lump through layers of cloth. *Did I really hear you in my mind, before that stupid quarrel?*

The roar and whine of Terranan machinery rumbled down the valley. Even here, they disturbed the peace of the day. The wind must have shifted, to bring the sounds to her so clearly. For just a moment she smelled hot metal, and felt as though something heavy muffled her ears.

Margali sighed. If she turned around right now, she'd have just time to get home before dark. She must do that; everyone in the house would be alarmed if she didn't. If she caused so much distress for no reason, she'd deserve every word of the scolding she'd get from her great-aunt. It did not become a Comyn maiden to cause scandal. It was just as well that Alan hadn't been out there.

No it isn't, protested part of her. She trudged on home. It should have been easier walking downhill, but it wasn't.

Margali came awake to find herself sitting bolt upright in bed. Beside her, Elorie snored softly; past her, their cousin Gabriela lay sprawled in the trundle bed with her feet thrust out from under the covers. A log in the banked fire settled in on itself. All was normal, including Gabriela's bare feet. *Still, something is wrong.*

Softly, Margali rose and thrust her own feet into ankle-high furred slippers. The heat from that fire didn't reach far. She wrapped an outdoor shawl over her nightdress.

As she went to pull the covers back over Gabriela's feet, her own room vanished from her eyes. Instead she saw a narrow bed where a boy twisted, half-rose, and cried, "Mama! Mama, make it stop!" His voice broke on the last word.

Margali groped for the side of her bed. Had that been Damian? She fished her starstone and reached out for her sister Camilla's mind.

"Margali? Oh Evanda, Margali!" Camilla cried. "Help me!"

"*How?*" But Camilla was gone. Margali wrapped her shawl

more closely around her and placed another log on the banked fire, nudging the ashes aside. It gave more smoke than heat, but this was no time to be fussing with the fire.

"*Camilla?*" Margali formed her sister's face in memory. "I am here," she murmured aloud. In the bed, Elorie shifted. Margali smoothed the girl's fine, red-brown hair back from her face. "Hush, Elorie. I'm just mending the fire." Elorie settled back into sound sleep.

Margali settled into the low chair by the fireplace and fished out her starstone from its silk bag. "*Camilla,*" Margali thought, "*Sister, tell me.*" She waited, forcing herself to take slow, even breaths.

Camilla's voice came to Margali again. "*Margali! Margali, oh I'm sorry, I shouldn't ask it, you have so many burdens—*" Then words tumbled over each other in a blur of mental images. Something was amiss with one of Camilla's children.

How could Margali help if she didn't even know the problem? She shoved her own annoyance and fatigue aside. One of them had to stay calm. *"What's wrong?"*

For a brief moment, Margali could See as well as Hear. Camilla twisted her hands together, staring off to her left in a candle-lit room. Layers of shawls covered her shoulders. *"Damian has threshold sickness."*

"Already?" The boy was what, eleven? Margali thought him the cleverest of Camilla's children, but cleverness usually had nothing to do with *laran*.

"No, I just wanted some excitement! Merciful Evanda, Margali!"

That had been a foolish thought. *"I'm sorry."*

"I haven't any kirian. None. What was I thinking? Was I thinking?"

No, why would she? Even in girls, *laran* didn't usually waken until twelve or later. With a boy, Camilla should have had at least two years before she'd any need of threshold sickness treatments.

"Margali? Sister? I don't know, Margali, what shall I do? I never had it much, I don't know what to do." The mental voice rose to a wail.

"You couldn't know. Shh, shh, it isn't your fault. You may not need kirian. Grandmother kept me walking when I had it, so that I didn't drift into illusions. You may have to haul him up out of bed to make him do it."

Margali could feel Camilla's revulsion at the idea of manhandling a sick child, any sick child, let alone one of her own beloved four. Margali repeated, *"You may have to,* breda.*"*

The contact snapped. Was Damian worse? Could Camilla get him up and walking, and if she could, would that be enough? Margali crouched near the fire, clutching her starstone as she waited.

Then Camilla's voice came again." He moans. Margali, he never cries, not when he broke that bone in his wrist—"

"Camilla!" Margali used her best bossy older sister voice. *"What did I say to do?"*

Camilla repeated the instructions. Then, "Come on, Damian. Come now, my big brave boy."

Big brave boy. Poor child, to go through this so soon! The boy was stubborn as Durraman's donkey; maybe that would help him.

Now Margali felt only a swirl of confusion and nausea that made her open her eyes and look around her own crowded room to orient herself. Damian had threshold sickness badly, if she felt it this strongly through another telepath's mind.

It seemed long until Camilla's voice came again. When it did, the frantic haste was gone from it. "It isn't working, Margali. Estevan has him walking right now, but it isn't—I think he almost had a convulsion."

Once convulsions began, few survived. Margali shivered, and not from the chill of the room.

Kirian was the best—no, the only—hope now. "Camilla! Send to the nearest Tower—you've *laran* enough for that—"

"And they get here how? Are we living in the Hundred Kingdoms, when the leroni could fly?"

Margali had a way to get there.

"Margali? Is there anything more we can do?"

Margali could tell what answer Camilla expected to get. Was there truly another?

A journey that would take a day and a half on foot, over dry roads, might not take more than a few hours on skis. She knew the way. Or she did when the road was clear. Well, the valley where the farm lay was the fourth in a rising series. How much different could the way be with snow on it?

Margali could almost hear Alan saying, grudgingly, that the skis were good enough for short runs. She wished she had his help, even if his arguments came along with it. This wouldn't be a short run. There would be no one to take a turn breaking trail.

And if she didn't try, then Damian would probably die.

"Camilla," Margali sent, *"put honey on his lips. He'll lick it off, and that will give him some energy. Keep him moving as much as you can. Talk to him. Tell him where he is. I have a way to get there. I'll be there with kirian by mid-morning. I'll be there."*

"How can you possibly—Margali, don't risk your life, sister, if I get you killed how can I live?"

"I won't risk my life. Truly I won't. I'll explain it all later." Margali detached gently from the contact and went to prepare for what was really only a somewhat longer ski touring practice session. Truly.

Margali tucked the precious bottle of *kirian* into the pocket in her underskirt. She fumbled with the tiny buttons, swearing softly in language unbecoming to her rank. There, that was done. Layered among her skirts, it would be as safe as it could possibly be. She sat and wrote a note for the cook, and another for the cook to give to Margali's great-uncle. He'd be furious that she hadn't consulted him. She could only hope that he'd forgive her; she certainly didn't have time to explain what she was doing.

In the kitchen, she grabbed a slab of the dried fruit, nuts and honey that cook kept handy for treats for the children, chewed her way through a bite of it, and wrapped the rest hastily in the first clean cloth she saw. A chunk of yesterday's bread and a bottle of cider joined it in a day pack that hung by the kitchen door. Last came a small chunk of cold-weather wax for the skis. Margali left silently.

The winter sun wouldn't be up for hours yet, but Idriel and tiny Mormallor lit her path through town. In the main part of town people had cleared at least a narrow path; as she made her way uphill to the northern edge of town there were stretches where she had to bash her way through drifts.

Before she reached the bothy Margali was sweating. Not good; sweat chilled on the body and invited the cold shivers. She unbuttoned her boiled wool jacket and loosened her neck scarf.

It was torture to take long enough to apply a fresh layer of wax to the skis, but she did it. If it were possible to do a mad thing sensibly, then that was what she must do.

Finally she could begin. The first part of the journey would be over familiar ground, though she'd never skied it with such deep, fresh snow.

The valley shimmered in the dual moonlight. Margali stood a moment to get her bearings; there, across the valley, lay the narrow gap where the road to Estevan's farm branched off from the main road. Good thing she already knew where it was. Too bad the ridge she stood on didn't continue that far; she'd have to traverse the valley.

The rhythm for breaking trail was different from skiing on someone else's tracks. It was more like a drumbeat than a song. And it was hard. The soft drifts yielded too easily for her to glide far. *But I need to be there as fast as I can!* Yes, but it wouldn't get her there any faster to exhaust herself in the first valley. She forced herself to set a slow, steady pace.

Out away from the trees, her journey grew easier. The wind had polished the snow just enough to let her skis glide smoothly, yet they still cut easily into the side of the valley. Back and forth, she worked her way up the hill like a dancer going up the line in a dance, swinging the ski poles in perfect counterbalance. Oh, she wished Alan could see her!

You're not doing this for fun, scolded a voice in her head. Margali winced, and lost the rhythm. *Be quiet,* she told the carping voice.

Ah, there was the trace of the horse path. She was where she should be. And the path would make a fairly level ski trail for her. It traced a long, irregular arc that shone against the downhill shadows in the two moons' light.

Shadows fell away to her left as she launched herself off down the path. It was a gentle slope, easier than several she'd done in her practice sessions. This wasn't going to be as hard as she'd feared. There would be a little uphill, from what she remembered, but she could do that.

A little downhill was a nice break. Margali tucked her poles up near her body and let herself enjoy the run. It was like flying.

It was too much like flying. She was going too fast. She knew it. The wind of her passing brought tears to her eyes. *I can't see.* Margali blinked frantically. *Oh Evanda.* What she saw was a drop off into a side-valley. The ledge that clung to a half-seen hill to her right was so narrow!

I will be calm. She'd just sit down. Never mind grace or dignity. What was dignity, out here where no one could see her anyway? She'd just lean into the hill to make sure she fell over there—not into that valley, no, valleys didn't really pull people down—she'd just lower herself a little more before she sat—

And she whipped around the curve of the buried road with a speed that made it hard to breathe. Icy air rasped in her throat, but she was safely past the drop off.

This was the fancy turn Alan had tried to teach her. *Alan, I've done it!* She laughed with delight. She longed to push on, as fast as she could, without stopping for food or water. She didn't; even though she'd always lived in Caer Donn and seldom left it, she knew what winter travel required.

It would have been easier if there had been anything like a flat place. Cross-slope would have to do. Now, how to get into the pack without losing her poles? The first time she tried she nearly slid away from them. Why hadn't Alan warned her about this?

Because he didn't expect you to be mad enough to take off alone, she thought. *Live and learn, in that order.* She managed better on her next try, and scooped some snow into the half-empty cider bottle to melt against the heat of her back.

The moons followed their own dance. Margali didn't know this valley as well. Shadows of trees confused her path. Each moon cast a different color; in places it was like skiing across a tumbled plaid. *If I could just stretch out, get some glide going!* But each tree had a danger zone around it, soft snow that could tip her into a drift, or onto a buried rock.

Twice she misjudged; once she landed against a tree and once she fell, hard enough to make her gasp for air. She clutched the nearest tree trunk, plastering her mittens with sap as she hauled herself back up.

Simply keeping going in the right direction was a challenge. New hills and valleys lay ahead of her, sculpted of snow and wind. Would she even know if she headed in the wrong direction? *Am I already going the wrong way?*

Clouds drifted across the sky. Margali slowed, peering around her. The snow seemed to grab her skis. She wrenched one loose and felt the other begin to slip off to one side. A thigh muscle protested as she forced her way against the pull of the slope. She flailed desperately; she had to stop. Finally, gasping, she stood across a narrow valley that led upwards into forested darkness.

But what valley was it? Too narrow, to winding, not steep enough...panic rose thick in Margali's throat as she tried to match what she saw with anything she'd seen near Estevan's farm. Tried, and failed.

Where am I? Oh, Camilla, I promised help and now I need help! Margali heard no answer. Behind her, the tracks of her skis wandered like a drunkard's scrawl. Margali's legs had begun to ache; her hands felt frozen in place on the ski poles. She could die out here. Who would ever find her?

I can't die. I have to get the kirian to Camilla. To Damian. Poor boy, how long have I taken? She pushed onwards.

Her skis sank into the soft snow until it covered all but the bindings. *Alan, I wish I could ask you to break trail for me.* He was so good at that, striding off across the snow like a god. Would she ever see him do that again?

Margali's legs were one solid ache. Her thighs trembled under her; she could feel her left ski chatter against a rock. She groaned aloud as she hauled herself away from it. Lots of short runs definitely didn't add up to one long one. Moving on through the deep snow felt as if she were lifting boulders. She had to keep going. Keep moving. She flexed her hands, trying to force warmth into them. Her feet were still amazingly warm.

She peered into the darkness. Shouldn't it be nearly dawn by now? Why was it darker, then?

Because I've been going downhill. Valley walls now blocked much of the light. Margali felt tears slide down her face. Stupid, stupid not to have noticed! She was just so tired.

Margali? This is weird.

The voice had a fuzzy, half-awake sound. Alan's voice.

Margali shook her head. *I must be even tireder than I thought.*

His voice came again. *"Okay. I think I may be nuts, but I'm going to go with this. Maybe it's only because I've been thinking about you so much since we fought, but maybe this is real."*

The voice was clear now.

"And if it's real then you need to listen to me. DO NOT STOP NOW."

"Ouch! Don't shout," Margali protested. She rubbed at one ear, then the other, through her woolen cap. It felt soggy under her fingers. Snow or sweat? Maybe both.

"Sorry." There was a pause, a sense of words she didn't know. Then Alan spoke again. *"I am new to this."*

Well, he had impressive reach.

"Alan. I don't know what to do. I'm lost out here, and I'm so tired."

"Margali. You have food? Water?"

Margali frowned. She didn't think she'd eaten the last of the food. Had she? Her throat felt too dry to swallow that awful fruit mash even if she had some.

"So drink something first. Now. All that sweating, you'll be—" another word she didn't know.

"Bossy damn Terranan."

"Yeah, I am. Do it anyway."

She hadn't meant to speak that to him.

"No problem. Just eat, and drink. Margali. Do it now. Come

on. Do it."

The refrain kept on until she gave in and dragged her pack out from under her. One she'd fumbled it open, her mouth watered at the scent of the fruit mash. Why had she ever thought it tasted too sweet? Margali chewed off a bit, and washed it down with half-melted snow from the bottle.

Energy rushed back into her body. Margali levered herself back onto her feet. There was still one problem. *"Alan, I have no idea where I am."*

"Sure you do. Follow your tracks back uphill until you can see something you recognize." He paused. When she heard his voice again, it sounded less certain. *"You've been wherever you're going before, right?"*

"Y-yes." Margali squinted back at the trail her skis had carved.

"Margali? Can you manage?"

Margali wondered if she could. The terrible weariness had faded, but her body still ached. *"I'll have to, won't I? Yes. I think you've saved my life, Alan."* Her tired mind searched for something better than, *"Thank you."*

"Just survive, and let me know when you're safe. Now ski to your sister's place."

She clumped her way gracelessly up to the crest of the hill. At least she didn't have to break trail! At the top, she fished out another small chunk of the fruit-and-nut mash, and drank a little more water. Now, calmly, look around.

Her tracks led downwards from here. There was a tangle of small trees across her tracks. That must be why she'd gone astray. So, the farm must be off on the other side of this wide valley. She set off again.

There had never been a more beautiful sunrise in all the mornings of the world. By its slanting light, she could see buildings off in the distance. They were still too far away for her to be sure in the dawn light, but she let herself hope they were her brother-in-law's farm.

She cleared the top of a snowdrift and scraped her skis against the top of a buried fence. There ahead of her were the farm buildings. Even half-buried under snow, they were recognizable. A man came to the door and lunged into the drifts, calling, "Margali!"

Her heart lifted. Estevan wouldn't have left Damian if the boy were in crisis. He wouldn't have left Camilla alone if—*Yes, I must be in time. Oh Evanda.*

It was downhill to the farmhouse front door. She swayed and laughed as she glided into the dooryard. Estevan muttered, "With permission," and took her elbow without waiting for it. Margali freed her boots clumsily from the bindings and limped into the house on Estevan's arm.

After the cold outside air, the kitchen felt steaming hot. She tried to speak, and failed. She hacked out a cough and tried again. "Damian?"

"He's conscious, I think. He was."

Camilla called down the narrow stairs that rose at the far end of the kitchen. "Oh, *breda*, is it you?"

"I'm here." One more hill, Margali thought. She groaned as she began hauling herself up the stairs. Estevan planted one large hand on her back and half-pushed her along.

The stairs ended in the middle of a wide room lined with box beds on two sides. Behind a wooden lattice half-wall, smoke rose from a brazier. Something bubbled on it, with honey in it by the scent. An older woman sat in a wide cushioned chair, cuddling a toddler; two children peered out from the curtains of one bed. She gave Margali an appraising look and rose, carrying the toddler. "Bless you, Mistress," she said. Margali nodded her thanks.

Camilla stood well away from the stairs, supporting a thin boy who was already half a head taller than she. His fiery hair hung lank with sweat. His eyes were closed, and he trembled. Estevan dodged around Margali and went to take his son's weight from his wife.

Buttons rattled to the floor as Margali pawed through her clothing for opening of the pocket. Fear hit her like a physical pain. Surely she would have noticed if the precious bottle had broken in one of her falls?

She touched it. Whole. The relief made her dizzy; she turned to her sister, holding out her skirts. "Camilla. Take it," Margali said. "I don't dare."

Someone thrust a mug of tea into Margali's hands. "Here, mistress," said the children's nurse. "Drink that, now. You've done your work."

The tea was thick with cream and honey. Margali gulped it down without really tasting it.

Camilla fished out the tiny bottle, ripped the wax away from its stopper and opened it. "Damian, sweetheart, open your mouth for me. Open up now, for Mama." She touched one corner of his mouth. Damian's mouth opened enough for his mother to tip a few drops of *kirian* into it.

"There, that's enough," Margali cautioned.

One handed, Camilla gave the bottle back. "Swallow, baby, swallow," she urged.

His throat moved. The fine tremors lessened. Damian opened his eyes and stared in bewilderment at them all. Camilla sobbed with relief; Estevan gathered the weary boy in his arms. "I can walk," he protested as his father helped him to a bed. "Father, I was somewhere so strange!" A huge yawn cut off the rest.

"Yes, Damian, you were. You're back safe with us now."

Somewhere, without being aware of doing it, Margali had shed her hat and heavy wool shirt. She wasn't sure how much longer she could keep going on tea and fruit bread, but she needed to tell Alan. She touched the lump her starstone made under her blouse. This time, the shift in focus came instantly.

"Alan, I did it! I got here, the kirian worked, it's all right."

"You're safe?"

She felt his joy before the words came clearly to her.

"Wonderful! See you soon?"

"Soon," she promised, and took her hand from the starstone.

It would be safe to let Damian sleep, now. Margali turned to meet her sister's embrace. *"Let the nurse watch over him for a little,* breda. *This isn't really over, you know. You have to take care of yourself, too, and Estevan."*

"I am a grown man, sister-in-law," Estevan protested as he tucked Damian in. Camilla turned to smile at him before she answered Margali.

"Oh, yes, Margali! You know so much about taking care of yourself. Can you even get down the stairs without falling? How did you manage—I always used to think you could work magic, older sister, and maybe I was right." She turned to the children's nurse. "If anything changes—if he says anything, call me," Camilla ordered.

The nurse nodded. "Be sure of it, *Maestra*."

They sat in the kitchen, dunking yesterday's bread into yet more tea. Margali refused, with a grimace, the offer of jam for the bread. Camilla took a roasted fowl from the larder, and they demolished it cold.

Camilla washed down a bite of bread. "Margali? Who were you talking to up there?"

"Oh. Did I speak aloud?"

"You did."

Margali felt herself blush. That meant Estevan had heard, too. Well, maybe this wouldn't come as a shock, then. "Alan. My *Terranan* friend. He saved my life out there in the snow. He taught me to ski—that's how I got here, Camilla." Margali smiled, and winced as her wind-burned skin objected.

Camilla blinked. "Terran friend? Ski?"

"Oh, is that what you call the boards you had tied to your feet?" Estevan sounded intrigued. "I could use something like that."

Camilla tilted her head to one side. "Later, I want to see those skis. But wait, Margali, you can't mean—Margali, the *Terranan* are all head-blind."

"This one isn't." Margali grinned.

Camilla shoved tangled hair back from her face. "And what have Great-Uncle and Great-Aunt got to say to all this?"

"They haven't met him—yet."

IMPOSSIBLE TASKS

by Marella Sands

I love it when an author "fills in the gaps" of Darkovan history in thoughtful and sometimes startling ways, with stories that don't take the easy, obvious path. One such gap concerns the founding and development of the *cristoforo* monastery at Nevarsin, St.-Valentine-of-the-Snows. Marella Sands describes her inspiration for the story in this way: "I felt that, even if Saint Valentine started a monastery, there was no reason the project couldn't have been interrupted for a generation or two during the Ages of Chaos. And as for the rumor that there was a cave somewhere above the monastery where a body lay that was presumed to be the saint himself, well, sometimes those kinds of things get a little messy if you know the real history. So, whose body is really in that cave? What person or persons got the project up and running again? What were their lives like? What brought them to Nevarsin? Here was my chance to find out."

Marella says she was born in a yurt on a windswept plain in Outer Mongolia (thereby preparing her to write stories set in the Hellers), but one especially frigid winter convinced her to move somewhere she could enjoy central heating. These days, she spends her time teaching, traveling, and enjoying life with her husband and pets. She has recently become a fan of cricket and is in giddy anticipation of the next T20 World Cup, which will be held in India in 2016. Besides writing stories for Darkover anthologies, she has three books out from Word Posse, the most recent of which was *Restless Bones*, an anthology of dark fantasy and horror.

Doubling back was supposed to put him behind his pursuers, but it hadn't worked that way. Carlo tried counting the number of footprints to see how many people might be following, but he was no tracker, and the calls of other men farther down the slopes meant another group was approaching. Perhaps the second group had nothing to do with him, and might offer him some warm food or shelter for the night. But he couldn't count on it. He couldn't imagine one group, let alone two, willingly climbing this pass at this time of year, unless the reward were very tempting. Knowing Damiella's family, they had probably made it quite tempting.

Darkness fell quickly this early in the spring, but Carlo couldn't stop for long. Of course, he couldn't light a fire, either, with no fuel and no tinder, so staying on the move was the only thing that could keep him from freezing to death. Having been born in the lowlands, Carlo had only seen mountains from afar, and at a distance, they were beautiful. Up close, they were horrific. Their slopes were covered in snow and ice, their passes few and far between. And over everything was the deep cold sliding down from their peaks. Carlo thought he'd known what cold was, until the mountains had touched him with their long shadows and frigid breath.

"You look like a man with a great deal on his mind," said a mild voice.

Carlo spun around, knife raised. He'd been careless and the second group of men must have caught up with him.

But before him stood only one man. Young, with red hair and green eyes, just like Damiella's own. Carlo pushed thoughts of his beloved aside. This man was apparently alone, and not powerfully built. Carlo could overpower him, though he wasn't sure he could do that before the man could call for help.

The other man only smiled benignly. "You look cold. Come, I've found shelter for the night. Share it with me."

That was a risk; what if the second group of men coming up the mountain should also end up sharing the stranger's fire?

The distant bloodcurdling wail of some wild creature decided him. He had heard stories of fantastic wild beasts and trailmen and who knew what else, and had always dismissed them as myth. But the howl coming from above chilled his blood far more than mere physical cold. Perhaps some of those stories were actually true. Carlo did not want to find out.

Carlo followed the man behind some boulders to a small rock shelter. The overhang barely protected the two men from the wind and certainly did nothing to ward off the distant cries of whatever terrible creature prowled this territory. Carlo glanced around, his hope of a warm fire and a meal fading into despair. He couldn't remember the last time he was warm, or well-fed.

The other man sat directly on the snow. Disbelieving, Carlo stood and hugged himself as tightly as he could. His clothing, which was more than adequate for the lowlands, was entirely insufficient here.

"Where is your fire?" he asked at last, hoping to prompt the man to start a friendly blaze, though Carlo saw nothing to burn. The glow of the moons wasn't terribly bright, though, so perhaps he had missed a cache of firewood somewhere.

"I don't need a fire," said the other man. "You can train your body to withstand the cold; it takes some practice, but all you really need to do is to focus your thoughts."

That surprised a laugh out of Carlo. "What? Impossible!"

The other man shrugged. "It's not so hard once you master it. But since you haven't, it is likely to be a long night for you. Here, I have a blanket I sometimes use to tie up my belongings." He held out a thin sheet; Carlo wrapped it around himself with ill-disguised poor humor. This was barely thicker than a summer shirt! But it did help a little.

"I'm Rinaldo," said the other man calmly. "Originally from the lowlands, but my life is here now."

"Here?" said Carlo with some shock. "In the mountains? No one lives here!'

"Of course people live here," said Rinaldo. "But I admit, they don't usually wander about alone after dark."

"Why aren't you with them, where you could be warm and fed and out of the weather?" asked Carlo.

Rinaldo chuckled, but without malice. In everything he did, he seemed calm and patient. It was beginning to wear on Carlo. The men he had been raised among had blustered, fought, and schemed for women, for wealth, for land. For any advantage.

They had fiery tempers and indulged them often. Both of his brothers had died in duels, and his father wore his scars proudly.

"I am warm enough," said Rinaldo cheerfully. "And do not need to eat today. Rather, I am here to find a good spot to build a retreat for myself and my brothers."

"So you have family."

"In a manner of speaking. They are my brothers by the blessing of the Bearer of Burdens."

Carlo scooted closer to the rock wall, hoping to avoid the new chill that had sidled into the rock shelter as soon as the last of twilight had fled. It would be a long sleepless night indeed. He closed his eyes; he needed time to consider Rinaldo's words. Nearly everything the other man said harkened to subjects Carlo had been raised to mock as false, superstitions that only the half-witted believed. Yet Rinaldo did not speak as if he were deranged, but as if these subjects were merest truth.

"I can hear by your accent you are from the lowlands, probably from a bit farther south than myself," said Rinaldo. "I can see why you haven't any knowledge of the mountains."

Again the wretched, bone-freezing cry sounded down the pass. "What *is* that?" Carlo couldn't help but press himself against the frigid rocks of the mountain.

"Banshee," said Rinaldo, bringing up another thing Carlo had been told was mythical rather than real. "They freeze their prey with their voices, and then rip them apart. I don't suppose you've heard one before."

Carlo merely shook his head.

"I admit their screaming makes my heart leap in alarm," said Rinaldo slowly. "Even though I have been trying for some time to accept the sound as part of the landscape, like the rocks and the snow. Some days I'm not sure I'll ever master my fear of their call." The other man sounded genuinely mournful.

"Master it? An impossible task!"

"You seem to think many things are impossible. But if we didn't set ourselves impossible tasks, there would be little reason to go on living, or to depend on the Bearer of Burdens."

The other man fell silent and Carlo was glad. He'd never met anyone like Rinaldo before; where he was from, everyone revered the Lord of Light, even if they weren't descended from him as the Hastur clan was. But this *Bearer of Burdens*? That was a figure so obscure, Carlo had barely heard whisper of him.

"What impossible task have you set yourself?" asked Rinaldo after minutes of silence. "I, as I said, am engaged in finding a space to build our retreat. I know there was one started here by St. Valentine himself, but its location was lost a generation ago. I want to find it, or, barring that, begin again. Right now, we wander homeless, driven out of most of the settlements on the continent. We need to find a place that will be ours, where we may worship and live as we see fit."

"I have no impossible task before me," mumbled Carlo darkly. "Unless you count surviving this night."

"Then, by all means, do your best to survive," said Rinaldo, his voice still pleasant and without a hint of stress or shivering, "and I will see you in the morning."

Dawn shed its crimson light weakly, as if hoarding the true wealth of the daylight for some other, more blessed, locale. Carlo blinked wearily, wishing he were home, wishing for breakfast, wanting nothing more than to put these horrible mountains behind him.

Rinaldo was awake already, of course, his pleasant smile still in place. In the daylight, Carlo was shocked to see that Rinaldo was not only sitting on the snow with merely a light robe between him and his frozen seat, but he had no shoes! Carlo shook his head in wonder. His own toes, firmly ensconced in stockings and boots, were numbed by well over a day at these frigid altitudes, as were his fingers, nose, and ears. He would never be warm again.

If he found nothing to eat, though, he wouldn't have to worry about warmth. Hunger and the cold together would finish him off, as certainly as a duel.

"I know a settlement near here," said his companion. "They will feed us. Come."

Carlo followed Rinaldo down the slope, grateful his knocking knees could still support him. His stomach twisted in eagerness at the thought of hot food, but he was wary. Any settlement near this path had likely been visited by those following him. The people would be on the lookout for a tall man with brown hair and eyes, a curly beard, and chipped tooth.

"Who is this Bearer of Burdens?" asked Carlo through chattering teeth, just to hear something besides their footsteps crunching in the snow.

"He is the one who carried the world child on his shoulders," said Rinaldo. "And though he bore the weight of the world, he was unbowed. You may cast your troubles upon him, and he will hold you up."

"I don't have any troubles." Carlo realized that was a ridiculous thing to say; no one without troubles would be wandering alone in the mountains without extra clothing, food, and equipment. A man traveling without any baggage into weather that could kill in hours, if not minutes, was desperate. But Rinaldo did not gainsay him or even behave as if Carlo had said something untoward.

If only Damiella's family hadn't been so strict! It wasn't as if they were truly accepted members of the Hastur clan; they were merely soldiers and farmers, like everyone else around. But Damiella's father's father had been recognized as a *nedestro* scion of a younger son of a minor Hastur lord. The connection was slim, but documented, and so Damiella must wed someone with better parentage than Carlo, whose father knew nothing but leather making and whose mother had worn out her eyesight, and her joints, with stitching gowns for fine ladies. She had died, blind and raving, two summers ago, the year Carlo had finally become old enough to stop dreaming of Damiella from afar and to step forward to ask her father for her hand.

But Tomas, her father, would not even hear his suit. Instead, Damiella had been betrothed to another man, a man whose connection to the Hasturs was just as obscure as Damiella's own. *This is what happens when the bastard grandchildren of younger sons have ambition*, his father had said when he had heard the news. *They get big heads. Mark my words, some other snot-filled lordling will take both Tomas and his wretched new son-in-law down a peg eventually.*

But that was not enough for Carlo. Damiella was his! Her delicate frame, auburn hair, and bright green eyes had captivated him the moment he first saw her. That had been five years ago, just after her mother had died and she had been brought back to Hastur lands from Arilinn, where she had been visiting her mother's kin. Carlo had courted, and sought, her from that day forward. She had always enjoyed their flirtations, only becoming more sad and withdrawn the closer her own wedding became.

He had thought he had her heart, but when he pressed her to run away with him, she had refused. At first, she had been demure and merely put him off with shy denials. But a tenday ago, when he had shown up to her father's house at dawn, waiting behind a bush for her to pass by, and pulled her aside to tell her his plan for their escape, she had firmly pushed him away.

"I may not have more than a drop of Hastur blood," she had said proudly, "but I can at least claim it, and perhaps even have a chance to serve a Hastur lord in his court! There's a chance that will happen if I marry Mikhail. With you, I will have nothing more—ever—than a husband who stinks of leather, and a life bounded by hard work and childbearing."

He had been shocked! Damiella had never spoken to him like that before. She must want him; she had to. Otherwise, what had the past five years of flirtation and dancing been about?

Well, there was one way to make her his that even her father could not ignore! If he could take her, she would be his, and no one in her family would be able to deny him his right to her after that. She would know how much he loved her, and love him in return, just as she always had. His temper, the same temper that had brought both his brothers to early graves, had overtaken him, and he had exploded in anger, grabbed at Damiella, ripped her dress, pinned an arm behind her back.

But, to his surprise, she had kicked him and screamed and run back to the house. Shock had made him let go; the rousing of the household had led him to flee. It had not taken long for him to notice he was being pursued, and so he had kept running long after he had thought to stop and turn back, and try to convince her once more.

"Here," said Rinaldo, bringing Carlo out of his melancholy and his memories.

The small settlement Rinaldo had brought them to was nestled in the folds of the mountains. A few fields, not yet plowed for spring, surrounded the homesteads.

Rinaldo seemed so lost in thought, Carlo wondered if he had forgotten about the necessity of finding food. Carlo was famished and the smoke rising from the homesteads promised that hot meals were being prepared even now.

At length Rinaldo smiled and continued toward the nearest homestead. A young boy wandered out of the farmhouse, saw them, and called for the people inside to pull more chairs up to the table for guests. The smile on the boy's face was the most welcome sight Carlo had seen for days.

The men pursuing him had either given up, been eaten by banshees, or had somehow gone on through the passes to hunt farther afield than any sane man would. After several weeks, Carlo no longer startled every time new people wandered through the settlement. He stopped looking over his shoulder. Perhaps most importantly for his peace, thoughts of Damiella no longer tormented him. One day, he would go back there, when Tomas had stopped looking for him, and he could win his place among the men of the community.

In the meantime, life in Nevarsin was pleasant. Some of the families in the valley, who kept to the old ways, had daughters who welcomed Carlo into their beds, and so his nights were warm and full of companionship. The fields were plowed, the crops planted. Flowers bloomed on the hillsides and the snow retreated a short way up the slopes.

But as the days passed, Carlo found that the appeal of physical pleasures began to pale in comparison with his fascination with Rinaldo's quest. Carlo wanted to go with him, but on most days, the people of Nevarsin prevailed upon him to help plant, or rebuild a damaged structure, or to get products made over the long winter ready for the spring market down in the foothills. Quickly, he had become a part of everyone's life, and the fabric of his days had become rich.

And yet, his thoughts were continually drawn up the mountain, to be with Rinaldo. When he was with the other man, he learned so much that was different than what he had always been taught about being a man, about women and family, about faith. He had also mastered the secret of staying warm without blankets and shoes, and he listened for hours to the stories of the Bearer of Burdens and of St. Valentine. The longer Carlo spent around Rinaldo, the more he felt at peace with himself and the other settlers, even with the land itself. The feeling was new, but Carlo loved it, and held on to it tightly.

Rinaldo had explained his plan of building a great stone edifice, where the sons of squabbling lordlings could come to learn the ways of peace. Carlo had scoffed, wondering which lordling would be the first to admit his sons might do well to learn something besides violence. Carlo's own childhood had been full of beatings at the hands of his father; and if it hadn't been his father, then he was bruised and battered from the way he and his brothers had fallen on each other upon a whim. Sometimes, he, his brothers, and his father, had united to form a nearly unbeatable wall of flesh that could physically dominate other men and force them to concede whatever it was they wanted. Having a common purpose had made them strong, his father had insisted. It would keep them alive.

In that, his father had been wrong. So very wrong. For the first time, Carlo felt pity when he thought of his father, and of the short pointless lives of his brothers. A man who had been raised to consider striking others as a form of love, who thought mere companionship with another male suspicious and unmanly, and who had considered women nothing more than bodies to be enjoyed and to sire children upon, was living only half a life.

He wondered now why it had seemed normal to be so wretched and unhappy, to think of destruction as the most ordinary, and necessary, of masculine skills. At night, in the arms of his lovers, he dreamt of his brothers, and wept.

The days had grown longer and the snows had retreated up the slopes a short distance. Carlo's heart called him to be up the slopes with Rinaldo, but today was a special day: the community of Nevarsin would come together to celebrate the nameday of its newest member, a child born over the winter. Carlo had assumed he was not invited. At home, no one would invite strangers, or near-strangers, to something like this.

So he had been shocked when Eduardo, the stooped bald leader of the small settlement, had personally invited him to attend. Carlo had stammered an acceptance and had blushed from gratitude for being included in something that was not rightly his. And now the day had arrived.

Carlo was put to work carrying tables and chairs outside. One of his lovers, Leonie, a girl of merry blue eyes and with long unbound hair as golden as the summer blooms on the slopes above Nevarsin, brought a pail of vegetables for him to peel once he had finished that task. "Make yourself useful," she said with a laugh. Carlo smiled at her and set to his task, happier than he could remember being in his entire life. The only thing that would make this day even more perfect would be Rinaldo's presence.

But the other man, though he had been made aware of the invitation, was not present when dinner was finally served. Carlo helped the oldest members of the community by cutting their food in to small enough pieces for them to chew, and listened to the stories of their youthful years when the community had been even smaller, and basked in the glow of their acceptance.

At last, when everyone was fed, Eduardo stood and gestured for the parents of the baby to come forward with her. They brought the seven-month-old to the front of the crowd.

The beaming parents could barely take their eyes off their child as Eduardo blessed the child and officially named her Carina with a prayer to the Bearer of Burdens. Then he asked, "And would you name others to be special guides and friends to this child?"

Carlo leaned forward, intrigued. In the lowlands, children often had several sets of parental figures, but he couldn't remember anyone actually making the position official with a ceremony at their naming.

The couple, whom Carlo had been helping build a barn for their animals, named another couple from a community several miles away, and then turned to him, "Would you also agree to be a guide and help to our child, Carlo?"

Carlo's mouth gaped open and he sat still, stunned, unable to speak. Finally, Leonie elbowed him. "Yes, he will," she said out loud.

Leonie's brother helped pull Carlo to his feet and he stumbled forward to stand with the parents, the other couple, and Eduardo. How could this be happening? He looked over the crowd, wondering how they could accept him so easily. He hadn't had to kill anyone in a duel to win land or women or riches. He hadn't had to challenge any of the men for anything at all. He had simply given them help when they'd asked; in return, they had given him so much more.

Eduardo laughed. "They must do things very differently in the lowlands."

"They do indeed," said a familiar voice. Rinaldo. Carlo turned to him and held out his hands in supplication.

"Rinaldo! How can this be? I'm not..."

"One of them?" Rinaldo finished for him. "You weren't one of them, not this spring. But you've been here some time now. You've made yourself a part of this community with your willingness to work. And as for belonging and becoming one of them in a more physical way, well, I think you are wrong there, as well." Rinaldo turned a measured gaze on Leonie, who crossed her arms and sighed.

"We were going to wait to announce it," she said, "But it's true. Janniya, Varielle, Cassia, and I will all be standing before you next summer with our own babes, and Carlo will be father to them all."

Carina's mother squealed in delight. "What a blessing!"

"Bearer of Burdens, we are blessed indeed," said Eduardo. He clapped Carlo on the shoulder.

For the second time, Carlo was stunned into muteness. A parade of well-wishers blurred before him as his eyes ran over with tears. He could think of nothing to say that could encompass what he felt. This community had adopted him, respected him, blessed him with love, friendship, and family. It had to be a miracle straight from the Bearer of Burdens himself. How impossible this all seemed, like a dream. Except he could never have dreamed something so extraordinary.

For the first time in tendays, he thought of Damiella, and the life he would have had with her, had she accepted him. Now, knowing how different life could be, he could throw off any remaining doubt and regret about leaving that life behind, about leaving Damiella behind. He prayed sincerely to the Bearer of Burdens that she would be happy with Mikhail, and his heart was content.

After the feast and the congratulations and the dancing and several rounds of wine and toasts to the health of Carina and her family, and to Carlo and his new and expanding family, Carlo was finally able to find a quiet moment to sit with Rinaldo.

"You've been gone so long," he said. "Everyone misses you."

Rinaldo's peaceful smile was just as Carlo remembered. "You mean *you* miss me. But you don't need to miss me any longer: I've come to ask you to travel up the pass with me tomorrow. I've found something exciting that you need to see."

"So you didn't come for Carina's naming?"

Rinaldo reddened with embarrassment. "I admit, I forgot about that. But what I found is the original site that St. Valentine himself began centuries ago! Some of the buildings are nearly finished; others just begun. Some chambers are already partially carved out of the living rock of the mountain. I'm not sure why it was abandoned, but it's a good site for the monastery. Even better, since it's the site St. Valentine himself chose! You must come with me tomorrow to see it."

"Very well, I will," said Carlo with a light laugh. Just then Leonie came out of her father's home and gestured toward Carlo.

Rinaldo patted him on the knee. "Your lady awaits," he said. "But one day, you will see that you do not need such pleasures. The Bearer of Burdens will consume your thoughts, your dreams, and your strength. You will no longer want for mere human companionship."

Privately, Carlo thought that was unlikely, but he did not contradict his friend. "Perhaps. But not tonight."

"Good night, *bredu*," he heard Rinaldo call softly as the other man walked away.

Bredu. Brother. A true brother, not just a man related to him by an accident of birth. Something else Nevarsin had provided for Carlo that he had never had. He smiled, took Leonie's hand, and followed her into the house.

The site Rinaldo had found was extremely steep, but the view was certainly incredible, with the towering ice of the Wall Around the World glinting off to the north while the small valley below looked valiantly green nestled among the harsh white peaks. As if it were defying the ice to come and defeat it.

As the days passed, and his lovers grew less interested in having both expanding bellies and a full-grown man in their beds, Carlo began staying at the building site more and more. One of the buildings began to feel like home, and Leonie even brought him blankets she had made herself. Carlo no longer felt the cold as he had when he had first come, but he was pleased with the gifts, and the love that had gone into their making.

But as much as this monastery building had become home to him, it was not to Rinaldo. The other man continued to explore the area, and stayed away many nights. He clearly had a favorite place, as the path he took grew more pronounced by the day. He never invited Carlo, or anyone else, to whatever he had found on the slopes above, but even when he was not present on the job site, his presence could be felt, strong and supportive.

Summer had started to retreat, but autumn had not beaten it back yet. The monastery progressed slowly, but that was as it should be. Carlo could feel the time it was taking to shape the stones, and carve the rooms out of the mountain as something tangible, just as he could note the passing of time it took for a babe to come to birth, or a boy to manhood. He had no illusions that the entirety of the site would be developed in his lifetime, or perhaps even his children's lifetimes, but that was good and proper. The construction of the monastery was more about the journey of finding and building than it was about completion. Even the strange fact it had been abandoned and was now rediscovered, had to be part of some larger purpose. It had taken him some time to understand that.

Sometimes, Carlo caught himself smiling benignly at nothing at all, and wondered if he ever looked like Rinaldo.

One of the others working on the site, Leonie's brother, shouted. "Look! Nevarsin burns!"

Carlo swiveled his head toward the homesteads in the valley. The dark crimson glow he had thought was sunset was fire. At least one building was ablaze.

Carlo raced down the path as quickly as he dared and arrived, out of breath, heart beating in both fear and exertion, at the settlement before the others. In front of him stood a small contingent of horses bearing strong, armed men on their backs. One of the men carried a flag, the silver tree on a blue field of the Hasturs.

Hasturs, here?

"Where is he?" demanded a broad-shouldered man whose red hair was accented by white streaks at the temples. "Where is my brother? You are hiding him here. Tell me where he is!"

The others looked at one another, but no one stepped forward. Carlo crossed his arms and tried to appear braver than he felt. He had always faced men on foot before, men like himself. He had never stood before men on horseback, who were armed with spears and bright swords. "Perhaps if we knew who your brother was, we would tell you…" He glanced at the weapons carried by all the men and forbore to add "…or maybe we wouldn't."

"I am Ruyal Hastur," the man said arrogantly. Carlo thought hard on the name; was Ruyal the overlord of the Hastur line that Damiella had been related to? The multiple sub-clans within the

Hastur lineage had never been important to him, but he was fairly sure he had heard of Ruyal. "I am looking for my brother Rinaldo."

The small crowd of settlers let out a collective gasp. Hastur! How could Rinaldo be a Hastur? They did not worship the Bearer of Burdens; they worshiped Aldones, the Lord of Light.

"Clearly, you know him," said the Hastur lord. "Where is he?"

Nearly as one, the villagers glanced up the mountain toward the building site. Ruyal's gaze was also drawn upward.

"Horses will be no good on the slopes," said one of the lord's men. "We will have to climb on foot."

"No," said Ruyal. "He will be brought to us."

"There is no need," said a gentle voice.

Everyone turned. The barefoot Rinaldo strode calmly through the gathering of settlers, smiled benignly at Carlo, and then faced the warriors. "I am here, brother. Leave these people in peace."

"They are nothing to me," said Ruyal, "now that I have you."

"You may have my body," said Rinaldo. "But not my mind." He glanced toward another figure, cloaked and riding a black horse. "Your *laranzu* will not succeed there."

Another gasp went through the crowd. A *laranzu*! Carlo's anxiety ratcheted upward. Though he didn't believe in magic, he also hadn't, until this spring, believed in banshees, either. What if he were wrong about *laran* as well? What kind of foul things could this *laranzu* do to Rinaldo?

Another small contingent of mounted soldiers entered the village. "No one else was along the road," the leader of the group said to Ruyal, who nodded in reply. The newly arrived soldier glanced at Rinaldo, and then spotted Carlo standing behind him. "Aha! Lord, here is another criminal—the man who took Tomas' daughter against her will!" The voice was familiar, though the face, at first, was not. But was that not Mikhail? Carlo had rarely met the man, and had never seen him armed and clothed as a soldier. His hair was short and beard trimmed more closely than it ever had been before; he had gained weight and had lost some of the predatory, hungry look he had always borne in the past. He was nearly unrecognizable.

The Hastur lord's gaze settled on Carlo. "You forced yourself on another man's bride?"

Even Rinaldo turned to watch Carlo's response. Carlo glanced around at the crowd of his new friends, his lovers. Their faces were concerned and curious, but not hostile; they were not prepared to believe this bellicose warrior over Carlo. Their faith in him was humbling, even though Carlo knew in his heart he had planned to commit the crime, would have committed it, if he had been able. Now, it was unthinkable. But last spring, he had been a different man.

"No," he said firmly. "I did not, but I admit I did try. When Damiella rejected my suit, I thought to take her by force. She fought her way free." Reddening, he realized the truth might be more embarrassing than the lie. After all, he had been raised to assume women were to be used; it was only that Damiella was already betrothed to Mikhail that made it a crime. But to admit a woman had gotten away from him? That was pure humiliation.

"You lie!" shouted Mikhail. "She says you took her violently against her will, and threatened to kill her should she tell anyone. Besides, are you telling us that a mere woman escaped you? You expect us to believe that?"

Carlo's heart squeezed itself tightly in pain, half from the humiliation and half from despair. Damiella had said such things about him? How could she? They had planned a life together.

No, that was folly. *He* had planned to have her. She had not planned anything, and had made her feelings quite clear in her rejection. She did not love him. She never had. The Damiella he had thought he loved was the one in his own mind, not the woman of flesh and blood.

As one, his lovers stepped forward. Leonie said, "I can testify that, since he has arrived here, this man has offered no woman any violence or insult. If this woman says he forced her, let her stand before the *laranzu* and make her accusation."

Ruyal Hastur grunted and spat on the ground. "The woman you speak of is my *barragana*, a scion of the Hasturs, and the word of a Hastur is without question." He waved a hand toward

Rinaldo and Carlo. "Take them both. The rest of you may go back to your homes."

Carlo was shocked. Damiella was a *barragana*? He glanced at Mikhail's cold and hard expression, and realized that Damiella's lie had gotten her what she wanted. Claiming she had been forced had, in turn, forced Mikhail to either take a shamed woman as his wife and suffer the loss of his own honor, or repudiate her and keep his honor. He had, as she had apparently counted on, chosen honor. Once free of her betrothal, Damiella had been able to worm her way into Ruyal Hastur's court and his bed. She was not well-bred enough to be wife to someone like Ruyal. But if she were clever enough, her children might be heirs to his holdings.

Carlo's anger faded into sadness. Yes, Damiella had lied, and she had schemed, but what other options had been open to her? Her life had been bounded by custom and law more tightly than if she'd been confined by unbreakable chains. In the old days, he had never considered what choices she had, or did not have, and how she might want to get more out of her life than the men who controlled it were willing to offer her.

The soldiers kicked their horses forward, but Leonie did not retreat back into the crowd. Surprisingly, she stood defiantly in front of the oncoming soldiers, placing herself between Carlo and Ruyal. "What of the home you burned? What of our stores of food your soldiers have already plundered! Return to us what is ours and leave us."

Mikhail spurred his horse forward and knocked Leonie aside. Carlo's heart leaped in his chest, but her father was quicker than he and covered her with his own body. Her brother stepped in between the horse and his sister to confront Mikhail, shouting, "You would run down a pregnant woman? We see the cut of your honor and we want none of it!"

Mikhail shouted back, "The Hastur lord has spoken!" His voice rang among the slopes and echoed back to the settlement. "We will have these two criminals and will brook no defiance. Back to your homes!"

No one moved. Rinaldo held up a hand. "Please, friends, it is all right. We will go with these men." He glanced at Carlo, a question in his eyes, and Carlo nodded. He would give himself up rather than see Leonie and the others harmed. He could not do that to his friends. To his *family*.

"We will go with you," he said to Ruyal.

Two of the soldiers dismounted. One tied Rinaldo's hands behind his back, and the other tied Carlo's. Without another word, Ruyal turned his horse to the path to the lower slopes. Someone prodded Carlo in the back with a spear, and he followed.

If Carlo retained any doubts that *laran* existed, he was disabused of that quickly. No sooner had they returned to the main camp, about two miles back down the mountain path, than the *laranzu*, Mikhail, Ruyal, and two others had Rinaldo and Carlo in a tent and the *laranzu* began staring into a blue stone. The light from the stone played over Rinaldo's face, making him wince, but he said nothing.

"Tell me what you did with them," insisted Ruyal over and over. "Tell me where they are!"

Both the *laranzu* and Rinaldo were covered in sweat, though neither moved as far as Carlo could tell. Their travails were internal. Whatever they were doing, it cost both greatly, but Rinaldo, as far as Carlo could see, was the one at a disadvantage. Twice the *laranzu* had to stop when Rinaldo passed out.

Carlo kept quiet, though his heart seized in agony every time a cry escaped Rinaldo's lips. He had little hope that Ruyal's men would be foolish enough to give him an opportunity for escape, but even so, he had to be alert for the possibility. Screaming or crying or struggling against his bonds would be pointless and waste strength. He needed to be smart, harbor his resources, and, should an opportunity arise for him to get Rinaldo out of here, he would need to take it.

Toward dawn, Rinaldo slumped to the ground. His face was ashen. The *laranzu* gestured toward him and confronted Ruyal. "Lord, he is almost spent, and I am no closer to getting the information you want. The mind of a Hastur is strong."

Ruyal growled and flung the man aside. "If you cannot do this thing, then I will find another who can. One way or another, my brother's mind will be opened."

Ruyal stomped out of the tent, Mikhail and the others following. The *laranzu* regained his feet, gave Rinaldo and Carlo a dark look, and then left as well.

Carlo crawled to Rinaldo awkwardly; his ankles were unbound but his legs were numb after a night of tense kneeling on the ground. His hands remained tied behind his back.

Rinaldo's skin was gray and his breathing irregular. Carlo knew nothing about nursing wounds, physical or otherwise, and could only pray to the Bearer of Burdens that Rinaldo could recover quickly.

Furtive footsteps approached the tent, and a cloaked figure sidled in. Carlo did his best to place himself between the stranger and Rinaldo, though what he could do to help his friend, he did not know.

The cloaked figure held up a hand for silence and gestured with a knife toward Carlo's back and made a cutting motion. He wanted to cut the rope keeping Carlo's hands bound. Carlo nodded warily and turned away from the man. If the man wanted to slip a knife between his ribs instead of cutting the rope, there wasn't much he'd be able to do about it. He trusted to the Bearer of Burdens and prayed the man cut the rope.

The rope was thick and it took the other man several tries to cut all the way through it, but within moments, Carlo's hands were free. He rubbed his wrists briefly but he was more worried about Rinaldo than himself. The other man's skin was cold to the touch.

His rescuer put away his knife, and then gestured toward the sky. It would be light soon, Carlo reasoned that to mean. He nodded. He got his arms around Rinaldo and lifted the other man off the ground. Rinaldo had some height but he was slimly built, unlike the men in Carlo's family, and weighed almost nothing.

The other man ducked out of the tent and was gone, but not before Carlo recognized the silver ring on the other man's little finger. He had last seen it on Damiella's hand. Stunned, he realized his rescuer was Mikhail.

That made no sense, but Carlo couldn't wait here to puzzle it out. He had to get Rinaldo up the slopes to safety. He carried Rinaldo outside, oriented himself, and slipped into the darkness.

The path to Nevarsin was fairly wide and he made good time, even though the moons had set and the sun had not yet touched the peaks with the first rays of dawn. Wearily, he trudged with his burden into Nevarsin and headed toward the path to the building site without pause.

Leonie and the rest of the settlement stood in his way.

"Please, let me through," he said. "They've nearly killed him."

Leonie gestured toward the limp form of Rinaldo. "Let someone else carry this burden now. You're tired; you need to rest."

Carlo only shook his head. "They'll be coming." Too late, he realized he had given Ruyal an excuse to kill everyone here. They would all look guilty of helping him escape. "I'm sorry; they'll take out their anger on you. You need to flee."

Leonie stepped forward and took one of his hands. "We've already made plans to flee. Most of us have run across Ruyal's kind before; we had no illusions he would leave us be, even after he had what he wanted. We'll head on up the mountain and trust in the Bearer of Burdens that he will send us salvation."

"I will take him for now," said Leonie's father, Orton.

"And I will take him after that," said her brother.

The other men in the village nodded. "We will all help," said Eduardo.

Leonie squeezed his hand before letting go. "Come; we women already have food packed and the children bundled against the chill of the high slopes."

Tears flooded Carlo's eyes and he nodded. Several men helped transfer his burden to Orton and everyone headed for the path to the building site.

Freed of his burden, Carlo walked more easily, but his heart remained heavy. The air on the higher slopes would be harder to breathe, and Rinaldo was so weak already. How could the other man hold on long enough to recover from whatever the *laranzu* had done to him?

The sun began sending spears of light into the sky, turning the snow-laden slopes pink and gold. The beauty was breathtaking but Carlo barely registered it; his heart was with Rinaldo, and with the people of Nevarsin, who loved and trusted him. Who had made him part of their community without him even being aware it was happening.

His father, his brothers, Tomas, Mikhail: they understood conquest and nothing else. Why, then, had Mikhail helped him?

As Carlo trudged along the trail, weary with the climb, he realized Mikhail and Damiella must have planned everything together. She would claim to have been forced; Mikhail would give her up. She would then, if she were clever enough, become *barragana* to the most powerful Hastur lord in the land, and Mikhail, if *he* were clever enough, would end up paxman to the same. Each one would improve their situation as far as custom and law would allow. All they needed was someone to provide a convenient excuse to begin the chain of lies. All they needed was one hothead to string along, for Damiella to smile at and dance with. One idiot to use to their mutual advantage. And Carlo had given them everything they could possibly have wanted.

They had *both* betrayed him, and had planned to do so for some time. The only hitch in their plan was when Mikhail had recognized Carlo. It would be risky to say later that he hadn't seen him, considering how Carlo had stepped out of the crowd to address Ruyal. But once Mikhail had pointed Carlo out, he had to make sure Carlo was never questioned by the *laranzu*, or the plot would come out. He had to see that Carlo escaped.

They neared the building site, but now Carlo could hear sounds of pursuit. Ruyal's men, unburdened by supplies, children, pregnant women, old people, and an unconscious man, had made good time, and had figured out quickly where they must have gone.

"Keep climbing!" Carlo shouted to those in front. "The path to the left—there, see? I don't know what's up there but it may be more easily defended than here."

Now the way became even more treacherous. Rinaldo's path was barely wide enough for one able-bodied person, let alone stumbling elders and exhausted children. Their pursuers grew ever closer, and Carlo despaired of reaching whatever shelter might be at the end of Rinaldo's private trail.

"Here!" shouted someone up ahead. "A cave!"

The cave mouth was low enough that Carlo had to duck, but it opened up into a large room illuminated by light streaming through the entrance.

The man carrying Rinaldo laid him gently in the center of the room. Carlo knelt by his unconscious friend and took the other man's cold hands in his own. Leonie and the other woman bundled Rinaldo in blankets, but even Carlo could see Rinaldo was failing. Tears dripped down Carlo's face and he ignored them. In his previous life, he would have preferred death to being seen to weep. Now, he did not care who saw. He only cared that Rinaldo was grievously injured, and he could not help.

The sounds of men approaching outside got louder. "There's a cave here, my lord!" shouted someone.

Orton walked to the entrance and shouted out, "Anyone who attempts to come in will be killed. You had best leave. We have supplies here to last us long enough for you to become cold and weary. Go home to your women and your families and your dreams of power and glory. They have no place here on the mountain."

Someone began to reply, but Carlo noted Rinaldo's mouth twitching and his eyes blinked open, and he focused on his friend alone. Let Orton handle Ruyal and his men.

Rinaldo looked at those surrounding him, but when his gaze landed on Carlo, his face became beatific in joy. "*Bredu*," he whispered. "You are still here with me."

"I will always be here," said Carlo.

"They wanted me to tell them where the others are, but I wouldn't. He wants to kill them all."

"Kill who?"

"The other brothers. Ruyal says no true Hastur can follow the Bearer of Burdens and that they must have turned my mind weak, made me over into an *ombredin.*" When he saw Carlo's confusion, he said, "A sandal-wearer."

That was a term Carlo had heard a long time ago, referring to a man who was too womanly to be considered a true man. In his former life, if a sandal-wearer had ever crossed his path, he would have killed the man, thinking it was the right thing to do, and would never had had a second thought over the incident. Men who were not prepared to fight and kill at a moment's notice were weak, unfit to live. At least, that was what he had believed until this spring.

"My brothers will start to arrive shortly," said Rinaldo. His voice was growing weaker. "You will need to lead them."

"Lead them? You must lead them!"

Rinaldo gave a slight shake of his head. "I denied the *laranzu* the knowledge he wished, and so he has broken me. I'm finished. But it's all right. They are safe, and you will be here to guide them and watch over them."

"Impossible! I am not a follower of the Bearer of Burdens. I am not one of you!"

Rinaldo only smiled again. "Are you not?"

Carlo felt arms around him and people touching him and he looked up. Leonie, Cassia, Varielle, Janniya, even some of the children, including little Carina, had their hands on him. "You are one of us," said Janniya. "We will help you."

Leonie smiled and nodded, tears in her eyes. Around him, men and women all nodded. "You're one of us," said Leonie's brother. "I want to be one of the first of the brethren to give my life and my soul to this place and its people. I'll follow you."

"But first," said Rinaldo, even more slowly and softly. "We must pray to the Bearer of Burdens for our salvation."

"They're going to come in!" shouted Orton.

"No," whispered Rinaldo. "They are not." His lips moved in silent prayer; Carlo could not help but do the same. Around him, men, women, and children muttered their own versions of their own prayers.

The men outside yelled at each other, clearly ready to attack but unsure how to do so on the narrow path where only one, especially if that person were wearing armor and holding weapons, could tread at a time.

From above came a rumble like thunder, but the light coming in to the cave was bright. The day was cloudless and perfect. Carlo could not understand what the noise was.

"Avalanche," said Janniya. Others whispered the word out loud as well. Janniya's brown eyes were wide with fear. "We'll be trapped in here!"

"We can dig out," said Leonie in her practical way. "But those out there will be swept off the mountain if they don't leave now. They should have known better than to make such a racket beneath the summer snow ledges."

Carlo had eyes only for Rinaldo. The other man's skin became whiter and somehow more translucent, as if he were burning out the flame of his life through his prayer.

It won't be enough. I am failing!

To his surprise, Carlo realized he was hearing Rinaldo's thoughts. Though he knew nothing of sorcery, if thoughts could go one way, why not the other? *I will help*, he thought in return. He grasped Rinaldo's hands and focused his whole being on the other man. It wasn't so difficult. Now that he had mastered the secret of keeping warm in the cold, he had the basic skill to focus his body's energy where he wanted it to go. In this case, he simply had to focus on Rinaldo. It seemed an impossible task, but Rinaldo always said that life was about attempting the impossible, to stand up when all you wanted was to lie down, to try again when all you wanted was to quit. Carlo pushed his very life force out of himself and into his friend. Even if Rinaldo used it all, he would give it gladly.

The rumbling, which had died away, came again, much louder. Carlo heard shouts of despair from outside as the roar became deafening. The floor of the cave vibrated with the power of the oncoming tons of snow, which now flowed over the cave mouth like a white and blue river. Boulders sailed by the entrance, leaping into the valley below. The noise and shaking continued for several minutes, but by then, everything human had been swept off the path.

The world grew quiet and still but still, Carlo only had eyes for his friend. His heart nearly burst in fear; Rinaldo was so pale; he was losing his grip on his body. Desperately, Carlo clutched at his friend, willing him to survive.

Thank you, my brother. Permanedál. The thought was so quiet, Carlo wasn't even sure he heard it.

Rinaldo's mind fell away into darkness. Carlo's thoughts collapsed in on themselves. The connection was gone. His brother was dead.

Carlo's mind reeled, grief clogging his senses, the emptiness in his own mind overwhelming. The grief was a searing, living thing scraping his internal organs, bursting through his thoughts, strumming along every nerve. It was more painful than anything Carlo had felt before. The deaths of his brothers and his mother was nothing compared to this.

Surviving this pain would be hard, nearly impossible. Living without his friend would be equally difficult. How could he bear it?

But Rinaldo would have expected him to shoulder that burden and hold up beneath it, just as the Bearer of Burdens had carried the entire world on his slight human frame without complaint.

"Are they really gone?" asked one of the children.

Carlo glanced toward the cave entrance, where Orton stood looking back down the trail toward Nevarsin, an exhausted Eduardo at his side.

"Snow took them down the mountain," said Orton. "A couple of us can deliver their animals down the pass tomorrow and let others know they were killed in an avalanche. Avalanches are common here in the summer, especially when strangers stumble about unwary and unconcerned for the danger."

Carlo felt a pang for Mikhail, someone who had grown up just like himself, but had not understood how dangerous ambition could be. Damiella would learn that lesson in a few days when word returned to Ruyal's court that its lord was dead. What use was a dead man's *barragana* to anyone? She would have nothing. But unless she came to Nevarsin, Carlo would be unable to help her.

Bearer of Burdens, please watch over her.

Leonie's brother began to lift Rinaldo's body.

"No," said Carlo. *Permanedál.* The old Hastur motto that even Tomas had taken as his own. *I remain.* Even if he had repudiated them, Rinaldo had been a Hastur. Carlo would take his brother's final thought as his last wish. "Let him remain here. If there is any trace of his spirit left in this place, I can't imagine where he would rather be than somewhere he can gaze down upon his good work, and on the valley whose people defended him to the end."

He leaned over and sadly kissed Rinaldo's ice-cold forehead in farewell, then walked out of the cave. He would not be back here. He would build the retreat, this monastery of St. Valentine of the Snows, on the slope below, and his brothers would come and live there, and worship, and train others to be wise and patient and kind.

Who knew, perhaps someday, a child or grandchild of Ruyal might come here and learn the ways of peace from one of Carlo's children or grandchildren. Nothing was truly impossible, not when you put your mind to it, and certainly not when the Bearer of Burdens was on your side.

Leonie came out of the cave and he put his arm around her shoulders; he knew he would never share her bed again. Such pleasures were in the past; his work on the monastery was his present and future. Let the Hasturs have their mind tricks; let other men have their feuds and wars over women and land. Here, there would be honest labor, and peace. A place built by hands alone, away from the vagaries of magic and clan strife.

Leonie stood on tiptoe to kiss his cheek and he smiled down at her and laid a hand on her belly, where his child was preparing its own entrance into this world. Carlo could see his life laid out before him, as Rinaldo must have done with his own life years ago, and the path he had chosen pleased him.

There was much to do. It was time to get started.

THE SNOWFLAKE FALLACY

by Michael Spence

Michael Spence describes himself as an expatriate Virginian living less than five hundred kilometers from the Canadian border, along the northern event horizon of the St. Paul-Minneapolis paradox. He is the narrator of several Darkover novel audio books, including Marion's *The Heirs of Hammerfell*. Recent publications include "Dark Speech" (with Elisabeth Waters, in *Sword and Sorceress 30*), "The Music of the Spheres" (*Music of Darkover*), "Requiem for the Harlequin: Two Perspectives on Time, and a Celebration of *Kairos,* in Three Stories by Harlan Ellison" (*Sci Phi Journal*), and "Why the Sea Is Boiling Hot" (Tales from the Archives of the Ministry of Peculiar Occurrences), a finalist for the 2014 Parsec Award.

He writes that stories in the Darkover anthologies serve at least two secondary purposes (the primary purpose being, of course, to entertain you!). Some explore new territory, while others fill in gaps in the existing lore. Here's a tale that provides the backstory to a principle well-known to Darkover readers.

Hiding behind a barely visible boulder, C.J. took stock of her situation, ticking off points on her fingers. Thumb: she was dead. Index finger: she was in hell. Middle finger: she heard war drums out there in the darkness. Something was coming for her.

Dead: Clearly this was no dream, at least not like any she'd ever known. It felt utterly different. She had heard about so-called lucid dreaming, but people she'd heard talk about it associated it with spirit guides and whatnot, and she wasn't ready to buy into that. And she certainly wasn't awake in any normal fashion, because what little she could see looked nothing like her home on the Ben Nevis Colony. That world had its mists, yes, but they were not only cool but cold and wet. The wisps of fog she could occasionally make out were on the cool side, but they didn't soak her the way the mists of home did.

As for dying, well, that was the natural consequence of being deathly sick, wasn't it? She had just left the classroom after a lesson on quantum elements when the blinding pain chiseled into her head and her stomach emptied itself onto her sweater, her jeans, and the school steps. Her father and the school authorities had decided that her university-prep study track would take a hiatus until she had a better chance of surviving it. Advanced mathematics would have to wait; but with her grades and the aptitude she'd shown, they were convinced she could pick up where she left off.

She snorted. Talk about optimism run wild. Four days she had spent in bed, surrounded by the remnants of a thirteenth-birthday celebration thrown by her father to encourage her, but too distracted by pain and nausea to notice them. Nothing stayed down, not even her favorite raspberry pudding, and intravenous feeds had done their best to keep her hydrated. Her father's friends, remembering how her mother had succumbed to a local bacterium shortly after their arrival a year ago, feared for C.J.'s life. One hour ago, on the fourth day, she fell asleep; the next thing she knew, she was here. Ergo: dead. Q.E.D.

As for where she was, that wasn't so clear-cut. Nothing could convince her, though, that this in any way resembled the "new heavens and new earth" her father spoke of in her mother's funeral sermon. And while he refused to describe heaven, claiming "insufficient data," current folklore was hardly so reticent—and what she could barely make out around her certainly did not look like the shining, cloud-paved fields commonly depicted as "heaven." Besides, there were those lingering headaches, even though their violence had lessened somewhat. One was not supposed to feel pain in the realm of the blessed.

For that matter, if this was heaven, where was everybody? She had awakened in near-total darkness and alone, outdoors, on dry ground. She sat up and glanced around her, hoping to see a familiar tree or cluster of buildings, but found none. There was no plant life to be seen, even if she could make out shapes beyond a few feet, and she could not. No stars, no moving lights of the orbital station that served the Colony in place of a moon. When she had closed her eyes in her sickbed she had been wearing her Commander Quasar pajamas; now she found herself clad in her favorite tee-shirt and jeans, her everyday school wear (vomit-free, happily). She creased the shirt fabric over her chest and felt the stiffer print of Maxwell's equations on it, even though she couldn't make them out by sight.

What did that leave, then? "When you have eliminated the impossible, then what remains, however improbable..."

Alone. Dark. Silent. Phrases from her father's sermons came back to visit her thoughts. "Cast out into the outer darkness," "wandering stars, for whom the blackest darkness is reserved forever"—surely they spoke of this. She thought of the Charles Williams book she had read two years ago, and the scenes of the recently deceased woman wandering the streets of a darkened, silent city that was and yet wasn't the London she had known. The way C.J. imagined that woman felt was much like the way she herself was feeling now.

Solitude was no stranger, of course. She had considerable experience being alone. Since she and her parents had shipped out from Nordgaard with the other colonists (their "mission," her parents had called it), C.J. had found socializing to be a continual source of defeat. Those who didn't shun her because of her lighter skin tone and her fire-red hair ("too weird," one had said, even after she colored it purple) often did so either because of her father's vocation or her own set of interests. A preacher's kid and a science nerd to boot: for now, "fitting in" was a phrase confined to her thesaurus. She kept to herself, taking refuge in books, her weekly online feed of superhero comics, and those times when she could drink in the night sky. The books and the telescope, her prized possessions on Nordgaard, were her closest companions on Ben Nevis.

And now they, along with anything else that made life worth living, were gone. Her father would agree with her that this was a capsule description of hell.

Something began to beat in the darkness. Not the joyful drum sounds of parades, but something more like the pounding of a war drum. She didn't know what it was, only that it could not be good. Although she didn't believe in the Dante-esque picture of myriad demons with pitchforks torturing the damned, she knew evil was real and that it bore no love for human life. Was it here? Was it preparing to enjoy her as its catch?

The drumbeats began to shake her very bones...

...and at that point she had broken and run.

Her father's advice returned: *When your resources are all you have, it's because God has determined that they will be enough, and if not, then he will give you the rest.* That sounded like a platitude, especially where she found herself now. And since being in hell meant God had turned his back on her, that possibility was gone. Nonetheless, she clung to the first clause. When it's all you have, you do what you can with it.

She ran at top speed, knowing that at length she would have to stop running because either something in her would give out or they—whatever *they* were—would catch up. The words of an old song ran through her mind:

Run to the rocks: O rocks, won't you hide me
Run to the rocks: O rocks, won't you hide me
Run to the rocks: O rocks, won't you hide me
All on that day

Yeah, that fits, she thought. *My own personal apocalypse. Oh sinner girl...*

The light level had increased slightly. (Light, in the outer darkness?) Around her a faint landscape crept into view: varied terrain, and the suggestion of a mountain ridge in the distance, a dark line against the deeper black. The drums were as audible as ever—were they following her? She kept moving.

She stepped on the stone before she saw it. Stumbling, her foot complaining (that's what it did when you stepped on a rock, no? The spirit remembers what the flesh experienced), she fell to the ground, scraping her hand against gravel (that too was bound to happen). In the darkness she could make out other stones scattered around her, with larger ones behind them. She slowed and maneuvered around the rocks until she came to the shoulder-high boulder and fell to her knees behind it.

She tried to determine if the drumbeats were getting louder. For the moment it appeared they were not. The sky was lighter, however, now more a charcoal gray with tinges of blue. It reminded her of the pre-dawn hours she loved back home. Here, though, no birds would sing, nor grazing animals bleat. All was still, except for the infernal drums.

So now here she was, done for. Eternally cursed, she could only await further doom.

She found herself wishing she could climb a tree. Perhaps if her pursuers were like hunters or beasts of prey, they might not think to look up. Did she have a scent? In the time-honored reflex, she pulled at the sleeve of her tee-shirt and sniffed the armpit. No scent that she could detect. Of course not. Fresh cadavers stank, not spirits. That didn't mean, of course, that some ghastly, predatory *thing* wouldn't detect her, but it encouraged her nonetheless. If there were a tree...

She raised her eyes and there it was. In the dim light she saw a red oak, tall, in full leaf, and clearly old. Where did that come from? No matter; she estimated the distance, decided to take a chance, and sprinted for the lowest branch. It was an easy jump to grab the branch, and quickly she swung herself up and onto it. It held her weight easily. She took the next three branches upward with ease.

Through the foliage she peered back the way she had come. No sign of pursuers. The light was a bit brighter now, though still the peculiar bluish hue not at all characteristic of the Colony. Her conviction that she was in the afterlife was growing shaky; could it be that she had somehow been translated to another planet, orbiting a blue-white sun? That would be a fascinating sight, except for the lack of her telescope. She missed it.

She glanced back toward the rocks and caught her breath in disbelief. It stood in front of the assemblage of boulders: a Starquest model T35-LV09 with brass fittings, motor drive, and teak tripod. The solar filters were already installed, ready to deploy.

C.J. dropped from the tree and approached the telescope, fearing it would vanish if she took her eyes off it. She put out her hand and touched it. It was no illusion. The main cylinder was as solid as the viewfinder; the motor drive whirred when she switched it on; the filters snicked into place one by one.

If this was hell, it was considerably different from any picture she had held up until now. The telescope, the mountains, the tree— She looked back toward the tree, but it was gone.

So were the rocks.

Huh.

In life, when an unexpected and baffling situation arose, her father would say, "It's one more puzzle, my snowflake! Don't freak; instead, work through it and find the answer." Clutching the telescope housing as if she could somehow keep it from dissolving into the ether, C.J. mentally retraced her steps. She had opened her eyes in the blackness, deduced where she was, panicked, run, found the boulders...

Wait. Back up one. The *song*. In her mind she had played the line about running to the rocks, and they had appeared. She had wanted a tree, and the tree had appeared. She wished for the telescope, and...

The *wish*. This was somehow a world in which wishing could make it so. Well, then. C.J. closed her eyes and said, "I wish I was back home! Healthy! Ready for school!"

She opened her eyes. She was still on the gray plain, holding her telescope. *Yeah, somehow I didn't think that was going to work.* Try something on a smaller scale, then. "The fountain in front of McKendrick Hall. I want to see it."

She opened her eyes and it was there. Three meters high,

adorned with the faces of famous researchers and inventors, water cascading from various spouts, it was the very image of the engineering building's fountain back on Nordgaard. The water splashed happily in the concrete basin. Sound, then, existed in this world.

Well, of course sound existed! She had heard the—

With a start C.J. realized that she had not heard the drums for some time. *Did I conjure them, too?* She wondered at that for a moment, then realized that she still felt a rhythm within her that roughly corresponded to the drumbeats. *My pulse.*

Her fear had come from within herself? She snorted. How many times had she heard *that* one before...

The rocks and the tree had vanished when she stopped thinking about them. The telescope remained because she clutched at it; evidently she had indeed kept it from disappearing. With a thought she released it, and it and the fountain ceased to be. Perhaps she could retrieve the scope later.

All of this suggested that she could create simply by picturing something and *wanting it to be so.* But to do so once wasn't enough—the wish had to be an ongoing process rather than a single event. That meant that she had to think of many things at once for them all to exist. How could she do that and at the same time get something done? It wouldn't work.

A focus, she thought, *that's what I need. Something that will channel a wish and maintain it while idling.* Some sort of mental routine, like Aladdin's genie? She couldn't see herself carrying around an ancient lamp. But wait: Aladdin had had two genies— one of the lamp, one of the—

And with that she had it. Not Aladdin, but another piece of mythology, one she knew like the back of her hand and thus could unconsciously maintain as long as she wanted.

Speaking of hands. With a will she stretched out her hand, and a white glove encased it. She drew it back, and there was the ring on her middle finger, above her closed hand's center of mass. The perfect device. The jewel in its center glowed with an internal vitality, lighting up the dimness.

She turned toward the flat ground where the rocks had been,

and *wished.* The tinges of blue light in the growing dawn were suddenly washed out by a ray of blue that streamed from her hand, digging into the ground and carving out an immense rectangle of rock, then another, and another, until five such shapes lay on the plain. Another *wish,* and in a wash of blue light the stone planes rose into the air and arranged themselves into the five upper sides of a cube. Four narrower rectangles joined themselves similarly atop the cube, forming a low wall she could duck behind. Wielding her ring's beam like a knife, she carved steps leading up the side of the cube to the top.

There we are. A fortress. She listened, but heard no drums. Nor, she reckoned, would she hear them again. At least she hoped not.

Now for the most important part. Turning away, with a wish she summoned her telescope, aimed it, and peered through it in the direction where she thought she had seen mountains in the dark. Whatever she had seen was no clearer than before. A gray fog not only covered the ground, it also made up most of the sky. If any other life-forms occupied this world, she might never learn of them unless she stumbled upon them in her wandering, or they her.

With a breath of anticipation she turned back to the fortress. It stood where she had left it, apparently as solid as before. With a whoop she ran up the stairs—*kind of a lot; I think I built too high*—to the upper story, where she sprang up and down in delight. "Yeeeee-*HA!* Beware my power, eh?"

Of course, she realized, there remained the trivial questions of where she could find food in this world—for whatever it was, it no longer looked like a place of punishment. Soberly she considered that she could be looking at the situation out of naïveté, and it had been far too soon to make any such evaluation. But for the moment she could think seriously about how to spend her days here: find food, water, *oh, and replace this cube with something prettier. Something with a potty.*

For the moment, in this her private world, she had become a superhero. That absolutely *rocked.* Should she make a costume? Nah, maybe later. She had the ring; that was what mattered. A name? That was easy. *Look out, world—here comes the mighty Blue-Ray!* Yeah, that would work. She could even change her hair color again to fit.

One question, after all this, still needed an answer. Before setting out to search throughout the land, she decided to create a bullhorn. Amped up to cosmic levels, of course. She raised it to her lips and called out, "IS THERE ANYBODY HERE?"

The silence continued. No crickets, no one even to drop a pin. Again she called, "IS THERE ANYBODY HERE?"

Again, nothing.

"IS THERE ANYB—"

Yes, yes, we're here. Please keep it down, for Avarra's sake! People are trying to get work done.

It took her a minute to recover her wits. She hadn't thought about what to do if someone actually answered.

Another voice said, *Do you think you could speak up a bit? I don't think they heard you out in the Dry Towns.*

Hush, said the first voice. *Are you lost? Where are you?*

She thought of reciting landmarks, then snickered. As if this plain had any. Well...that itself might be something. "I'm on a large flat plain, and I think there's a mountain range some distance from here. There's enough light to see by, but it's like I'm surrounded by a bluish-gray cloud. There's fog everywhere."

A pause. Then, *Interesting. Can you display a beacon of some sort? We'll try to find you.*

It was worth a try. "Okay, how's this?" She extended her ring hand skyward, and a brilliant beam shot from it into where the heavens would be back home. "Will this work?"

Excellent! We'll be there at once.

Almost before she had the chance to wonder why, after fleeing from presumed demonic pursuers, she would invite persons unknown to rendezvous with her, she heard a noise below her and saw a small cluster of oddly dressed people milling about in front of the fortress. They looked around them, evidently wondering where their summoner was.

"Oh." She had forgotten she was still on the roof. "I'll be right down!" She raced down the steps along the wall—*that was dumb, not putting a hand-rail on this thing*—and joined the arrivals.

A woman of quiet, elegant demeanor stepped forward and gestured. "Greetings." Her voice was clear but non-committal, her bearing regal but not unapproachable. She looked like one of the otherworldly queens C.J. had seen in fantasy posters, and C.J. couldn't help thinking of her as The Lady.

"Uh, hello! Where am I? *Am* I in hell?" Immediately she wanted to kick herself, but then figured, what if the answer were yes after all?

Someone in the group said, "Which one?" before the others shushed him.

That stopped her. "There's more than one?"

A small smile pulled at the Lady's lips. "Nine that I'm aware of. But no, child, this isn't one of them. It's too warm by far. You are very much alive. It sounds as though you are a long way from home, though. Which kingdom are you from?"

"I'm from the Ben Nevis Colony. I just woke up here this, uh, this morning."

The Lady considered. "I am not familiar with the Ben-nevis lands; but then, Darkover has many realms that I do not know. I hope you will not take offense."

"Er, no ma'am. The Colony has its own planet, and I'm told there are no other humans there. I take it this is a different planet?" C.J. looked around her to see if the view had cleared any. No, this was probably as bright as it got, and the mists continued to swirl around them.

The Lady, apparently unsure of the best response, turned to the others. A massive man who looked as though he'd be right at home leading one of the Colony's construction firms answered. "Well, yes and no. Yes, this is not your colony planet. Our home is a world we call Darkover, and our group comes from various regions there. But no, we are not standing on Darkover itself. This is what we call the Overworld—and you are the first person we've encountered here who is not Darkovan. At least, we don't think you are. This is passing strange, for a number of reasons—"

A young female voice spoke up. "And I think one of those reasons is me." She came forward and stood face to face with C.J., who wasn't sure whether to blink or faint.

The girl was C.J. herself. Her hair was different, her clothing radically different, but seeing her made C.J. wonder whether she herself had ever been alive or was merely this girl's dream.

As C.J. stood dumbfounded, the girl giggled. "Nice mask. Isn't it rather early for the Midsummer Festival?"

Abashed, C.J. felt at her cheeks, tore the mask off and threw it away. She hadn't been aware of creating it.

The man who had spoken before—she labeled him the Workman—whistled. "Lenore, do you see this? Am I imagining it?"

"No. I see it, too," said the Lady. "Apart from their hair and dress they appear to be identical." She turned to another of the group. "Kevin, please scan her if you can. What do you see?"

The tall man toward the back of the cluster nodded. He held a blue stone in his hand, translucent and regular in shape like a crystal. It scintillated softly, casting eerie sparkles on him and those around him. C.J. glanced at the others in the group—the Lady, the Workman, and five others—and saw that each was holding a similar stone. Their radiance was like the light that illumined this world, but far brighter. The man said, "She is closely connected to her body, enough so that I can observe many physical traits. In these she is indeed identical to Cherilly, with one difference. This girl is still in the grip of threshold sickness."

"Oh, dear," said the Lady. She asked C.J., "Do they have *kirian* on your world? Can they give you the treatment you need?"

"I don't know that word. I don't think so," C.J. replied, quite at a loss. She told them about her experiences at school, and how the Colony medics had failed to understand what had happened to her.

The Lady—no, the Workman had called her *Lenore*—took a sharp breath. "There's no question, then. We must get her to

Neskaya." To one of the other women she said, "Andrea, have the large screen readied for teleportation. If this girl is truly a match for Cherilly, then we can use her as a search pattern. We need to try, at least."

Andrea nodded, and one by one the members of the group vanished, leaving Lenore and the man called Kevin behind. Lenore said, "I would take you with us, but to be honest, I do not know exactly where in the Overworld we are. In fact, the notion of 'place' is quite awkward here. You will have to come to us, as we came to you. Our Tower is present in the Overworld as well as in the physical world, so—"

"Wait, wait," said C.J. "Physical world? So this isn't a real place?"

Kevin chuckled. "Oh, it's quite real. It's just not made of matter as we know it. It's real because people are real, because minds are real; under the right conditions, they manifest here. We can meet here unbounded by limits of space, sometimes even unbounded by time. Indeed, you could call this a world of meeting."

Something clicked. "Ah!" C.J. said. "It's the noösphere!"

"Excuse me?" said Lenore. "My starstone creates a bridge for our thoughts, but specific words...this is one I do not know."

C.J. was delighted to find something she could connect to from home. "My dad talks about many theologians—uh, people who work with spiritual knowledge—and one that he likes wrote about the noösphere. It's a world of thought. Interaction. You have a planet, you've got the geosphere. The planet has life, you've got the biosphere. Living things have sentience, minds, you've got the noösphere. There's lots more; I think he imagined the noösphere waking up to become the next stage of humanity, or something like that, but...wow. The noösphere really exists, and I'm in it! I've gotta tell Dad about this!"

She suddenly recalled where she was and what had put her there. "I will get to see him again, won't I?"

Lenore laughed. "Yes, child, you will. We'll help you heal, and then we can send you back to your Ben-nevis world. But tell me, where did this building come from? Did you build it?"

C.J. nodded. "Want to see?"

"Of course," said the Lady. C.J. brandished her ring and created a maple tree, then her telescope. Then, just to see if it would work, she crafted a full-scale replica of her home exterior on Nordgaard. Finally, she used the ring to disassemble the fortress, carve the walls into the appropriate shapes, and rebuild them into an old style of house called "Cape Cod." She stepped forward, turned, and struck a pose beside all her creations.

Lenore and Kevin watched, astonished. "Look at this!" Lenore exclaimed. "Her first day in the Overworld, and she's already showing skills that our children take months to develop! How is this possible?"

"Intriguing," said Kevin. "Tell me about this ring. Did you make it here, or is it part of your picture of yourself?" Laughing at that—"In my dreams!"—C.J. explained her comic books, the concept of "superheroes," and the particular books from which she had borrowed the ring. Lenore nodded, fascinated. Kevin grinned as if he'd discovered a new toy. "A cultural touchstone used as a framework! Lenore, we need to make note of this. Such a technique could make a significant improvement in our training."

"I'm certainly impressed," said Lenore. "Before you came here, did you even know you had *laran*?"

"Loran?" said C.J., puzzled. "No. I have a computer, and we have an InterStel subscription for books and stuff, but no, we don't have any navigational equipment at all."

"Nav—oh," said Lenore. "Words again."

Kevin took over. *It appears, my dear, that you are a telepath.*

"Me? You're kidding, right? You mean, like mind-reading and stuff?"

Kevin raised his eyebrows. "I'm sorry, were you talking to me?"

"You know I was! You just called me a telepath."

He grinned. "I did? Did you see my lips move?"

"Of course I di—" Wait. Had she?

You're "reading" my thoughts because I'm presenting them to you, he said silently. *You can also pick up the thoughts of others who don't shield them, and before we go much further we'll have to teach you ways to shield your own mind so that you're not bombarded with everyone's mental noise. Although from what I see here, I suspect you would be able to work it out for yourself.*

"Wow," she said. "My grandmother said her mother had the Sight, and that always sounded cool. But I never thought I— Wait a minute. You said this isn't a physical world, and so we're not really here, not physically. That means all this is going on mentally, right? So maybe I'm just 'hearing' you because you've been projecting to me all along, even when I *did* see your lips move, and it's not me at all. True?"

"No," said Lenore, "but that's good thinking. There's another reason we know you're a telepath, and that's your very presence here. The word I used earlier is *laran*—it's what enables telepathy, the use of starstones, and related gifts. It makes itself known around puberty by causing what we refer to as 'threshold sickness,' because the body's systems that handle *laran* are the same ones that change to bring you into adulthood, and they're caught between the two purposes. What you told us you experienced before coming here sounds exactly like threshold sickness."

"More than that," said Kevin, "my scan earlier showed that you *do* have threshold sickness. It seems unlikely that anyone who doesn't come from Darkover could experience this—I assume you're not descended directly from us, and the factors that led to the emergence of *laran* in humans seem unique to Darkover—" ("Spacefaring *chieri*?" said the Lady; Kevin shrugged) "—but whatever the source, you have it, and we need to deal with it as soon as possible."

"I see," C.J. said. *Huh—an internal conflict of interest, eh? I can't even socialize within myself!* "Let's do it, then. How do I get to...what was the name of your place?"

"Neskaya," said Lenore. "We have the proper medicines there, and we're taking steps to bring your physical body there even now."

"'Neskaya.' Right. Got it. And you're sure that you can put

me back in there once I find you?"

"Theoretically," said Kevin, "it shouldn't even be necessary for you to move from this spot. But this is a new experience for us, since you've come to the Overworld from elsewhere in the heavens, and we'd like to remove as many unknowns as possible. And as we said earlier, it's not clear to us where this part of the Overworld is in relation to our Tower, if any such relationship can even be charted. You told us you were able to move from place to place, didn't you?"

"That's true," she said. "I ran, and it felt like some distance. I don't know if running will work in this case...but you know, I think I'd like to try flying."

Lenore smiled broadly. "That sounds interesting. I've never tried it myself."

"Oh, it often comes with the superhero package." She *wished,* and found herself rising into the sky. She stopped and hovered. *Holey cheese! It works!* "How will I find you?"

"We'll send up our own beacon. Keep your eyes on it, and it should lead you to us." The Lady held her stone cupped in both hands and closed her eyes.

Far off, through the gray mists, a bright blue glow appeared. From it a beam shot skyward, similar to the one C.J. had projected. "There we go," she said. "That shouldn't be too hard to follow. See you there!" She started to move toward the beam.

"Look for a tower built from bluish stone. It should be hard to miss," Kevin called. "We'll be waiting." They vanished.

This was *incredible.* She had flown through clouds in aircraft, and the view then was much like what she saw now, except for the lack of sunlight. They must all live on one continent, she decided. That would explain why it was so dark when she got here: if this was a realm of mind, then the level of illumination might correspond with the level of mental activity on Darkover, and she arrived when most people were sleeping.

But then she recalled them saying that the Overworld's relation to time itself was unusual, so perhaps that explanation was silly. Ah, well.

From her "aircraft" perspective she looked down to what would be the ground at ten thousand meters, and forgot to breathe. (Breathe? Here she had probably breathed only out of habit.)

The sight of the ground was *gorgeous*. Lights shifted and danced in kaleidoscopic patterns. She saw areas of special brilliance—Towers, she guessed—but also hundreds of thousands of points of light in twinkling, swirling clouds: people meeting, conversing, bidding hello, bidding farewell, sharing memories, loving, working, simply *experiencing* each other. Were these only the people who had *laran,* she wondered? It didn't sound like it. She suspected she was looking at "just another day on Darkover"...and it was glorious. *Charles Williams would have loved this.*

She started. *Hey, you! Pull it together. Keep your eyes on the beacon, they said. Is it still there? Have we lost it?* In a near-panic she searched the distance—and yes, there it was! She hurtled forward, leading with closed fists, ring blazing in blue fury. *You know, monochrome can get to you. We should add some orange here. Or green. Yeah. Green would be good.*

Onward she sped, fixing her gaze on the vertical blue light. As she flew, she felt more and more comfortable in this strange environment, and that thought filled her with wonder. Suddenly she realized that the feeling of comfort had subtly changed to one of *presence*. She was not alone. Speeding through the fog, the light on her finger seeking the light on the horizon, she said, "Hello?"

Hello, C.J.

"Mom?! Where are you?"

I'm here in Ben Nevis, darling. But I won't be here long, I'm afraid.

"I—I don't understand. Are you...dead?"

Oh, good heavens, no. But I know it will be soon. This bug is vicious and takes no prisoners, they tell me.

Her heart sank. "So you're still alive...but that means I'm talking to you in my past. Are you seeing me in your future?"

Yes. I have no idea how, but I've been watching you there—

how you were lost but bravely faced the unknown; how you kept your head when you thought you were being hunted; how you thought through what was happening and came out of it a hero. I don't know if I'll awaken to tell you, dearest, so I'll tell you now: I'm proud of you. Very, very proud.

"Oh, Mom, I wish I was there with you!"

I know, sweetheart. I can't stay, but at least I know you and your father will be okay. I hate leaving you. I know I'll see you again, but it's hard to leave now. Just know that I love you and always will. And that I'm proud of you, proud that you're my daughter.

"I love you, Mom."

I love you too, C.J. God bless you.

The voice was silent, the presence gone. She sped on through the pale gray sky. This was as suitable a time for a good cry as any.

The beacon continued its upward thrust through the mists, and before she knew it she was there. A stone tower, they had said... there it stood on that hillside, massive and defiant. (Hillside? This Overworld wasn't completely flat after all.) *Okay, just like an airspeeder, the tricky part is the landing. How would Commander Quasar handle this?*

She slowed, adjusted her pitch, and dropped toward the tower feet first. It wasn't like an airspeeder after all. More like a dandelion seed.

On a balcony below she could see the forms of Lenore and Kevin waiting to welcome her. Slowly she descended...

She touched down.

C.J. opened her eyes and took a breath—a genuine breath this time, full of sweetness and mountain air. She lay on a low cot, again wearing her Quasar pajamas. Faces looked down at her, concern in their eyes. Most of those faces she knew because she had seen them on the gray plain. "Kevin... Workman—"

"Robert," the big man said.

"Robert... Lady Lenore."

The Lady smiled. "Welcome to Neskaya Tower. Several

circles work here; ours is the one that met you in the Overworld. I serve as the Keeper, and Kevin is our monitor. And Maureen—" she indicated a woman busy at a nearby table, mixing something in a cup—"is our principal healer. She'll give you the best care available in this world . . . or the other."

Robert turned to Kevin. "So what do you think? Still think she's identical?"

The tall man frowned. "More now than ever. Even down to the molecular level, they're exact duplicates. The hair looks different, yes, but without the dye it's as red as Cherilly's. I can't deny it, I'm baffled."

"Me, too," said another voice, and C.J. turned her head to see the face of the girl who was C.J. and yet wasn't. "You're me, only from the sky. This is really strange."

C.J. chuckled. "And the kids at school said I was weird before. They should see us now."

She turned to Kevin. "Do people here say that no two snowflakes are alike?" When he nodded, she spread her fingers and said, "We used to say that about fingerprints too. But that was before we went out into space, and eventually there were more people than there are parts of a fingerprint, so they started finding prints that went with two people or more. I always figured the thing about snowflakes was the same, that the only reason we thought they were all different was that nobody had ever seen every snowflake at once. And you'd have to compare them all. I'm good at math, but I can't prove that they have to be different, and I haven't heard that anyone has. And now—" she looked at the girl and grinned—"I'm even more convinced."

"You are saying, then, that this is a huge coincidence?" said the Lady, frowning. "I am finding that difficult to believe."

"How far does it go?" said the girl. "My name is Cherilly Leynier-Alton. What's yours?"

"Charis Josephine Niemczyk," C.J. replied, and her grin turned sheepish. "Sorry."

"But you and I got sick at the same time, from what I understand," Cherilly said. "That's a really big coincidence. It seems as though something else is at work, and I think I want to find out what it is."

"Me too," said C.J. "The only guess I can come up with right now is that it has something to do with quantum entanglement. We induce entanglement in particle arrays for communications—it's the only way we can talk between planets and star systems. Entangled particles come in pairs, and what happens to one affects the other. You and I are a pair, and we not only get creepy-sick together, but somehow we're sharing this *laran* thing. That's a *mammoth* coincidence, right? Okay, I know it's a big jump from subatomic particles to whole people. And who or what entangled us in the first place, and when? Before we were born? Those are giant questions, but we've got a *monster* foundation right here to start the process. Right?...Am I right?"

She looked around her and had to chuckle. She had never seen this many glazed-over eyes outside of math class. Robert offered, "I'm picking up scraps of ideas from you, but...I think this is one of those areas where unless you have the proper background, nothing is going to make any sense."

"That's fair. That's certainly fair," C.J. replied. "But no, ma'am, I agree with you. It's hard to think that all this with Cherilly and me is just coincidence. I want to follow this up."

"I as well," said Cherilly. "Could we collaborate? Is there a way our twin-ness could make it work?"

"I seriously doubt it," said Lenore. "For one thing, we would need to furnish Karris—"

C.J. held up a hand. "'C.J.' is fine. The rest is too big a mouthful."

"—C.J. with a starstone, and I don't think that is wise. She needs to return home to her family. They must be frantic by now, wondering where she has gone."

"Yeah," C.J. said soberly. "Dad probably will be. I think...I think my mom's okay with it."

"Nonetheless," said the Lady.

Kevin frowned. "Lenore...I think that issue may have been taken out of our hands." He pointed to C.J. The Lady followed his gaze and gasped. "No," said Kevin, "I've never seen one either. I've heard stories about them, but this is the first I've actually laid eyes on."

"What?" said C.J. She saw Kevin pointing at her hands. Back and forth she turned them, searching, until she saw it. On her middle finger, where the ring had been in the Overworld, was the lightly sketched shape of a stone such as the circle used. It was geometrically regular, and she knew immediately that it was much more than a tattoo. There was...*something*...going on inside.

"A shadow matrix," breathed Lenore. To C.J. she said with a wry smile, "Call it a souvenir of the Overworld. I suspect we will hear from you again whether we plan to or not."

"So we can talk again?" asked Cherilly with delight.

"Sure," said C.J. "Call me anytime. In brightest day, in blackest night."

"Wonderful! We can share the things we each learn, and who knows? One day we can publish, and you'll be famous here."

Robert the Workman hrumphed. C.J. glanced at Lenore, who frowned and gave her head a faint, worried shake. "Not sure that's such a great idea," C.J. said. "I take it people on Darkover aren't likely to go along with the idea of offworlders visiting?"

"Ah...not really, no," said Kevin. "I don't know how we'd tell them, and even if we could, how they would react."

C.J. snorted. " *'Space aliens working in the Towers! Details at twenty-three hundred!'* Yeah, that'd go over well. Tell you what: If we publish, we do it both on and off Darkover. Offworld, it's under my name. Here, under yours. How does that sound?"

Kevin chuckled. "Interesting. Do you really think something could come of this?"

"No idea," C.J. said. "But why not—who knows what we might find. Besides, if we really do discover what's going on..." She grinned. "'C.J.'s Law' sounds kinda neat."

"Clouds of light, eh?" her father said. It was evening, and they sat together on the patio he had built. Flames from a small firepit warmed their feet. He sipped at his coffee. "You're right. I think Teilhard would have loved it."

"It was breathtaking," C.J. said, "especially after a morning that started out really scary."

He frowned. "I bet. And it sounds as though you handled it like an expert." The frown turned into a smile. "I really am proud of you. You know, all this sounds like a dream. And I would probably be convinced that it *was* a dream—*if* there had been any place in the Colony where we could have found you. And hiding is something you don't do well. But you were gone, vanished, *pfffft!* for days. No one had any idea what to do."

"I know, Dad. I'm so sorry," she sighed. "It really wasn't something I had planned on."

"I know it wasn't, sweetie." He put an arm around her shoulder and held her close. "I'm just glad you're here again."

"I learned something in the Overworld," she said. "Hamlet trumps Holmes."

"Come again?"

"You know, when Hamlet says 'there are more things in heaven and earth than are dreamt of in your philosophy'? It's true."

"Ooooooookay. And—?"

"So I guess I'd have to tell Sherlock, when you've eliminated the impossible, what remains, however improbable, may only be an alternative to something you haven't thought of yet."

Her father laughed, then gulped the last of his coffee and got up to add wood to the fire. She stretched and looked up at the stars. *So much I hadn't thought of yet.*

He brought back two containers of soda, handed her one, and sat back down. "I learned something too," he said, "for the second time: how much it hurts to lose someone you love." He smiled and nodded. "My one and only snowflake."

C.J. smiled. "That reminds me, Dad. I think I know what to tell the University Prep people about my study plans. You'll get a kick out of this...."

OLD PURITY

by Leslie Fish

The *chieri*, a nonhuman sapient race native to Darkover, have fascinated readers for decades. Once space-farers, they have long ago retreated to the planet of their origin, dwindling into a reclusive, dying race. The *chieri* may be hidden, for reasons of their own, but they are still a vital part of Darkover. This story takes place about the time of *The Alton Gift*, four years after the departure of the Terran Federation in *Traitor's Sun*.

Leslie Fish learned to sing and to read at a very young age, playing guitar at sixteen, and writing the first of hundreds of songs shortly thereafter, including settings of Rudyard Kipling's poetry and the "all-time most notorious" Star Trek filksong ever written: "Banned From Argo". She's recorded a number of albums and composed songs, both alone and collaborative, on albums from every major filk label. She was elected to the Filk Hall Of Fame as one of the first inductees. In college, she majored in English and minoring in psychology, protest and politics, joined the Industrial Workers of the World, and did psychology counseling for veterans. Her other jobs included railroad yard clerk, go-go dancer, and social worker. She currently lives in Arizona with her husband Rasty and a variable number of cats, which she breeds for intelligence.

Old Robard knew perfectly well that his current duty was a polite sinecure, make-work given to a faithful old retainer, to keep him from feeling like a useless beggar at the Aldaran table. After all, the Terrans had been gone from Darkover for better than four years, and no ship had landed at old Port Chicago in far longer than that. On the other hand, it was important to remember the past, including its skills and techniques. Who better than an old Terran-trained radio operator to be the maintainer of the former control tower, like the docent of a museum?

Besides, he liked playing with the antique equipment, seeing to it that the wind-generator still worked, the lights still glowed, and the radio still hummed. When there were no tour-groups of schoolchildren visiting, he could still sit in the glow of the indicator-lights and listen to that comforting hum, and be comfortably warm no matter what the weather was doing outside. Whatever else one could say of them, the Terrans had built well.

Consequently, he was shocked out of his chair when one of the indicator lights flashed and a distinct voice rasped out of the speakers.

"Hay-lo?" it said. "This is the *Green Angel,* aysking purmission to laynd at Port Chicago fee-yuld. Is aynybody they-ur? Hay-lo?"

The language was undoubtedly Terran, but with a bizarre accent.

Robard gaped for a stunned moment, and then his training took over. He automatically poked the response buttons, grabbed the microphone, and said the first thing that came into his head.

"Who *are* you?!"

There was a pause, then an impatient snort, then: "Laik I said, this is the *Green Angel*—payssenger and cargo—aysking to laynd. Nobody aynswered at old Thendara, so we-yur trying here. Glad to hee-yur from you. Can we laynd already?"

A ship! Some kind of a Terran ship! Again, Robard answered automatically. "We don't want any Terrans here! We threw them off Darkover four years ago. Go away!"

The reply was fiercely indignant. "We-yur no dayum Terrans! We-yur Vainwalers—and we threw out the dayum Empa-yur too, just layst year. We-yur your neighbors, and we want to trade with you. We've also got some of your citizens, wanting to come home. Now cayn we please laynd?"

Robard opened and shut his mouth several times, concluded that this was too deep a decision for him to make alone, and dived into the classic response. "Wait here. I'll have to go ask the lord."

"…the Lord?" the voice puzzled.

But Robard was already out of his chair and grabbing for his cloak and walking-staff. He hurried out of the control tower as fast as he could hobble, straight toward Aldaran Castle. Indeed, let someone with higher rank deal with this! He was just a museum docent, after all.

Within half an hour, Lord Aldaran, his secretary, Under-Keeper Sharalynn, and even elder Keeper Ventellin stood in the old control tower, crowded around the antique radio, listening intently while the captain of the *Green Angel* wearily repeated his request and his explanation.

"You say you threw the Terrans off Vainwal?" Aldaran asked cautiously. "Why did you do that, and how?"

The unseen captain gave a patient sigh. "They got too demaynding, too pushy, and too expey-ensive, thayt's why. Ays for how, did you ever he-yur the term, 'General Strike'? Or 'guerilla war-fayr'? We-ud been ha-yudding and stockpa-eeling our harvests and goods for a couple yee-urs, and then we all up and fled the cities and hid out in the wilderness. Gave 'em nothing but guerilla ray-uds, cost 'em money until they had to let us go. Besides, they were getting trouble all over the gaylaxy by then—spread thin, had to cut they-ur losses."

Aldaran raised his eyebrows significantly at his secretary, who was taking furious notes. He turned to the two Keepers and whispered: "Could you pick up anything from him?"

Sharalynn, peering intently into her matrix, sighed and shook her head, but old Ventellin gave a brief nod. "He's sincere," she reported. "He's telling the truth, at least as he knows it. Ask further."

Lord Aldaran turned back to the microphone. "And why are you here, now?" he asked.

"Laik I say-ud, trade!" the captain snapped. "When the

Empah-ur was hee-yur, they used our world for a—" The could all hear the sneer in his voice. "—a *'play-zhur planet'*, one big amusement park. Well, you cain't run a world on pure fun, especially when the vacation crowds have gone. We've stee-yill got the medical complex, fee-yishing and some farming, and we've started up some ma-eens, but we need a wa-eeder range of crops and la-eevstock, especially some cold-weather breeds— such ays you've got. We need to expaynd way north and south of our equator."

"Sincere," Ventellin murmured again.

"And what do you have to exchange?" Aldaran queried in a totally neutral voice.

"We've got medicines, feeyish, and a kiloton of metay-lic copper; we hee-yur that's stuff you're short on."

The secretary's jaw dropped. "A *kiloton* of copper?!" he mouthed.

Aldaran bounced eagerly on his toes, but still managed to keep his voice calm. "Yes, I think we can trade for that," he purred. "Very well, you have our permission to land. Alas, you'll have to handle the landing yourselves; Port Chicago has been nonfunctional, except for the radio, for close upon fifty years."

"That's fa-een," the captain enthused. "We can laynd and launch rough. Just stay away from the pad, and we'll do the rest. Oh, I forgot to mention: we-uv got some payssengers to let off: Darkover folks who got stray-unded on Vainwal until now. See you soon."

With that the radio-voice clicked off, leaving the Aldaran officials looking at each other.

"A *kiloton* of copper?!" the secretary repeated aloud.

"I wonder just what medicines they have," Lord Aldaran considered.

"And what kind of fish," Sharalynn added, tucking back a wayward lock of sandy-red hair. "Our city-folk have been plagued by some dietary deficiencies of late."

"And I'd like to meet those Darkovans who were stranded on Vainwal for the last four of their years," Ventellin murmured. "Yes, I believe we should go out to meet these Vainwalers as soon as they land."

"Not yet!" Robard spoke up. "Let's stay in here until they're safely down—" He really didn't want to go out into all that strangeness.

At that moment they all heard the growing roar of approaching engines rumbling out of the sky.

"Which shouldn't be much longer," Aldaran noted. "They're not wasting any time."

Water-vapor was still steaming away from the base of the ship when the Aldaran delegation came out to meet the strangers. Lord Aldaran had thoughtfully sent for a small contingent of guards, all wearing the last issued lot of beam-pistols rather than bows or swords, and he warned them to "Look friendly, and be ready to help them unload if need be." One could almost see glimmers of copper in his eyes.

"You might send for some carts," Sharalynn frowned, holding her treasured notebook and stylus ready to take notes. "Where and how shall we transport the medicines and the fish?"

Ventellin brushed silver hair out of her almost equally silver grey eyes, smiled, and said nothing.

A large port hissed and opened, extruding a ramp, and a man came out. He was wearing ridiculously colorful clothes—knee-high bright red boots, tight blue trousers, and a thick red-gold-and-blue striped jacket—and his skin, hair, and eyes were three different shades of dark brown.

"Definitely a Vainwaler," the secretary murmured.

The captain strode up to the waiting quartet, smiled widely and asked "Whee-ich of you is Lord Aldaran?"

"I am," Aldaran said affably, stepping forward and presenting an empty hand in the old Terran fashion. "This is my secretary, and the, ah, Ladies Sharalynn and Ventellin. Welcome."

The captain smiled wider, took the proffered hand and shook it briefly. "Pleeztameetcha. Ahm Morgan Smith, and hayppy to be here. Let's get ma-ee payssengers out first." He waved toward the open port, and four people emerged.

The first two were a middle-aged couple, both brown-haired

and hazel-eyed, wearing a mixture of worn Darkovan clothing and newer Vainwal garb, who hurried to Lord Aldaran and introduced themselves as Danilo and Laurelinn Lindir-Aillard, who had gone to the Vainwal medical center to seek healing for their brother, Stefan. Here they turned to the third passenger, a tall older man wearing aged and worn but entirely Darkovan clothing—but he had stopped to kneel down, take up a handful of dust from the ground and clutch it to his chest, while tears trickled from his eyes. "I thought I'd never get home," he murmured getting to his feet. "I thank Vainwal for my life, but I thank all the gods in agreement that I'm finally home."

Sharalynn didn't need her matrix to feel the gratitude flooding off him. While Aldaran formally welcomed the three of them, she looked to Ventellin to see how she was affected by Stefan's sincerity.

But Ventellin wasn't looking at the other arrivals. Her gaze was fixed on the fourth passenger—a tall, slender man in nondescript clothes, with hair and eyes as silver as her own—who was walking quietly toward her. "T'thanyel," she breathed.

He only smiled and grasped the tips of her fingers, and led her a step closer to Lord Aldaran. "I greet you also, *Dom,*" he said softly. "I am Danyel Macfarr of Arilinn, brother of your Keeper."

"Brother?" Lord Aldaran's eyebrows shot up, as did Sharalynn's. "My Keeper's brother? How is it I've never heard of you?"

"Or I," Sharalynn whispered, feeling betrayed. Ventellin had been her teacher since she was ten years old—as close to a mother as she'd ever known, growing up in the domain orphanage. Of course, Ventellin had never said much at all about her family…

"Ah, that's because I rather scandalized my grandmother by studying Terran sciences, and societies," Danyel replied smoothly. "I daresay the family hasn't mentioned me in decades."

"Oh, indeed," Aldaran fumbled. "Well, I welcome you back to Darkover. You and your companions are welcome to my house, and I'll expect you all for dinner."

"If it please you," Ventellin cut in. "I'll lead them thence and get them settled in, *Dom.* No doubt you'll have much to discuss with the good Captain Smith."

The glance she gave Danyel clearly expressed that she had much to discuss with her brother, too. As Aldaran gestured polite dismissal and Ventellin began to lead the party of newcomers away, Sharalynn turned to follow them—but the lord stopped her with a peremptory, "Bide, Sharalynn. I suspect I'll need you for a…verifier."

Sharalynn dutifully turned back and bowed her head, and silently ground her teeth. She badly wanted to watch more interaction between Ventellin and her mysterious brother, and Aldaran didn't need her to truth-check the clownish Vainwaler. One would have to be totally mind-blind not to see that the man was sincere—and desperate. She caught a glimpse from his mind of colorfully-dressed people lining up at a warehouse to buy tiny packets of precious seeds, and an underlying dismay that there were so few species available. *Fruits and herbs and leafy vegetables,* she caught from him, *And no grain but sweet corn and amaranth! Can't feed millions on that…*

She stepped a little closer as Smith and Lord Aldaran and his secretary began to confer about the cargo, preparing for some serious haggling. The names and natures of the medicines were decidedly interesting, including some not listed in the pharmacopeia texts that she had deliberately read into the memory in her starstone—a tactic she'd invented after pining for the lost data-crystals in the orphanage. That was a feat which had impressed Ventellin. Very well, the mystery of her teacher's family could wait; she was getting a fascinating picture of Vainwal and its people and its knowledge.

Let the rest of Darkover forget the Terran sciences if they chose; Aldaran had always been the renegade domain—willing to experiment and learn, and willing to keep the best of the Terrans' knowledge to add to their own. This was a priceless opportunity to increase that knowledge without having to deal with the Terrans themselves.

Sharalynn didn't get to see Ventellin again until dinner, and by then she had her notebook, immediate memory and matrix memory stuffed with exciting information. Now more than ever she needed to talk to her teacher, but first she needed to get through this interminable semi-formal dinner.

Not that she begrudged the food—mostly roast rabbit-horn, various greens and roots with cheese or butter, and nut-breads with assorted fruit jams—for she was ravenous after all that work. She noticed that Captain Smith was studying the food even as he and Lord Aldaran kept haggling, to the point where the other guests could barely get a word in edgewise. She also noted that Danyel, for all his self-effacing silence, was covertly studying the captain and his earnest chatter. With a slight shock she realized that he was lightly probing the Vainwaler with the aid of an unseen matrix. It didn't surprise her that Ventellin's brother had *laran,* or could use it so well; what did puzzle her was finding a skilled *laranzu* not only outside of a Tower but having traveled to other planets. How had he put up with the noise of all those untrained and unshielded minds? What had he been doing on Vainwal? Studying? Studying what? Could he be a spy, and if so, for whom?

She caught Ventellin smirking at her, blushed, and concentrated on her food.

At last—at last!—the final dish and drink were finished, and Aldaran stood up to formally bid the guests and staff good evening, and send them off to their sleeping quarters. No one looked twice as Sharalynn followed her teacher into the Keepers' apartments, but she found it intriguing that nobody seemed to notice that Danyel did, too.

The moment the main door was shut and the shielding put up, Ventellin turned to Sharalynn and asked, with a sly smile, if she wanted to report or ask questions first.

Danyel, dropping into the nearest chair, answered for her: "Oh, report first, child; I daresay that will include downloading your matrix—a clever trick, that, by the way—and we may as well get that done first."

Blushing, Sharalynn went to the little round table in the center of the cluster of chairs, pulled her starstone out of its insulating bag and laid it in the middle of the tabletop. Ventellin took a seat beside Danyel and did likewise, so that the stones just touched. Not surprisingly, so did Danyel—and his matrix was not small. Sharalynn settled on the remaining chair, set her mind into matrix-working state, and sank into the recorded memories. She could feel Ventellin's presence, combing and guiding the memories, and Danyel's as well. He was indeed very well trained, and she wondered why he had abandoned tower-work. She felt him reply with a silent ironic chuckle before all three of them became absorbed in the work.

A measureless time later, Ventellin pulled them all out of the working and up to a fresh sense of exhaustion and elation.

"A kiloton of copper!" Danyel laughed. "Oh yes, Aldaran is the richest man in the Domains right now. Smith can ask for almost anything he likes—including..." He gave Ventellin a keen look. "...transport to the coast and the loan of a sturdy boat."

"For us, not for Smith," Ventellin noted. "We'll have to do some dickering with Aldaran to let us go, but I think I can come up with an effective argument."

"...Boat?" Sharalynn puzzled.

"Smith and his crew will spend the next few cycles of Idriel, at least, hunting up and packing breeding-stock and seeds of everything edible within Aldaran lands," Danyel went on. "Vainwal needs crops and livestock that can flourish in the temperate and even arctic zones; the planet's climate is much warmer than Darkover's, so anything that grows here should do well outside the equatorial zones there. That would also include cold-water fish..." He gave Ventellin a keen look. "Such as thrive near Kuithal."

Sharalynn had never heard the name, but obviously Ventellin was familiar with it.

"Will this not disrupt the natural life-system of the planet?" Ventellin frowned, as if that were a long-held concern.

Danyel shook his head. "Vainwal is as young a world as

Darkover is old. When the Terrans arrived, the only life there was at the microbial stage: nothing more advanced than algae. That was enough to create workable topsoil, and the Terrans brought in everything else. Unfortunately, they meant to keep the planet—as the articulate Captain Smith put it—as an amusement park and a medical center, dependent on the empire for food and manufacture. Well, they couldn't do that entirely; entertainment included exotic foods, which were best served fresh, and it was cheaper to make building materials on-site, which involved some mining and industry. When the population grew big enough, it had to at least partly feed and supply itself. The Vainwalers did manage to supply themselves for the revolution, but they badly need more diversified crops, livestock, and timber. They have good reason to be our allies for a long time to come."

"So…" Ventellin leaned back and steepled her twelve fingers. "Now is the time to go to Kuithal?"

Danyel nodded once. "I believe it's time to report to Grandmother again."

"Grandmother?!" Sharalynn almost bolted from her chair, gaping at the two of them. Simple facts that she'd known half her life connected with a jolt. *Silver eyes and hair, unguessable age, the look of the Old Blood—How much Old Blood?!* She snatched her matrix from the table, shoved it back in its silk bag and pulled the drawstring shut. "Teacher," she gasped, "Just how old *are* you?!"

The other two exchanged looks, and a resolve. "Older than you'd readily believe, child," Danyel said gently. "Yes, we're both half *chieri.*"

"…Half?" was all Sharalynn managed to say.

"Our mother had a human lover," Ventellin almost whispered. "Our grandmother did not approve." Thoughtfully, she picked up her own matrix, as did her brother.

"They haven't spoken in centuries," Danyel smiled, leaning back in his chair. "We went out among the humans, and have studied them, and brought back reports to Grandmother ever since. She still doesn't approve, but she has difficulty arguing with the facts. It's definitely time to report to her again."

"At…" Sharalynn remembered the name. "…Kuithal? Where is that?"

"Almost halfway around the world," Danyel smiled sadly. "A large island, in the middle of an archipelago, out where humans never bothered to venture, thanks to the rather fierce winds at sea."

"In fact," Ventellin added, "I think we had better take that little air-ship that Lord Aldaran keeps in hiding. It would shorten the journey considerably, and I assume that your weather-working abilities have not withered."

"Not at all," Danyel agreed. "It might even impress Grandmother."

"She would more likely complain that we didn't transport through the Overworld," Ventellin gloomed.

"Tell her that no one on the mainland builds big enough screens these days, and ask if she really wants us to draw attention to ourselves by creating them." Danyel cast a thoughtful glance at Sharalynn. "And let's bring your daughter, too. Her clever trick with storing such great amounts of symbolic memory—and so clearly—in her matrix really would impress the old dragon."

Sharalynn caught on that one word. "…Daughter?"

Danyel did a classically human double-take. "You haven't told her?"

Ventellin gave a long sigh. "Sharalynn, my dear, do you recall what was happening here seventeen years ago? …Ah, no, of course not. Suffice it to say, it was not safe to keep you with me. I could not even find a safe fostering-family. That's why I left you at the Aldaran domain orphanage, and only guarded you, unseen, from a distance."

Sharalynn couldn't think of a thing to say. She only pulled a deep breath and clutched her starstone in its bag, remembering the past seven years. *No wonder she was so motherly toward me. No wonder…* She finally thought of a question. "…Seven years since you took me from there, took me into what passes for a Tower in Aldaran Domain these days. In all that time, why did you never tell me?"

Ventellin fixed her with a sad look. "Dearest, how many times have I reprimanded you for being headstrong, impulsive, and likely to speak before you think? You're much like Mother that way... I feared you could not keep the secret, but might blurt it out in a moment of excitement. Society is not so settled yet, nor our position so secure, as to risk letting everyone know about... well, aliens in their midst."

"We're not the aliens..." Sharalynn began, then caught herself. Despite the revelations of recent years, *chieri* were still regarded as legendary creatures, and most Darkovans didn't quite know how to deal with legends come to life. ...And yes, she knew that she did tend to speak before she thought. Still, the knowledge rankled.

"I realize you've suffered several shocks today," Danyel said gently, "Yet I would ask you to risk another. Would you come with us to Kuithal, to meet Grandmother?"

"Yes!" Sharalynn snapped—without thinking, she had to admit. "I...have had no family for so long..."

The other two exchanged looks again. "In that case, dearest," Ventellin murmured, "I think I should give you a gift that I've been planning for awhile."

She reached into her belt-pouch, pulled out what looked like a simple piece of jewelry and handed it to Sharalynn. On closer inspection it was revealed as a small open-work locket of silver wire, hung on a silver chain. It contained nothing.

"Place your matrix inside, love, and tie the insulating silk over that," Ventellin explained. "Then you need only pull the bag away, and the stone will touch your flesh without occupying your hand. That may be necessary where we are going. I recommend practicing with it while you have time."

Sharalynn did indeed practice with her locketted matrix, ignoring almost everything else. She practiced until she could speak mind-to-mind clearly with Ventellin or Danyel while strolling through the house garden, or through the ruined parts of the old castle. She practiced until she could scan any creature from a bird to a human at twenty paces. She practiced until she could identify mold-damage on a flower, comparing the images with the memorized books in her matrix, and heal it within an hour. She ate ferociously and fell asleep, exhausted, early.

Consequently, she kept little track of Ventellin's and Danyel's machinations, still less of Lord Aldaran's dickerings with Captain Smith, until Ventellin caught up to her at dinner on the third day and told her, "Pack one change of light clothes, but lay out your heavy cloak and boots, beloved. We'll leave tomorrow soon after dawn, and I can't guarantee that the airship can be kept warm. Also, bring a box of several sample-bags. We will indeed be gathering seeds for Vainwal."

Despite her hunger and fatigue, Sharalynn pulled herself upright and away from her plate. "Pack nothing else? And how shall we bring back livestock? Should I bring my prettiest clothes or the sturdiest? How shall I—"

"Enough, enough," Ventellin laughed. "Just wear your sturdy red wool dress, and pack the light silk one. Grandmother will pay no attention to surface appearances. ...Oh, and bring a fresh notebook and stylus. Don't worry about livestock; Lord Aldaran has already arranged for as many local animals as the *Green Angel* can safely carry. Captain Smith will be well compensated for his cargo. I daresay he'll be back for more within the year."

For a moment she looked about to say more, but instead just patted Sharalynn's hand and walked away. Sharalynn regretted that she'd insulated her matrix, but then hunger reminded her of the immediate task, and she turned back to her plate.

For all her weariness, it took a long time for her to fall asleep.

Dawn found her dressed and packed and waiting impatiently at her mother's door. When Ventellin came out, similarly garbed for the journey, she only smiled and took Sharalynn's hand and led her through the castle by the back hallways.

Where are we going? Sharalynn asked through her unshielded starstone.

So eager? Ventellin chuckled back through the link. *We're going to a side door, out to a disused field, where Aldaran has thoughtfully pulled his airship into place. No one but ourselves and a trusted few of his guards know it is there.*

Sharalynn caught some of the implications behind that thought, and smiled in her turn. *We must take care to return it in pristine condition.*

Ventellin's reply was a ripple of silent laughter.

The trim little ship waited in the middle of the field, and the half-dozen guards discreetly pulled away as they saw the Keepers coming. Danyel, likewise dressed in warm clothing, stood waiting by its near door. Sharalynn ventured to give him a silent greeting as they approached, and he raised an appreciative eyebrow. *You do indeed learn quickly, niece,* he replied as he pulled the ship's door open. Ventellin entered first, towed Sharalynn after her, and settled her on one of the rear two seats while she and Danyel took the forward two. Sharalynn was surprised to see a wire-netted matrix set into the dashboard. She had seen pictures of aircraft, of course, and of their cockpits, and none of them had ever sported a matrix in the control panel.

She also noticed that both Ventellin and Danyel pulled out their starstones and stripped away the insulating bags. Immediately, the stones began to glow faintly. A moment later, so did the one set in the dashboard.

"Strap in," said Danyel, pulling up belts from either side of his chair. "We have a very long way to go, and this ship carries only so much fuel, so I mean to ride the high winds for most of the voyage."

"Which will mean a lively ride," Ventellin added, pulling up and fastening her own belts.

Sharalynn made haste to copy her. "How high are we going?" she asked.

"Very," grinned Danyel, an image forming in his mind of a distance nearly the height of the Hellers.

And I'd best concentrate air and warmth... Ventellin considered, seeing patterns of how to accomplish that.

Sharalynn observed both their minds, fascinated, as the engine purred to life and the sleek little craft began rolling down the smoothed center of the field. They thought not in words now but in patterns, mechanics of the ship's hydrogen-jet engine, automatic monitoring of the fuel-containment system, the birdlike wings pulling the ship upward and the wind pushing from below, concentrating certain molecules in the air to condense inside the cabin, pulling heat from air-friction through the metal skin and around their bodies, trapping it there with an invisible field of force... *Not too much, Mother. We don't want to roast.* The precision, the skill, felt glorious. *Ah, the fruits of Science!* Almost without thinking, Sharalynn impressed those thoughts into her matrix.

Watching the fuel, minding the air-currents, Danyel pulled the craft higher and higher still, like a stiff-winged hawk, seeking a particular invisible river of wind somewhere above them that he could vaguely sense. *There! Ah, there...* The ship cut into the edge of that wind-river like a boat launching into water, and immediately it began to buck and lunge. Danyel held it firmly on course, working his way deeper into the current, until at last they reached the heart of the flow. Sharalynn could feel that wind-core taking hold of the ship and carrying it forward, much faster than it had flown on its own power. "There!" Danyel said aloud, and deliberately cut back on the ship's fuel-flow, damping it down to just enough to keep the engine running—idling, really—while the vast wind thrust the ship southwestward.

Danyel leaned back in his seat and relaxed, intending to ride the wind for several hours yet, noting that it was time to look down and take bearings. Sharalynn looked too, surprised to see nothing below but the wrinkled gray sheet of the sea. *We've made good time,* Danyel agreed. *Fast wind this time of year, and faster today than usual.*

How long since you've flown on Darkover? Ventellin countered. *The weather changes...in slow increments, but it changes.*

True... Danyel's thoughts closed off behind a private shield, but Sharalynn caught a sense of gloom and brooding, and wondered what that portended.

Still, the sight of the sea so far below whipping past them was hypnotic, and she was soon lost in the fascinating sight. Now that she thought of it, she had never seen the ocean nor traveled across it.

The sight of a small green islet passing underneath was startling; she had never thought much about islands in the sea, either. There was supposed to be an island within sight of the Elhalyn lands that people lived on, but she'd never met anyone who'd been there. Why was the sea so little known and unexplored, after all these centuries? The usual explanation was ferocious winds that could sink a boat, or thrust an airship out of the sky, but the more she thought about it, the thinner that explanation seemed, especially now when she could look down on the ocean and see—and feel—that the surface winds were nothing so fierce as that. Why had Darkovans never explored the sea?

I'm afraid that's our doing, child, Ventellin nudged at her thoughts. *We have always...discouraged the humans from venturing out of sight of the mainland.*

Sharalynn understood that such discouragement had not been done with words, and was indignant. Influencing another person's mind without their permission, or at least without serious cause, was simply Not Done. *Why?* she snapped, letting her disapproval show.

We had serious cause, Danyel answered, and then slipped behind his shield again, trailing a hint of that grimness she'd noticed earlier.

Ventellin, with a flicker of annoyance that Danyel had left her to do all the explaining, spread out a vision before Sharalyn's mind—an image as complex as a vast tapestry, with a sense of immense age...

Twelve thousand years, to be precise.

...And Sharalynn saw Darkover as it had been then, before ever the humans came.

Before humans were anything more than the Trailmen are, as we have cause to know.

The sun was slightly, but noticeably, larger and brighter then. The weather was noticeably warmer. Forests grew a thousand meters higher up the Hellers, and the Dry Towns were not dry. There were cities where none stood today, made of crystal stone. Their inhabitants were the *chieri*.

And they were quietly, deeply, frightened.

Another image: the interior of a working tower, filled with elaborate equipment, much of it large and intricately linked screens, with several dismayed *chieri* looking into them. They all shared the knowledge that something was wrong with the sun. Oldest memories showed it, at dawn on midsummer day, rising between two famous mountain peaks—as seen from the top of a third—and filling the space completely. Now it could not touch both peaks at once. The sun was shrinking, dying, cooling, and their world with it.

...Or else Darkover's orbit is slipping further away, Sharalynn thought to herself.

And that was only half of the immense danger.

Other *chieri* peered into a small screen suspended over a glass dish which contained...living cells, and their dismay was aimed at themselves.

Diminished fertility. With our extended life spans we bred less and less. Too late did we realize that this was no longer by choice.

Sharalynn saw what they were seeing—and realized what they were not seeing, or understanding.

Didn't they have tools for reading DNA? Couldn't they comprehend what they saw?

Ventellin's reply was tinged with an old impatience. *No, we had no such knowledge then, nor any idea of what to look for. So we searched elsewhere.*

Another image: determined *chieri* explorers, stepping through a large screen...

Into the Overworld, and then another solid world.

Several other worlds, Ventellin detailed. *Earth was one of them. First we sought out any people with knowledge we could use. Then we sought people with whom our seed might be compatible. We found none, but there are hints that our explorers tinkered with the seed of humans, with what skill we had then, to make them—eventually—more compatible. The explorers came home with only that thin thread of hope.*

And that, Danyel cut in, *was where our great philosophical division began.*

"Politics," Ventellin muttered aloud.

The image this time was more a pattern than a vision: three branching and often conflicting solutions to those two monstrous problems.

There were those who chose to work with their own geneplasm, to study the mechanisms of reproduction, to experiment and alter what they already had. (With a start, Sharalynn saw that one of those experiments were the creation—or more accurately, re-creation—of the creatures called *kyrri*, originally an ancestor of the *chieri*, which had normal fertility, near-human intelligence, and a shorter-than-human lifespan.) The intention was to restore the fertility of the *chieri* and give them adaptability to the growing cold.

Sharalynn wondered briefly about the other sentient creatures on the planet: Catmen, Ya-men, Trailmen—were they experiments too? She dared not ask.

There were others who continued to search for compatible worlds where they might transport themselves and their whole ecosystem. The searching was, of necessity, done through the Overworld. Quite often they worked in tandem with the first group.

Then there were still others, who likewise searched through the Overworld for other planets, but the purpose of their search was, still, to find another species with whom they could interbreed and restore their species' earlier vigor. These still hoped that the species they had encountered earlier might progress to the point where they could offer more knowledge. They were completely at odds with the first group, and took up residence in different parts of the world from them, on the mainland.

Guess which group includes Grandmother, a thought from Danyel darted past.

Sharalynn noticed that when speaking mind-to-mind Danyel used a concept which had less sense of gender; "grandmother" could as easily mean "grandfather".

Thus we remained, Ventellin went on, *until humans*

progressed to the point where they began traveling the galaxy. Then we noticed them again.

The balance between the three groups then shifted fiercely. The Interbreeders, feeling justified, redoubled their efforts to bring humans to Darkover. Now the World-Seekers allied with them, hoping the humans' knowledge of space-travel could find a compatible world for the *chieri*. The Purists, feeling isolated, withdrew to their geographical fortress in the Islands—the center of which was, yes, Kuithal.

Sharalynn thought of Ventellin's and Danyel's renegade mother (father?). *How did s/he come to desert the Purists?*

The answer was an image of a human ship, over a thousand years past, pulled out of its course to land on Darkover—on the one continent, where the *chieri* had been clearing and preparing for them, where the grand experiment began.

Breeding experiment, Sharalynn understood. She glanced down at her own six fingers. *We know what the humans gained from the crossbreeding. What did the chieri gain?*

There was a moment of almost embarrassed silence, then a sly chuckle from Danyel, then an image of a group of children playing in the forest: all of them half-breeds, and all of them with the distinctly c*hieri* look. Adult c*hieri* looked on, studying the children, and quietly selecting future mates for them. *Back-breeding*, Danyel clarified. *Three-quarter-breds, seven-eighths—and the genetic knowledge from the minds of the humans helped—they had the improved fertility while keeping all the other characteristics of our kind, exactly as the Interbreeders had hoped. The experiment was a success. That was what inspired our mother to join them. Only the old purists held out.*

Like your Grandmother, Sharalynn finished. *Why did you resume contact with her?*

There was another briefly embarrassed silence before Ventellin took up the tale. *We grew painfully tired of being used as breeding studs*, she said bluntly. *We...escaped from the mainland enclave and joined with the World-Seekers. I specialized in seeking through the Overworld, while T'thanyel studied the pilfered knowledge of the humans. He was among those who found a way to lure the humans here a second time.*

You brought the Empire here?! Sharalynn didn't know whether to be shocked or grateful.

It wasn't so corrupt then, Danyel admitted. *And we needed their knowledge of the galaxy—and their ships.*

Right there Sharalynn saw the real gap between the factions. Ages of matrix-work had shaped the way the *chieri* thought; the most analytical of them could not match the precision of the humans' thinking, and it was their means of recording knowledge that made the difference. Without *laran* or starstones, humans had been obliged to record thoughts with precise marks, which led to a reverence for precision itself. It was no wonder that human mathematics and physical sciences had leapt ahead of the *chieris'*.

It was humbling for the *chieri* to admit that this younger species had, because of its very lack of *laran*, surpassed the ancient people in everything but the psychic sciences.

Not that we couldn't learn from these upstarts, Danyel chuckled. *It only takes study, for which we certainly have time. It's simply...embarrassing.*

And Grandmother, Sharalynn guessed, *was proud.*

But she dearly wished, Ventellin went on, *to reestablish the alliance between the Purists and the World-Seekers. That much we could give her.*

Sharalynn pondered that as the island-studded sea whipped past, far below. The very idea that the near-mythical Beautiful People of the Forest indulged in squabbling politics was almost beyond belief. Yet she could see the sense of it. The goal was survival, when their world and sun were slowly dying. Purist or Interbreeder, the *chieri* knew they had to escape to some other world, and the psychic sciences that were their great skill had failed to find them one, but the alien sciences of the humans could do it.

Both factions would court the World-seekers.

But she could see a problem. *We drove the Terrans away, four years ago. Where now shall we get the ships? Can the chieri use Overworld travel to reach worlds that human sciences found for us?*

Ventellin laughed aloud. "We've been trying!" she said. "It's gone slowly, but now…"

If that fails, Danyel finished, *we now have another way.*

That was followed by a vivid image of Captain Smith, in his laughable clothes, stepping down from the port of the *Green Angel.*

Vainwal has ships, Sharalynn understood, *And badly wants our help…*

She saw it all, in a burst of comprehension as complex, unified and beautiful as an unfolding flower.

Not so loud, girl, she felt Ventellin wince.

An instant later, the ship lurched forward as if a giant hand had grasped it, and rushed forward at twice its previous speed.

Danyel snapped a thoughtless oath and struggled to keep the aircraft level. Ventellin linked with him, also worrying about keeping the ship intact under that pressure. At once the cabin's warmth bled away.

Sharalynn realized that the air would thin next, without Ventellin maintaining it. She checked her starstone's memory for the pattern of how her mother had managed the trick, attracting and concentrating molecules of oxygen, and took over the task herself.

Just past the threshold of her concentration she noted Danyel sparking a flash of recognition, realization, and then near-outrage.

Grandmother, stop it! he roared mentally. *You'll wreck the ship and bring us down in the sea!*

Sharalynn knew she couldn't afford to take attention off the task of maintaining breathable air, but one corner of her mind marveled at the thought of any *laranzu* with telekinetic power like this—and at such a distance. Land and sea were whipping past below, fast enough to blur, but still Kuithal must be thousands of kilometers away… *Air, air, concentrate upon air. Oxygen molecules. Air…*

There was a sense of a powerful mind observing, then making an adjustment. The ship's nose pointed down, and the blurred sea rushed closer. Danyel swore again, actually grasped the aircraft's matrix, then gave up and sat back. "She's taken over," he said aloud. "Let's hope she doesn't rip the wings off, bringing us in."

The plane's nose rose away from the water, and the craft leveled out. Sharalynn noted that the air was thicker, and warmer, though their speed was no less. She also observed that Ventellin was concentrating solely on holding the ship together. After a moment Danyel joined her.

Sharalynn, her effort no longer needed, leaned back in her seat and considered all she'd just learned. Grandmother's display of power aside, the timing of her takeover was significant. *It was right after I saw...*

Oh, that implied much!

Ventellin reached for the bundle on the floor and pulled out some wrapped meat-rolls and a classic Terran thermos bottle. "We'd best eat now," she said aloud, handing out the food, mentally adding, *If the old dragon is this impatient to meet us, she won't give us time for any formal meal.*

Added to that was a brief image of a real dragon, shooting its igniting breath at a small banshee-bird. The details were too vivid to be imagination.

You've seen a live dragon?! Sharalynn queried, reaching for the thermos. *How long ago? They're said to be extinct...*

On the mainland, they are, Ventellin answered, thoughtfully chewing. *They're maintained on the islands.*

Sharalynn thought about that as she sipped from the thermos' contents—a light wine-and-fruit punch, she noted. *What other supposedly lost species survive there?*

Danyel laughed briefly, then politely reached for the thermos. *Primarily us.* He flicked her an image of the Interbreeders carefully moving the whole population of the lone continent out to the islands, making room for the humans, leaving only the study-teams and experimenters. *...and a few distant individuals who didn't get the call...* There was a flash of pity for "poor lost Narzain-ye", and the hint of a sad story there.

Sharalynn guessed the rest of it. *So you kept the humans confined to the continent, and the rest of the world—all the islands*... She tapped her matrix-memory for the statistics on just how much land that encompassed. The final figure was impressive. "Mother," she asked aloud, "just how big is our—the *chieri*—population now?"

There was another exchange of glances and private thoughts between the siblings. Then Danyel stated, "Among the purebreds, at last count, half a million. There are at least another half-million half-breeds, like us, and the gods only know how many apparent humans are carrying a quarter or less of *chieri* genes."

"Probably most of the humans on Darkover, by now," Ventellin added. "Yes, our species is very likely to survive."

"Provided we can get to another world," Danyel finished, "which is now also very likely."

Sharalynn thought that over as she munched through a fruit-roll, and made a good guess as to how important their news was, and why the Grandmother was so anxious to meet them.

Their only warning was that the ship's speed slacked, a little at first, then more. Sharalynn looked out the viewport and saw land approaching—a very large shore, its ends invisible in the distance. Matrix-stored memory provided Terran comparisons: Iceland, New Zealand, Britain. The land looked rocky, bleak and barren, its sky smoky from distant sullen volcanoes, totally uninteresting to the Terran aerial survey teams that had provided the only map. The airship slowed further, and with the faintest whisper of a parting veil, the illusion faded and the true land was revealed.

It was all green in variegated patches, thick forests and wide meadows, threaded with streams running from a string of cloud-wreathed central mountains, with not a patch of snow anywhere. Sharalynn wondered if the land's obvious warmth came from some actual volcano among those hidden peaks, or if there was some other explanation.

The sense of that watching mind—or network of minds—grew stronger as the ship, with no action from Danyel, slowed and sank to hover near a crystal-blue lake. Sharalynn saw a single building on the lake's shore, what looked like a simple tower, made of crystal stone as blue as the water. It was backed against a thick forest and fronted by a smooth green meadow, where the aircraft finally landed as softly as a feather. The door seals withdrew, and amazingly warm, humid, plant-perfumed air filled the cockpit.

Danyel sighed and turned off the engine. "Now we wait," he said. "If Grandmother's in a good mood, she'll come out to meet us."

The feel of the watching mind gave an almost audible snort of impatience, and withdrew—toward the crystal tower. A moment later, a door opened and several figures emerged from it. Sharalynn realized that not only were they all c*hieri* but they wore color-coded robes: white, blue, green—and the leader wore red. *Colors of rank,* she knew, and recognized them. With a start, she realized that this was the circle of a working matrix tower, and the lead figure was their Keeper. *A Tower of chieri!* she marveled, wondering what powers such a circle could command. Was this the original model of a Tower circle, which humans had later copied? "Do they even bother to speak audibly?" she murmured, "Or have they forgotten their voices?"

Ventellin didn't answer, but opened the cockpit door and stepped out to meet the approaching delegation. Danyel followed, Sharalynn bringing up the rear. They waited by the ship, a fine point of manners, until the Tower's crew drew close and halted.

The lead figure took a few more steps closer, and Sharalynn saw that she—or he—was very tall, silver-haired, silver-eyed, slender but giving an impression of immense power, and very old. Beyond doubt, this was the Grandmother. Sharalynn had carefully shielded herself, but she felt the ancient Keeper scanning the three of them.

"Report," Grandmother snapped, in a strong and perfectly capable voice. "First, who is this?"

Sharalynn caught the unspoken addition: *The one who trumpets so loudly of matters better kept quiet.*

Ventellin took Sharalynn by the fingertips and led her a few steps forward. "Sharalynn, my daughter," she said.

Sharalynn pulled back the hood of her too-heavy cloak and gave a polite curtsy.

Grandmother stared at her sandy-red hair and distinctly blue eyes, thinking: *A quarter-bred, of course.* The contempt in the thought was obvious.

Sharalynn's impulsive temper flared. She thought, vividly, of reaching out and slapping the sneer off that arrogant old woman's face.

Nobody was more surprised than she when Grandmother's head snapped back, and she stumbled and almost fell.

Sharalynn! Ventellin winced, and everyone stared.

It was Grandmother who recovered first. "Quarter-bred," she said aloud, eyeing Sharalynn with amazed respect. "And that strong?!"

Danyel stepped forward quickly. "Hybrid vigor," he said. "I believe I've mentioned it before."

Grandmother straightened, rubbing her cheek. *You must breed her back into the line,* she noted. *At the mainland enclave, of course.* "Meanwhile, what is the news you were so eager to tell me?"

Danyel stepped forward, pulling out his starstone. "That I've found us an ideal world, Grandmother," he said. "I've been there and studied it, and it's perfect, and they desperately want our life-forms, and they have ships."

Vainwal! Sharalynn understood, staring, as Danyel stepped close to Grandmother and held out his matrix.

After a moment's hesitation, Grandmother pulled a similar locket from her own robes and held it out until the stones touched. For long moments they stood motionless, and the rest of the Tower's circle, too, clearly receiving the information stored in Danyel's matrix-memory.

Sharalynn wondered if Ventellin had taught Danyel that trick, after seeing her do it with the medical texts. *Vainwal,* she considered, turning to aim a look and a thought at Ventellin. *How long have you been planning to invade Vainwal? And what then will become of the humans there? And why is it so perfect?*

She felt Ventellin smile back. *Not precisely an invasion, child; we'll pay well for the land we'll settle. The humans will survive and prosper in the warm lands they're used to, with the help of ourselves and the whole ecosystem we'll bring with us. As to why it's perfect... Dearest, why do you think Grandmother and her circle have kept this land so warm?*

For a moment, Sharalynn couldn't imagine why. She was beginning to sweat under her thick wool dress and cloak. Why would anyone want to live in a climate like this?

Then she remembered what Ventellin had said earlier about the planet cooling over the ages, and the c*hieris'* fertility problem. ...*Fertility?!*

Precisely, Ventellin confirmed, smiling. *Much of it depends on our symbiosis with the kireseth flower, which needs warmer weather to thrive—and so do we, really. Despite our best efforts, we can't maintain our fertility in colder climates. Humans can manage, but we can't. We need Vainwal, and Vainwal needs us.*

Sharalynn nodded, seeing—again—the whole picture. She had no doubt that the Purist *chieri* could transport themselves—and every native life-form on Darkover—to the temperate and even arctic zones of Vainwal. They would leave Darkover to the humans and the Interbreeders, and the interbred—like herself—and make Vainwal into a revival of the earlier, younger Darkover. On that younger planet, with its younger sun, they and their companion species could survive for millions—or billions—of years. Indeed, the c*hieri* thought in long, long terms.

And Darkover? *Hybrid vigor,* she remembered. Between crossbreeding of genes and ideas, the people—and ecosystem—of Darkover would survive, too, in altered form no doubt, but vigorous. *Surviving.*

Without degenerating, as Grandmother feared, Ventellin confirmed. *Besides, the Bloody Sun has probably a million more years to go before the planet becomes uninhabitable. By that time, who knows what we can accomplish?*

There was a brief, playful, fantasy image of a circle of *laranzu* moving the whole planet, and its moons, closer to the sullen sun.

Not impossible... Sharalynn agreed, and then shielded the

thought right there. If Darkover could be moved in its orbit, just a few centimeters every year, closer to its primary, then there might be no need for the migration to Vainwal—and Grandmother just might prefer that course, and so must never know. Vainwal needed their help, and—to quote an ancient Terran saying—it wasn't wise to keep all one's eggs in one basket.

Her thoughts were safely distracted by the sight of Grandmother and Danyel stepping apart, and then a sudden flurry of activity. The rest of the *chieri* scattered to different tasks, Danyel hurried back into the ship, then re-emerged a moment later carrying the sample-bags. Grandmother turned toward the Tower, still holding her starstone, silently giving commands.

A few moments later, knots of *kyrri*—clearly servants—came hurrying out of the Tower, carrying large and small containers. Danyel hastened to meet them, taking some of the smaller containers himself, silently ordering others into the ship.

"Hold," Grandmother snapped, and all activity came to a halt—except for a dozen *kyrri* coming out of the Tower doorway, carefully rolling between them what looked like a man-high disk of polished dull gray metal. "Fit that in the ship first," she commanded. "It will take the most room."

Ventellin gasped as she recognized the object, and Sharalynn caught the thought.

Yes, a screen, Grandmother confirmed for both of them. *Next time, use that to visit me. Lord Aldaran's airship may not always be available.* Then she turned her attention back to Danyel. *Yes, eventually take it to Vainwal. We can make more, given the right minerals. And yes, from your information, those minerals are abundant on Vainwal. We are no longer bound to naturally-occurring starstones.*

There was a barely-shielded image from Ventellin, something about the age-long stagnation in the physical sciences having finally come to an end.

Grandmother clearly caught it, for she returned a glare and unshielded reply. *Not stagnant: stalled—for lack of new information. I grant you, we learned much from the Terrans. Be assured, we made good use of it.* Then she turned her silent attention back to the kyrri, who rolled the featureless gray disk to the ship.

The next several minutes were a flurry of loading and packing, the *kyrri* moving with far more speed and efficiency than was natural for them. Sharalynn noticed Grandmother studying her, and—on impulse, again—pulled out her locket and held it out, hoping the ancient Keeper would take it as a peace-offering. "It contains medical texts," she explained.

"Medical?" The Grandmother pondered for a moment, then gestured to one of her circle—green-robed, almost certainly a Monitor. "Zhainthille," she snapped. "This is your field of study."

The Monitor almost tiptoed up to Sharalynn and nervously held out his matrix.

"Just draw it directly into the stone," Sharalynn explained, touching her starstone to his. Through the contact she realized that the hapless Zhainthille—and, amazingly, Grandmother—were a little afraid of her, of this trick she'd invented, of her almost-alien thought-patterns. She guided the transfer of information as smoothly and gently as she could, beginning and ending with the guide/index for retrieving the knowledge as needed. Even so, the Monitor looked a little overwhelmed by the time he broke contact. He moved back and shot a quick report at Grandmother.

Massive, he judged—and Sharalynn caught. *Organized. Useful.*

Grandmother raised an eyebrow, silently dismissed him on another errand, and turned her attention back to Sharalynn. "My apologies, Great-granddaughter," she said, formally. "You do indeed have much of value to teach us." Hidden under that, but not so far that Sharalynn didn't catch it, was: *Must back-breed her! Valuable genes, wherever they came from...*

Sharalynn managed to keep her own reactions hidden as she politely curtsied again, but it wasn't easy.

At that point Danyel returned. "Everything's packed," he said.

"With the help of your circle—and a slightly gentler carrying—we can be back in Caer Donn before nightfall."

"Not quite everything," Grandmother murmured, turning toward Zhainthille, who came cautiously up to them. He was holding a large, sealed clay jug as if it were a newborn babe. Very carefully, he held it out to Danyel, who took it with much the same care.

"Is this...?" he asked, sounding a bit awed.

Yes, Grandmother confirmed, *Kireseth seeds. Enough to seed a small continent, if you're careful. Take them to Vainwal, and sow them in the temperate zones. Be thorough, Grandchild. Our future is in them.*

Danyel raised an eyebrow, and with no further words turned and walked, very carefully, to the ship—trailing thoughts of Vainwal weather records and rainfall predictions.

Ventellin stepped forward, and Sharalynn realized that she had heard everything, and was firmly suppressing a slow boil of anger. Very politely, she projected: *If I might be so bold as to ask a rude question, Grandmother...*

Grandmother sighed. *You will anyway. Ask.*

Ventellin smiled tightly. *You never did tell me. How many children have you yourself begotten since first the humans came?*

Sharalynn smothered a gasp. Everyone knew—now—that humans had first landed on Darkover a little over a thousand years ago.

Grandmother blinked for a moment, then straightened proudly. *Both bred and sired, all of 97. I have done my part.*

Ventellin actually blushed, nodded formally and stepped back. Her thoughts were shielded so tightly that if Sharalynn hadn't been looking at her, she wouldn't have known Ventellin was there.

But Sharalynn was calculating; 97 children in a thousand years came to slightly less than one every ten years. That couldn't be too burdensome, could it?

"Ventellin-zhe..." Grandmother called, relenting. "Do one thing for me?"

"What?" Ventellin asked, not turning.

"Tell Lehantliss: please come home, all is forgiven."

Ventellin looked around, startled. An unshielded thought revealed that Lehantliss was the name of her mother, the renegade who had run off to join the Interbreeders. "I will," she promised.

Grandmother smiled benignly, leaking another thought. *I've found the perfect mate for her. His genes are flawless...*

Whether or not Ventellin heard that, she resumed her march to the airship.

Great-grandmother! Sharalynn tight-beamed, exasperated. *Must you be so obsessed with breeding?*

The ancient chieri smiled at her. *If I had not been, child, we would still be a dying species. Now there is more than hope for us.*

Sharalynn thought of what Danyel had said about population numbers, and realized that her great-grandmother was more than a Keeper; she was the leading political force among the Purists. *...A queen?*

Grandmother smiled wider. *You came at just the right time, too. Another Idriel, and the Kireseth flowers will be blooming. Every meadow will be golden with them, all over the island. And the winds will blow...*

Accompanying that was an astounding image of a vast number of *chieri*—thousands of them, tens of thousands, more— all over the island, clinging to each other and rolling on the ground in a grand frenzy of mating as the sweet wind blew...

Sharalynn blushed furiously, and all but ran back to the ship.

As promised, the airship landed in the field beside the castle a little before sundown. Lord Aldaran's guardsmen hastened out to help unload the craft, and Danyel gave sharp orders as to how and where to carry the metal disk. Ventellin took charge of the seed-jug herself, leaving Sharalynn to manage their personal gear.

Nonetheless, the three of them had a fine presentation for Lord Aldaran and his guests at dinner. Captain Smith's eyes practically bulged out of his head as Sharalynn, Ventellin and her brother displayed jar after jar of seeds, and described the properties and growing requirements of each.

"Stars and all," he muttered. "We cayn playnt the whole northeast continent …"

"And I'll be happy to assist," Danyel purred, "If you'll but take me back to Vainwal with you. I daresay you'll need my help with the animals, too."

"Oh hayl, yes," Smith agreed. He raised his cup in a clearly heartfelt salute. "Mee-lord, he-yur's to the start of a beautee-ful friendship."

"Agreed," Aldaran smiled. "We'll have more livestock next time you visit."

"I'll drink to thayt!"

"Astonishing," muttered Stefan Lindir-Aillard. "I'd thought the *saranath*-kale was extinct."

"It survives down by the seacoast," Ventellin smiled glibly, "In odd corners here and there."

"Ah, on the Macfarr family lands, eh?" Aldaran thought he'd guessed. He turned to Sharalynn, almost as an afterthought. "And you, *damisela,* did you add to your knowledge too?"

Sharalynn couldn't resist. "Oh, a few things," she improvised, grinning. "A rude folksong, for one:

"My mother's a renegade's daughter,
"My uncle plots invasions,
"My great-grandmother became a queen
"By organizing orgies,
"And, gods, how we all prosper!"

Ventellin shot her a horrified look, but Danyel laughed. "I recall an old Terran song with a similar theme," he said, "But all I remember now is the chorus: 'My gods, how the money rolls in.'"

"Indeed," Lord Aldaran chuckled, raising his cup. "Here's to the money continuing to roll in."

"Ay-men," Smith agreed.

Sharalynn only smiled, content with how few of the dinner crowd understood what she meant.

A WALK IN THE MOUNTAINS

by Margaret L. Carter & Leslie Roy Carter

Darkover's snows practically beg for adventures, and what better one than a rescue mission? Instead of the skis in Jane M. H. Bigelow's "Snow Dancing," the characters in "A Walk in the Mountains" team up with that most iconic of dog rescuer breeds, the St. Bernard.

Margaret L. Carter specializes in vampires, having been marked for life by reading *Dracula* at the age of twelve. Her Ph.D. dissertation even included a chapter on *Dracula*. Her vampire novel *Dark Changeling* won an Eppie Award in the horror category in 2000. Other creatures she writes about include werewolves, dragons, ghosts, and Lovecraftian entities with tentacles. In addition to her horror, fantasy, and paranormal romance fiction, she has had several nonfiction books and articles published on vampires in literature, including *Different Blood: The Vampire As Alien*. Recent work includes *Passion In The Blood* (a vampire romance), *Sealing The Dark Portal* (a paranormal romance with Lovecraftian elements), and "Crossing the Border" (horror erotic romance novella with Lovecraftian elements). Explore love among the monsters at her website, Carter's Crypt: http://www.margaretlcarter.com.

Les and Margaret Carter attended the College of William and Mary together as a married couple and earned their bachelors' degrees there. Les later received an MS in Electronics Engineering from the Naval Postgraduate School. He retired from the U.S. Navy as a Captain after thirty years of service. He and Margaret co-wrote "Carmen's Flight," published in one of the early Darkover anthologies. They have also collaborated on a fantasy series, beginning with *Wild Sorceress*, for which he's the primary author. "A Walk in the Mountains" draws upon Les's fifty-plus years of experience in search and rescue as a member of the Civil Air Patrol. Les and Margaret have four children, eight grandchildren, and two great-grandchildren. Over the years they've owned five St. Bernards.

The young *Terranan* security officer stared across the tavern table at his Darkovan Guard friend and said, "You want me to do what?"

"Help me search for my lost cousin, Eddard Ridenow. A simple walk in the mountains—nothing too tasking for a skilled warrior of your people."

Laughing, Senior Lieutenant David Fairechild shook his head in feigned disbelief at the answer to his question. "You know how they feel about that, Mikhail, and I doubt if your people would allow it, anyway."

"The Hastur has already asked for *Terranan* help. Your Legate conducted a survey of the area from space but found nothing. He told us that a severe storm over the mountains would prevent an air search using flyers. He offered the use of ground forces, but the Hastur wouldn't go that far." Mikhail Leynier drained his beer. "That storm kept us from putting out our own search teams, but it is supposed to clear by late tomorrow."

David emptied his own mug and signaled for refills. "Your cousin must be a very important person, a VIP, for everyone to go to this much trouble. Who, or what, is he?"

"A young lad, half-child, half-man. Wants to be a Thendara City Guard. His father insisted he spend a couple of years getting an education at Saint Valentine's-of-the-Snows at Nevarsin, and Eddard was not too happy with that decision. He stuck it out for a year but disappeared yesterday morning before the storm hit."

Sitting back in the booth, David slowly twirled the newly filled mug on the table, studying the thick, white foam on top. "Cold up there this time of year. Mikhail, I am not too well versed on Darkovan politics, and I know the word cousin has a lot of meanings, and..."

"He is a favorite of the Hastur, but that has no real import for our relationship. He is a third son to a second son of a sister of the Hastur. He stands to inherit nothing, his marriage will be for love, not power, and he has no special gifts to bring to our family. He's just a fourteen-year-old boy. His disappearance could be for any reason."

Taking a gulp of his drink, David looked at Mikhail, a slender young man with the flame-red hair typical of the local aristocracy. "Why ask me to help? I've known you only a couple of years. We don't work that closely in our jobs. You're Guard, I am a mere lieutenant in the Terran Security office. We occasionally share drinks."

Mikhail smiled. "More than occasionally, but that is because we share the same interests. We both like mountaineering, hunting, outdoor life. I know you are the Search and Rescue Officer for the security detachment assigned to my world. You have special training, you are in superb physical condition, and I have seen how you handle yourself in the wild where very few of your people are allowed or even want to go. Will you help me?"

"I'm game, and I'm sure the Legate will jump at the chance to get a Terran out in the field. I'll need to sleep off this beer and arrange a flyer for us. I'll grab my gear and meet you at the main gate at sunrise. Sound all right to you?"

Mikhail stared down at his drink. Something was bothering him.

"Keep in mind, Saint Valentine's is a monastery, and their beliefs don't hold with Terran magic. They will not allow the machine within their gates."

David held up a hand to interrupt, hoping his frustration didn't show on his face. Nice enough folk in most ways, but bloody stubborn about their archaic customs. "Yeah, I know, and no ranged weapons. I'll go armed with whatever you approve. It would be nice if we had something against those blind banshee birds..."

Mikhail cut in, "Sightless, not blind. Banshees hunt by sensing body heat."

Shaking his head, David sighed. "Infrared sensors in a frozen environment! The bird has all the advantages."

"You underestimate our adjustment to our world's environment." Pushing aside his mug, Mikhail stood. "Let us plan on meeting at the castle gate at the time you suggest. And, David, thank you in advance for your help."

The ride in the flyer was no worse than vertlifts David had made in Scout Recon training. There was almost no acceleration associated with the takeoff, but the positive and negative G's from the sudden updrafts and downdrafts were brutal on the stomach. Mikhail was sick almost the whole half-day flight to Nevarsin. Ground-hugging all the way, the flyer leaped over the mountain ridge surrounding Nevarsin and dropped down into the valley toward the monastery north of the town. During the too-rapid approach to the landing site picked by the pilot, David almost joined the Guard officer in his misery. They set down on a fallow field nestled up against the outside wall of Saint Valentine's. Getting off that flyer occupied both their minds for several minutes.

"You all right?" David asked, sitting on his backpack to avoid the snow-covered ground. Mikhail lay sprawled face down, pawing snow onto his face.

"Give me a moment," Mikhail moaned.

"Take your time. Our hosts are just exiting what looks like the main gate of the monastery. I do expect I'll need your help when they get here. I doubt if my *cahuenga* is good enough to answer their questions about why we all of a sudden dropped out of their sky."

Rolling on his back, Mikhail croaked, "They knew we were coming."

"How? Heliograph in this weather?"

"You know, our magic…"

"*Laran*? If this stuff does all I've heard, finding your cousin should be a snap. Can't you just contact him by telepathy or something?"

"It's more complicated than that."

It always is with psionics, David thought. *Never works predictably.* "Is it affected by weather? I've heard stories it controls the weather." *And I'd be amazed if half of them were true.*

Rising slowly to his feet, Mikhail glanced at the approaching monks before giving him a glare. "It's complicated. Weather control has been tried and abandoned."

"Too bad. I'm feeling chilled, and we haven't even started. Something about this place attracts the cold. Is it me, or do these monks appear to be not wearing coats?"

"They are, I believe the word you use is, 'acclimated.'" Addressing in *casta* the white-haired monk in the forefront of the approaching trio, he said, "Good morning, Father Marius. Any further developments?"

"No, Captain Mikhail Leynier. No sign of the young Hastur." The Father Superior of the monastery looked at David standing next to the young Guard officer. "This must be the *Terranan* specialist I was told to expect. Does he speak our language?"

David saluted. "My name Senior Lieutenant David Fairechild. More *cahuenga*, little *casta*, Honorable One. I have a good man talker, he speak for me."

"He means translator, Father," Mikhail cut in. "They rely heavily on their mechanical devices for communications."

The priest acknowledged the Terran with a slight bow. "This is Brother Cyril, our novice master..." indicating the tall, middle-aged man to his left, "...and Brother Bernardo, the kennel master, on my right."

Bows and salutes followed. Father Marius turned toward the nearest building and held out his arm to direct the group to proceed in that direction. "Hand signals. Works for me. Best way to deliver commands I know," David said to Mikhail.

David stood before the map tacked up on the wall and slowly shook his head.

Mikhail gave him a questioning look. *What was David expecting anyway?* "It's the largest map we have of the area. The detail is a little lacking, but it shows the general lay of the land."

"General lay is right. If I were planning a campaign, I would be happy to start with this. This doesn't tell me anything about the ground we'll be searching. About the only thing it tells me is, I hope, that the top of the map is north. That is your symbol for north, isn't it?"

Mikhail looked where David's finger was pointing. "Yes, and the scale markings are in what you call kilometers. The map is as accurate as our cartographers can make it. The salient points are in the right place—this mountaintop is that far away and in the right direction. The brothers can fill us in on the conditions of the trails…"

David wiped his hand wearily across his brow. "Mikhail, I know you have fought many wars here on Darkover. I don't think you relied on native guides to lead you into battle. How did you do it back then?"

Mikhail fumbled for a brief answer, one which did not contain the word *laran*. "Um, we used, what is the word—scouts! Aerial scouts. Much like those things that fly around the parameter of Thendara—drones, only ours are alive."

"Alive!"

Mikhail suppressed a sigh at the need to keep explaining and justifying his people's ways. "Birds. It's complicated. Must we talk about such things in front of the brothers? It will upset them."

David leaned closer to Mikhail. "Birds? Is this more of your psionics magic? You look through their eyes or something? Can you still do this?"

"The skill was once widespread, but was—discouraged, shall we say. There are very few technicians left that can read animals." Mikhail glanced toward the Father Superior. "*Laran* was badly misused centuries ago, creating horrible casualties like in your nuclear wars on Terra that I have read about. Use of *laran* for pursuit of war purposes is severely punished on our world."

David stood back from the map and walked over to where the monks were sitting around a wooden table. It was one of twenty in the building they had been ushered to, apparently a dining hall. Father Marius glanced up from the conversation he was holding with his fellow monks. "Are we ready to send out the search parties yet? A thorough search of the monastery has been conducted. We have been waiting for you to start outside."

While Mikhail translated, David shook his head. "First we gather information and use that to assemble facts. Then we organize the search." Pulling out a data pad, which drew a collective frown from the assembled monks, he began to ask a rapid-fire list of questions. "We need to know some basic information. Where was the last point Eddard was seen? The time when seen? What was he wearing? When he last ate and what…"

Most of the questions could not be answered by Father Marius and his fellow monks. Messengers were sent to find those who did have the information. Mikhail was impressed with the thoroughness of the questions, but they reminded him too much of what police asked in an investigation. He queried the scout lieutenant during a lull while the messengers were out seeking answers.

"I told you there was no question of foul play, David. Your 'victim profile' seems to imply there is." Thoroughness was admirable, but David seemed to be dragging out the preliminaries when they should be taking action.

"I know, but it is a sad fact that many missing-person searches end up in a crime scene. After all, a child from a noble family might become a target of kidnapping. We have been capturing search statistics since before the beginning of space travel, and they have led us to a scientific approach to finding victims. The method takes in the psychological, sociological, medical, cultural—just about all the 'cals' you can imagine.

David noticed an increase in the activity around the Father Superior. "It looks like the last of our questions have answers waiting for us. Time to do some serious planning."

The victim profile took several hours to compile. David briefed his findings to Mikhail. "The last time anyone remembered seeing Eddard in person was at evening prayer. Shortly thereafter, he was seen in bed. Now since his robes were arranged under the blankets to make it appear he were sleeping, he could have left just after evening prayer. That means he'd have made further progress than we would have guessed if he had left yesterday morning."

Brother Cyril cut in. "He left his cell wearing the clothes he arrived in. He was prepared to leave us for good."

"So you're certain he was running away?" David asked. "Well, if so, that assumption puts him in the category of not wanting to be found, which could change our search strategy if we have to plan on him trying to evade us."

David explained how a victim's mental condition could skew the findings of the "histories"—he didn't think "databases" would translate well here. He ascertained by careful questioning of both Eddard's cousin and his monk mentor that the boy had shown no classic mental retardation, autism, depression, or bipolar behavior. Eddard was apparently a kid tired of doing what he didn't want to do and running from it. This was good news and also bad. In absconding he had made some preparations for the environment he was escaping through, but on the other hand he was more than likely not going to respond to the searchers unless he was really in trouble.

David spread out the topological map on the table and waited for the murmuring from the assembled monks to die down. The map was only a compilation of sub-maps taped together, because the strip printer he had crammed into his pack was limited in size. It had been a long shot that he would be able to convince the Darkovans who operated printing presses that the digital machine was hardly more complex than what they possessed already. The need for a map to search from overrode their reluctance to use Terran technology.

A comm feed to the main computer allowed him to tap into the mapping data on Cottman IV, and he had printed out a hundred-square-kilometer segment centered on the monastery. He had segmented the map using the roads and trails radiating out and also streams and ravines that could possibly be used. What he had created was a piece puzzle over the real world map, each piece representing an area of thirty to fifty hectares, about as much as a search team could cover in three to six hours. He pointed at the map and began to explain what he had drawn.

"Our histories tell us that almost all lost teenage children are found within ten kilometers from the initial planning point of a search. This circle on the map represents that distance drawn from our present location. You have told me that he was last seen in his bed. That was forty-eight hours ago." Father Marius nodded in confirmation.

"The histories show that for mountain wilderness the survivability in good weather drops to none in four days—gets even worse with bad weather like we have now. Truthfully I'd say he is dead as I speak…" David glanced at Mikhail. The young Guard officer's eyes stared back pleadingly. "…but I've been told that Eddard has survived up here for a year.

"What was the weather here like the night he ran?" David asked the Father Superior.

"Clear, but the snow squall blew through before sunrise. It covered any traces of his leaving. He had taken a set of snowshoes with him. We found tracks of them a short distance away from the walls."

"Where? Show me on this map."

The priest pointed to a sector immediately south of the monastery. David said, "We'll start there. It is an area of highest probability." David lined out a pattern on the segmented map. He traced a track on either side of the area and told Brother Cyril to arrange for a four-man team to sweep those tracks back and forth in a south and north direction until the area was covered. David emphatically ordered that the team have a leader with as much knowledge of the area he was to search as possible, who could mark his team's progress on a copy of the map area he would be given.

"I'll take charge of coordinating other teams in the following area." David pointed to segments lying adjacent to the ones where track lines were already laid out. "We will set the priority in which we search them, depending on how much experience your team leaders have and their knowledge of the terrain. Send me monks who know the lay of the land. I'll form additional teams to search these areas. Each area should take several hours to cover."

With Mikhail translating rapidly at his side, David spent the next few hours coordinating teams, producing maps from his little printer, and teaching the Terran symbology used on the topo maps to the monk team leaders. He told them, "Return your teams here when they finish their areas. Don't let them loose on their own. Go to the assigned area, search it, and then come back. Call Eddard's name and wait for a response. Be aware that there are other teams searching next to you, and don't respond to their calls. It will add to confusion if you chase after them. Stay in your area as well as you can. If you find something, send a runner back to us to report. Do not pursue the clue unless you have the victim in sight. Running off without telling us will most likely result in chasing a faulty lead and/or losing the clue because nobody secured it."

When the two soldiers had a moment to take a break, a novice brought them hot *jaco*. Sipping the Darkovan stimulant, David became freshly aware of the cold and relished the warmth of the sweetened beverage going down. Sitting at an open table next to Mikhail, he said, "We're going to have to prepare relief teams next. The returning teams will need a couple of hours' rehab before we send them out again. People will tend to work themselves to exhaustion with the anxiety of a search and will become ineffective rapidly."

Mikhail drained his *jaco* and reached for the pitcher to refill his cup. "Speaking of anxiety, Brother Bernardo has been pestering me constantly because we are not using his charges. He could not go out earlier because of the storm. He has several new dogs that he has been training especially for this type of search. He calls them his animal brethren."

"Brethren? Is he one of those animal mind readers?" David asked. Clairvoyance and telepathy had some evidence in their support, but the concept of speaking with dogs roused his inborn skepticism.

The Guard officer blinked with a puzzled expression on his face. "Mind reader? Oh, you mean, does he have *laran*? I don't think so."

Would you tell me if he did? David wondered.

Mikhail smiled. "No, they are, what is your word? 'Namesakes.' They are from a line of dogs that the *Terranan* had brought with them when they established your first base at Caer Donn. Large, heavily-furred, mostly brown- and white-coated monsters of work dogs. Bred for hauling heavy loads and breaking a trail in the snow. You know them as Saint Bernards."

David nodded. "Our histories mention them. Used long ago but went nearly extinct because better dogs were bred for search and rescue. Lots of stamina in the snow but not much where cold isn't. I guess that is why we brought them to such a frozen planet as Cottman IV."

Finishing his *jaco*, David moved to the master map on the table and waved his hand at the segmented areas depicted there. "We don't usually employ scent dogs for wide area search. They are better used for search after a clue is found. Do we have a scent article they can use?"

Mikhail nodded. "Eddard left his robes behind, and the dogs have gotten a good whiff of his smell."

A sudden rise in the noise volume announced the return of one of the teams. The two soldiers headed to the table where Father Superior sat, arriving to hear the news that Eddard's tracks had been sighted. Studying the map, the team lead traced a line parallel to the road heading south from the monastery. The young lad was avoiding the road for fear of being found.

Under questioning, the monk said that his team had followed the footprints to the edge of their assigned sector but, as instructed, had not gone beyond. They had made their discovery at the end of their time, and the monk decided to leave two of his team to guide the next searchers to the find. He reported that the snowshoe tracks were filling with snow and urged Father Marius to send his team out again, as they knew the area.

David cautioned against that. The group had been out there for four hours and looked exhausted. The snow was knee deep, and even with the snowshoes, the trek was a slog. David wished he had convinced Mikhail to let him bring a motorized sled. They had horses and those strange deer pack animals, but other than conserving energy by riding, they would not make any more speed.

Pointing to a set of buildings depicted on the map, David asked what they were. He was told they were an outlying village that served as a way station. "We'll move our base camp to that location. Muster the teams there and set up containment locations here, here, and there. Two-man teams in place, with fires to make them visible. If Eddard realizes he is in trouble, he may head for them if he is mobile."

David turned to Brother Cyril. "Or he may have thought to head east toward the village after the storm hit. If they have him, though, I would have thought they would have sent a messenger to the monastery. That makes me believe he is still out. Captain Mikhail and I will take Brother Bernardo and his dogs to where the tracks were found."

"What about the teams still out in the field?" Father Marius asked.

"Muster them here and see that they rest for at least several hours before sending them to the new base camp." Tracing a line through the containment sites, David worried that Eddard could have gotten beyond the line. In the heart of the storm, the boy might have tried to gut it out. The containment circle depicted the edge of the distance within which most victims were found. He would need to send teams to the segmented areas that lay beyond the circle, but he was running out of personnel.

Looking over to Mikhail, David said, "Unfortunately, we can't expect help from the air. Our weather report predicts another storm tonight."

Mikhail nodded. "A Renunciate guide we consulted with confirms that report."

David bit back the sharp answer that leaped to mind. Yet another example of distrusting technology and falling back on their deep-rooted customs. He walked over to where the backpacks had been stored. He hoisted his equipment harness on and checked the items hanging from it. Brother Cyril brought over a pair of snowshoes and handed them to him. The monk started to explain how to put them on, but the Scout officer took them out of his hands and waved him away. This was one low-tech device David approved of. He turned to Mikhail and said, "Some things never change. Snowshoes are an old friend to winter operations. Tell him, 'Thanks.' Let's head out."

They followed the tracks of the returning search party and found the two members they had left. Sensibly the monks had made a fire and were eating a meal. Mikhail told them to return to the monastery. With the storm approaching, it was too dangerous for the tired men to try to hike cross-country to intercept the group traveling to the base camp.

The two dogs were reacquainted with the scent articles, and they began circling the area where Eddard's tracks had been sighted. David found it fascinating to watch the huge balls of fur race around with their noses literally buried in the snow. Their floppy ears perking forward and tails wagging back and forth, they converged on the spot where Eddard had switched from walking boots only and donned his snowshoes.

Staring at the ground, they seemed to be memorizing every impression in the snow as if the scent were telling them what the boy had done standing there. Brother Bernardo explained to the two officers, with Mikhail translating, that dogs could break down the composition of a meal to what spices were in it, the amount of each, every vegetable used, where they were grown, the meat in it, how fresh it was, and what part of the Hellers it was shot in. David translated that to mean the dog could smell the chemicals that made up the scent and distinguish their proportionality almost as well as a mass spectrometer.

The dogs seemed to agree simultaneously on their findings and took off following the scent, noses buried and ears flopping. David took a reading with his tracker of the heading they were on. It would be downloaded to his printer back at the monastery and stored in memory. Unfortunately, Mikhail was the only non-Terran he'd had time to train in retrieving info from the search database, but his commanding officer would know where he was.

The trail led through the narrow valley and onto the slope up a ridge where the valley ended. The three men had a harder time keeping up with the dogs when the trail led over the bare, rocky ground. The wind, blowing from behind them, pushed them forward off the vertical and made trudging in the snowshoes more like stepping sideways in ski fashion. The climb was not steep, but it made an exhausting struggle. Mikhail stopped the men and suggested they remove their snowshoes while they struggled up the wind-blown gravel.

The trail crested with a slight pass between two tree-covered hills and disappeared from sight. The ceiling had been lowering steadily since they left the base camp and would soon completely cover the valley behind them. Brother Bernard signaled the dogs to return to the men and expressed his worry that they were losing the scent trail. Any scent in the air was of course gone with the freshening wind and would not linger on the bare ground as it had in the snow. The two dogs lay on the ground but kept staring at the crest.

"Well, he made it over the ridge. The topo map shows descending terrain sloping toward the village to the east. I don't know about you, but from the distance we've traveled, I am really feeling the stress. I need a rest," David said, lowering his butt to the ground with a thump.

Mikhail sat at David's side. David shared his canteen. "It's water from our base. That grimace you just made is probably from the taste of the electrolytes we put in there. Absolutely engineered for this environment."

Mikhail handed it back after only one sip. "Except for taste. I'll stick with watered wine. I know it works out here."

David took the canteen back and gulped another swig. He offered it to Brother Bernardo, but the monk took the cue from Mikhail and drank from his own flask. David removed an object from his vest and tore off the wrapping. He offered it to Mikhail. "Energy bar?"

Shaking his head, Mikhail instead accepted a lump of something from the monk and thanked him. The monk bowed and turned to feed his animals. David finished his energy bar and stuffed the wrapper into a side pocket. Mikhail offered him a chew from the dried meat he'd gotten from the monk. "It's rabbit-horn."

"Er, no thanks! Makes the stomach concentrate too much on digesting that. Takes more energy to process than it gives back quickly. Our scientists have made a lot of studies to determine the best food for survival in the wild."

"You *Terranan* make a study of everything and seek efficiency and economy in all you do. We have discovered over centuries what works for our world and are content to leave it alone." Mikhail finished his piece of rabbit-horn and wiped his gloves on the ground. "Which is why we are reluctant to accept the things you offer—that and the destruction your weapons bring, showing the cheapness you place on human life. We learned that mistake centuries ago also."

David updated their position with his tracker and scanned the descending clouds. "You can't reach the stars and the worlds that are out there by accepting what has worked in the past as sufficient." He stood and offered a hand to assist Mikhail up.

The Guard Captain took it and pulled himself erect. "It all depends on what your goals in life are. Ours were never to leave this world, only to live with it."

Brother Bernardo released his charges, and they scrambled toward the crest.

The dogs picked up Eddard's trail soon after cresting the hill. The winds slacked off, and the ceiling loosed its burden of snow. The village to the east was obscured by the lowering clouds and quickly blocked by snow squalls. Eddard's trail did not swerve in that direction, so either he had not seen the village or he was not in trouble yet and continued to avoid it. The slope had accumulated enough snow from the last storm that wearing snowshoes became feasible again.

Eddard's footprints were almost invisible and becoming more so each passing moment. The Saint Bernards started a weaving pattern across the trail and stopped at one point, ears perked toward the mountains to their west. A low growl rumbled from the lead dog as an eerie, high-pitched sound floated down from that direction. David glanced at the cloud-covered trees upslope. "Banshee? I'm actually going to meet a banshee. Me, with no range weapons."

Mikhail shifted his coat and checked the sword hanging at his side. Bernardo called to the dogs and ordered them to resume the search. He spoke with Mikhail and motioned down the disappearing trail.

The Guard Captain eyed David. "Unless we need to go after the banshee, the situation warrants leaving the bird alone to avoid attracting it to our position. I agree with him."

David made no attempt to conceal his worry. "The team who found his tracks—I don't remember their reporting a banshee. This would certainly be a finding they should have told us about. Are they so common in this area that people ignore their presence?"

Mikhail asked the monk that question and got a short reply from Bernardo. "He says the banshees are not that common, but they can be handled by leaving them alone."

David shook his head in exasperation. "The presence of predators in the search area where they are not normally found is a major clue. That bird may be on the trail of Eddard!"

"Then let us hurry and hope we find him before the banshee does." The three men raced after the dogs.

The trail disappeared to human eyes, and the dogs tracked the scent, turning downhill. Eddard was no longer trying to avoid the village, but he must have known it was down slope and was taking the path of least resistance. It led to a sharp drop-off. The dogs crossed back and forth along the ledge and waited for the men to catch up.

"He likely went over this ledge," Mikhail said. "The drop looks to be ten feet or so. No telling how deep the snow is at the bottom."

Bernardo, peering over the edge, pointed excitedly and said something rapidly in *casta*. Mikhail translated. "He says the boy is down there somewhere in the ravine. The snow down there came from up here. A small avalanche. The dogs know he is there."

All David could see was a smooth sheet of snow fanning

away from the rocky face of the ledge. He glanced at the two dogs prancing at the edge and making little whining noises. "We can go around by this side and get to the start of the ravine, but I don't see how we will find Eddard in that mess."

The monk smiled. "They can scent through twenty feet of snow and hear noises that deep. They will find him." Bernardo released the dogs, and they bolted down slope of the ledge and onto the covered ravine, the men sliding in their wake.

Zigzagging across the face of the ravine, their noses buried and plowing up snow, the dogs converged on a spot twenty feet from the rock face and frantically started digging. Mikhail called for Eddard while David and Bernardo listened for a reply. The men, not being equipped with large, efficient paws, stayed away from the digging animals.

A faint response came from the depth of the snow in front of the dogs, which paused in their digging. Mikhail called again and told Eddard help had arrived and to hold on. The boy begged them to hurry, because he couldn't feel his feet and hands. The dogs continued to tunnel and soon reached the buried figure. When they lay down on either side of Eddard, he was effectively now buried in fur instead of snow.

Mikhail, with David crouched next to him, looked at the dogs licking at his cousin's face and laughed in obvious relief. "That will warm you up better than anything we can give you. You are very lucky to be alive."

A muffled, sheepish voice arose from the fur mound. "The meditations taught by the monks saved me. I was wrong thinking I had wasted my time at the monastery. I'm sorry I ran away."

Mikhail backed away from the entrance and turned to face David. "We're going to need help clearing this snow pile off him. I'll stay with him. You take Brother Bernardo and head for the village—"

An ear-shattering cry split the air. Looking up, David saw the nightmare image of a huge beak atop seven feet of death with claws pointed at him. The bird leaped off the rock and dropped to the snow below the ledge. It gave another horrendous cry. Mikhail fought his sword out, struggling to clear it from under his coat. He was closest, and the banshee turned its eyeless head toward him.

David yanked a canister off his harness and pulled the pin, tossing it overhand. The bird was turning its body and starting to leap at the Guard Captain when the canister exploded with a white-hot hiss in front of the bird, throwing it back against the cliff face.

"Get it, Mikhail. Stab it while it's stunned."

The Guard Caption shook his head to clear his own eyes and charged the banshee, swinging his sword in an arc to connect with the neck and sever it. He dove to his right, rolled out of the way of the thrashing claws. Looking up at the Security Officer, he gasped out, "By the gods, what kind of a weapon was that?"

"Not a weapon at all. It is a solar flare I intended to use to mark our position for the space-borne infrared sensors my people are using to search for us. Now that they know where we are, they will send a flyer to execute a rescue pickup," David said.

Stepping over to help his friend up, David added, "It was not in violation of your Compact. You told me earlier that the banshee uses body heat to track its victims and that terrible scream to stun them. I used the infrared signaling device to even out the playing field by blinding its heat sensing. By the way, nice job of close-combat killing. Now let's get Eddard out of the hole he managed to get himself in."

The flyer delivered the rescue party to the monastery, and Eddard was soon seated in front of a fireplace wrapped in blankets, a hot drink in hand. The two Saint Bernards lay close underfoot, turning their huge heads to look at him every time he spoke as he told his story to the assembled leaders of the rescue effort.

"I thought if I could make it to Thendara on my own in the dead of winter, they would have to let me join the Guard now instead of later, after I showed how tough I had become. Stupid, eh?"

David shook his head. "Not stupid, just young. It's amazing that you didn't freeze to death out there. Those 'meditations' work better than I would have imagined." He glanced at Mikhail. "Even so, you must have a natural gift for wilderness survival. You have had a real learning experience. After finishing your education, instead of the Guard, would you consider trying out for our Search and Rescue service? Our government is eager to encourage that kind of crossover between cultures. That is, if your family will agree to it."

The boy's eyes shone with eagerness.

After a thoughtful pause, Mikhail said, "Perhaps they might."

THE FIFTH MOON

by Ty Nolan

My cats inform me that in order to maintain the cosmic equilibrium, their cousins must enjoy a fair share in these stories. I'm sure the characters in Ty Nolan's "The Fifth Moon" would agree. Like his "Climbing to the Moons" (*Gifts of Darkover*), this tale fits into the category of "alternate but faithful to the spirit" Darkover stories.

Trained as a traditional Native American Storyteller, Ty Nolan had his first short story published by Marion Zimmer Bradley in *Sword of Chaos*. His book, *Coyote Still Going: Native American Legends and Contemporary Stories*, received the 2014 BP Readers Choice Award for Short Story Collections and Anthologies. He is a *New York Times* and *USA Today* Best Selling Author. He currently splits his time between Arizona and Washington State.

Arisa watched the four moons of Darkover with the same intensity that she did everything. She found them beautiful. She felt their alien energy call to her—it danced on her skin and she so wanted to join the dance.

"She will see you now." The Free Amazon was shorter than Arisa and much heavier. Arisa followed her back into the warmth of the Guildhouse. They passed the dining hall and entered a large meeting room. A middle-aged woman with kind eyes looked up from her reading and smiled. "We don't get a lot of visitors," she said. "And I'm just a simple country woman— you're the first Terran I've ever even seen." She stood and the younger guide lowered her head and backed out of the room, leaving the two of them alone.

"Tea?" the Head of the House asked. Not waiting for an answer she walked to the far end of the table and poured out two cups. "My name is Fiona," she said, "but I'm sure you know that just as I know your name."

Arisa gratefully received hers. The steam brought a sweet and minty scent.

"Before we begin," the older woman said after her first sip, "Rafaella—one of our members—was concerned that your— presence is not that of others she's known."

"*Presence? Is that what they call it here?*" Arisa thought. Aloud she replied, "I'm not surprised. I may not look it, but I'm only half Terran. My mother is from Kaliph—a distant world, even by Terran standards. There are enough differences in my genetic structure to trigger medical scans, and I suspect that's what—Rafaella?—is picking up."

"I suppose that would make sense. And while I've read your proposal, I'd like to hear from you directly what brings a child of Terra and Kaliph to our home." She sat down at the table and Arisa mirrored her.

"I'm a Xenoanthropologist. I study the cultures of entities from other worlds. I'm here to learn more about the Cat People."

"What does Terra know of them?"

Arisa froze, her cup halfway to her lips. It wasn't a question she had anticipated. This House was far from the Space Port (at least by Arisa's former reliance on Terran transportation). They lacked the technology for easy communication, so perhaps the House was isolated enough to be hungry for knowledge of what the elites of the world thought and what they might have shared with her. She knew the Free Amazons were a mixture of women, a number of whom started off as members of the Comyn. She also knew they renounced their status when they joined a House. Maybe they wondered what their families were doing.

"The Cat People are one of the indigenous peoples of Darkover. There is reportedly a long history of conflict between your people and theirs. It's a common humanoid experience to exaggerate differences and engage in disputes, particularly if a new group is moving into the established territory of another.

Just so, I'm quite curious to see firsthand a group that's never been formally studied before. Frankly, the Darkover records available to us end up sounding more like folklore than accurate information. For example, I'm unclear if the Cat People manufacture their more advanced items—like their curved swords—or obtain them through trade. A number of commenters insist the Cat People are barely functioning savages whose only interest is in killing humans. I suspect this is fairly standard propaganda, and I'd like to discover the Cat People's point of view. Other records indicate they are articulate and maintain regular trade with the Dry Towns."

Fiona looked into the green darkness of her cup. "In my experience," she said softly, "people looking for something already have in mind what they want to find."

"Oh, I won't deny I have a hypothesis. I expect to find the Cat People a rich and evolved culture. I'm also aware some members of the Comyn would find the—eradication—of the Cat People to be—convenient. Such individuals would not be happy for an academic to share with a much larger audience not only how civilized an indigenous species is, but the implications of universal civil rights. The majority of worlds are increasingly concerned about the exploitation of Native peoples." Arisa put her cup down, growing more animated. "I was actually supposed to have been here nearly a year ago, but I've been told my proposal was shelved as too controversial."

"I can't imagine the Comyn were thrilled at the thought of a solitary Terran—half or otherwise—poking into their affairs." Fiona sipped at her tea and Arisa watched her relax. The older woman's own scent had also shifted, indicating a gradual lowering of anxiety. She smelled of trust. Arisa smiled.

Eyes shut and the cup loosely held in both hands, Fiona continued, "I have arranged for you to meet with Rakhal. I'd say you were lucky, but when you run a House like this you learn to question that anything has to do with luck rather than opportunity. Let's just say Rakhal has done more to open up trade and interaction in a positive way than we've ever known. He's—friendly towards humans and..." She hesitated in what

Arisa recognized as an internal edit. "…others. If you had come even twenty years ago, I doubt you'd have been able to achieve an interview with the Cat People, let alone an invitation to spend time with them."

"What's so different about Rakhal? I only know him as the current leader—the Big Cat."

"That was a title hard fought for and worthily won," she said. There was an odd spark in her eye and Arisa wondered how the older woman was connected to the fur-clad aboriginals. It felt like more than simple admiration, and her heartbeat had sped up. There was a faint tang of excitement rising from her. Arisa rubbed her nose in response. "But I respect the privacy of others. Let him share what he will. I'll only tell you Rakhal is unique and has been working for several years to change attitudes and heal the rifts between his people and ours."

"But why?" Arisa asked. "In so many civilizations, such major shifts for a leader don't just happen. Such leaders are often born of unusual circumstance or thrust into situations that force them to re-evaluate the status quo."

"It's best you save your questions for him." Fiona put her cup in front of her. "I'd prefer he tell his own story, rather than handing you my version."

"Does he speak *cahuenga*?"

"Not only the trade language, but *casta* as well. He's also worked hard to learn Terran Standard."

Arisa was caught up in the woman's enthusiasm. "He sounds like a most remarkable individual."

"Even his enemies would agree with that description."

"Has he many enemies?"

Fiona developed a deep interest in her cup. "All agents of change have enemies. You used the term *status quo* a moment ago. Many—those with fur and those without—are not comfortable with change." She took another sip. "Even with positive change. It's been over five years since a substantiated raid by or against the Cat People. Throw a pebble into a pond and it's hard to see how far the ripples flow. Remove the Cat People as a perceived danger and merchant lords in faraway towns end up changing routes. Innkeepers and shop owners suddenly find the familiar traffic has been diverted elsewhere and others will grow fat on the new business. I'm sure Rakhal doesn't even know who some of his enemies might be."

In the distance, Arisa heard a ringing bell. "We are called to dinner," Fiona said, putting her cup down. "We have a proud history of being blessed with a healthy and productive garden. It has sustained us when hunting has gone lean. It will give you a chance to get used to the taste of some of the foods the Cat People will feed you."

The next morning found Arisa sitting with Fiona at a table and bench in the garden. It was the largest one the younger woman had ever seen—even in media. Her home in San Francisco had one large container that had been the closest thing to a garden she had known. Terrestrial real estate had always been at a premium. Gwennis—the young woman who had first brought the two of them together—appeared with a tray. It featured a teapot, three cups, dried meats, and fresh fruit. She set it down and left. Arisa had never actually heard her speak more than a handful of words.

"I'm really looking forward to meeting Rakhal," Arisa said.

"You'll meet him soon enough." The older woman turned and addressed a fruit tree. "Haven't I told you it's rude to snoop on people? Come out and meet each other."

Arisa was stunned. She hadn't known he was there. It was rare for her to be surprised this way. As Rakhal stepped in front of the tree she now grew aware of his scent—both comforting and alien. Definitely more like the big cats of Terra, rather than anything domesticated. Or like the Khyanne of Kaliph. He was taller than either of them. He—and the masculine power radiated off him—was covered in gray fur. His eyes were a brilliant green, and when he smiled his fangs were sharp and white.

"Rakhal," said Fiona, "meet Arisa. Arisa—Rakhal."

He took her hand in a stiff Terran manner and then cocked his head, looking more bird than cat. "Why do you smell so familiar?"

Before she could answer, Fiona said, "Our guest's mother is from a world so distant the Terrans think of it as far away. Maybe that's why."

"Maybe," he said, holding Arisa with his eyes. His eyes did not say, "Maybe." They said, "Yes."

After sharing the food and casual conversation, Arisa picked up her backpack and followed Rakhal into the woods. They walked for a while in silence. "You two seem to know each other very well," she said as she watched his tail twitching as he walked.

"She's my mother," he said, turning to look back at her and catch her reaction.

"Did she adopt you?"

He laughed. "Unlike you, I don't think I could pass as half human. The family story is that Fiona was walking and heard my cry. She followed the sound and found me clutching to the body of my dead mother. She rescued me and I grew up in the Kadarin Guild House."

"That explains a lot."

"What do you mean?"

"Why you work so hard to be a bridge between your two peoples. It may not be easy for some to see, but I think in many ways you are like me. Born of two worlds, even if in your case you are a child of the heart rather than of the body."

They had come to a large boulder a few feet away from a small river. "Speaking of the body," he began. He sat on the rock and looked serious. "Before I take you into our home, I need to know why you smell as if you could be one of us. If I notice it so much, then all will. They'll have questions and I'd like to have answers. Kiya told me it was because you're only half Terran, but I don't believe that's true. I don't want to walk into our home with secrets between us."

Arisa breathed deeply, analyzing his scent. Curiosity— determination. No hint of hostility. Everything rode on a constant level of arousal. He was responding to her. She had expected it, but it was a relief to have it confirmed.

She put her backpack down and then quickly stripped off her

clothes. The morning was chilly enough to harden her nipples. She looked at Rakhal in a challenging way. "What I am about to share comes not from my mother's people, but my father's." As he continued to watch her, black fur, the color of her hair, began to spread across her skin. Her face moved, reshaping itself and a muzzle shoved out, opening up to show fangs as sharp as his but her canines were much larger. Her eye color had shifted to a molten gold. Her slender hands were now tipped with claws thicker and longer than his. A tail that he had not seen until now, whipped back and forth as she stood before him.

"Are you one of us? Did our ancestors meet with yours in the old days when those of Darkover first knew other worlds?"

"Wait," she said. Her voice was a little lower. "Are you talking about Creation stories or history?" She sat down next to him.

"Know then that when the world was young, the *chieri* could not contain their wanderlust."

She leaned forward, recognizing a structure similar to most of the cultures she knew—this was oral history. "Wait, who are the *chieri*?"

He leaned back, considering. "They are our relatives. They opened the portals to other places." Arisa repeated what he had just said inside of her head, not sure if she had understood him correctly.

"How do you know about these other places?"

He smiled, flashing his fangs, "Know then that when the world was young, the *chieri* could not contain their wanderlust." She nodded and he continued, "A bargain was made that's never been made before or since. The coin they used was Tarrise, the fifth moon of Darkover."

"A fifth moon?"

"Do you always interrupt people?"

"Sorry."

"Yes, a fifth moon." He crossed his arms and said, "The coin they used was Tarrise, the fifth moon of Darkover. The moon was shattered into a thousand stars and its Power was released, as if the moon had been a great cosmic egg cracked open—they channeled it into pools deep with Power. These became portals to other planets. Freed of the ties to the world of the bloody sun, the *chieri* roamed the galaxy." He paused and looked into the sky.

"Is there more?"

"The full cycle runs through the winter. One story is told per night."

"Did the *chieri* live happily ever after?"

"I suppose you'd have to ask them. They—faded. I don't know a better way of putting it. It was as if the further they got from Darkover, the more diminished they became, like a plant hidden from the light. One by one they drifted from the palaces and enchanted machines they built on the other worlds. One by one they abandoned those things and drifted back to where the circle began. None of us have forgotten the *chieri* destroyed Tarrise. Once every five cycles the *chieri* gather and we join hands and remember Tarrise and wonder if they had traded poorly."

"Did your people accompany the *chieri* in their travels?"

"Our Stories say we hesitated for many years, uncomfortable with leaving our homes. When some did, they did not tend to stay but returned to Darkover. There are tales of the many people we met while traveling, but none of other Cat People."

"I don't know exactly how much we have in common, or if we share some long ago ancestor. We can shift shape into three forms. You've seen my human form." She touched her face and said, in standard, "We call this our meta-human form." Then she lowered herself to the ground and seemed to pull into herself until a black panther looked up at Rakhal.

"Oh, if I had the Power to shift into human form, I would have used it long ago." He pulled off the clothes he was wearing and knelt. He fell forward, expanding into a grey tiger-like shape. Startled, Arisa snarled at him. Both pulled back and shifted into their initial forms.

She began to put her clothes back on, chilly with the loss of her fur. Rakhal did the same. "On Terra, there are some who can shape shift. There are some rare ones who can take several different forms, but most of us are species specific. A werewolf can take on a canine meta-human form, or the shape of a true wolf, for example."

"Not even my mother knows we have two forms. As required by Guildhouse Law, when I was five I was required to leave because I was male. When I entered puberty and was first able to shift, I had found others like me. The older ones told me what to expect and helped me through my first change. I would hate to think what that would have been like if I didn't know what was happening to me. I would also have hated Fiona to have watched me become full Cat while she was raising me. I think that was her constant nightmare, since she tried so hard to teach me to be human."

"And humans have never seen your full cat shape?"

"Oh, they have, but they don't make the connection to us. Our females don't show themselves like this—" he touched his chest, "—but prefer to only appear to humans in their full Cat shape."

"It is very important for you to understand those of us who can shift have kept our truth a secret from humans. It is a vicious history we learn as children that at one point the humans massacred many of the Supernatural Community—not only shifters like me but others who were—different. The solution chosen was to hide in plain sight. My ancestors carefully wove themselves into legends and folktales so that humans grew to laugh at the idea the Supernatural was real. There was a Compact of Silence signed where to reveal The Secret of our existence to humans would result in a death sentence."

"Yet you share this Secret without hesitation."

"You are also a shifter. Of a different sort but part of what we would consider Supernatural as well."

He laughed. "For Darkover, we are simply natural."

"Oh, I've read as many of the Terran records as I could and we've trained them so well, they describe your peoples as superstitious and babble on about Supernatural powers the members of the Terran Empire mock. There are references to so-called magic jewels."

"Oh, you're talking about a type of living matrix that can be used to manipulate and transform matter and energy. The way you describe your shifters is similar to being able to use the star stones. Those of us truly of Darkover can make use of the stones, but not all humans can. It's like a genetic talent. The ones who were most gifted eventually formed the Comyn. They would not be able to survive without their use. When I was growing up, Fiona would tell me stories of how those of Darkover were as suspicious and uncomfortable with the reliance Terrans have on the mechanical—just as Terrans mock the matrix technology."

"There is a genetic range of talent for us as well. Most shifters can only change form when our single moon is full." She smiled as she smelled confusion rising from Rakhal. How odd it must seem to think of a world with only one moon. "Those tied to our moon are unable to travel to other planets. They would be the way you describe the *chieri*. They would eventually sicken and die if they were unable to *Change* on a regular basis."

"But you are not tied to your moon?"

"No—I am an Alpha and that means—just as your Comyn—we are the natural leaders of our communities. We can shift at will. We are also able to shift parts of our body rather than having to totally transform." She held up her right hand and as he watched, her fingernails shifted back into black claws.

"You share so much," he said in wonder. He reached into an inside pocket of his jacket and pulled out a small leather pouch. He looked at her and removed a grey silk wrapped object. He smiled and pulled the silk away and held a blue stone in his palm. She leaned closer. There were colors moving inside of it and she could feel a tingle of energy. She reached out to touch it and Rakhal pulled it away.

"No," he said quickly. "A matrix stone is keyed to its owner. If someone else even brushes against it the owner can experience great pain." He stopped and held the stone as he turned in a circle. "There," he inclined his head. He quickly replaced the stone in its silk insulation and returned it to the leather pouch. "Danger is approaching," he whispered. "I assume you have a dagger or sword. It would be a good time to bring out a weapon."

His own claw sword was in his hand and he was slowly

spinning it. In the additional year she had spent on Terra, waiting for her clearance to do research on Cottman IV—the Terran designation of Darkover—she had studied sword play. The reports she had read emphasized how primitive the local society was and how they favored hand weapons. As an Alpha shifter, she had no need of a weapon. Her body was a weapon. Just so, she found the training to be an interesting discipline she enjoyed. Her non-human strength and speed had made her a formidable opponent with her sword. Her first instructor had insisted she begin competing and she had won a number of titles.

Rakhal called out in an unfamiliar mixture of growls and mewls that she assumed was the language of the Cat People. In the distance she heard an answer. Five Cat People emerged from the woods with their own swords out and ready. They formed a V shape with the largest one in front. He said something else, and Arisa asked Rakhal to translate.

Before he could respond, the other Cat Man looked at her and said in heavily accented trade language, "I, Nadan, am here to call Challenge. I am here to claim the rights of a new Big Cat."

"Rethink your Challenge," Rakhal replied. "Are you willing to give up your lives for something you cannot win?"

Nadan laughed and said something in the other language and then spit on the ground. Arisa needed no translation.

"Wait," she said in a loud voice. "Where I am from, a Challenge is one of our most formal rituals. It has to be done in public and witnessed. What are the rules that both parties will observe or will this simply be a free-for-all and the one who survives is declared the winner?"

"Who is this human?" And Nadan used a word in his own language that triggered a snarl from Rakhal, so Arisa assumed she had just been insulted. "Even from here I can smell your scent on her. It is an abomination to rut with a human. For that alone you should be stripped of your position and killed."

"Answer my question," she continued. "I want to avoid making any mistakes that might invalidate Rakhal remaining the Leader of his Pack after we kill you. Also—will it be necessary for us to kill all five of you, or will the others surrender after you die?"

The challenger lowered his sword in disbelief. "You are even crazier than a Dry Towner," he said. Then he glanced at his men. "They follow me. They will not serve the one you lie with."

"Fine," she nodded and then stepped closer to Rakhal. "Just to clarify, we're about to kill all of them." The other five laughed. "If you deal with the usurper, I'll take out his supporters."

He looked at her with wide eyes. "I'm an Alpha," she said simply. "This is what we do. It is what we are born to do."

Rakhal began to spin his curved sword the way the others were doing. Arisa had never seen their fighting technique before, but she could see it left them vulnerable to a direct attack with her longer sword. Rakhal gave a battle cry and ran towards his challenger. Arisa leapt, covering the space of several body lengths, and thrust her sword into one of the Cat Men even as he was frozen in the shock of what seemed to be a flying human. She pulled out the sword as she spun. She was much faster than the others and killed her second foe before Rakhal had even reached Nadan. She dove beneath a strike one of the surviving men attempted, but she was far too swift. She knocked the curved sword from his hand and then grabbed him by the throat and lifted him into the air. He struggled, and she laughed. The native Cats might look like Terran shifters, but they were not stronger or faster than humans. She shifted the hand she held him with and her claws tore out his throat. She tossed him aside and smiled at her last opponent with fangs longer and deadlier than his.

He cried out and spun his sword and rushed towards her. But she was no longer there. She was just too fast for him to track. As he missed her she swung the sword one more time and slashed him open. She was excited now—the smell of blood always did that. She took deep breaths to calm herself as she watched Rakhal battle Nadan. Both of them moved with grace. They were testing each other out, assuming they might be very evenly matched. Then Rakhal's stance changed and he moved more confidently. He feigned a thrust and when Nadan reacted, he moved in the opposite direction and slashed Nadan. Blood rushed from the deep gash he had opened on the other's throat. Crazed with anger and pain, Nadan jerked awkwardly forward and Rakhal finished him. He turned and looked at Arisa and the carnage around her. While they were both covered in blood, none of it was theirs.

"Are all Terran Alphas as skilled as you?"

"Pretty much. Otherwise they tend to die early on. It's true for all the predatory shifters." She lifted her hand and shifted it back to human form as she spoke. His reached into his pocket and pulled out the starstone once more.

"I'm still picking up on danger. I thought it was just these five but there are others out there."

"More challengers?"

He closed his eyes. "No, these are humans. But their intent is no different. They want me dead."

"Why?"

He laughed. "The matrix stone does not give me such details. It amplifies my own gifts of precognition and telepathy, but it doesn't provide every answer."

"How far away are they? How many?"

"Close. Many."

Arisa's hearing was also better than a human's, and she picked up the sound of horses approaching from the opposite direction of the Guild House. They stepped away from the broken bodies around them and moved away from the river.

"Hard to sneak up on anyone when you're riding horses," she said. Knowing horses were used as one of the primary forms of Darkover transportation, she had also learned to ride while waiting for her clearance. As a resident of San Francisco, she had never been around horses before. Horses tended to shy away from shifters as too alien. She wondered if she might use that to her advantage. She was frustrated because she would not shift in front of humans. Killing all the humans was not a choice she preferred, but it was one she would make without hesitation. She worried how a mass killing of humans by what others might assume was Rakhal's action would damage the rapport he had spent so much time building between the two groups.

Men on horseback rode into sight. They looked different from the others she had so far seen on Darkover. They were uniformly lean and lanky, and their hair was various shades of butterscotch instead of the red hair she found so common.

"Dry Towners," Rakhal said. He jumped on the rock where they had been sitting so he was at eye level with the riders. They kept coming. Arisa counted twenty-five. She disliked the odds. She would need to disable or kill the horses to get to their riders. "What do you seek?" he called out to the lead rider. They looked at Rakhal and Arisa, not immediately answering but letting their presence serve as intimidation. It was working. Rakhal carried a scent of fear that he had not had with his own people. She had found references to the Dry Towns in her research, but there was no record of contact between them and the Terrans. All negotiations of the Empire had been with the Comyn.

"We're here to end your interference," the leader said. His *cahuenga* had an odd drawl and she had problems following his words. "Now that the Cats have had their claws pulled by you as you try to suck at the teats of the Free Amazons and the Comyn, trade routes are changing. You're not seen as a threat anymore and we of the Dry Towns are robbed of our rightful place."

"If the Dry Towns had a better reputation for honest and fair trade, perhaps you wouldn't be so threatened." Rakhal stood defiantly before the riders.

"It's simple. We take you out and word spreads that the Cats are once again the unpredictable and wild menace that scare away travelers from your territory. Things return to normal."

Rakhal spoke so softly, Arisa knew the riders could not hear him. "Even with you I don't think we can defeat them all. One option is to assume our full Cat forms and make a run for it. I'm faster than a horse but I don't have the endurance to outlast them. The only other option I can think of is to use my matrix stone to spook the horses."

"Do it," she whispered back. "The horses give them too much advantage."

"Talk to them," he said as he reached into his pocket. "Distract them. I'll need a moment or two."

"I am Terran," she called out in an authoritative way. "I want to know your name so I can let my people know who tried to end a carefully constructed peace. Do you represent all of the Dry Towns or just yours?"

"So you're a Terran," he laughed. "We're told Terrans are hideous aliens who are barely human. You look like you just wandered in from a Guild House. How—ordinary. I am Lykos, and all you need to know is I am the Dry Towner who will bring an end to a peace we never sought and will not tolerate."

"Arisa," she heard without hearing. She shook her head to clear it, but Rakhal's voice was still there. "I'm about to use my matrix to form an illusion to frighten the horses, but I should warn you so you are not caught up in the deception as well." She nodded her head.

"Lykos," she shouted. "You'll find how strong peace can be." The Dry Towners laughed in derision.

A charcoal-colored mist began to form around the riders. It rose as they pointed at it—and began to condense into the shape of an enormous winged beast that reminded Arisa of a dragon. It lowered its snake-like head to hiss. The horses were terrified. Lykos was tossed off as his horse reared while the others began to break formation to pull away from what seemed to be so real to her. If she were not aware that Rakhal was controlling it, she would be frightened as well.

"*Hold!*" She froze at the command that was suddenly inside her head. It was not Rakhal, but a woman. Even the horses seemed frozen and the dragon thing faded away.

Arisa turned at the sound of movement and Free Amazons were suddenly everywhere, greatly outnumbering the Dry Towners. They were all armed. Arisa caught sight of Gwennis standing near Fiona. All the gentleness and kindness she had seen in them had vanished. They were all truly warrior women.

The mind voice resumed. "So far no lives have been claimed. Even Dry Towners are not crazy enough to try to overcome Free Amazons who outnumber them. Begone and live. Stay and die."

Lykos stood up, bloodied from his fall and radiating waves of anger. Sullen, he mounted his horse and rode off, the other Dry

Towners following him.

"Grateful am I to see you all," Rakhal said, replacing his matrix stone into its silk insulation and then returning it to the leather pouch.

"Rafaella could feel you in danger," Fiona said, moving towards him. "In her vision she saw you under attack by rival Cat People and then the Dry Towners. We rallied all who could help and came as quickly as we could." She looked at the five bodies of the strangers who had found Rakhal a greater foe than they had anticipated. "Obviously you did not need our help with them." She pulled him into a hug and said, "And that was impressive work with your starstone. I don't think you really needed our help with the Dry Towners, but there's been enough death already. Let them take word back to the Dry Towns they are not welcome here and that the Big Cat is allied with the Kadarin Guild House."

"I am honored," he said, his head bowed as he stepped away from her. "But are you sure? Such an alliance has never been made before."

"You are my child," she said proudly. "Both our people seek peace and perhaps our action will provide a healthier model for other human communities. Before you were born, the Comyn sent out raiding parties when a Big Cat of great evil had kidnapped Lady Callista Lanart-Alton. It is important the Comyn see clearly that time is of the past and one psychotic leader does not mean that all the Cat People are to be hated and feared, any more than innocent humans should be blamed for the behavior of Dry Towners."

"I can only hope they will listen," he said softly.

"I will add my voice," Arisa said. "If it is known the Terra Empire respects the Cat People, perhaps it will inspire respect from others as well."

A tall woman with a hawkish face pulled Arisa aside. "In my vision," Rafaella spoke inside the Terran's head, "when you were fighting against the Cat Men, I saw you as almost like one of them. Sometimes visions use metaphors—symbolism. Perhaps that is why I saw you as non-human. If there is another explanation I don't know if I want to hear it."

Arisa smiled innocently and decided silence was the best response. Rafaella's scent was that of fading excitement and rising relief. There was a mild curiosity she could sense, but no hostility directed towards her.

Fiona called out orders to have the bodies buried. "Return to the Guild House," she said to Rakhal. "Clean yourselves of the blood that covers you. It would frighten your people to see you as you both are now. Let us formalize the alliance and have it recorded. Then you can begin on your journey."

"It's exciting to see cultures changing in front of me," Arisa said.

"We have a great deal to learn from each other," Rakhal said, touching Arisa's face gently. If she claimed leadership, he would have no way of defeating her. But if she stood by his side, his position would become even more secure. All he had been working towards was now something he felt he could reach out and touch as easily as he did her.

"I promise I'll be a better listener and not interrupt you so much," Arisa said, returning the light caress to his face.

He laughed. "I don't think that's a promise you'll be able to keep."

"You already know me so well." She grabbed her backpack and they headed back toward the Guild House.

SUDDEN TEMPEST

by Deborah Millitello

Psychic gifts, like magic, come with a price, at least in thoughtfully-crafted stories they do. Both require energy, training, and both carry the risk of terrible consequences. It goes without saying that both can be devastating in the hands of the untrained. Or, as Marion Zimmer Bradley wrote, "an untrained telepath is a danger to himself and everyone around him."

Deborah Millitello published her first story in 1989 in *Marion Zimmer Bradley's Fantasy Magazine*. Since then her stories have appeared in various magazines such as *Dragon Magazine*; *Marion Zimmer Bradley's Fantasy Magazine,* including the third-place Cauldron winner "Do Virgins Taste Better?"; *Science Fiction Age*; and anthologies such as *Aladdin, Master of the Lamp; Sword and Sorceress; Tales of Talislanta*; and *Bruce Coville's Book of Nightmares*. Her novels include *Thief's Luck* and *The Water Girl*. Her collection, *Do Virgins Taste Better? and Other Strange Tales* came out in 2015 Word Posse. She spends her free time baking, making jams and marmalades, knitting and crocheting, and gardening. A member of the Alternate Historians writers group, she lives in southern Illinois with her husband Carl, has three children, eight grandchildren, and a great-grandchild. She works at a doctor's answering service as her day job.

The air felt electric, and thunder mumbled far away. Startled, Gareth Marius-Danvan Elhalyn y Hastur searched the horizon for clouds, but the sky was completely clear. Seldom were there clouds in the Dry Lands, and rain was nearly unknown. Still, the air felt as if a storm were coming.

For the last week the weather had felt strangely turbulent, hot and dry as usual but with sudden wind shifts. Dust devils would spring up and just as quickly disappear. And on occasion the air actually felt humid. Gareth had felt that often in Thendara or Elhalyn, but never in the six years he had lived in the city of Carthon had he ever felt moisture in the air. Was something affecting the climate of the Dry Towns? What if something were changing the weather on all of Darkover?

The clatter of a slamming door drew his attention from his unease. Cyrillon's son Alric stomped from the house toward the barn. The sullen look on the youth's tanned face was so out of character for the boy, Gareth stared at him.

"Can I help?" Gareth asked.

"No," Alric said bitterly as he strode by, finger-combing his sandy-blond hair back from his face. "No one can." He went straight to the *oudrakhi* barn and slammed the door after him, his anger like the distant thunder threatening a storm coming toward them.

Puzzled by the boy's behavior, Gareth shrugged, shook his head, and walked toward the house.

Cyrillon, Gareth's father-in-law, was sitting at a low table in the dining area, staring at the glazed cup in his hand.

"What is bothering Alric?" Gareth asked.

"I don't know," the caravan master said, a worried frown creasing his deeply tanned forehead. "He's as changeable as the weather in midspring in the Domains and as irritable as an *oudrakhi* at the end of a caravan. He's always been obedient and respectful, but now—I hardly know him."

"He's young," Gareth said, remembering how difficult his own youth had been. "He'll find his way. It just might take a while. I didn't find mine until I came here."

Cyrillon smiled at that.

"What I'm concerned about is the weather," Gareth said. "Something isn't..." He searched for the right word. "Something isn't normal. I can't sense exactly what is wrong, but it worries me. The air even smells different, like ashes and burning resin, but I've heard no reports of fires in the forests."

"Do you think you should delay leaving?" Cyrillon asked.

Gareth considered his answer. Tomorrow evening he and his

wife Rahelle were planning to lead a caravan to Thendara and some of the other nearby cities. It would be the last chance they had to visit his family before Rahelle delivered their first child. Gareth had worried about the long journey with her being six months pregnant, but she'd laughed at him.

"A Dry Town woman could ride a horse, stop, deliver a child, and get back up on the horse," she had said. "I can ride for at least three more months. And I'm going."

Gareth had finally given in and agreed to go with her.

Rubbing his chin, Gareth studied Cyrillon. "I don't think there will be a problem, but I might consult my grandmother or my aunt to see if they have any misgivings about traveling. Is Alric coming with us?"

Cyrillon sighed. "He had said he was excited to go, but now..."

"We still have until tomorrow. He might change his mind."

"I hope so."

Gareth headed for the room his shared with Rahelle. She was there, packing for the trip. The gold silk blouse and skirt she wore made her skin glow. Her dark hair seemed to shine, and her eyes—her dark eyes always drew Gareth like hematite draws steel. Her abdomen was rounded with their growing child.

On their bed lay several piles of heavy tunics, trousers, cloaks, everything for the colder climate in the Domains. She'd also laid out a few dresses for herself and Gareth's dress clothes for the inevitable gatherings his family and the Comyn would hold to welcome him home.

"Have you spoken with Alric?" Gareth asked.

"Not this morning," she said as she folded the clothes and put them in a travel bag. "I did last night. He's very moody, but I don't know why. I'm not sure *he* knows, either. I think he feels as if he doesn't belong here or anywhere."

"What do you mean?"

She stopped folding clothes and caressed her abdomen. "Our child will have a mother and father who are married, and he will have a name and a large family. Alric only has a father."

"And us," Gareth said.

"But he doesn't have a mother or a name. It's hard for him, knowing he is illegitimate. Father has tried to give him a place here, and that was enough when he was younger. But now he's a young man. What can he hope for when he has no name? What woman of the Dry Towns would marry him?"

Gareth had never thoroughly considered the boy's situation before. Was he destined to be alone for the rest of his life?

"It's not his fault. In the Domains he could be fostered in my family or one of my relatives. I think it would be good for him to see places where his birth wouldn't matter as much."

"Maybe," Rahelle said.

"Do you know anything about his mother?"

"Very little."

"Was she from Carthon?"

"No, she lived in the Domains."

Startled, Gareth stared pensively at her. "The Domains?" A thought tickled in the back of his head.

"Father came home from one of his caravans, carrying Alric, who was only three years old. You'd have to ask Father for the rest of the story."

"I will." He kissed her. "I'm going to check on the trade goods and see if I can find anything else in the market that might do well in the Domains."

"Try Hakka the Jeweler," she said as she returned to packing the travel bag. "He had some fine pieces that the Comyn ladies would fine attractive."

The market was crowded despite the growing heat of the day. Only a few women were at stalls, buying vegetables and grains. Although Carthon had belonged to the Domains at various times, it was still more of a Dry Town city. The rules governing women in public were not as rigid as in the great city of Shainsa, but women seldom ventured out during the day without a male relative.

Gareth had become accustomed to the ever present odor of horses, *oudrakhi*, dust, and sweat, and even some more noxious odors, but he didn't mind them any longer. Thendara was much cleaner, but it had felt like a prison. A clean prison, but still a prison. The Dry Towns were sometimes dangerous, but he felt freer than he ever had in the Domains.

He stopped at several stalls, but found nothing he thought would be good for trade until he reached Hakka's shop. He bought several gold necklaces set with gems and crystals, matching bracelets, earrings, and rings. He almost bought a jeweled-handled knife, but decided against it.

Stowing his purchases in a shoulder bag, he walked out of the shop when he suddenly felt an electric sensation crawling over his arms. A beggar shouted and pointed to the west, terror on his face. Gareth turned to where the beggar was pointing and gasped. A high wall of dust and sand swept toward the city, screaming like a banshee.

Gareth ran back inside Hakka's shop and slammed the door. "Quickly," he shouted at Hakka, "close the shutters!"

Hakka pulled the shutters on his front window together and set the brace in place. Gareth leaned his shoulder against the door to brace it against the wind. Dust blew through cracks and under the door, causing Gareth and Hakka to cough. Gareth held a corner of his cloak over his nose and mouth to keep from choking. Finally, the wind stopped.

Opening the door slightly, Gareth gazed outside. The street was covered in dust and sand, some places only ankle deep, other places drifted knee high. Merchandise in many stalls was hidden under a thick layer of dust. Many sellers huddled under their carts, faces covered with scarves.

Gazing east, Gareth saw no sign of the dust storm, as if it had suddenly disappeared. Something strange is happening, he thought. This isn't a natural occurrence. It almost feels...like *laran*! But that's impossible!

Sprinting eastward for home, he arrived to find no dust anywhere in Cyrillon's compound.

How could it not affect here when it covered the rest of the town? he wondered.

Quickly, he entered the house and sought out Rahelle. "Did you hear the wind or see the dust storm?" he asked.

"I heard some wind over the argument."

"What argument?"

Rahelle looked anxious. "Alric confronted me, asking why I was to be the caravan master, that he should be in charge instead of a woman. We argued until he stormed out of here."

Suspicion filled Gareth's heart. "I need to speak to your father. Do you know where he is?"

"He left before Alric and I started arguing. I think he was checking that we had enough drovers for the caravan."

"Where is Alric now?"

Rahelle's shoulders slumped. "I don't know. He ran out and slammed the side door as he left. I don't know him anymore. He's like a stranger to me."

"I need to find your father urgently. I suspect..."

"What?"

"If what I suspect is true, Alric is in severe danger."

Gareth turned, ran out to the yard, and headed toward the stables, hoping Cyrillon was there with the stable hands. The stable smelled of straw and dust and a faint odor of manure, although the stalls were cleaned. Horses shuffled in their stalls, including Gareth's own black mount. But Cyrillon wasn't there, and the stable hands hadn't seen him.

Suddenly, Gareth heard *oudrakhi* bellowing. He ran from the stable and saw Cyrillon and Alric beside the corral, Alric shouting at his father.

"Why can't I be the caravan master?" Alric said. "I've run several caravans already!"

"With your sister's guidance," Cyrillon said.

"I don't need her guidance! I can run a caravan by myself!"

"It's too soon. You're not ready."

"I'm old enough to do it on my own!"

"Only in years but not in wisdom!"

Alric's hazel eyes blazed with rage. The louder he shouted, the more the *oudrakhi* bellowed in panic. Gareth felt static electricity crackling in the air and running over his body. A small whirlwind formed in the yard, growing larger and stronger. The *oudrakhi* began to skitter about the corral, frightened, frantic, bumping into each other and the wooden fence.

"Stop!" Gareth yelled as he ran to the two, grabbing Cyrillon's and Alric's arms. "You have to stop this! If you don't, the animals will panic and crash through the fence! And something worse may happen to Alric!"

Cyrillon stared at Gareth, a bewildered frown on his face. "Something worse?"

Alric jerked free of Gareth's hold. "Leave me alone! This is between me and Father! You... don't... have... any right..." His eyes rolled back in his head, and he collapsed to the ground. His face was as pale as milk, and his breathing was so shallow, it was barely audible. Instantly, the whirlwind disappeared.

Gareth felt the boy's forehead. It was burning hot. *What I feared,* he thought. *Threshold sickness.*

"We have to get him to bed immediately," Gareth said, kneeling and lifting the boy in his arms. "Get the door and send for cold water and a cloth."

Cyrillon ran ahead of Gareth and opened the door. Gareth carried Alric to the small room the boy slept in and laid him on the bed. Rahelle followed Gareth, worry in her eyes.

"What happened?" she asked, taking her brother's hand. "His skin—it's like fire! What's wrong with him?"

Gareth sat beside the bed, took out his starstone, and placed his other hand on Alric's forehead. Concentrating, Gareth searched the boy's mind. There it was—*laran*, long hidden, just awakened, and severe threshold sickness threatening to destroy him. Gareth sat back and rubbed his eyes, afraid, unsure he could keep the boy alive.

Cyrillon entered the room as did his wife, who carried a basin of water and a clean white cloth. Silently, his wife sat on the other side of the bed, dipped the cloth in the water, wrung it out, and began dabbing Alric's forehead.

"What is it?" Cyrillon pleaded. "What's happening to him?"

"Who was his mother? And where was she from?" Gareth said.

Guilt on his face, Cyrillon glanced at his wife, then hung his head. "I met her on a caravan to the Domains. She was from Ridenow. She was kind and generous, and I didn't intend to care

180

for her, but I did. I saw her again when I returned, and she was several months pregnant. Normally, I wouldn't have come back to that area so soon, but I couldn't keep away. I was there when he was born. Every chance I had to see him, I did."

He paused and cleared his throat. "I love my wife and daughter, but he was my child, too. She was a good mother to him, but she wasn't well after Alric was born. Every time I saw her, she was weaker. I gave her what I could, but she was no better. Alric was three when she died."

"Did she have any family?"

"No, she'd been an orphan since she was fourteen."

"So you brought him home."

Cyrillon nodded, silent.

Gareth searched his memory for anything about Ridenow. "They were Dry Towners—the Ridenow. They invaded the Serrais lands, killed all the men, and married the women in hopes of developing *laran,* as well as gaining the gentler and more fertile lands of the Domains. It seems they succeeded with Alric."

"*Laran?*" Cyrillon said. "Alric has *laran?* The same power you have?"

"Not quite. He seems to have different talents, controlling wind, maybe others. Only a *leronis*—a specially trained user of *laran*—could determine what his talents are. But right now he is in danger of dying of threshold sickness which affects children when they first come into their power. It can be mild if caught early and cared for by those who are well versed in the treatment. Usually, someone from one of the Towers would come to help the child through the sickness. But there's no one from the Towers here, and Alric is much older that most children who have the sickness, which makes the sickness more dangerous. I don't know if I can help him through it. I've never done this before."

"Save him," Cyrillon said, tears in his eyes. "Please save him."

Gareth gazed at Alric. *Am I strong enough?* he thought. *Can I reach Grandmother for help? And can I save him even with her help? All I can do is try.*

Clutching his starstone, Gareth reached out to his grandmother, Keeper of the Tower in Thendara. *Grandmother, if you can hear me, I need your help. There is a youth in threshold sickness, and I don't know what to do. I fear he may die if I can't help him. Please help me!*

He concentrated with all his strength, waiting, listening, hoping. Slowly, he felt power filling his mind, his body, growing stronger. He sensed his grandmother's power and also his aunt and others, many others, all lending him strength.

Entering Alric's mind, Gareth felt the boy's confusion and anger, swirling like a snowstorm in the Hellers, raging like a fire in the resin forests. The boy was lost in his fears, huddled like a child afraid of the dark, feeling so alone.

Help me, Alric cried. *Someone help me!*

I'm here, Gareth said to him. *Listen to me. Don't be afraid. Just follow my voice and come to me. I'll help you.*

Please! Someone help me! Alric said as if he hadn't heard Gareth speak. *I'm scared and I'm cold, so cold!*

Alric, I'm here. I'm trying to find you. Can you hear me?

There was silence for so long, Gareth was afraid the boy was so terrified, he was unreachable.

Gareth? the boy said.

Yes, it's me.

I can hear you, but I can't see you! Where are you?

I'm here, so close. Just listen to my voice and reach out for me.

Suddenly, another voice spoke, a woman's voice, Gareth's grandmother. *You are not alone, son,* she said. *We are here. Just come to us. We will keep you safe.*

Mama? Is that you? Alric said. *Help me! I'm lost in the snowstorm and can't find my way home!*

Follow my voice, child, Grandmother said. *We are your family, and we're here to help you. The snow is not as thick now. The air is clearing. Look and you will see the way. Come to us. Reach out and take Gareth's hand. He will lead you back home.*

Gareth felt Alric's fears diminish slightly, but he was still gripped by dread. Slowly, the boy reached out, grasping for hope and help. Gareth enveloped Alric's mind, surrounding the boy with a warm and caring refuge from the turmoil that had threatened to destroy him.

Alric opened his eyes and gazed up at Gareth. Tears filled the boy's eyes, and he reached out and hugged Gareth. "You found me," he said, his voice wavering. The boy's forehead felt sweaty but cool against Gareth's cheek.

"Of course," Gareth said gently. "You are my brother. How could I not find you?"

Alric said nothing, just held onto him. Gareth explained that Alric had suffered threshold sickness from the onset of *laran*, but that he was over the most dangerous part.

"*Laran?* Like you*?*"

"Yes, but you may have different abilities than I have. And you'll need to be trained to use them so you won't be overwhelmed by them. You'll need to go to one of the Towers in the Domains to learn."

Cyrillon gazed steadily at Gareth. "He'll have to leave us? But for how long?"

"I don't know," Gareth said. "But he has always been quick to learn. Maybe only a few months or a year if he studies hard."

Distress filled Cyrillon's eyes. "A year? A whole year?"

"Or less. Some of your caravans last many months. He'll be away just a little longer."

Cyrillon bowed his head and nodded.

Gareth turned his attention back to Alric. "You need to rest now. We can delay the caravan for a few days. There will still be time to reach the Domains. Until then, sleep as much as you can. And when we get to Thendara, I'll introduce you to my grandmother. And she will help you find your talents, your family, and your name."

Looking exhausted, Alric lay back and smiled up at Gareth, then drifted off to sleep.

HOUSEBOUND

by Diana L. Paxson

Some characters and their adventures come to live so vividly that they refused to be limited to a single short story. (Thus are novels born, and readers who insist on hearing more are satisfied.) Adriana, the protagonist of "Housebound," is one of my favorites and I am always delighted to see more of her and her friends. She is a transgender woman, and thus faces not only the skepticism of the Free Amazons she seeks to join, but the prejudice against women on the part of many Darkovan men. The following story is one of a cluster of tales that include "Blood-Kin" (Gifts of Darkover), "The Motherquest" (Free Amazons of Darkover), "A Season of Butterflies" (Renunciates of Darkover), and "Evanda's Mirror" (Stars of Darkover). And there is snow. Much snow.

Diana L. Paxson is the author of twenty-nine novels, including the books that continue Marion Zimmer Bradley's Avalon series. She has also written eighty-six short stories, including appearances in most of Marion's Darkover anthologies. She is currently working on a novel about the first century German seeress Veleda.

"Adriana, come on!" Kiera's voice echoed against the rock face where the trail to Nevarsin had been cut through.

Great banks of snow loomed over the trail and continued well down the mountainside. Another week and we would not have made it through the pass. I took a deep breath of the crisp air, wondering why I didn't want to move. Last night's wind had cleared the skies, and in the light of the ruddy sun the snowfields to either side of the pass shone like the inside of the shell Kiera kept on her shelf in our bedroom. It was the last gift her father had given her before he died and she joined the Free Amazons.

"All is well," I replied. "I was admiring the view."

I nudged my pony's shaggy sides and we moved forward. We were above the tree-line here, but dark resin trees clung to the slopes below. Cassilda was already down among them. Huddled on her mount in a swathing of shawls, she looked like a ragman's stock-in-trade. The trip had been hardest for her. Kiera made her living as a licensed guide and was used to mountains, but Cassi had never left Thendara before. On this journey both of my lovers had tried to care for me. I did not remind them that when I was growing up in the Hellers I had herded chervines in all weathers. No surprise if they did not remember. These days even I was forgetting I'd not always been a girl.

But for the journey I had to put on the sensible breeches that the Renunciates had fought so hard to earn the right to wear. *I'm only changing clothes, not who I am*, I told myself, but that new person Kiera and Cassi's love had helped me to become was afraid. I told myself that I could get into skirts again when we reached the Guildhouse, and shook the reins to get my pony moving once more.

Across the valley rose another mountain, from whose peak the walls and towers of the *cristoforo* monastery seemed to have grown. On the slope below it, the chimneys of the slate roofed houses sent spirals of smoke into the clear air.

Nevarsin of the Snows...

One of those buildings was the Guildhouse where I was to spend my housebound half-year. I had longed for this, but now I was wondering if I could endure the confinement. Maybe that was why I did not want to move.

"As our new sisters may have noticed, Nevarsin is not like Thendara—" at the ripple of laughter that greeted this, Mother Suzel smiled.

I looked at the women gathered in the dining hall, a jumble of faces now, but by the end of six months no doubt I'd know them all too well. They looked back at me and Kiera and Cassi with equal curiosity.

"...the members of the Guild of Free Amazons shall be to me, each and everyone, as my mother, my sister or my daughter, born of one blood with me..." The words of the Oath echoed in my mind. The night when the Comii Letz'ii of Thendara House had accepted my oath still shone in my memory. With the medicine made from my blood still protecting them from the Yellow Plague, they were grateful.

But not forgetful. I had learned how to be a woman. It would be easier to learn how to be a Renunciate here, where no one knew that when I was born they had thought I was male.

On the wall behind Mother Suzel was a mosaic of the Lake of Hali, pieced together from different kinds of wood. The hall was decorated with pictures and hangings, the fruit of endless hours when women were confined to the Guildhouse by blizzards that prevented any activity outside. Some featured abstract patterns while others showed summer scenes. I supposed a snow scene would be redundant, here.

"When Mother Keitha came to Nevarsin to start a training school for midwives, there was not even a Guildhouse," From her place at the high table Mother Suzel went on. She was a strongly-built woman of middle years, her skills as a healer respected even by the *cristoforos*. "This was a workshop for tanning and working leather, which is still one of our specialties—so we are especially glad to welcome you among us, Cassilde!"

Cassi blushed and smiled. She smoothed the gloves she was wearing, of her own making, sewn from thin leather finely stitched with an edging of embroidery. They would not do much good outdoors, but Nevarsin's weather was another difference from Thendara, cold even inside with a roaring fire in the hearth at the end of the room. The scent of the whiteroot and rabbit-horn stew that had been served for dinner reminded me of home.

"A woman named Arlinda owned the business, and Renunciates stayed with her often enough that they used to call the place the Nevarsin Guildhouse in fun. When she died she left it to us, and the joke became truth. Gwendis," she pointed at a young woman with fair hair like a Dry Towner, "Give us another reason why Nevarsin is not like other places in the Domains—"

"The *cristoforos*," she replied. "Elsewhere, men treat a woman like a lesser being, or if they know we are Amazons, sometimes with scorn. But the monks, if they are forced to take notice, look at us like something foul you find on the bottom of your shoe."

"Indeed, and that brings me to the point of tonight's discussion," said the Guild Mother. I stilled, listening. I had heard about these sessions from Kiera and Cassi, but since I was going to Nevarsin for my training, Mother Doria had not insisted I attend one at Thendara House.

"When a man looks at you, what is he seeing?" She pointed at a dark-haired girl who looked barely old enough to take the oath.

"If I am lucky, he thinks of his daughter and scolds me for running about alone. If I am unlucky, he thinks I am a good-time girl and looks around for my pimp so he can make a deal."

"And you, Adriana—" I jumped as the Guild Mother turned suddenly to me. "You are pretty enough to attract attention. How does that make you feel?"

Like a real woman, I thought, but I knew better than to say so. I was always aware of a flicker of triumph when I heard the catcalls, though to be honest, I had also received unwelcome attentions when I was a boy.

"It makes me want to run away," I said at last, which was sensible, if not entirely true. I tried not to show my relief as several of the others nodded.

"But don't you see that is exactly what we have to fight?" one of the older women exclaimed. She had been introduced as Rebecca, and she worked as a farrier. "We have to stand our ground, short hair, breeches and all, and force them to truly *see* us—not as men, and not as the kind of women they know, but each one of us as unique—as *ourselves!*"

I shivered, though a moment before I had not been cold, and wrapped my woolen skirts more closely around my knees. In the days before the Goddess changed my body, the kind of women most men knew were the only models I had. Learning that role had been too hard for me to abandon it for some nebulous image on which even the Free Amazons could not agree. As for the rest of it—I was unique enough already. I leaned against Kiera, who sat on one side of me, and squeezed Cassi's hand. To be their sister and lover was identity enough for me.

One major source of income for the Guildhouse was the women's baths. The Guildhouse was located near the edge of the city, where the presence of hot and cold springs assured us of water for both the tanning operation and the bathhouse. Mother Suzel had seemed a little disappointed when I listed my skills—I wrote a fair hand, could play the *ryll*, do mending when I had to, and herd chervines, none of which were likely to contribute much to the welfare of the Guildhouse, but my job at the tavern in Thendara had made me an expert at cleaning, and in a bathhouse, where each wooden tub had to be completely emptied and scrubbed at regular intervals, that was at least useful.

"You are stronger than you look," said Gwendis as I hefted the bucket of vinegar wash and lowered it into the empty tub. The slightly organic smell from the hot springs mingled oddly with the tang of the vinegar in the steamy air, but the heat kept the chamber warm enough so that we could work in shirt and under drawers.

Because I was housebound the work fell more often on me, but the task was rotated, and Gwendis was my partner for the day. I suppressed an impulse to roll the sleeves of my shirt back down over my forearms. Were they too sinewy for a woman? I reminded myself that there were many women in the House who were stronger than me.

"I grew up in the Hellers and worked on the farm." I dipped the bristle brush into the liquid and began to scrub at the stain along the water line.

No need to explain that I had not done the daily labor of a farmer's daughter, but helped out as even the son of a minor lord might be expected to do when there was need. The *chieri* inheritance that had changed my sex to match my soul hadn't actually done much to the rest of me. If I seemed smaller, it was other people's perceptions that had changed.

"You don't talk like a farm girl," Gwendis replied, hopping

down into the tub and dipping her own brush into the bucket.

"I ran away to Thendara and scrubbed floors in an inn."

Her eyes rounded. "An inn! Did the men try to paw you there? Did they—"

"At Thendara House I was taught that it's impolite to ask people about their past!" I snapped.

"Well I'm *sorry*! I only—" She turned away and began to work at the wood on the other side.

We finished the tub in silence. Better she should think I had been raped than guess the truth, which was that the one man who had managed to pin me long enough to get beneath my skirts had been so surprised by what he found that I was able to hit him and get away. But the innkeeper had fired me. After that I slept on the streets until I nerved myself to seek refuge at Thendara House, and was forced to reveal my secret and thrown out into the snow.

I scrubbed at the wood as if to obliterate the memory. I was a Free Amazon now, and Cassi and Kiera loved me. When I doubted, I saw my identity confirmed in the mirror of their eyes.

Snow had been falling for three days, sometimes with a blustering fury that could at least provide a thrill of danger, and sometimes with a depressingly steady persistence. We were all housebound when winter closed in. Today it was my turn to shovel the snow off the cold frames where we tried to keep a few greens alive. They were built above the pipes that carried water from the hot springs into the baths, which kept the soil from freezing, but they needed whatever light a short winter day could provide.

Cassi was waiting for me in the mud room when I came back in, with a kiss, dry clothes, and a warmed towel. Sweet Cassi! She considered herself ungifted, but she had a remarkable knack for finding you the thing you were going to need before you thought to ask. I hugged her, in that moment as grateful for her warmth as for the feel of her sweetly curved body against mine.

"Has there been any word about Kiera?" I asked when I stopped shivering. Our lover had gone off with a hunting expedition a little before the blizzard arrived. If Cassilde was thoughtful, Kiera had the courage of the Comyn caste she had rejected. No weather was *safe*, here at the edge of the world, but an impending snowstorm had not stopped her from going out when she knew we needed food.

And I am good at scrubbing and shoveling, I thought then. And loving—I added to the mental tally. At least I can return their love.

"We should not expect it," Cassi answered, more emphatically than there was need. "They will have taken refuge in one of the herdsmans' shelters. Kiera has too much experience to venture out before it is safe, and the others all know this land."

True, I thought, but hunger could argue louder than common sense. In the Hellers we had stories about people who had been trapped by blizzards that lasted longer than their supplies. I had fretted at being housebound, but being snowbound was worse.

As we came through the door into the kitchen, the air heavy now with the scent of baking spice bread, Gwendis called my name. Since our shared duty at the tubs we had not spoken. I turned in surprise.

"Mother Suzel wants to see you in her office!" she said with a kind of suppressed glee. I traded glances with Cassi, but clearly she knew no more than I.

The Guildhouse was built around a square yard, and the Guildmother's chamber was at one corner in a little tower. The original building dated from a time when the city was smaller and the bandits more bold. Situated at the edge of town as the tannery required, no doubt a watchtower had been a necessary precaution.

Not that any attackers could have been sighted today. The only thing visible through the long, multi-paned windows was swirling snow. As I climbed the stairs I began to shiver. I told myself that one of the window frames must be a little warped and be letting in cold air. I passed my hand across the window but felt no draft, and realized that I was afraid.

As I entered, Mother Suzel looked up from her papers and smiled. I took the three-legged stool on the other side of the desk.

I wondered whether it was backless to keep those called into the Guild Mother's presence from relaxing, or just another assumption of Free Amazon fortitude. For a few moments she simply looked at me.

"You have been here for most of a moon," she said finally. "Long enough to settle in. I hope you are not feeling suffocated by all this snow."

"I was brought up in the Hellers, *mestra*. I don't mind a little snow. And anyway, this is my housebound time."

"True—I was forgetting you were not from Thendara."

What else, I wondered, was she forgetting, or pretending to? When Mother Doria requested that Nevarsin take me she had to tell Mother Suzel the whole story of why the Free Amazons of Thendara had initially rejected me. There was no need for the other women to know. Everyone had seen me naked in the baths. There would be, *could* be, no doubt that I was a woman here.

"How are you getting along?" she asked. "Are you happy here?"

"Just now I'm fearing for Kiera, but aye, I'm content—" I replied.

"And the other women, have they been kind to you?"

"Kind enough, given I'm still a stranger—" I frowned. "Have there been complaints about me?"

"There are some who feel that you three, but especially you, Adriana, are not opening up to the others, not trying to fit in."

I felt myself flushing up. "You know my story! I try, but you know there's things I cannot say—"

"Yes, yes," she sighed. "I met Camilla n'ha Kyria, you know, and she made me think about how a person's inside and outside might not be the same. That is why I agreed to let you come to us here."

I bristled. Camilla was a legend in Thendara House. She had rejected her womanhood to become *emmasca*. I had always been female inside, and now my body was the same.

She nodded. "But it might have been a mistake to let all three of you come."

I stared at her in panic, achingly aware of how much I

depended on my lovers to confirm my identity.

"Tell them it's on account of my fearing for Kiera—that's surely true. Has there been any word from the hunters? Can they no send folk to search for them?"

"How?" Mother Suzel gestured toward the window, where for a moment wind had swirled away the blizzard to reveal range upon range of white peaks. "Any tracks they might have left are under several feet of snow! Ah, child—Rebecca is with them and we are all worried, too. Do your best to be friendly with the others, and if there is need we'll speak again when our lost ones have come home."

Cold! Wind like a knife that rips at cloak and sears the skin! Clouds part, I recoil from the glare of sun on snow, through slitted eyes I see an abyss where the path should be. "Trapped! Cassi, Adriana, I'm sorry!" Tears freeze before they can fall....

I opened my eyes. Somehow I was on the floor, still shuddering beneath that wave of despair.

"Adriana! What is it? What's wrong?" Gwendis was bending over me. Mother Suzel had ordered us to work together in hopes we'd learn to get along. At that moment I didn't care.

I struggled to sit up, gripping her hands. "It was Kyria! I heard her call!"

Gwendis looked dubious, but one of the others was nodding. "Kiera is Comyn, and look at Adriana's hands! They both have the blood, it could be!"

Gwendis looked down at the six fingers on the hand that gripped hers. "Somebody get Mother Suzel!"

I was drinking from the cup of water someone else had brought when she arrived.

"It was Kiera. I've touched... her mind before. They are trapped in the snow."

Everyone was still arguing about my vision when the visitor came. Men were rarely admitted to a Guildhouse, and when the *cristoforos* had business with Amazons the Guildmistress was usually summoned to the monastery. But when the bell clanged, what I saw from the upstairs window was a shaven-headed monk wearing only sandals and a simple garment of wool. I had been told that some of the monks had practiced austerities so long that they could use their body heat to melt snow. Was this one of them, and if so, what was he doing here?

A few minutes later someone called me to the Visitors' parlor. Sipping tea with Mother Suzel was the monk, so ancient that all marks of gender were blurred, and all one saw was age.

"Adriana, this is Brother Gabriel. Brother, this is the girl who says she heard a call—" The Guild Mistress sounded as if she neither believed nor denied my word. I suppose I could not blame her.

The monk's eyes, faded with age but clear as a forest pool, met mine. "Tell me, child, what did you see?"

"A path that ended in a gap, and on the other side a bare knob of rock—"

"Like the head of a banshee," the monk replied.

I stared. "Aye, just so!"

The monk turned to Mother Suzel. "In meditation I travel. I saw a woman with the cropped hair of a Renunciate and the ginger color of the Comyn. Her *laran*, I think, is more powerful than she knows."

"Could you find the place?" I cried. "She had no hope. I think their food is gone."

The monk nodded. "It is our duty to help those in danger. I will speak to the men in the village who know these mountains. We can take wood and ropes, and perhaps build a bridge to get them out."

"I will go with you!"

Mother Suzel shook her head. "You are bound to stay within."

"Except in an emergency!"

"And you do not know these mountains," she continued sternly.

"I grew up in the Hellers," I exclaimed. "I have climbed peaks as high as any I saw. They may need me to find her."

Mother Suzel frowned. "We will think about it—" she said at last.

193

I bowed my head, but it was to hide my expression, not to agree. I was going with the rescue party if I had to go out the window on a rope with my boots tied together around my neck to get there.

A storm demon was breathing ice down my back. I fumbled with gloved hands to tighten the knitted scarf I had wrapped around my head, pulled down my sheepskin cap, and hunched my shoulders against the blast. I would not have admitted it, but I was glad that Rinald Maclain, the local man who was leading the rescue party, knew the road well enough to find his way, and I need do nothing more than stay on the sure-footed mountain pony, which was proving challenge enough in this storm.

Even a moon housebound had been enough to soften me. The first step outside had shaken my resolve, but I kept silent, too grateful for the sheepskin leggings over my woolen breeches and knitted stockings to resent the necessity for male attire. I had worn clothing like this often enough when I was a boy, unlike newcomers to the Amazons who had to be instructed on the folds and ties. Indeed, it was becoming far too easy to wear these clothes. If I had not been so cold that would have bothered me.

The first night we camped at a travelers' shelter, grateful that the weather had allowed the preceding visitors to gather more wood to replace what they had used. From the neat stacking, I guessed that this was the party we were looking for. I smiled as I fitted sticks into the little fire, thinking I could feel Kiera's touch. In addition to Maclain, our group included Anndro Gonsalvez, the town smith, a forester called Esequial and his twin Esteban, Rebecca Alleyn, who was said to be the strongest woman in the Guildhouse, and of course Brother Gabriel, who sat in the drafty spot near the doorway, feet tucked beneath his robe and hands open on his knees. If by escaping into meditation one could ignore the cold, I thought that the *cristoforos* might have something after all.

"We'll be needin' more afore the morning," said Esequial. "You there, give me a hand!" I got to my feet, shrugged back into my coat, and followed him out into the storm. I did not suspect him of ulterior motives—he was right about the wood, and in this weather any man who exposed his poker long enough to try rape risked losing it.

Snow crunched beneath my boots as we stamped toward the woods. I was relieved to see a series of tall poles topped with fluttering rags and connected by a rope spanning the space between the hut and the trees. The snow was blowing sideways, and once out of sight of the building it might be hard to find it again.

Any wood that fell at the edge of the edge of the forest had been taken by earlier travelers. We had to go a fair way into the trees before we found anything we could use.

"Come on, lad!" Esequial called from ahead. "Need your help to get this branch down!"

I bristled. Was I somehow giving off masculine signals? Had my body language changed to match my garb? The Amazons spent so much time teaching women to walk free and proud—like men. Could I tell the difference between the way a free man and a free woman moved? Could Esequial?

I shook myself and hurried forward. Trying to second-guess myself could drive me crazy. Better to assume that beneath all these layers I could be a Ya-man for all he knew, and that neither sex nor species mattered when survival was at stake.

The forester had hold of an evergreen bough that had been torn off by the wind but was too tangled in other branches to fall. I grabbed one of its smaller branches, and together we tugged until we could get it free. While I held it braced, Esequial took his hand-axe, and with swift, efficient strokes, lopped branches and chopped the limb into pieces we could carry.

By the time we got back to shelter, the tip of my nose was numb. As the fire began to warm the space, Esequial spun a highly colored tale of our trek to bring the wood in. Finally I felt warm enough to unwind my scarf. Rather defiantly, I shook out my black hair.

"Cold as a banshee's heart it was!" exclaimed the forester. "An' this lad—" he turned, eyes widening as I favored him with my sweetest smile.

"Bearer of Burdens! 'Tis a lass!"

"A Renunciate woman," Rebecca corrected in her most dampening tones.

"*Mestra*, I ask pardon. I meant no offense."

"'Tis no matter," I replied. "You said nothing to me that could not be said in the presence of my oathmother and my sisters."

I could see Rebecca trying not to laugh. I sat down next to her and she handed me a mug of dillyflower tea, good to boost circulation. There had not been many opportunities for me to know her, or more to the point, for her to know me. Perhaps this trip could win me another friend in the Guildhouse.

In the morning the snow, for the moment, had ceased and we set out once more, this time towing a load of firewood and two young tree trunks. The monk's vision had shown him a gap. All I remembered was Kiera's despair. We climbed high enough that some of the men began to joke that our lost ones must have been hunting banshees., while others started looking around uneasily in case the banshees were hunting *us*. When I found I myself swearing the same oaths that they did, I moved my pony back down the line to ride with Rebecca.

Did the person I had become only exist when I was with women? What was I, if the change that had transformed me into a woman was so vulnerable? *Kiera! Cassi!* My heart cried, *Let me be the goddess I see reflected in your eyes!*

The sun was casting ruddy shadows across the snow when we halted and the word came down the line for me. Brother Gabriel had dismounted and was standing where the trail began one of its precipitous descents, peering beneath his hand.

"Come here, child. The eyes in my body are old and may betray me. Is this like what you saw?"

Child! I thought, a term that transcended gender. I supposed that to one so old, and so detached from fleshly concerns, we were all the same.

I swung down from the saddle and stumped through the snow to stand beside him. We were above the tree line. The trail, if you could call it that, dipped down and up again to an outcropping of granite too steep for snow. Some ways beyond it was another bulge of black stone that could be likened to a head.

"Something like," I answered, "but the angle is wrong. We would need to be higher, to look across and down."

At my words, someone groaned, but if this had been easy, my beloved would have been home by now, toasting her toes before the fire. Rinald had already strapped on his snowshoes and taken up his two walking sticks and was seeking a trail up the slope. The cold was beginning to seep through my shoes when he returned.

"There is a way—but we cannot take the ponies. Dark is coming. We'll camp here, in the morning climb."

I noticed that he had not said there was a *trail*.

"But how will we know if they are even there?" said Esequial. "We'd risk our lives for nothing. They could be dead by now!"

"Any one of us could die at any moment!" the monk's deep rumble got everyone's attention. "We must live as if there is hope or we are no more alive than these stones!"

I was not so sure about that—we had stories in the Hellers about stones that moved of themselves and crushed impious men. And this was a country of stones. Who knew what they got up to when unobserved by humankind?

"'Tis true that it is a great risk to take without some confirmation that they are there." Rinald sighed.

I looked at him in alarm. He had been so confident a leader, I had never thought he would falter.

"When we have rested we will seek them, this child and I," the monk said in reply.

That night we had a makeshift camp in the snow. When we had boiled up a meal of dried meat and porridge, Brother Gabriel motioned to me to follow him. Liriel had risen, casting a ghostly light that turned the peaks that had seemed such solid barriers to transparent shapes against the sky.

"And which is the illusion?" asked the monk, as if he had read my mind, "the rock that resists or the beauty that veils? You think you have lost the one you love, but she is as close as breath."

"In my heart, yes," I agreed, though how could I be sure, when I did not even know my own heart half the time? And how could he know what Kiera was to me?

"Sit down, and we will breathe together," he said then, assuming his usual position cross-legged in the snow. More awkwardly I followed his example, wrapping myself in the extra blanket that Rebecca had given me.

"Match my breaths, and when we are in unison, sink deep within yourself, and bring to mind the image of your beloved. Call to her, tell her we are here. Tell her to come to the edge of the gap in the trail."

I bowed my head, watching my breath puff white as I exhaled, but I was supposed to be seeking within. I closed my eyes.

Kiera! I called, *my beautiful bright one, falcon fierce, but so patient with me, so tender!!* A hundred images chased through my memory, of Kiera practicing her sword moves, or facing down the mob that threatened the Thendara Guildhouse, Kiera sighing as she scrubbed whiteroot or laughing at Cassi's wry comments on people we knew. *Kiera, hear me! See me! I'm here!*

I sent my soul winging like a thrown stone, and like a stone above the abyss, began to fall. And then there was something beneath me, a presence like a warm wind that bore me up again. *Kiera!* Hope propelled me further. *Kiera where are you?*

Adriana? The mental touch held both love and fear. I glimpsed a cave, several figures clinging together.

We've come to rescue you! Come to the edge of the gap when it is day. We'll find a way across.

In the morning I thought I must have dreamed, but the monk had shared my vision, and Rinald believed him where he might have doubted me. The storm had passed, but it was mortal cold. We left the horses with Rebecca and, switching to snowshoes, began to make our way over terrain that even one bred up in the Hellers hesitated to call a trail. But the shape of the banshee rock grew ever more like the image in my vision. Presently we came to a place where a path had been hacked into the side of a cliff, and stopped, seeing the scar where a section of it had fallen away.

I went forward as far as I dared. The missing pieces of the trail lay tumbled at the bottom of the cliff below. Far below. It made me dizzy even to look down.

On the other side, what I had thought was a humped rock stirred. My heart lurched as I recognized Kiera's bright hair. Did she hear my shout? I moved to the back as some of the men went back for the logs we had dragged along with such toil. Esequial, who had the best throwing arm, managed to toss a packet of dried meat across the gap, and Kiera took it back to the others.

"And how are we going to get the logs across the gap?" I asked Rinald, as the men came puffing along the trail with their load.

"That is why you need foresters who know how a tree will fall!" exclaimed Esteban.

Kiera had returned with two men behind her. One of them leaned heavily on the arm of the other. Even if we could bridge the gap I wondered if they would be able to make it across.

The foresters were bringing up the first of the logs, a young resin tree a little less than a foot wide and fifteen feet long. The second trunk was a bit smaller. They laid them down and began to weave and knot a kind of web between them, bracing it at intervals with some of the branches. More ropes had been tied around the ends of the trees. The ones on the near ends had already been snagged around outcrops of rock. Esequial was binding the end of the longer rope at the far end around a stone. He walked to the edge of the trail.

"Can ye catch this?" he called.

As Kiera nodded, he gathered the loose rope into a coil, swung the end a few times around his head, and threw. A gust of wind caught it and it smacked against the cliff wall, but he was already reeling it back in. He waited, wetting a finger to test the direction of the wind, then cast again. This time Kiera was able to grab it as it went by, and in a few minutes she had the rope from the other pole as well.

"Is there a bit of rock on your side secure enough to take some strain? Angle your ropes around it and hang on. If we can't tip the ladder right the first time, ye may have to haul it up."

Or we would have to do so from our side, but every movement increased the chances that something would give way.

Men grasped each pole and lifted until the makeshift ladder was standing on end, then frog-walked it to within a foot of the edge, while others secured the loose ropes at its base to rocks on our side. Rinald tested the wind.

"In the name of the Bearer of Burdens, may this bridge hold!" Brother Gabriel made a sign of blessing and the foresters let go.

For a moment the construction shivered in the wind, but Kiera was already hauling on the rope from her side. The ladder dropped, bounced, and was still. For a few moments all of us simply stared. Those logs had been heavy when we had to carry them, but they seemed fragile when compared to the gulf they spanned.

Then Kiera called to the others. *Come first,* my heart called, but at moments like this one remembered that she was Comyn-born, and it was in her blood to take responsibility. I could see her explaining, and the stronger of the men got down and began to inch his way across. He tried to keep his weight on the logs, but once or twice his knee slipped and his weight came down on the ropes, pulling the poles closer together. One of the bracing posts snapped, and the whole structure sagged and groaned. All of us began to breathe again when he reached our side.

Kiera was arguing with the other man, who seemed to have injured his arm. They moved forward together.

Rinald shook his head. "'Twill not bear the weight of two—"

"Not those two, maybe," said Esequial, "but the lass here is lighter, an' if it breaks, we might be able to haul her back again—"

I glanced at the cliff again and felt my blood run cold.

"Nay, that's no task for a girl!" said Rinald. I remembered that he had been against my coming along.

He sees me as a weak woman, I thought. *Just what I wanted to be.* Suddenly I understood what it was that the Amazon training sessions were intended to help us overcome. Kiera or I would both be in danger, but her weight was more likely to break the bridge than mine. Words came to me unwilled.

"Then call it man's work," I said, "and call me what you will. I will go, but Kiera must come across before I try." I began to strip off my heavy coat, itself weighing several pounds, but my blood was pumping furiously, and I did not feel the cold.

Beloved, you cannot fault my logic! I sent the mental message with all my strength, and when I saw Kiera's shoulders slump I knew that she had understood.

Once more we held our breaths as she inched across. When she was safe, she hugged me hard.

"You don't have to go—Aran frees you from your word. He took a foolish chance and broke his arm, and would not have another pay the price."

"But that word still binds me," I replied. "I think this is something I have to do." As I let her go, she swayed, and I thought she would not have had the strength to help the man if she had tried. They wound a rope around my chest and shoulders. I tried to persuade myself that they could hold me if I fell.

"Don't look down," said Rinald as I gripped the poles and began to wriggle forward.

"The angels will bear you upon their wings—" came the voice of the monk, and though I was still acutely aware of the drop below, a glow of calm began to banish the terror that had threatened to freeze my limbs. I thought the poles swayed less beneath me than they had with the others who crossed. I told myself I was feeling the touch of those wings in the wind that swirled around me and kept my eyes on the injured man, who had gotten himself down on the poles. One arm hung limply.

"Can you get your arm up onto the pole at all?"

The poles quivered as he reached with his other hand, grasped his sleeve, and pulled. His face was white by the time the arm was where I could get a grip on the wristband.

"Stay with me, Aran. I'm going to lift and pull the arm forward to keep you balanced, but you will have to move your legs."

The ladder flexed alarmingly as Aran's weight came fully

onto it, but I thought that there was perhaps less sway. Focusing on keeping the man going, I had less time to care. At least, I thought in one of the moments when we both paused for breath, if we fell, it would be over soon.

Inch by painful inch we moved. The bridge began to lose stability behind us as another of the bracing sticks gave way, but I was too intent on encouraging the man to give way to fear. I had taken off my mittens to get a better grip. The supple leather of the gloves Cassi had made for me did little against the cold, but the need of the moment kept blood pulsing through my veins.

And then I felt a touch on my ankle. A strong hand closed around it, then around the other. Hope renewed my strength as the men drew me back to solid ground. Aran screamed and fainted as they grabbed his injured arm, but they had him now. I felt like fainting myself, but Kiera was holding me. As she kissed me I felt on my face a spatter of burning spots and knew they were her tears.

Brother Gabriel was able to set Aran's broken arm, and the continuing good weather made getting home much easier than it had been to come. As I had feared, the hunting party had run out of food some days ago and had been subsisting on moss and melted snow.

"We had not quite come to the point of deciding between freezing, sitting out for the banshees, or leaping to a quick death on the rocks below," said Kiera when she reported to Mother Suzel, " but we were thinking about it."

Thinking about it certainly made me want to weep, though Kiera laughed. I had spent much of the journey back fighting tears, but so did Aran. Whether that made me more of a girl or him less a man I did not know. It did not seem to matter anymore.

The Guild Mother looked at me. "We did discuss whether we should add a week to your housebound time to make up for the time you spent away." Kiera bristled, but Mother Suzel was smiling..

"So long as it is warm, I will not complain." I answered her.

"Rebecca gives a good report of you. Your actions have won us some credit in the town, and it seemed to me that last time I encountered one of the monks, he actually looked at me. I would think that Brother Gabriel had been praising us, but I gather that the other monks don't understand him any better than we do."

"Then I can stay?"

"Nevarsin Guildhouse is in your debt, my dear."

I nodded and straightened the skirts I had so gratefully put on once more. But I knew now that I would be just as happy to put on trousers the next time I had to go out into the snow.

SEA OF DREAMS

by Robin Wayne Bailey

Every human society has developed its own forms of pharmaceutical escape from reality, whether natural substances or psychedelic drugs created in a laboratory. Earlier Darkover stories (such as *Darkover* Landfall) portrayed the hallucinogenic qualities of the pollen of the *kireseth* flower and various psychoactive distillations like *kirian*, as well as more prosaic intoxicants like wine and *shallan*. In "Kira Ann" (*Stars of Darkover*) by Steven Harper, an ex-narcotics cop tracks down a highly addictive designer drug, Darkovan style. In Robin Wayne Bailey's darkly gritty "Sea of Dreams," another Terran makes his way to the back alleys of Thendara in search of quite another drug... and for quite different reasons.

Robin Wayne Bailey is the author of numerous novels, including the *Dragonkin* trilogy and the *Frost* series, as well as *Shadowdance* and the Fritz Leiber-inspired *Swords Against The Shadowland.* His short fiction has appeared in many magazines and anthologies with numerous appearances in Marion Zimmer Bradley's *Sword And Sorceress* series and Deborah J. Ross's *Lace And Blade* volumes. Some of his stories have been collected in two volumes, *Turn Left To Tomorrow* and *The Fantastikon,* from Yard Dog Books. He's a former two-term president of the Science Fiction and Fantasy Writers of America and a founder of the Science Fiction Hall of Fame. He's the co-editor, along with Bryan Thomas Schmidt, of *Little Green Men - Attack!*

John Stark kept to the shadows with his hood up and his cloak drawn close. The dark Old Town streets, lit only by occasional lanterns, made his movements easier. Still, he kept one hand on his concealed blast pistol, grateful for his watchfulness training

and good instincts as he slipped nervously through the twisty
ways.

He stopped at a corner. Looking in all directions to be sure the
streets were empty, he parted his cloak, lifted one gloved hand
and glanced only for a second at an electronic map. The dim blue
light briefly illuminated his neat features and dark eyes before
winking out. Clipping the device to his belt, he moved along
again.

A chilly breeze gusted through the streets, bearing the muddy
fish-scent of the nearby river and setting the lanterns to swaying
on their hooks. The walls of abandoned warehouses creaked as,
overhead, thick gray clouds raced to occlude the few visible
stars. The air turned even colder, and John Stark shivered.

I hate this planet, he thought, *with all its freaks and freakish
weather.*

In a glum mood, he reached his destination. Down the next
corner, a door opened. Music spilled into the night. A couple of
stranyos stumbled out arm in arm. Another *stranyo* appeared
from around the next corner and stumbled in. From the shifting
silhouettes on the walls inside, the tavern was full. John Stark
crossed the street quickly and caught the edge of the door before
it closed.

He hesitated on the threshold until the closing door nudged
him from behind. He looked around for a table, surprised by the
smoke in the air, the chaotic smells of incense and herbal blends
and God knew what else. It stung his eyes, but he ignored the
discomfort and moved around the edge of the room to an empty
table in a corner. Without removing his cloak, he sat down,
leaned on his elbows, and peered out from under his hood.

The place was ungodly warm. Fires burned in two fireplaces,
pouring out the heat, lighting up the faces of customers with
crazy flame-flickering. A half dozen men on the opposite side of
the tavern beat pulse-stirring rhythms on stringed instruments
and drums, their faces sweating, heads banging in time while a
pair of women and a willowy boy/man, all in scant garments,
writhed to their music. Women with loose hair sat brazenly in the
laps of men whose hands knew no boundaries. A laughing

serving woman seemed to be everywhere at once with mugs of beer and vessels of wine. She skirted among revelers, sometimes twirling, spilling nary a drop as she flirted and cavorted.

It was all so different from the mannered, almost ritualized pomposity of the Darkover he knew. These *stranyos* had pumping blood in their veins and fire in their eyes. They grinned and laughed easily as they drank, and their open lusts burned as hotly as the flames in the fireplaces. Here was an aspect of the planet he had only heard about in whispers.

Without quite realizing, he began to nod in time to the music, to those infectious rhythms. Perhaps that was why he didn't see when the serving woman approached. Without warning, she appeared at his side, set down a beer before him, then playfully swept back his hood.

She gasped, stumbled back, spilled her tray of drinks. Drawn by the clatter, eyes turned his way. A few men pushed back their chairs and stood up. Laughter turned to suspicious glares, and the music stopped.

John Stark kept his hands in plain sight on the table. As casually as he could manage, he reached for the beer before him, lifted it to his lips, took a taste, and then raised it in a universal gesture of salute. He said nothing.

"A Terran," someone sneered, "an earthworm."

"So he's peaceful, it matters nothing," said another.

The serving woman recovered. "If he pays, he's welcome as any," she announced. "Now don't you be staring. He can't help how he looks."

Vaguely insulted, John Stark nevertheless smiled. What could he expect from these people? Even in the studied politeness of diplomacy and politics among the Thendaran upper crust, he had encountered bigotry. His dark skin and dark eyes marked him among Darkover's pale people, and he sensed their palpable distrust.

"I can pay," he said, pulling up his hood again. Then lowering his voice so that only the serving woman could hear, he added, "Tell Gwynn Connell an earthworm would like to see him."

She frowned as if taken aback, then twirled away, and it was a sign for the music to resume. The musicians picked up their instruments, beat their drums, and the dancers began to dance again. The tavern filled with muttering, but that turned to old conversations, and soon, to laughter once more. John Stark sighed and leaned back in his wooden chair as he tasted his beer again.

Yet beneath his cloak, he was shaking.

The serving woman disappeared, and a younger serving girl took her place. She did not come near John Stark, although he noticed her glances from time to time. It didn't matter; he sipped his beverage slowly, having no intention to become drunk. He watched everyone, studied everything, and memorized much. More than once, he felt himself aroused by some salacious sight or action around the tavern—these *stranyos* were brazen!—but he shut off such emotions, refusing to be distracted.

He had, after all, come to Old Town with a purpose.

Even with all his watchfulness training, he failed to notice the figure that appeared first behind him, then right at his side. Only when a small, thin man sat silently down in the chair opposite him, did John Stark notice. He reacted with surprise and pushed his hood back just a little, although not completely off. "Not many men can sneak up on me," he said evenly.

The pale Darkovan inclined his head. "Was I sneaking?" he said. "Why would I sneak in my own establishment?" He stared at the space behind John Stark. "Now *they* were probably sneaking. Yes, you could say that of them. They are both natural sneaks."

John Stark half-rose from his chair, irritated and frowning, aware now of the two men who stood just behind and on either side of him. They should not have been able to approach him in such surreptitious manner. Neither did anything menacing or made any move to touch him, but he understood their clear purpose.

"I am Gwynn Connell," the small man continued. "Perhaps you knew that, although I suspect you did not. The names of my two associates..." he nodded toward the men behind John Stark, "...are irrelevant. As you Terrans would say, they are only *muscle.*"

John Stark resumed his seat, stared across the table and tried to look unimpressed. "You're safe with me," he said.

Gwynn Connell allowed a tight smile and then waved his associates back into the shadows. He crooked a finger then, and the original serving woman appeared with two crystal vessels of sweet, golden wine. Taking up the glasses of beer, she placed the new vessels on the table. The liquor sparkled in the firelight as if the crystal contained flames. Gwynn Connell picked one up and sipped as he studied John Stark.

"You're outside the Terran Zone," he noted quietly, yet audibly over the music and laughter that surrounded them, "in a part of Thendara where your kind aren't allowed."

"I have the necessary permissions," John Stark answered. Moving carefully, deliberately exposing the butt of his blast pistol, he reached into a pocket of his cloak and withdrew a thin packet of papers. He passed them across the table.

Gwynn Connell picked them up, glanced at the several pages, folded them and slid them back again. "Passable forgeries," he pronounced, smiling at his joke. "But forgeries. One criminal shouldn't try to fool another criminal, Mr. Stark," he continued. "It's not courteous."

Though he tried hard to control it, John Stark began to shake again. He looked around the tavern, noting the faces, automatically memorizing the music and the movements of the dancers. Subconsciously, he filed it all away. With careful calm, he picked up his wine, savored the bouquet, and finally tasted it

"Forgive me. I'm a bit out of my element," he admitted when he no longer shook. "Old Town isn't quite as I anticipated." He looked across the table and fought back the fear that his host could read his mind—not an impossibility on this planet.

Gwynn Connell leaned back and laughed. Over interlaced fingertips, he looked thoughtful as he observed John Stark. Then his expression turned cold even as he adopted a casual air. "Every culture, no matter how advanced or refined, has its dark underbelly, Mr. Stark. Darkovan society is no different. While the Comyn and the Eight Great Families build their soaring towers and immerse themselves in wars and schemes and plots and petty jealousies, we thrive ignored and out of sight in the oldest run-down parts of the city. And if, once in a while, a few lords or ladies take notice and do come down to join us, they do so on our terms, wearing their titles around their ankles. If you take my meaning."

He took another taste of his wine and crossed his legs as he continued to regard John Stark. His tone turned hard. "You Terrans are no different. You look around this room and you lift your nose without even knowing that you do it. You think of us..." he gestured around the room, "...in pejoratives—*stranyos*. Strange people. Unnaturals, even though we are not Comyn. You think we are not to be trusted, that we are inferior." He fixed John Stark with a cold glare. "That is exactly the way the Comyn think of you and all Terrans." He grinned suddenly and winked. "We are all inferior to someone," he added with a shrug. "It's the way of the world—this world and all the worlds ever known."

Gwynn Connell leaned forward, picked up his crystal vessel and clinked it against John Stark's, turning convivial once again. "So I ask, you, my sloppy forger with your blast pistol and your belt gadgets and your shiny dark skin and dark off-world eyes— what do you want of a poor tavern owner?"

Without thinking about it, John Stark committed every detail of Gwynn Connell's face to deep memory. It was not an unpleasant face at all, and he found a certain appeal in the Darkovan's lively eyes and frank manner. Even the name, *Gwynn Connell,* attracted him with its hard musicality. As he regarded the man across the table, John Stark felt a wave of heat that had nothing to do with the blazing fireplaces.

He pushed that to the back of his mind, though. This was not the time for such an attraction.

He reminded himself for a second time that he had come here—dared much to come here—with a purpose.

Lifting his glass, John Stark drained all the wine and twirled the glass between his fingertips.. He stared at the empty crystal for a moment. The delicate, glittering facets shone with prismatic fascination. Then, setting the vessel down, he leaned toward

Gwynn Connell and whispered three words: "*Sea of dreams.*"

It was Gwynn Connell's turn to look startled. He inclined his head, his gaze suspicious. "That is a body of water at the southernmost end of the continent. A paradise, some say, with white sand beaches and the bluest water." He drained the last of his wine, too. "I've never been there, but I'm sure you can find it on your belt-map."

John Stark touched the device he thought was out of sight. Then he shook his head and finally pushed his hood away. "One criminal to another," he said, "who is being discourteous now?" He leaned closer across the table. "You know what I mean, Gwynn Connell. I'm a careful and thorough man. I asked around, and one name came up repeatedly. Your name."

Gwynn Connell pursed his lips and folded his fingers together again. "But you're not really a criminal," he said. "You're a diplomat."

The butt of the blast pistol became visible under the hem of John Stark's cloak, a clear and threatening gesture. He wondered again if Gwynn Connell was reading his mind, and he recoiled at the thought. Still, he sat back and calmed himself, and then leaned forward again. He had been taught, as part of his watchfulness training, to resist telepathy or at least to sense it. Nevertheless, this was Darkover.

"Are you reading my mind?"

Gwynn Connell gave a disapproving look and beckoned for more wine. "I haven't the power, the *laran,* as we call it." The serving woman, never far from Gwynn Connell, refilled their glasses. She appeared to be serving them exclusively. "Your papers give you away," he reminded John Stark. "Clever little forgeries, but the best forgeries only ever rely upon a single falsehood that hides among the truths. Yours say that you are a diplomat with the Terran Empire. Therefore, since the lie is that you're authorized to leave the Zone, you really are a diplomat."

"I hate telepaths," John Stark muttered, letting the words slip out. In truth, he hated all the psychic freaks on this crazy planet. If the Empire listened to him, they would quarantine the entire world. No secrets were safe here and no one could be trusted.

How could there be diplomacy between the Empire and Darkover on such an unequal footing?

The crowd had thinned in the tavern. When, he wondered, had the customers begun to drift out? How had he not noticed? Still, the musicians played. The rhythms of the drums soared over the strings. The sound pulsed in his head. He rubbed a finger over one temple.

"And yet you ask about the Sea of Dreams," Gwynn Connell pressed.

"I want to try it," John Stark continued. "I want to know what it's like. *I have to know!*" He spread his hands upon the table and scraped his nails over the wood. Half rising from his chair, he loomed over the smaller Darkovan.

Gwynn Connell merely looked up at John Stark, and the Terran slowly sat down again. "I'm sorry," John Stark apologized, taking another sip from the second glass of wine the serving woman had placed before him.

"The watchfulness training your kind receives," Gwynn Connell said. "I hear it makes your kind sensitive to things."

Your kind. That was twice Gwynn Connell had said it. John Stark let it go and said nothing. The training taught him to be alert. And to read people—their body language, their faces, their vocal inflections. It was not the same as telepathy, but it was as close as humans could come in a lopsided game with the Darkovans.

At least, so far.

"Assuming I did have this drug you seek, this *Sea of Dreams*," Gwynn Connell said, after a lengthy pause. "Why would a Terran want to ingest such a potentially dangerous and mind-altering substance?"

John Stark assumed an air of nonchalance. "I'm always interested in new experiences," he answered. "That's why I joined the Terran Service, to see and experience new things. Now, I'm assigned to a post on Darkover, and still I feel this drive to seek out the *novel* and the *unusual.* I'm an addict for excitement, you might say." He shrugged, sure that he was convincing. "So I forge documents, and I wander alone in parts of Thendara few Terrans ever have seen, and I pay courtesy calls on the city's crime lords."

Gwynn Connell arched an eyebrow. "You do it for the thrill." His voice was easy, sardonic, relaxed, with just the proper hint of menace. "So, if I had this drug—and I said *if I had it*—do you have any idea what it does? How it works? How it might affect you?" He gave a spare smile. "Assuming it affects your kind at all?"

John Stark resisted the impulse to grind his teeth. Gwynn Connell was baiting him. "I told you , I'm a careful and thorough man, Gwynn Connell. I do my research, and I know a hawk from a handsaw."

Gwynn Connell sat still as stone, not a muscle twitching, unblinking. "But do you know what it does?" he asked again.

John Stark concealed his annoyance. Of course, he knew. At least, he knew what it was *purported* to do. *Sea of Dreams,* it was said, granted euphoric peace and powerful sense of well-being, along with the most intense dreams a man could ever hope to experience. *But in some, who possessed even a hint of latent psychic ability, it granted far more. For a brief period, it allowed some users to experience a range of mental talents reserved only to the Darkovan high families.*

Including telepathy.

John Stark wanted that experience. He felt sure that his awareness training, natural instincts and frequent hunches made him a prime candidate for the drug. He would risk anything for a chance to possess, even briefly, the mind-reading power that gave the Comyn the upper hand in every single negotiation with the Terran Empire. Even if he could not keep the power, he hoped to gain insights into how it worked, or at least how better to defend against his telepathic foes.

John Stark gazed at the *stranyo* across the table. Gwynn Connell wasn't even one of the Comyn. He was nobody, really, a common criminal like criminals on a hundred other worlds. Shrewd, no doubt, and clever, even attractive, but in the end, serving only his own interests. "What I know," he said coldly, "is that I want it."

Gwynn Connell took another sip of wine. "What would a Terran ambassador offer a lowly tavern owner if the poor fellow had this legendary drug?"

John Stark smiled inwardly. *...in the end, serving only his own interests.* He had read Gwynn Connell accurately. He waved a casual hand. "Drugs for drugs," he suggested. "There is a shipment bound for the Terran Medical Services sitting on the docks at the starport. I can arrange for the guards to be looking in other directions. A clever tavern owner with a little *muscle* might take advantage of that and reap considerable profit."

Gwynn Connell thought for a long moment. "I could be recording this conversation," he said in a low voice. "I could turn you in to your own people."

"You could," John Stark felt confident. "But you won't."

Gwynn Connell's eyes lit up and he held out his glass to the serving woman, who refilled it. "You are a criminal after all, John Stark," he said, making it sound like a compliment. John Stark held up his own glass, and the woman poured. "Go easy, Terran," Gwynn Connell advised. "You don't want to dull your carefully honed senses to the experience that awaits you." He crooked a finger, and the serving woman set down the wine bottle and bent low. Gwynn Connell whispered in her ear. She disappeared into the tavern's back room.

John Stark watched her depart. Only a few Darkovans remained in the tavern now—Gwynn Connell's *muscle,* the younger serving girl, the band musicians and the trio of dancers. The customers were gone. He quickly assessed the situation.

"Now?" he said, frowning.

"You Terrans have a saying," Gwynn Connell answered with a subtle smirk. *"No time like the present."*

John Stark felt himself seized. The pair of thugs caught his arms, twisted them behind the wooden chair and swiftly bound him. "What's this ...?"

Gwynn Connell waved a hand. "It's for your own protection," he assured. "The initial ingestion can be painful and a bit violent. We don't want you to hurt yourself." He leaned across the table suddenly, his gaze narrow and challenging. "I thought you had researched this?"

"I have!" John Stark shot back. With an effort, he forced the stress and surprise out of his facial muscles and tried to relax into his bonds. In fact, nobody had told him anything about pain or violence, but he wouldn't let Gwynn Connell know that.

The serving woman reappeared. In her right hand, she carried something that looked like a straw about fifty centimeters in length. In her left hand, she carried a bulb-shaped phial containing a bright blue powder that she set in the middle of the table. The powder seemed to give off tiny flashes of light or electric flickers. A tenuous cloud of it floated near the top of the phial as if it sought to escape.

John Stark stared. "What is that?"

Gwynn Connell arched one mocking eyebrow. "A sea of dreams," he answered. "Nothing like you have ever experienced before. It may not be what you hoped for, Terran, but it will not disappoint."

"But what is it?"

The Darkovans remaining in the tavern drew closer and exchanged glances with one another. The younger serving girl bent for a better look at the phial. The older woman pulled her away. "You Terrans are aware of the Matrix crystals—the so-called *starstones*—from which the Comyn largely draw their powers."

"It's old news among the Imperial worlds," John Stark interrupted.

Gwynn Connell moved a fingertip around the phial, and the contents seemed to shift and follow, as if his finger was a magnet. "Well, you might think of this as matrix dust," he continued. "Where the *starstones* sat for millennia, the very ground in which they nestled accumulated some faint traces of their properties. The Comyn, in their arrogant obsession with the crystals, paid as much attention to the dirt as they pay to the rest of Darkovans who are not part of the Great Families." He took the straw from the serving woman and ran his fingers along its length. "But we are not above a little dirt. We collect it when we can, as our ancestors did, in secret. And we expose still more dirt to it, passing its properties along yet again so that we maintain a carefully guarded supply. Our chemists then work to refine it until we have what you see before you."

The serving woman spoke for the first time. "Are you ready, Terran?"

Gwynn Connell gave her back the straw, then rose and gave her his chair. "This is Shierra," he said. "She will administer your ingestion."

"Why?" John Stark asked, growing nervous as the pair of thugs removed his cloak and opened the neck of his shirt.

"Because not everyone can handle the dust," Gwynn Connell said. "I never touch the stuff, myself, but like you, Shierra has special training." He came around and patted John Stark's shoulder. "Don't worry, she'll be as gentle as she can be. However, it's a bit messy at first with quite a lot of mucus."

John Stark watched fascinated, forgetting his bonds, as Shierra carefully broke off the smallest piece of the phial's wax seal. The dust in the bottle wafted up, but she quickly pushed the straw through the opening, preventing any diffusion of the precious dust. Then, she tapped the end of the straw deep into the powder, packing the slender tube to perhaps a half centimeter.

He still did not understand what the straw was for or how they would administer the strange powder.

"Hold him," Gwynn Connell ordered. The thugs gripped John Stark's shoulders and neck, immobilized his head. The musicians and dancers pressed in to watch. The younger serving girl seized up the phial as Shierra extracted the long straw, while two others removed the table.

John Stark's eyes widened as he sat facing Shierra. She pressed the packed end of the straw against his left nostril, but she did not stop there. She pushed it further up into his nose, into his sinus cavity. The pain was intense. John Stark's eyes flooded with tears, but the thugs held his head firmly.

Shierra set her mouth to the opposite end of the straw—and blew.

The powder hit him with great force. John Stark cried out as if thousands of tiny razor blades blasted into his skull. He felt the straw withdrawn and opened his eyes briefly to see Shierra's face close to his. For the first time, he noted her red hair streaked with gray, and the emerald intensity of her green eyes, the intricate lacework of laugh lines and crow's feet, the dryness of her pores, the fine hairs around the tips of her ears.

He saw Shierra in startling and vivid detail. As the thugs released his head and he looked around, he saw them all that way, as if the drug was already magnifying his senses. The bonds burned his wrists; his clothing abraded his skin, and every nerve ending screamed as if individually tortured. He tasted the flavors of his own mouth, the nectar of his spit.

Then, as suddenly as it had started, it stopped, and John Stark fell into a vast calm sea of darkness—*a sea of dreams*. All torture ended, all pain dissolved, he sank into a rolling bliss, forsaking senses, pure tranquil existence, and bodiless peace.

Through such euphoria, he began to perceive a heartbeat, a small and distant sound. He knew it was his own. A tiny part of the darkness swirled around that soft flutter, nurtured and protected it, and the darkness expressed itself to him. *Here is the face I wore in the hour before my parents conceived me!* He wept eyeless tears at the wonder.

Time passed. Or maybe it didn't. Maybe there was no time at all.

Tiny sparks of light flashed suddenly in the darkness, like stars winking into existence only to explode. Electric webs danced across his awareness and diffused away. He was no longer alone. He felt Shierra's curiosity and disdain. The bigotry of the big Darkovans behind him who hated his skin, the indifference of Gwynn Connell—an attraction not shared—the young serving girl carefully resealing the blue drug in a back room.

Abruptly, tranquility shattered. The darkness heaved upon itself. John Stark's brain became shards of glass. In every shard, he saw something new, and he saw them all at once. Explosions, dying men, angry faces, desperate faces, and his face the most desperate of all. Blood on his hands! Gwynn Connell dead! Shierra dead! The serving girl and the willowy boy dancer running.

With a small part of his mind, he untied his bonds and raised his hands to his eyes.

Blood on his free hands!

John Stark tried to scream. Maybe he screamed a thousand times. Another part of his mind uncoiled itself and reached out to seize the flames from the fireplaces. Fire snaked out across the wooden floor to engulf the tavern. He heard tempestuous rhythms in a young drummers head, but those rhythms were in his head now, and the drummer was gone. Somewhere outside the tavern, a man made love to his wife, and their passions filled John Stark. He heard a conversation in the street, another conversation beyond the boundaries of Old Town, and still another in the highest recesses of Comyn Tower.

So many thoughts, an entire city in his head all at once!

He couldn't process it all.

Gwynn Connell should have taken his blast pistol! The horrible echoing explosions of his weapon were too loud in his mind. His host had thought him no threat—only an effete Terran. That thought alone lingered clear and sharp as the tavern burned around him.

Cloakless and exposed, John Stark stumbled outside. He groped his way unseeing through mysterious streets until he cowered finally in an alleyway. A small crowd gathered around him. He couldn't sort their chaotic thoughts nor control his own. He clutched his head and screamed, wishing he could tear out his brain.

Then, unexpectedly someone spoke to him, someone inside his mind. *Shierra!*

"Be calm, Terran," she urged. "This will pass. You have killed no one; the tavern is not burning."

John Stark did not believe her. Shierra was a telepath! He saw it now! Gwynn Connell had deceived him. Even as the drug began to weaken in his system, he felt her digging through his thoughts, prying secrets from him, information that Gwynn Connell would sell for profit.

He forced his eyes painfully open and looked about the alley.

A passerby took mercy on him and draped a cloak around his shoulders to ward off the cold of Darkover. He did not thank the person; he couldn't. Hugging his knees, he rocked himself in the mud against a wall and tried to draw together the broken pieces of his mind.

A new thought took slow form, and he held up his hands in the dim light. Blood on his hands! If he hadn't killed anyone, why was there blood on his hands?

Shierra spoke again in his mind. "It is your own blood. You cut your wrists as you twisted free of your bonds, but your wounds are not fatal. Return to us. I can guide you through this."

John Stark rose shakily to his feet, his back against a warehouse wall, sweat stinging his eyes. How could he trust her? How could he ever trust any *stranyo*? All he could think about was getting away.

"You must return!" Shierra's lies churned in his head. "The drug is fracturing your mind! Nothing you are seeing is real! Let me help!"

John Stark tried to shut her out. The *Sea of Dreams* was in his blood now. It might be extracted and analyzed, even controlled. Then Terran diplomats would no longer bargain from positions of weakness.

All he had to do was get out of Old Town, back to the Terran Zone and the spaceport.

He lurched out of the alley. A blue, flickering dust wafted in the street and at the center of it stood Shierra and Gwynn Connell. He spun about, and there was Gwynn Connell again. No matter which way he turned, there was Gwynn Connell.

He was mad, he realized. An icy chill shivered through him. He could not deny it. *The drug is driving me mad!*

He spun about again, and there was Shierra. "Help me!" he begged.

"I will," she promised. *"I am."* The flickering mist stirred and shifted. New figures appeared behind Shierra. Stepping around her, they advanced, tall and stiff and dark-skinned in smart uniforms—Terran police.

John Stark laughed as they seized him. "Earthworms!" he

cried.

He was safe among his own kind. They would take him home away from this nightmare.

He cast a final glance over his shoulder. Gwynn Connell and Shierra and all the musicians and dancers stood on a street corner watching him go. In their hands, they clutched his every private thought and secret—but he didn't care.

He knew now and for certain what he had always known.

You could not trust a Darkovan.

STORMCROW

by Rosemary Edghill & Rebecca Fox

Some short fiction has the "feel" of longer stories, either in the expanse of landscape, intricacies of character, or—as in "Stormcrow" by Rosemary Edghill and Rebecca Fox—the span of time. Readers get a sense of Darkovan history unfolding, with glimpses of events and characters they know from other stories. These intersections and echoes evoke a larger world beyond the pages of the individual story. Astute readers will recognize a few of their favorite characters, including Ercan Waltrud from "Learning to Breathe Snow" (*Gifts of Darkover*).

Rosemary Edghill describes herself as the keeper of the Eddystone Light, corny as Kansas in August, normal as blueberry pie, and only a paper moon. She says she was found floating down the Amazon in a hatbox, and, because criminals are a cowardly and superstitious lot, she became a creature of the night (black, terrible). She began her professional career working as a time-traveling vampire killer and has never looked back. She's also a New York Times Bestselling Writer and hangs out on Facebook a lot.

Rebecca ("Becky") Fox started writing stories when she was seven years old and hasn't stopped since. She lives in Lexington, Kentucky with three parrots, a chestnut mare, and a Jack Russell terrier who is not-so-secretly an evil canine genius, but no flamingos, pink or otherwise. In her other life, she's a professional biologist with an interest in bird behavior.

At the rim of the galaxy the suns are scattered and few. The races that once called them home have left those homes behind, finding either extinction or apotheosis. But their forsaken cradles remain, and one such is Cottman's Star. Cottman's Star is an aging red star attended by seven planets. All of them are barren of life save the fourth one. Its name, in the stellagraphy catalogues of the Empire, is Cottman IV.

Its inhabitants call it Darkover.

There are seven Domains on Darkover, seven Ruling Houses, seven Comyn lords: Elhalyn, Hastur, Ardais, Aillard, Alton, Ridenow, and Aldaran. During the Ages of Chaos, each Comyn lord ruled as an undisputed prince, but those days are long gone. Now the Comyn lords meet in the Council Hall at Thendara instead of on the battlefield; Stephen Elhalyn of Elhalyn rules six of the seven, and Istvan-Regis Hastur of Hastur, Warden of Hastur, Lord of Thendara and Carcosa, rules Stephen.

Long ago, each Comyn Line had a hereditary Gift, a *laran* uniquely its own. To Alton, the Gift of forcing rapport; to Aldaran, precognition. The Ardais were able to waken *laran* where it lay dormant, just as Aillard could rouse desire and fertility. To the Ridenow line came the twin Gifts of empathy and xenotelepathy, but the Hastur Gift was the greatest of them all, nameless, its secret passed from each Hastur lord to his successor. Once Elhalyn was no more than a sept of Hastur, but to the Elhalyn Line had been given the most terrifying Gift of all: the ability to see not one future, but every future that might be. Through that Gift, Elhalyn rose to become the Seventh Domain, the royal house of Darkover.

But Elhalyn's Gift was double-edged. Those who bore it did not live long, nor did they leave many children behind them. For centuries, Elhalyn dwindled, and with it, the power and the influence of the royal line. Stephen Elhalyn, eighth of his name, was crowned without displaying the Elhalyn Gift, and everyone believed that the *laran* of the Elhalyn Line was truly lost.

They were wrong.

Cyrillon Elhalyn was a distant cousin of the king. He married where Stephen commanded—to Merelda Aillard—and they lived happily (if distantly) together, for Cyrillon came virgin to his marriage-bed, and gossip said that he remained so on the following morn.

And so, for many years, no child graced their marriage.

No one yet alive can say what brought Merelda to do what she did. The rumors said that she took a trusted companion and journeyed to the Yellow Forest, walking there beneath its branches, her head bent in prayer. What she prayed to, or whom, could not be known, but what is known is that soon after her return to her husband's house, all could see that she grew great with child at last. Not once did her husband show even the smallest hint of surprise, and, when the child was born he acknowledged the boy as his true son.

And so Felix Javiar Hermes-Reuel Aillard y Elhalyn was born to a world that had not yet known the print of a Terran boot.

Felix was a small boy and slender, with rose-gold hair and eyes the unflinching amber of the mountain hawks. When he was barely beyond the care of his nurse, his mother died of one of the swift summer fevers, and less than a year later, his father joined his wife in death. Felix barely noticed—or to be absolutely accurate, they had both died so many times in his visions that when one of those visions came true, it had little effect on him. It was a rarity indeed for any of the Comyn to come into their birthright at such an early age, and his halting attempts to explain his visions, or to ask about what they meant, were ignored or misunderstood by the servants and family retainers to whom he brought them.

When Felix's father was laid beside his mother on the shores of Hali, Istvan Hastur was among those who attended the ceremony. Afterward, he took Felix back to Castle Hastur with him. The castle was filled with children of his own age, for Hastur held many hostages, and for the first time Felix learned what it was like to be both bullied and toadied to, for he was a cousin of the king, and the king was known to be Hastur's man.

Here, the thousand thousand futures that spilled out from every action were blinding, and Felix quickly developed the reputation of being both sickly and simple-minded. Lord Istvan thought he would die young, or if he survived, would never be fit to take a seat in Council.

That assumption saved Felix's life, for the Comyn chafed

under the rule of Elhalyn and Hastur, and rebellion was never impossible. Every year at Council season came the inevitable challenge from one of the other Domains, the accusation that Stephen could not be considered properly to be crowned without showing the Gift of his Line. Istvan's answer was always the same: no Elhalyn now possessed it. Should a candidate possessing the Gift come forward, by Comyn law, the crown would pass to him—and to whatever supporters of his claim lurked in the shadows.

And that was something Istvan Hastur would not allow.

In later years, Felix could never name the day when he *knew* his life hung by such a slender thread. It was just something that had always been, just like his ability to see every future that could ever be. He learned to conceal his *laran,* but as he grew older, he realized concealment was not a tactic that would work forever. In many Domains, testing for *laran* was scattered and perfunctory, but Hastur tested every boy as a part of his coming of age, and Felix's Gift would be discovered.

So be it, Felix thought. *But let it be on my terms and no one else's.*

And so Felix perfected his masquerade of dull-witted foolishness. He fell off horses. He dropped swords. He trod hard upon the feet of any partner unlucky enough to dance with him. He complained of constant headaches, of nebulous pains. And in the end, when a *leronis* came from Arilinn to test Istvan Hastur's hostages for *laran,* she very nearly did not test Felix Elhalyn— the weakling, the simpleton—at all.

And she saw nothing in him he did not mean her to see.

Of the great Towers that had once held all of Darkover together in a great web of *laran*, only a dozen remained, all watched over by Arilinn Tower as a mother hen her chicks. All of them had retreated from their former glories: Dalereuth, Tramontana, Neskaya, Corandolis; all the others were lightly-tenanted, for few Comyn wished to subject themselves to the rules and privations of a Tower Circle.

If Felix entered a Tower, he was unlikely to be commanded to

leave it. His absence would suit Istvan as well as his death—
better, perhaps, since no one could say his life had been
shortened as a result of Hastur scheming. But which Tower
would be best? No matter which he chose, most of the futures he
saw ended with his death. Only Tramontana, far to the north,
offered any hope of safety.

When Felix spoke to Lord Hastur of his desire to enter
Tramontana Tower, Lord Hastur agreed without hesitation:
though Tramontana was in Aldaran lands, the Towers were
neutral by long-held custom. Lord Hastur spoke vaguely of
arranging a proper marriage for Felix when he left Tramontana,
to which Felix responded with polite and meaningless phrases.
He already knew that he had no appetite for women and never
would, and (should he reach the future he saw only dimly) Istvan
Hastur would never try to compel him into a marriage.

And so Felix Elhalyn rode north, with a dozen guardsmen to
see him (and the copper in his saddlebags) safe to his destination.

It would be more than fifteen years before he left Tramontana
again.

Life in Tramontana was unlike anything Felix had ever known.
Gone was the need to play the fool, to deny his Gift, to *lie*. The
work was demanding, and with training his visions were few, the
warnings they held easily conveyed to Sherna MacAran, Keeper
of Tramontana Tower.

If not for Anjuli Aldaran, it would have been paradise.

She was cousin to Lord Aldaran, and that alone should have
been enough to keep her from Tower work. Marriage alliances
were more important to the Comyn lords than manning the
Towers; that was something every child of the Comyn knew. But
Kazal Aldaran had sent Anjuli to Tramontana, and before he had
been in Tramontana a single tenday, Felix understood why.

She had visions.

It was not unheard-of. The Aldaran Gift was Foresight, after
all. But Anjuli spoke of seeing impossible things. Great metal
beasts descending from the sky on clouds of white fire. Strangers
from the stars. All of Darkover plunged into darkness, cowering

under a threat so long forgotten that it seemed like an impossible dream. They had called her "Mad Anjuli" before Kazal had sent her to Tramontana, and only the empathic closeness of a Tower circle kept the name from following her.

But the visions she had—everyone agreed—were beyond reason.

And yet Mad Anjuli's visions had been the things of Felix Elhalyn's nightmares for longer than he could remember. He had always dismissed them as the instability of his line, a terrible forecast of the insanity that claimed so many of the Elhalyn line. But hearing the others speak of what Anjuli saw, Felix knew them for truth. Strangers from the stars were coming. And Darkover would be...changed, transmuted, *destroyed...*

Felix could not bring himself to believe it was possible to find a future that the star-men had not overrun, but still he clung to hope. If he, if Anjuli, could stop them—somehow—the world of the *Comyn'imyn* could go on as it always had.

Untouched.

Free.

Safe.

The years passed. The workers in Tramontana left, one by one, until not enough remained to work the circle. Only Anjuli and Keeper Sherna remained when Felix at last took his leave. Lady Sherna was bound for Neskaya, as soon as her escort arrived, to relieve the Keeper there.

And for many years to come, Felix would believe that Anjuli had returned to Castle Aldaran.

As for Felix, he had always known where he must go when he left Tramontana and what he must say when he arrived. It was not a matter of *laran,* but of desperate and careful planning: he would have only one chance to sway Istvan Hastur to agreement.

One chance to survive. One chance to summon the future.

He followed the servant to Lord Hastur's rooms in Comyn Castle. Despite his Tower-trained self control, his heart pounded fiercely and his mouth was sour with fear. So many of his futures had ended here.

The servant bowed and departed, and Felix knocked. A moment later, a servant opened the door. Felix stepped inside.

The room was windowless, for Comyn Castle had been built as a great labyrinth anchored by Old Tower, and few of its rooms were windowed. Lord Hastur's private chamber was filled with fine wood furniture, with rich fabrics, with all the opulence that came with power. The only thing that struck Felix, momentarily, as odd, was the lack of books and papers, for Lady Sherna had given him a love of learning. But of course Lord Hastur could not read.

He stepped forward and bowed punctiliously as Lord Hastur rose to his feet.

"I present myself with all a son's duty, foster-father," Felix said.

Lord Hastur waved him to a chair and seated himself once more. He regarded Felix for a moment in silence. "Tramontana seems to have agreed with you," he said at last.

"Unfortunately, it did not agree with most of those sent to it," Felix said. "It has been closed. I imagine the news to have reached you long before I did."

For all the times this scene had played itself out in his visions, the reality of it was subtly different. *He looks old,* Felix thought in surprise. Felix had not seen Lord Hastur since he left for Tramontana, and rarely enough before that. He knew intellectually that Lord Hastur was a man of only middle years, but Felix now saw that his hair was already streaked with grey, and deep lines of worry and care were graven into his features.

Lord Hastur frowned a little. "Why should I care what happens in Aldaran when there are things to occupy me here? You, for example. Why are you here? Have you not estates to your liking?" His pale eyes narrowed with suspicion.

"I have come to beg you for my life," Felix said. "And to tell you why it is to your benefit to grant it to me."

For a moment Lord Hastur stared at him, then he began to chuckle, and then to laugh. "And here I thought you changed!" he said, his voice hoarse with mirth. "You are as much a mooncalf as you ever were."

"Not a mooncalf, but a stormcrow," Felix said levelly. "Nor simple-minded. You thought me so, I admit, because my Gift came early. The Elhalyn Gift is a heavy burden for a child to bear. But I am no longer a child."

The laughter was gone now from Lord Hastur's face. For a long moment there was silence.

"You have the Gift of your Line and you have come to tell me of it?" Lord Hastur's voice was filled with disbelief.

"As I have said, I have come to beg for my life," Felix said. "It is no secret that the Council presses my cousin to stand aside because he lacks the Elhalyn Gift. What would happen, do you think, were I to come before it and demand to be recognized as Elhalyn of Elhalyn?"

Lord Hastur did not answer, and the ice-pale eyes were narrow now.

"Yet it suits you—and me as well—that Cousin Stephen should remain king," Felix continued. "And it suits me—though perhaps not you—that I remain alive. And so I have come to plead my case."

"You know the future," Lord Hastur said, a sour smile twisting his lips. "You already know my answer."

Felix smiled slightly. "My lord, I know every answer you *could* make, but not the one you *will* make. That is the curse of the Elhalyn Gift: to see all possible futures, but not to know which one will come to pass."

"And so," Lord Hastur said at last, "you wish to change the future you see, Lord Felix."

Felix shook his head slightly. "I wish to summon the future that best suits both of us, Lord Hastur," he answered. "One in which I am alive—and not king. Stephen was crowned when I was but a child. By now you have had ample time to discover that one may rule a king, or rule his council—but not both."

"And if that is so?" Lord Hastur said warily.

"Then you will welcome my help," Felix said. "The Lords Comyn plot, each for his own advantage, yet you can overturn their scheming if you know of it. For that you do not need the

Elhalyn Gift. You need me."

"I am not yet convinced," Lord Hastur said tightly.

"My lord is wise," Felix said, with a small seated bow. "When I brought you the news of Tramontana's abandonment, you did not know of it, though it has been known in the Towers for many tendays. No one brought word to you, because they felt, as you did, that it did not matter. But how can the news that Aldaran is without a working Tower within its borders not matter? Without the *leronyn*, Aldaran must rely on messengers to bear word, nor will his people have any forewarning of trouble when Fire Season comes. There will be no one within *Dom* Kazal's borders to train the *laran* of his children, to become healers. Such a thing might make him cautious. Or reckless. Or determined to take his rightful place among you in this Council—"

Lord Hastur said nothing, and Felix went on, explaining what a useful tool a spy network could be. Of course, the Compact forbid entering another's mind without permission, and good manners forbade the use of *laran* to gather intelligence. "—but there is no obstacle to having a network of informers, without *laran*, to bring information to someone who can husband each piece until he holds the whole of the tale. And this is what I shall do for you—if you will have me do it."

He had grown more hopeful as each turning point he had foreseen was reached and safely passed. But hope turned to despair as he reached the end of his speech and was met with silence. He had seen this as well: Lord Hastur would smile, and nod, and summon his paxman. And Felix would be dead before the moons changed once more.

At last Lord Hastur spoke. "And if I say yes, will you become my sworn man? Will you repudiate your allegiance to Elhalyn, and take oath that you will serve Hastur all your days?"

"I shall," Felix said, his voice barely a whisper. *Hastur is Darkover itself, and to serve Hastur is to serve Darkover. It has always been so—it must always be so.*

"Then let it be so," Lord Hastur said in unconscious echo, rising to his feet again. "And welcome home, my dutiful and obedient foster-son."

The oath he had taken was a secret between the two of them; Felix had expected nothing else. He took apartments in Comyn Castle; he took his seat in Council. When Council season was over, Felix moved into a house in the Trade City, saying he had no taste for life at Elhalyn. He developed a circle of lovers and friends, each chosen for what advantage they could bring him, and a steadily increasing network of trustworthy informants, all to one end: to avert the future his visions had shown him. Every move he made in Council, every alliance he helped build or shatter, every word he put into Istvan Hastur's ear, was done with the sure knowledge that the strangers from the stars were coming. If Darkover was to survive, the Comyn had to be ready.

And more years passed.

The day when everything changed was a day like any other. It was already spring here in the south, though the passes through the Hellers and the Hyades would be blocked for some time to come. Felix had taken a couple of clandestine meetings with his agents in Thendara, then gone riding to clear his head for the report he must prepare. That evening he attended a quiet party, and then retired to bed with his current *bredu*.

And as he slept, a vision came: a great ship, a shining (impossible) vessel of metal soaring over Darkover as if it were a fifth moon. From its belly it spat out tiny silver dragons that fell from the sky with a sound that seemed to shake the world. He saw one plow into the ground near the Wall Around the World, raising great clouds of hissing steam when the metal of its hull touched the eternal snows.

He thrashed his way out of the entangling blankets and was on his feet before the vision had even fully dissipated. Young Lord Padreik (new come to Thendara and willing to be dazzled) sat up in the wreckage of the bed, blinking sleepily. "*Dom* Felix?" he asked around a yawn, drawing the covers up around his bare thighs.

"Go back to sleep," Felix said in the gentlest voice he could muster. "It was an ill dream. Nothing you need to fret over. I just need to see about something before morning."

No reason to disturb Padreik's rest more than he already had. Peace was about to be in short supply indeed.

The *Terranan* had come to Darkover at last.

His hope of somehow eliminating the *Terranan* before they could take root in Darkovan soil had always been a remote one, and now it died completely: he could not leave Thendara during Council Season, and there was no one he could send. It did not take spycraft to know that Aldaran would see the strangers and their metal beasts as tools with which to secure wealth and advantage for himself. Aldaran might be outlaw, but it was a rare Comyn lord who didn't treasure the dream that someday he might be king.

Lord Hastur greeted Felix's report that men from the stars had come to Darkover with little interest, and Felix suspected he simply didn't believe it. His attitude hardly changed when word reached Felix that *Dom* Barak had presented the strangers with land near Caer Donn: they weren't Comyn, therefore they were beneath a Hastur's notice.

Once again Felix's dreams were filled with fire and darkness, and the waking visions were harder to push away. He'd spent half a lifetime trying to avert this future, and his failure was bitter. Over and over, he saw Darkover burning, poisoned, dead, and he didn't need his spies or his Gift to tell him these *Terranan* were only the first of the hordes to come.

All that was left was for him to go to Caer Donn as soon as he could. He would see the strangers with his own eyes, learn as much of their language as he could. Determine what threads of the futures he'd seen might yet be salvaged.

And which prevented.

"I hear the *Terranan* call this place *Port Chicago*," Felix said to Daniskar, pronouncing the alien words with care. He and his paxman stood on a rise that overlooked both Caer Donn and the alien city that looked to devour it. If Felix had not seen this with his own eyes, he would never have believed it could be done.

Less than a year ago, the land beyond the town had been covered in dense forest, close to useless even for hunting. Undoubtedly, *Dom* Barak had granted those lands to the *Terranan* because he had no other use for them.

Now the forest was gone as if it had never been. A mirror-smooth plain swept through the landscape as if some ancient matrix weapon out of the Ages of Chaos had touched down here. Clustered along the side nearest to Caer Donn (in some pattern that, presumably, made sense to the *Terranan*) were strange, squat huts made of some gray material. Here and there the frameworks of larger buildings—made, improbably, of metal—rose into the air. Outlandish wagons moved between them, emitting a faint whining sound as they moved.

"The metal in one of those structures would buy every treasure on Darkover," Daniskar said softly.

"And more," Felix agreed, struggling to conceal his unease. What *were* these *Terranan* strangers?

They were a month in Caer Donn before Felix had a basic understanding of the strangers' language. He spent his days eavesdropping wherever he could find *Terranan* gathered, and even performed menial tasks for the strangers, much to Daniskar's outrage. Wherever they had come from must have been very different than Darkover, because they went about so bundled that they resembled shiny, brightly-colored berries. (*Or ticks,* Felix could not help but think. *Here to suck the blood of Darkover with no thought of the damage they will do.*) As he had hoped, he and Daniskar did not come to anyone's notice: they had donned the guise and the manner of a wealthy—and curious—merchant and his bodyguard. They were hardly the only ones here hoping to profit from the strangers.

As the days crept closer to winter and the closing of the passes, Daniskar constantly urged him to depart before they were trapped in the Hellers until spring, but Felix delayed. This might be his only chance to study his enemy up close, and he dared not risk failing to discover the one fact that might save Darkover.

Daniskar wrinkled his nose in distaste as a couple of the strangers made their way gracelessly through the streets of Caer Donn, talking with the loud confidence of men certain their words were incomprehensible to anyone around them. Felix heard his paxman sigh in resignation as Felix turned to follow them.

"I'd love to know who the hell decided it was a good idea to build a spaceport here," one of the men said. "What these barbarians call broad daylight is twilight anywhere else, and I've spent the last six months freezing my balls off."

"The system is in a perfect place for a transport hub," his companion pointed out. "Be glad the 'barbarians' were easy to buy off: you'd like Cottman V even less."

"Yeah, but if we ever want to open this place up for development, we're going to have to terraform the whole goddamned place," the first man replied disgustedly.

Felix wasn't sure what *"terraform"* meant, though it sounded a bit like *Terranan*. Did they mean to make Darkover like their homeworld? Even the great *leronyn* of the Ages of Chaos could not have worked such a change!

He heard the two men laugh together, and suddenly a vision took him so strongly that he was blinded and senseless, cut loose from his body.

At first the images were a roaring geyser of incomprehensible flashes. But in Tramontana Felix had learned to steady his breathing and slow the torrent of potential futures, letting them surface one by one so that he could examine each individually. But as these visions steadied, he wished with all his heart he'd never learned to do any such thing; that these possibilities could rush past unseen.

He saw the surface of Darkover charred, blackened, lifeless, the light of the four moons hidden behind choking clouds of poison smoke.

He saw a warm green world filled with the calls of unfamiliar birds. Saw Thendara erased, saw the courtyard of Comyn Castle choked with a mad tangle of too-bright greenery and a profusion of alien blooms. Saw the skeletons of long-abandoned Towers crumbling under thick blankets of vines.

He saw the trees of the Yellow Forest rotted from within and the *chieri* lying dead; no Trailmen alive to dance between the treetops of High Kimbi, the *cralmacs* and *kyrri*, the Forge-folk, the Ya-men, all the life Darkover held lying dead, all of them dead, so many dead that it would take years just to bury them all.

He saw the Comyn in chains, toiling for *Terranan* overlords.

He saw a chained woman wreathed in flames. She met his eyes and laughed.

There must be something else—there *must!*

There was. The image was trembling and faint, barely-possible, but Felix clung to it with all his strength.

He saw Darkovan and *Terranan* side by side in the Council chamber. He saw the children of Darkover spreading across the galaxy as Darkover rose to take her place as an equal among the worlds of the *Terranan*. He saw peace.

This was the future he must summon.

No matter what the cost.

When Felix came back to himself at last, he opened his eyes warily.

The room was dark. Unfamiliar. By the dim glow of the brazier flickering in the corner, he could make out Daniskar dozing nearby in a thickly upholstered chair. The image of the chained woman in flames still danced behind his eyes. That future could not be allowed to come to pass.

He cleared his throat quietly.

Startled out of sleep, Daniskar leapt to his feet, reaching automatically for his sword. When he realized what had roused him, he came to Felix's bedside, looking stricken.

"I am sorry, *vai dom,*" he said, sinking to his knees beside the bed. "I did not know what else to do. The *Terranan* would have taken you to their healers..."

Felix shuddered at the thought. "And so you told them I was from the castle," he said, realizing where he must be. He noted that their packs had been brought from the inn and winced inwardly. All they needed now was for *Dom* Barak to complain to Lord Hastur and King Stephen about *spying*. "I can only imagine what *Dom* Barak said upon being informed we had been his guests all autumn," Felix said, struggling to sit up.

Daniskar looked guilty. "*Dom* Barak extends every courtesy, and tenders his regrets that the press of business has denied him your company. He vows to repair this deficiency with all haste. Probably first thing tomorrow," Daniskar added dolefully.

"I'm certain it's purely a formality," Felix said wryly. *And that he will let us leave once he is done with us.*

Felix chose to breakfast in his rooms to spare everyone the awkwardness of meeting him before Lord Aldaran's intentions were known. He knew little of the current Lord Aldaran: Kazal Aldaran had been Lord of Aldaran when Felix had been at Tramontana, but his grandson now ruled here.

While he was dressing, a servant came to tell him that *Dom* Barak awaited him at his leisure. Felix hurried to finish and allowed the servant to conduct him to the meeting he would so much rather avoid.

Dom Barak received Felix in his private study, a utilitarian and almost shabby room entirely at odds with the ostentation of the rest of Castle Aldaran. When Felix entered, Barak got stiffly to his feet, strode over to the sideboard, and poured two cups of wine with his own hands, waving Felix to a seat. This was to be a private meeting, then.

He glanced around the room. It was cluttered with maps, hawking furniture, and hunting trophies. Objects made of metal and of an odd material Felix didn't recognize sat atop the disorder on the table; Felix supposed that they must be *Terranan* artifacts.

"I can only suppose you've come to steal my *Terranan* for Stephen," Barak said without preamble, setting one goblet in front of Felix and taking a sip from the other.

"I only came here to see them," Felix said neutrally. "You can't blame me for being curious."

Barak snorted. "Curious?" he said. "That explains, I suppose, why you decided to skulk around in Caer Donn, pretending to be a tinker."

"I felt it would save both of us embarrassment. Aldaran isn't a signatory to the Compact."

"Oh, not that damned nonsense about the Compact again," Barak said irritably. The chair creaked as he leaned back and set his cup down on the single bare space on the desk. "Aldaran honors it."

"Even now?" Felix let his gaze rest meaningfully on the *Terranan* objects.

"Even now," Barak said, his scowl deepening. "I don't like what you're implying, *Dom* Felix."

"I am implying nothing," Felix said, "other than that these *Terranan* might be dangerous."

"Or that Hastur wants their wealth for himself," Barak scoffed.

Felix sipped his wine. "If Aldaran and the *Terranan* form an alliance, Lord Aldaran, the Council will have to take notice. You know that as well as I."

It was satisfying to see the effort *Dom* Barak had to spend to keep his temper in check. "If you have delivered your message, Lord Felix," Barak finally said, in a voice that *almost* approximated cordiality, "I think perhaps it is time I let you return to Thendara. I am sure you have urgent business awaiting you there."

Felix smiled pleasantly at Barak and set his own goblet aside. "I think I do," he said. "But before I go, I really must satisfy my curiosity: how do you plan to force your subjects to welcome a bunch of rude star-men who fell the forests they use for hunting and treat autumn as if it's midwinter?"

The journey south was quicker than the journey north, for Felix and Daniskar were attempting to outrun the winter. Even with their breakneck turn of speed and frequent remounts, they failed, and were forced to beg hospitality of Lord Alton at Armida. It was luck alone that there was a hard, cold frost a few tendays after their arrival, or they might have had to overwinter there. Lord Alton was a gracious host, but he shared Lord Hastur's views on the *Terranan*—they were as irrelevant to the affairs of the Comyn as were the Dry Towners or the Trailmen.

Felix wished with all his heart that were true. Since the disastrous vision that had ended his time at Caer Donn, his mind had been occupied with only one thing: how to summon the single future of hope from the abattoir of possibilities he'd seen. If only it was a matter of choosing and wishing, but it was not—every single moment, every decision, was a crossroads. Make even one wrong choice in the days—or years—to come, and see Darkover utterly destroyed.

And the worst of it was, he had absolutely no idea of what the right choices were.

His thoughts remained bleak through Council Season. He had shared something of his visions with Lord Hastur, coming as close to pleading for help as he could, but it had done no good, The Council's mind was fixed on other matters beyond anyone's ability to influence them. What use was foreknowledge of disaster without knowledge of how to avert it? Felix sent as many agents as he dared northward to gather information, and wondered in idle moments whether he dared kidnap one of the *Terranan* for questioning. Tenday after tenday passed, and he could not see a useful course of action. Nebulous warnings alone would not move the Comyn to defend Darkover, especially since he could not suggest any practical way to do it. The most he could do was encourage the Council to see the strangers as a resource to be removed from an enemy's grasp. Bring them south, where they could be easily seen, and perhaps others would convince themselves of what he already knew.

Perhaps.

Summer turned to autumn, and Felix still had no answers. His agents, running before the winter storms like leaves before the wind, brought him their harvest of rumor and gossip and truth—among them, the disturbing news that Anjuli Aldaran had never left Tramontana Tower at all. And that a *Terranan* had—somehow—caused her death.

A generation ago such a thing would have been impossible, Felix thought bleakly. The *leroni* were sacrosanct—any man who raised their hand to one would be slain instantly for the sacrilege. But even when he'd been a boy, half a century ago, the Towers and their inhabitants had already been half legend, a thing belonging to the time of Varzil the Good.

And now, it seemed, the *Terranan* would erase even those legends.

To think of Anjuli Aldaran, *Comynara* and *leronis*, dying old and frail in her crumbling tower, was a weight upon his heart. He had loved her in his way, all those years ago, and she had died alone and terrified.

He could have saved her. If he had gone to Tramontana while he was at Caer Donn— If he had convinced her to return to her home— He knew what she had Foreseen. Her word would have bolstered his. Barak might have been willing to see the danger. Done something. Sent the *Terranan* away.

It had been a chance, and he had missed it. *How many other chances have I let slip by unseen? How few are yet to come?*

Am I to be nothing more than a witness to the death of our world?

He ate little and slept less. He abandoned his friends, rejected old lovers and did not take new ones; even Daniskar walked warily about his master. Felix roamed for hours through Thendara— Comyn Castle, Old Town, Trade City—returning to his rooms late at night to pace sleeplessly until the dawn. The visions he had managed to shut out for so many years returned now with a vengeance; there were times he could not tell what was happening in the here-and-now from what only might have happened, or would happen. In his visions, the Yellow Forest burned. The peaks of the Hellers were bare of snow. *Chieri* and Trailmen and *kyrri* and humans lay dead or dying in the ruins of great forests. And still the great metal ships of the *Terranan* came.

Darkover lay naked and helpless before the star-men who had come to ravish her. She could not fight and must not die and

Felix did not know how to guide her to that future he had only just glimpsed.

At last, in the depths of winter, anguish and desperation drove him to accept that there was only one course open to him. A decade ago, he wouldn't have flinched away from it, but he wasn't a young man anymore.

Tell the truth, if only to yourself. A decade ago, you did not hold your life so dear. Only now, with Lorill about to step into Istvan's place, with the Comyn fewer in each generation, who can give shape to the future if you do not? And they would call it arrogance, did they know I held myself so indispensable, but I have seen what might be and they have not.

He made his arrangements carefully. The Castle was nearly empty at this season and he had sent Daniskar to his bed long before. In the days preceding, he had gathered together the things he would need: a small brazier, a heavy stormcloak, a lantern.

He thought longingly of a cup of hot wine to steady his nerves, but he dared not indulge himself—not when he was about to drink something far more dangerous. It had been a small matter to acquire it clandestinely: as he closed his fingers around the small glass bottle in the pocket of his half-cape, it seemed to burn with an eldritch fire.

Kirian. The bitter liquor distilled from *kireseth* flowers. It was used, in small doses, to help children through their threshold sickness. In larger doses, it overthrew the natural barriers the mind created to defend itself. With it, Felix hoped to be able to stay submerged in his visions long enough see the path on which his people could reach safety.

Or die.

He would have no monitor, no Keeper, no working circle to support him. He smiled painfully, thinking of what Sherna MacAran would have said about this idea. Certainly nothing good. (Did she still live? he wondered. Did she grieve for Anjuli Aldaran?)

But there was no other choice. From the moment of his first vision of the great metal ships descending from the sky, Felix had sworn his service not to Hastur or Elhalyn or even to the

Comyn, but to Darkover herself. If there was a road to safety, he had to discover it.

Before it was too late.

A storm raged over Thendara that night, a creature of wind and ice screaming through the towers of Comyn Castle as if it stalked its prey. Here in the upper levels of Comyn Castle it was a palpable thing, evident in the faint rattling of shutters, the whistle of wind through every crack and opening. Once it had been said that nights like these were the best for Tower work. Tonight Felix would test that old superstition.

Thendara was unique among the Domains in having two Towers. Legend held that Old Tower—called Ashara's Tower—had stood before the city, let alone Comyn Castle. There were so many legends built up around it that not all of them could be true, but among them stood one fact: no one entered Ashara's Tower without invitation.

It was fortunate, in that case, that the Castle held a second Tower, called simply "New Tower". It had been built in Felix's great-grandsires time, perhaps in a spirit of happy optimism regarding the future of the Comyn. Whatever its impetus and purpose, it stood empty now. And to do what he intended, he required its shielding.

In winter, the Castle was but lightly-occupied, and none of the servants who inhabited it at this season would dare to question one of the Comyn anyway. Felix moved swiftly and unimpeded to his destination, passing quickly through the wards and shields of the empty Tower as he made for his goal: the Working Room, where the circle would gather to work the relays—and in ancient days, to perform far darker acts. Habit brought him to the center of the chamber, to the wide circular bench where the circle would gather. He opened his pack, set his brazier in the center of the floor, and lit it before draping his storm cloak loosely over his shoulders and seating himself.

Everything was ready.

He held the bottle of *kirian* in his hand for a long moment before he could bring himself to break the seal. As the bitterness filled his mouth and throat, he experienced a moment of pure terror. *Too late,* a voice from nowhere and everywhere said. *Too late to turn back now...*

And then he was gone.

This time there was no familiar dreamlike procession of confusing images. This time he did not experience a vision, but created it. Over and over, he navigated the shining silver maze in the Overlight—

—the maze that was an echo of the bones of Comyn Castle—

—just as you did so long ago, when Lady Sherna set you such puzzles to teach you how to move through the Overlight—

—finding only the things he had found before.

Darkover destroyed, barren, its people enslaved.

The world transformed to a desert that suffered beneath a hot white sun.

His people, exiles. Scattered among a hundred alien worlds.

The Yellow Forest burning. The Beautiful Ones dead, slain, gone.

The laughing woman in chains, flames clothing her naked body, setting forests alight in mountain and valley until all Darkover was in flames.

Each time the maze led him to such a destination it took all his strength to turn back, fight free, begin again. It seemed to him that the maze shifted every time he ran it, the futures he rejected vanishing, new ones appearing. He did not know how many dead ends he turned back from, how long he hunted. Was the body he had left behind failing, dying, while he searched for a future that might not exist? Even here he felt his strength fading, the self he wore in this place-not-place beginning to dissolve like summer frost...

But there is a way! There is! There must be! I will not surrender before I find it!

He forced himself to begin again. This time there was no maze, no puzzle to solve. All the possibilities had been rejected, and all that was left was a grey mist with no beginning and no end.

There!

A gleam of silver, a faint brightness in the mists. He followed it, the shape he chose as mutable as the mists: hound, then horse, and at last as a hawk, keen-eyed, relentless, soaring through a world that held neither up nor down, near or far, his only guide that faint and wavering silver thread...

Between one moment and the next, the mist vanished, and he stood in an utterly alien place.

The chamber was dim and held nothing of Darkover about it. Garish forms of colored light hung in the air, striking multicolored glints from surfaces of glass and metal and substances he could not name. Despite the fact that nothing he saw was familiar, he knew this place. A tavern. A place where men came to rejoice. Or to grieve.

Where am I? Why here? I seek a living future for Darkover...not this.

He looked around carefully. If this was where he had been brought, he would learn what it had to teach him.

There were tables and booths, and men were gathered here. Many were garbed alike, in an unfamiliar black uniform. He turned, looking for a door, and saw a dim booth at the far end of the room. A man sat there, drunk nearly to the point of oblivion. He wore a uniform like the others, but the collar had been pulled open as if it pained him. *Terranan.* Alien.

Grief surrounded the man, visible, a pall of dark smoke. It fed on him and he welcomed it gladly, for it promised him an ending to his agony. In the eternal "Now" of the Overlight, Felix understood that he knew this man. Would know him. Had known him.

Why you? Who are you?

There was no answer, but suddenly, standing beside the *Terranan*, he saw another. A woman, colorless and insubstantial as a ghost, also clad in alien garb, reaching out to him. Or to both of them?

Not someone he knows. Someone he will know. But...?

Suddenly—as if it had always been there and he had just now noticed it—he saw the silver cord that he had followed. It coiled

Rosemary Edghill & Rebecca Fox

about him; about the man and the woman. He held it in his hands, a ribbon of light...

A tool. A promise. Hope.

Find the man and the woman both, and he would save Darkover.

There was a way.

As if that realization had taken the very last of his strength, his surroundings were whipped away like smoke in a high wind. When they were gone, there was nothing.

Nothing at all.

The next thing he was aware of was the taste of hot honeyed wine. It did little to quell his thirst, or his aching gnawing hunger. He tried to reach for the cup, but could only manage a clumsy flailing.

"Blessed Aldones! No, drink it all, *vai dom.* You're far too weak."

Daniskar.

Felix gulped greedily until the cup was taken away. The wine had done little more than to awaken his body to its pain and exhaustion. The room was sweltering—he could smell the logs burning on the hearth—but the heat did not seem to reach him. He struggled to open his eyes and finally managed it.

This was his bedchamber. He lay in his great canopied bed, bolstered in a half-sitting position by a number of cushions, and lying beneath what was surely every blanket in Comyn Castle. In addition to the roaring fire in the fireplace, the room was filled with half a dozen braziers. Daniskar was stripped to his breeches, and his body gleamed with sweat. He returned to Felix's side with a bowl of rich pudding. At the first spoonful, the taste carried Felix back to Tramontana; it had been Keeper Sherna's favorite, one of the things always on the table after a Circle.

When he had finished it, he felt stronger, though he knew better than to try his strength too soon.

"How did you find me?" he asked.

"Do you think I am stupid, *vai dom?*" Fear had loosened his paxman's tongue. "Where else would you be but in that unholy place, looking for things no man can find!"

Felix studied Daniskar's face. Daniskar had come to his service just after he had made his pact with *Dom* Istvan. It had been at Istvan's suggestion, of course, and neither Daniskar nor Felix had felt it prudent to refuse.

That was a long time ago. They had both grown old, but Daniskar did not have a bloodline that would keep him alive long beyond a man's appointed time.

He reached out and put a hand on Daniskar's arm, suddenly contrite. "I did what I must, for Darkover's sake," he said gently. "And now I have hope."

Daniskar sank to his knees beside the bed. "My lord," he said brokenly, and then words seemed to fail him. He pressed his face into the mound of blankets so Felix could not see his face.

Felix stroked his paxman's hair gently. *Have I overlooked the love I could have found on my own doorstep?* he wondered. But no. Daniskar had always been a man for women, without the urge of marriage and family. Of course, to marry would have given him hostages to fortune, and Felix had made many enemies in his time. It was why he held his own lovers so lightly, that none of them could be imagined to possess enough of his heart to sway him. But Daniskar's love, though chaste, was deep and true...

He was wandering in his thoughts, he realized. He would need to sleep soon.

"So you followed me to the Tower," he said, stroking Daniskar's hair. "And followed me in, I suppose."

"Certainly not!" Daniskar said hotly. He had recovered some of his composure and regarded Felix with familiar exasperation. "What good would I do you if I were struck dead by sorcery? But I remembered that Lord Dawyd was overwintering here, and I went to beg him for the loan of one of his *kyrri*."

Felix smiled. "Neatly done," he said approvingly. The Towers were nearly gone, but the inhuman servants the Comyn had bred up during the Age of Chaos to serve their needs remained. None of the veils and barriers that stopped a man would stop a *kyrri*. "And did Dawyd think to ask why?"

"I told him you had expressed a need for a servant who could be discreet," Daniskar said blandly. "He did not ask further. No one saw us, my lord. I swear to you."

"And I believe you, for there is no man living I trust as I do you," Felix said. "And I promise you, tonight's work achieved its purpose."

"If you say so," Daniskar said, with a touch of his usual disapproval. "But it will come to naught if you do not rest yourself now."

Felix was asleep almost before Daniskar had removed the pillows and straightened the blankets to his own satisfaction, but the dreams that followed were not gentle. They were filled with blood and death, with the screams of parents lamenting their murdered children, with fertile and pleasant lands turned to ash and waste.

But this time it was not Darkover's future that he saw. This was the inferno in which his weapons were even now being forged. Out of this suffering and loss would come Darkover's salvation.

If Felix were clever enough.

The rest of the winter passed quietly enough, and by the time spring came again, one of Felix's plots had borne fruit. The *Terranan* had abandoned Caer Donn and were building a new spaceport on the eastern side of Thendara.

It was said the *Terranan* had come south by their own choice, two winters in the Hellers being more than they could stand. Their commander, Carroll Stone, had by then heard of Thendara, and had petitioned Lord Hastur for permission to settle here—a permission Lord Hastur willingly gave. To save face, and perhaps to placate *Dom* Barak, the *Terranan* were not leaving Caer Donn entirely (as if even they could turn a desert of stone back into a lush forest, Felix thought derisively), but it would only be a "backup" site, one which would have little contact with the Darkovans. Perhaps Commander Stone had realized that Lord Aldaran considered the *Terranan* and all their devices to be his property, and perhaps he had not liked it. At least here in the south, the *Terranan* wouldn't belong to any of the Comyn: the Trade City and its vicinity were neutral ground.

There was an additional bonus to the *Terranan* relocation. As the Trade City was neutral territory, it fell to the head of Comyn Council to deal with them. As spring turned to summer, Istvan Hastur developed as much dislike for the aliens as even Felix could ask for—and at last began to realize what a danger they were.

"A babe unweaned would have better sense!" he snarled, banging his goblet down on the table. Felix reached for the jug and refilled it. They were in Istvan's private chambers, unobserved by anyone, even Istvan's servants. What had been a report each tenday on matters of general interest had, since the spring, become a venue for Lord Hastur to vent his anger.

"The *Terranan* have no honor, no shame, and no self-respect!" Istvan snarled. "Demanding to be put in leading-strings at one moment and the next insisting the Comyn bow down to them!"

Felix sighed. "They are what they are, *vai dom*. And what they are, and have always been, is trouble."

He had never shared, even with Lord Hastur, the full extent of his foreknowings about the *Terranan*, and he was glad of it now. Istvan Hastur was no longer the vigorous man who had first accepted Felix's service. He had become an old man, prey to an old man's sudden furies. To lead them into war against the strangers...there would be no quicker way to set Darkover on the road to the bleakest of Felix's visions.

"I should send them packing," Istvan grumbled, staring into his wine. "That damned puppy Stone had the insolence to offer to pay me for the right to extend the spaceport! *Me!*"

Felix winced inwardly at the thought of anyone treating Hastur of Hastur as a common laborer. "They are fools," he said flatly. "But like the *cralmac* and the firetower, now that we have let them in, it is much harder to tell them to go."

"At least it will be Lorill's problem soon," Istvan muttered. "And I wish him joy of it."

"Surely you intend to live forever?" Felix said lightly, hoping to cajole Istvan out of his dark mood.

"Bah! Should I condemn myself to an eternity of Council sessions? I think rather it is *you* who plans to live forever, Stormcrow," Istvan said, allowing himself to be mollified.

"I can but hope," Felix said. "Someone must be here to advise your son, after all."

"And he trusts you," Istvan said with a faint bitterness. "Will you swear to him as you have sworn to me? And serve him as you have served me?"

Istvan's mood had undergone another mercurial shift; he glared at Felix with angry suspicion. *It is age, nothing more,* Felix told himself. *I have as much of his trust as he gives to any man. I have earned it, after all.* "I shall," Felix said simply, and Istvan's dark expression eased.

"Then I suppose I can deal with those damnable *Terranan* for another year or two, if I must," Istvan grumbled. "I should order you to do it."

"The best weapon is the one the enemy does not see," Felix reminded him.

"Just as you say," Istvan grumbled. "Now go. I have much work to do, if the idiot *Terranan* will allow me to do any of it."

Daniskar fell in behind him as Felix stepped out into the corridor. His destination was one of Comyn Castle's highest points. The Council Chamber had been built to give the illusion of floating in the sky, a place of polished stone and crystal mirrors. The seating areas for each of the Seven Domains (Aldaran's place was never filled, but it still remained) divided the chamber into seven sections; at the back of each of the railed-off sections a door led to an outside hallway, so that during Council sessions the Comyn could take their seats without crossing the chamber floor. At the turn in that hallway, a short flight of steps led up to a small open balcony, its original purpose unknown.

Here, all of Thendara was laid out before him as if he were a bird in flight. The Venza Hills cradled the ancient Trade City; north, beyond the Venzas, lay the Plains of Arilinn. And beyond that...home. Hali and Elhalyn. He wondered if he would ever see them again.

But to dream of home was not the reason Felix had come here. At the far side of the Trade City stood the growing *Terranan* spaceport. Here, as in Caer Donn, the ground had been flattened, leveled, and sheathed in an artificial stone. The setting sun drew glints of light from the machines that flitted back and forth between the great metal bulk of the *Terranan* ships they serviced, and there was already a warren of what Commander Stone called "temporary" buildings. The *Terranan* also meant to mirror the Darkovan Trade City with one of their own, a place filled with strange shops and strange wares.

And weapons? Felix wondered. *They think our Compact is a foolish child's game, and perhaps it is good that they think so, but no matter what lip-service they pay it, they will not keep their weapons out of our hands. And there are many, both foolish and venal, who would seek to profit from their carelessness.*

"It doesn't look as though they're planning to leave Darkover anytime soon, does it?" Daniskar said disgustedly. Felix could hardly blame him for the implied criticism. He had told Daniskar, months before, that he had found a way to save Darkover, and the *Terranan* were still here.

"They're building a home for themselves," Felix said. *Have patience, my old friend. My tools are still a-forging.* "Their commander has told the Hastur that they mean to stay."

"But we don't want them here!" Daniskar protested. "They hate our weather, and they already have a home somewhere else. Why don't they go back to it?"

They say our world lies in a strategic location among their stars, and so they mean to take it. And give us in fee what will destroy us. "They say we are their long-lost kin," Felix said aloud. He needed neither *laran* nor sight to know Daniskar's lips quirked skeptically. "Whether or not it's true doesn't matter," Felix said with a shrug. "They are here now."

"Like a forest fire raging out of control," Daniskar answered.

"And a fire can be tamed, if one knows how," Felix said.

With the proper tools.

It was three years more before the first of Felix's tools was ready, but he had not been idle. The *Terranan* had finished their spaceport, only to say that all its structures were temporary, and to ask for Darkover to lend them the labor to make them permanent. The Council had balked, but Felix had been delighted. Every laborer sent to the *Terranan* was another set of eyes and ears to gather precious information. He spent many days coaching *Dom* Lorill in the things to demand, the things to delay, and the things to ignore. The strangers seemed to be even fonder of endless meetings than the Comyn Council was, and Istvan had willingly left his heir to deal with it.

Despite the growing presence of the strangers, Felix felt a sense of peace. Every small act, no matter how inconsequential, closed off—or opened—another possible future. He had never been a trusting soul, but the vision he had seen—the man and the woman who lay in his future—had given him confidence. If the *Terranan* were like a forest fire raging wildly out of control, well and good; a fire could be fought with cunning, with guile, with the proper tools.

That was what the *Terranan* would provide. In due time.

Caer Donn had grown since he had last seen it, its character changing as if it were some hapless creature infested by a parasite. It was no longer a walled village, but a town filled with taverns and lodging houses and such places as a traveler would seek out at the end of a long journey. The "abandoned" *Terranan* port just beyond was brightly lit, as if the *Terranan* would command day where there was night.

A light snow was falling as a *Terranan* ship came in for a landing. By now their landing and departure had lost its novelty value, but still Felix watched. The craft settled itself to the ground beneath a pool of light, and Felix was near enough to hear the whine of machinery as its hatch opened and a gangway unfolded. The men who exited the ship walked toward the customs house, their talk and laughter carried on the wind as they moved toward its promise of refuge and warmth.

Felix continued to wait.

There.

Another uniformed man appeared in the hatchway, holding onto its edge as if he was mustering his courage. After a long moment, he stepped down the gangway, moving as one who had lately received some terrible injury.

No injury of the body, I think, but of the spirit, Felix thought.

At the foot of the ramp the man hesitated, glancing from the direction his fellows had taken to the road that led down into the town. Felix watched as he made up his mind and hurried toward the gate, his steps unsteady.

When he reached the town, the man hesitated, looking from one tavern to the next. Felix stepped out of the doorway to meet him, and for the first time, saw him clearly.

The laugh-lines in his face were deep, but they had been graven over by a mask of sorrow. Even in the wind and the cold Felix could smell the reek of alcohol and drugs that hung about him. They were not enough, Felix imagined, to truly dull the self-hatred that was killing him. He put a hand on the man's arm. *Laran* gave him the images from his dreams. And a name.

"Welcome, stranger. What do you seek here?" he asked in his carefully-learned Common.

Ercan Waltrud regarded him with glazed indifference. "Oblivion," he said harshly. "Are you selling it?"

"No," Felix said. "But I will give it to you. And perhaps redemption as well." He had been a fool to imagine the Comyn could stand against an utterly unknown enemy and prevail—that had always been the flaw in all his plans. To win against such an enemy one must know him as well as one knew one's self, and to know an enemy as *alien* as the *Terranan* seemed impossible. But there was always a way to do the impossible, Felix had learned.

Ercan laughed gratingly. "Redemption! You have no idea what I've done, old man."

"Perhaps not," Felix answered. "But I have some understanding of what you may yet do. Come. I will take you to a place you can rest."

If one needed to learn, all that was needed was the proper teacher. And what better teacher than this man, who had done elsewhere that which Felix must prevent here?

He felt as much as saw Ercan Waltrud's surrender; his thought that to place himself in the hands of an *alien barbarian* would at least be a way to give up the terrible burden of knowing what he knew. He felt an unexpected pang of tenderness for a mind and heart so terribly bruised by the duty the *Terranan* had called him to.

This is how we will win our safety. Both Darkover's, and your Terran Empire's. Darkover will take up those tools it has discarded, and make them our own. And in the end, it will free us both.

"Come," Felix said again. "I will bring you to a place where you can forget."

The two men walked deeper into the town through the falling snow.

FIONA, COURT CLERK IN TRAINING

by Barb Caffrey

"Fiona, Court Clerk in Training" by Barb Caffrey is another story that continues and develops characters from previous tales. This sequence began with the author wondering, "There was a mention of a judge who happened to be a Renunciate at the end of *The Shattered Chain*, so I got to thinking about her. How did she get to be where she is?" In order to answer that question, she wrote "At The Crossroads" (*Stars of Darkover*) and "A Problem of Punishment (*Gifts of Darkover*), both of which explored the family background of Fiona n'ha Gorsali. Here Fiona herself takes center stage in her own inimitably resourceful fashion.

Barb Caffrey has written three novels, An Elfy On The Loose (2014), A Little Elfy in Big Trouble (2015), and Changing Faces (forthcoming), and is the co-writer of the Adventures of Joey Maverick series (with late husband Michael B. Caffrey) Previous stories and poems have appeared in Stars Of Darkover, First Contact Café, How Beer Saved The World, Bearing North, And Bedlam's Edge (with Michael B. Caffrey).

Wooden staves clashed as two women—one young, the other not-so-young—sparred in the outdoor practice area behind the Nevarsin Guild House. It was a cloudless midsummer day, maybe two hours before supper—the perfect time to fight. After a few minutes of hard-fought staff drill, the elder neatly disarmed the younger and pushed her to the ground.

"You're better, but you'll never make a fighter this way, Fiona," Cassilde n'ha Elorie said as she helped the girl up. "You need to keep practicing. What would you do if your mother was robbed in the market?"

The teen-aged girl who one day would be called Fiona n'ha Gorsali considered it carefully. Although her mother was a Renunciate herself, she wasn't much of a fighter. "I'd run after the thief while memorizing what he looked like, what he was wearing…if I couldn't catch him, I'd do my best to bring the matter up before my father in court."

"Assume your father is at the other end of his circuit, and you're still around here for some reason," Cassilde suggested. "What would you do then?"

"I'd run even faster. And I'd catch the thief."

Cassilde chuckled. "Just do your best, that's all I ask."

"I'll keep working." Fiona scowled. Why hadn't she been able to last more than a few minutes against Cassilde today? She'd tried so hard…being disarmed within moments hadn't been what she'd been hoping for.

Soon, Fiona would have to choose a profession. Everyone from her father and mother to the head of the Nevarsin Guild House said so. And Fiona knew she must figure out what she was going to do with her life long before she actually took the Oath of Renunciates. She was in an odd position, as her father Dominic, who was a judge, had been training her to become a court clerk—and Fiona actually liked the work.

But there had never been a female court clerk in the entire history of the Hellers. So was all of her training pointless, then?

Her parents had argued last night, in fact. She couldn't hear everything they said, but heard her name several times during the heated discussion. Fiona had the impression that Dominic had tried hard to get Gorsali to listen to something…but of course her mother wasn't about to do that.

Fiona wished she knew what was going on, but as usual, no one told her anything. She hated being thirteen. So many things were kept from her, supposedly for her own good. *Someday,* she vowed, *I'll be older. And they'll* have *to tell me everything.*

"A *sekal* for your thoughts?" Cassilde asked.

"I'd wanted to do better today—" Fiona started.

"And you did," Cassilde replied. "Haven't you figured out yet that the better you get, the harder I am on you?"

Now that was a new thought. Fiona pondered it.

"That's not all I'm thinking about," she finally ventured.

"Figured as much. What's going on with you today?" Cassilde led the way to a nearby bench. "I've taught you long enough to know when you're distracted. Spill it!"

Fiona smiled, but her heart wasn't in it. "My parents argued last night. I'm sure it was about me, about what I'm going to do with myself."

"You have years yet before you take the Oath. And I've never had the sense Dominic macAnndra was against that—"

"Oh, he isn't," Fiona hastened to assure her. "Grand-sire macAnndra doesn't like it much, but Da said he wants me to be happy and make my own choices." *Otherwise, why would I be working as his court clerk right now?* she thought. *Unless it's for the free labor...*

"Makes sense." Cassilde put her chin on her hand. "We've never had a situation like this before in the Guild House, Fiona. Most men are against everything Renunciates stand for. But your father is not most men, and we count him as a friend, here in Nevarsin. I truly believe he wants what's best for you. Otherwise, why would he be paying me to teach you weapons?"

Fiona laughed. "I thought you were supposed to pretend my mother wanted that?"

"Why pretend when we both know it's not the truth?" Cassilde gave her a sidelong look, and added, "Isn't it time to go help your mother with her hives?"

"Yeah, yeah. I know." Fiona hated going to the hives. She always got stung. And she didn't like dealing with her mother, either...but her duty was plain. "I'll go."

"Oh, and the Guild Mother will be seeing you later."

"Why?"

"She didn't say," Cassilde said blandly. "But I know about it, because she and I have been invited to dinner at your parents' house."

Fiona raised impressed brows. Dominic and Gorsali rarely entertained...could this be about Fiona's future, then? Because what else could the Guild Mother want?

Or had Fiona done something wrong? Was Cassilde tired of training her already? Cassilde's deep blue eyes gave her no clues; worse yet, her body language was muted.

Something strange was definitely going on. But before she could figure it out, she heard a familiar male voice ask, "Is practice over?"

Fiona turned around and almost smiled. "Hi, Da." Her father's grey eyes lit up; he was always happy to see her. "Yes, we just finished. Cassilde told me I have to go help Ma with the hives."

"You should do that, then." He came up and rumpled her hair, something she pretended to hate. But at least her father had come by to watch her fight; her mother was never anywhere to be found during fighting practice, for reasons no one would ever explain.

"Good to see you, Judge," Cassilde said easily. "I'm looking forward to dinner. I haven't had Gorsali's honey-cakes in ages!"

"You always did love her honey-cakes," Dominic said with a laugh. "Fiona, you'd best go help your mother now, all right?"

"All right. I'll go help mother with the bees." As Cassilde and her father nodded in unison, Fiona tried to smile. Then she started trudging down the path to the hives. They were near the Guild House itself, which was quite unusual as Fiona understood it. Originally, the Nevarsin Guild House had been only grudgingly accepted by the *cristoforo* brethren, as they'd been afraid women would leave their homes willy-nilly. So having the hives nearby was a subtle point of protection.

Over time, though, her father had told her that the *cristoforos* realized that the Guild House didn't admit that many women—you had to truly *want* to take the Oath if you were to study at Nevarsin, and you had to have a trade the other Renunciates actually needed. So the *cristoforos* had come to terms with them…and even allowed some limited access to their priceless archives, providing you'd actually sworn to be a Renunciate already.

Fiona wanted access to those records, too. She dreamed of them in the night. There was so much about the law she didn't yet know—and she wanted to know it all. Right now.

But she wasn't allowed in there. She was only thirteen.

Worst of all, without seeing and studying those records, she couldn't officially become a court clerk. Much less a judge in time, which she knew in her heart she wanted to be—but how would it ever happen?

Fiona worried about that, most days. She didn't want to do anything else. While she knew her letters backward and forward, she knew she'd not enjoy teaching others. She wasn't much of a rider, she wasn't much of a fighter, either, and she couldn't cook at all. And if anyone was to depend on her supposed acumen with bees, well…they'd all starve.

What she *was* good at was helping her father. If only she could get at the records the *cristoforos* had, she could become a court clerk in truth, and do her job even better.

But so far, everyone said she was too young.

Once she got to the small out-building where her mother kept the heavy clothes she used for beekeeping, Fiona did her best to clear her mind. Today, she'd not get stung—at least, if her wits were as sharp as her father always said.

Fiona and her mother had returned to their small but comfortable brick home on the outskirts of Nevarsin. This time, Fiona had been stung only twice—once on the forearm as she'd reached in to get some honey her mother needed for tonight's meal, and once on the neck. She supposed this was progress…even so, she never wanted to see another bee again as long as she lived.

As her mother went to check on the meal she'd set to simmering before going to work with her hives, Fiona went outside to the pump and washed her face, neck, and arms thoroughly. This seemed to take some of the pain away…and anyway, she had to wash up for dinner, right?

When she went back inside, her father, Cassilde, and Guild Mother Kestra n'ha Piedra were seated at the wooden dinner table, making conversation with Gorsali. The good tablecloth—the one depicting bees frolicking in the woods—was out, and the best dishes and glassware were set out, too. And eight honey-cakes glistened in the middle of the table.

Clearly something important was in the offing. But what?

Fiona ate, not really tasting the meal. She even passed up the last two honey-cakes, as she knew Cassilde liked them; besides, Fiona wasn't hungry.

What was going on?

After Fiona helped Gorsali and Dominic clear the table—a nightly ritual all three enjoyed whenever her father was home from riding circuit—they went back to the table. Dominic brought out a small cask of ale, and poured five small glasses.

She looked again. Yes. There were *five* glasses. Not four.

She'd never been allowed to drink unwatered ale before, at least not with the adults…now she *knew* something was seriously wrong. But before she could ask, Dominic started talking.

"Fiona, we need to discuss something with you." His grey eyes were kind, unthreatening.

But Fiona saw that look in court all the time, usually before her father pronounced some criminal or other guilty and sent him to hard labor at the monastery—or some other dread fate. She distrusted it.

"What did I do wrong?" she yelped. She took a drink of ale to calm her nerves, but it was strong and she nearly gagged before it finally went down.

"Nothing, dear," Gorsali said, patting Fiona's hand as if Fiona were only a toddler. "But we need to decide your future. I'd hoped for a few more years alone with you—" she gave the others a stormy look "—before we needed to talk in earnest. You're only thirteen, after all. But—" She waved at Guild Mother Kestra, who took up the thread next.

"Fiona, dear, what do *you* want to do with your life?" Her dark eyes held nothing but interest. She seemed like she truly wanted to know.

So Fiona told her. "I want to be a judge. Like my father. And I definitely *don't* want to have to take care of the bees ever again!"

Kestra, Cassilde, and Dominic laughed, while Gorsali looked crestfallen. "I love the bees, dear…I'd hoped to show you what I see in them. You truly don't like them?"

"I'm not good with them, the way you are." How could Fiona say this without hurting her mother's feelings? She did love her, even if they didn't get along most of the time. "I always get stung. And it doesn't seem worth it—even though I know how important they are, that nothing would grow without them. I can see why you love them, even though I don't. But I do appreciate them."

"Don't forget the honey-cakes," Cassilde put in. "Evanda knows I don't." She patted her flat stomach. Fiona stifled a laugh, while Dominic's eyes twinkled. But when he turned to her again, his mien turned serious.

"So you want to be a judge, like me," he said. All eyes turned to him. "That's what I thought, child. But it won't be an easy road. Many people, most of them men, will be unhappy you've made this choice. You're prepared for this?"

"I don't know if anyone is truly prepared for anything," Fiona said, trying to keep the bitterness out of her voice. "But yes, I know there has never been a female judge. As far as I know, I'm the only female court clerk, too—even without portfolio. And I can't be an official one without seeing those records at Nevarsin—and I don't know how that can even *happen*. But yes, even with knowing all that, I want to be a judge more than anything."

Many questions followed, some about the law—when had Guild Mother Kestra learned about circumstantial evidence, anyway?—some about Fiona's thoughts on learning, and others, oddly enough, about the *cristoforos*. They even asked her what she thought of people with *laran*...not that Fiona knew that much about it, but legal precedent was clear: anything having to do with *laran* was dealt with by others with the same gift. And if, say, Neskaya Tower couldn't handle their own issues, they'd ask Arilinn for help...that was clear from what she and her father had discussed.

After thirty minutes of questions, Guild Mother Kestra said, "Enough. I can tell this is your heart's desire, child...and I think we've found a way to give you at least part of what you want."

"What does that mean?" Fiona asked. She hoped the table

completely hid how she'd clenched her fists. Would these adults ever get to the point?

"Another judge will be here in three weeks to test you, Fiona." Dominic's voice was level, even. His face gave away nothing. "He'll give you the same test I was given, years ago, when I became a court clerk—long before I became a judge. That means you'll have to go to Nevarsin's archives—"

"But...I'm not a Renunciate. Not yet..." She looked beseechingly at the Guild Mother.

"No, you're not. You won't be for years yet. But you can still go there—under your father's protection."

"What?" Fiona couldn't believe her ears. "They don't let girls in there!"

"They've made an exception," Dominic murmured. "Something about the additional labor I've been sending them through the court, I believe." His eyes twinkled.

"You'll have to cover your head, behave yourself, and stay beside your father at all times," Gorsali put in tartly. Her body was tense, but her eyes looked oddly peaceful, almost as if a weight had lifted from her shoulders. "You'll have to have a female chaperone stay with you while you study, too. Someone who's not a Renunciate, so I can't go with you. And you'll have to wear a long skirt. Even on the ride up there."

Before Fiona could erupt, her father spoke again. "Think of it as a judicial robe. I wear those all the time. It doesn't make me any less of a man. And it won't make you anything less of a woman, either."

"But—I've never worn a long skirt before. And I don't ride side-saddle!"

"I'll teach you," Cassilde put in. "I learned, years ago, and I've never forgotten. Though granted, I'd never thought this would be part of my teaching."

"Child, I wish there were another way," Mother Kestra said, her dark eyes kind. "But this is it—you have to take this test. Your father can instruct you, but he needs those materials at Nevarsin... Will you take this chance, even though you must humble yourself to do it? Or will you spurn it, and become less than you are? It's your choice."

"We'll give you a day to think it over, if you need it," her father said.

"I don't need any time," Fiona said. "I *have* to get to Nevarsin and study those records. So in service to the law—and to myself—" she gave the Guild Mother a long, steady look "—I will do whatever is required." *Even wear a long skirt,* she thought, stifling a shudder.

"Then it's settled," Dominic said. They all shook on it.

"I'll be by in the morning to teach you how to ride side-saddle," Cassilde told her. "I'll bring along a long skirt, too—it won't be fashionable, but the *cristoforos* won't care."

"I won't, either…I just want to study the law. Who cares what I'm wearing?"

"That's the spirit," Mother Kestra said, before turning to Gorsali and Dominic. "Thank you for an excellent evening, my friends." Then Kestra and Cassilde took their leave.

Cassilde arrived with the dreaded long skirt the next day, and brought a guest with her. The girl's name was Miralys Baker, as her parents made most of the bread everyone in Nevarsin ate, and she wore a long, dun-colored dress plus a pleated white headscarf, with a bright blue cloak atop it all. She looked much the same as anyone who might be a *nedestra* child of the *Hali'imyn.* Fiona hadn't any idea how Cassilde had acquired Miralys's services.

But before she could ask any questions, Cassilde made Fiona put on the long skirt. It was plaid, durable, and inoffensive—and as Cassilde had said, it was far from stylish, but it would do the job. And it was warm, which Fiona appreciated; even in midsummer, she was often cold. She also donned a matching plaid headscarf, to better conform to the monks' "delicate sensibilities," as Cassilde called them.

They walked to the nearest stable, where Fiona's trusty mare, Star, awaited them. She wore the dreaded side-saddle, and looked nearly as uncomfortable with it as Fiona felt…but Fiona knew from long practice that she must project confidence.

Otherwise Star would feel it, and who knew what would happen then?

She got on her horse, waited for Miralys to mount a roan gelding (also hampered with the side-saddle), and allowed Cassilde to walk the two of them up and back to the Guild House. As it was still early, they didn't see anyone on the streets save a few Renunciates and Miralys's mother Mistress Baker, who waved before ducking back inside her bakery.

Walking the horses slowly wasn't too difficult with the sidesaddle and the long skirt, Fiona found. But her balance on the horse was off, and Star felt it; worse yet, after she'd dismounted, her nether regions actually felt sore.

When she'd been a regular rider since the age of three!

"Why do I hurt so much?" she asked, feeling crabby but hoping she didn't show it.

Miralys, a raw-boned redhead, gave her a quizzical look. "Riding side-saddle takes different muscles than riding astride. It took me a while to learn this, too, last year. I'm sure you'll get it, in time."

"But I don't have much time," she murmured, before a sharp look from Cassilde quieted her. *This stinks*, Fiona thought. *Why must I wear these ridiculous clothes and ride side-saddle, anyway? Do the cristoforos care that much about proper deportment?*

The rest of the day went the way it normally did when her father was home. She took her place as his court clerk, and wrote down the day's proceedings. Then, afterward, she talked about what she'd witnessed with her father. Then they walked home, ate supper with her mother, and went to bed.

Tomorrow, she thought sleepily. *Tomorrow we go to the monastery.*

Tomorrow couldn't come fast enough to suit her.

As they rode toward the monastery, Fiona's thoughts roiled around in her head. *What if I can't learn this stuff in time? What if I fail? What will I do then?* But she couldn't say this, not to her father, and certainly not to Miralys, whom she barely knew.

"Don't worry, Fiona," Dominic murmured as they approached the monastery's entrance gate. "Everything will be all right. But let me handle these monks, all right? I know what to say to them."

"Of course, Da," Fiona said, while Miralys just nodded.

When they actually got to the gate, an officious, elderly monk stopped them. "What do you here? And why are these women with you? We don't allow—"

Dominic waved a hand, and said mildly, "I'm Justice Dominic macAnndra. The Reverend Mikael is expecting me, and these ladies also. Will you please allow us to enter?"

"This is quite irregular," the monk muttered. "Who did you say you were, again?"

Her father got out his judicial seal, and showed it to the monk. "I'm Justice Dominic macAnndra," he repeated calmly. "I'm expected. Please pass us through."

The monk gave them all a still, heavy-lidded look, but finally allowed them passage through the gate.

"What a rude little man!" Miralys said.

My thoughts exactly, Fiona agreed silently.

"The monks are, shall we say, a little behind-times in their thinking," her Da said, seemingly casual. But his posture was peculiar, and his face had flushed bright red. By these signs, Fiona knew her father was deeply unhappy over the confrontation they'd just endured. "Rest assured that Reverend Mikael promised me we'd have access to the archives, so we will. Have a little faith."

They stopped at the stable, where another monk helped them to stable their horses. This one seemed kind. But when Fiona tried to curry Star, as she always did after a ride, the monk waved her off. "Oh, no, miss," he assured her. "I'll take care of it for you."

She decided to accept this with outward good grace, but inside where it mattered, she seethed. Didn't that monk think she could handle her own horse? What was wrong with him?

Once they'd been ushered inside, her father was taken to an office of some sort while she and Miralys were forced to cool their heels in the hallway. But after only a few minutes, Dominic came back out again. His color was high again, and his shoulders were up and tight—her Da was agitated—but he assured them in a calm, deep voice that the Nevarsin archives were indeed open to the three of them. They would have two hours until lunch to study; then they'd have to leave for two hours, and could come back for two hours later on. They would be allowed no writing materials, either; they'd have to remember everything they'd seen.

Well, Fiona had somewhat expected that...if anyone could copy their archives out, willy-nilly, the *cristoforos* wouldn't have a monopoly on the information. But she knew better than to say that now; it wouldn't be polite.

Though goodness knows, these monks mostly hadn't been polite to them so far. Still, her mother would have sharp words if Fiona couldn't keep her temper leashed. So she did her best to project serenity, the same as her Da, and walked along as if nothing bothered her at all.

When they sat down inside the archives, a different monk, Cassio—a scholarly sort, Fiona thought, considering the ink stains on his hands—fussed over them, to the point Fiona wanted to scream.

But she couldn't lose her temper here. Her father was counting on her. And she really did need to see the archives.

She wrestled her temper down, and waited for the scholar to bring out what her father had requested. One scroll had nothing to do with the law—apparently this was something Miralys needed, as Dominic passed it right to her and kept going—but the others were all about how the Domains had been started. How law had been created, and about how the Courts of Arbitration had been set up. During the times of the Hundred Kingdoms, being a judge must've been absolutely fascinating!

Before she knew it, their first two hour study-block was up.

When Fiona started to argue over it, her father gave her a long, heavy-lidded look. She shut up, and instead thanked Cassio gently for his care.

This made the scholar smile faintly, but he did nothing other than bow over her hand, then Miralys's in turn. Then he waved them out again.

They went off in search of food, and found the main commissary. There were beans, plain brown bread, and watered ale. It was filling, but it wasn't very tasty. Apparently the monks knew far less about food preparation than did her mother. They were not allowed to speak during lunch.

In the hour between lunch and being able to dive back into the archives, they walked around the monastery's grounds. There was an interesting rock garden set up almost like a maze, and from the center, Fiona could see the tree line all the way down the mountain to Nevarsin proper. It was serene up here, if colder than Fiona preferred; there was still a goodly amount of snow on the ground, in fact, which was strange as Nevarsin itself had no snow to speak of at all.

"It's the higher elevation," Dominic told her, when she asked. "It's colder up here, so the snow sticks around longer."

She nodded. "That's sensible."

"Are you finding what you needed, Miralys?" Dominic asked the girl gently.

"I'm not sure," she mumbled. "Can you ask for the second file for me?"

"Of course I will," Dominic answered.

Fiona had no idea what they were talking about, but nodded anyway. It was good that Miralys get something out of this trip; otherwise, she was chaperoning Fiona for nothing.

But the whole idea of chaperonage burned inside her…why must she be chaperoned at all? Her father was with her, and he'd never harm her…why did these silly monks think she needed additional protection?

But it would be the height of rudeness to talk about it here. She'd have to wait until she got home. Of course.

And then, she'd need to talk about what she'd actually learned in the archives with her father. Or this experience would be wasted.

She vowed to study harder, and keep her head down. She couldn't change these monks, certainly not today…she knew that, but she was still quite frustrated.

Their next two-hour study session passed without incident. Then they were on their horses and riding out of there, just as the afternoon light was starting to angle down the mountain. She felt much freer once they'd passed the gates of the monastery, but did nothing other than to sigh and turn her head toward home.

Once they were back in Nevarsin, proper, they stabled their horses, bid goodbye to Miralys, and walked home. Fiona had many questions for her father, but didn't know how to even begin asking them.

Her Ma was not home yet, which was probably just as well. Fiona wasn't up to discussing this with her right now, or the Guild Mother either.

When they took off their cloaks and Fiona shook herself out of the hated headscarf, her father surprised her. "I know that wasn't easy, daughter," he said with an intent look. "The monks don't see you as a scholar. They see you as a young woman who needs to be protected. And they don't know how to see both at the same time, as I do…"

"You truly think I need protection?" Fiona asked, startled.

"Everyone needs protection, whether he or she realizes it or not," her father replied gently. "Otherwise, why study the law at all?"

"Good point," she admitted.

Then they hunkered down and studied for a few hours, until her mother returned with fresh chicken eggs for supper.

Over the next fortnight, Fiona, her father, and Miralys made the trek to the *cristoforo* monastery six more times. Every time, Cassio let them study a tiny bit longer, until on the final day, he surprised them all by allowing their party to stay an uninterrupted eight hours straight.

"Thank you very much for all your help, Brother Cassio," Dominic told the scholarly monk. "We truly appreciate it."

Cassio nodded, then took her father's arm to lead them outside. Once they had reached the stable, Cassio murmured, "My sister Angelica is a Renunciate down Thendara-way. She taught me, long before I came here, that women want much the same things as men. While she's not a scholar, she told me some were—and your daughter, Judge macAnndra, most definitely is."

Then before any of them could speak, he bowed to the three of them. "May the Holy Bearer of Burdens lighten your load. And may the young lady pass her test with flying colors." Then he smiled brilliantly, and went back inside to his duties.

"Well, that was unexpected," Dominic muttered. "But welcome, nevertheless." He helped the girls get their horses ready to go, as none of the other monks seemed to be about. Then they mounted, and left the monastery.

Two days later, the testing judge, Lorill di Asturien, came to Nevarsin with his wife, Miranda, his daughter, Cassilinde, and six men-at-arms. Fiona was at the bakery getting some good, white bread from the Bakers, as Judge di Asturien had sent word from Caer Donn that he'd be there soon, when they rode into town.

"That's the judge?" Miralys asked, deftly making change and wrapping up the loaf in clean linen. "He doesn't look like much."

No, Fiona decided, he didn't. He was short—her father must top him by at least a few finger-lengths—and his hair was already starting to gray at the temples. He wore traveling leathers, same as anyone might who had any sense at all...and his wife and daughter were garbed in sedate woolens, with only a tartan around the shoulders to show their family pride.

Then the judge looked toward the bakery, and Fiona was startled. She didn't know why, but his grey eyes somehow reminded her of Mother Kestra—they seemed those of a man who had power, and knew exactly how to wield it.

Fiona hurried home, carrying the wrapped bread under her arm. But the judge and his family beat her there (Fiona had no idea where the six guards had gone), and was already being greeted by her father and mother. All she could do was say stupidly, "Welcome, Judge di Asturien. Welcome, Mistress di Asturien," and nod at the daughter, as Fiona couldn't remember right now how she was supposed to address the daughter of a seated judge.

"Ah, but we are cousins, are we not?" Miranda di Asturien was raven-haired and blue eyed, and wore her dignity like a cloak. "Dominic, how could you not have told your daughter that—"

"It slipped my mind," Dominic admitted. "So glad to see you, cousin. And Cassilinde! My, how you've grown!"

The slight, dark-haired girl giggled nervously, but said nothing.

Fiona wasn't sure what to do. She'd never once thought that the judge who'd come to test her would be married to one of her father's distant cousins. But she knew she had to make them feel welcome; that was part of highlander hospitality. So she stuck out her hand, and prepared to say something gracious.

Instead of a handshake, Cousin Miranda pulled her into a hug. It felt strange, being hugged by a woman she didn't even know, but she endured it without complaint. This woman was part of the family; Fiona would just have to get used to her effusiveness, that was all.

"I'm so happy to meet you at last, Fiona," Miranda said warmly. "Dominic's letters have told me a great deal about you—"

But he's told me nothing at all about you, Fiona thought, but had the wit to keep back.

Her mother said brusquely, "I'm sure he's told you many things, Mistress di Asturien."

"Please, call me Miranda. We're family, after all!"

"Miranda, then," Gorsali said. Her eyes grew a trifle warmer. "Can I get you anything? Some tea or toast; something to break your fast?"

"My wife makes a great honey-cake," Dominic said fondly. "And we do have some ready, I believe—"

"I've heard much about your famous honey-cakes," the judge said with a smile. "But later would be better, I think. Right now I just want a bit of rest and a good, cold bath before we partake of your hospitality. Is there anywhere close by that you'd recommend?"

"We can put you up here, if you like," Gorsali said, exchanging a firm nod with her husband.

"But the Dew Drop Inn down the street has a very nice suite, and I reserved it especially for you," Dominic added smoothly. "I thought that would be far more comfortable for your family than our little place."

"Then let us go there," the judge proclaimed. "And we'll be back later. When would you like us to come back?"

"I'll have lunch ready in an hour," her mother told them.

"I look forward to getting to know you all better," Miranda said. Then she prodded her daughter, who mumbled something at Fiona.

"I look forward to getting to know all of you better, as well," Fiona replied.

Then, with the niceties observed, her father insisted on accompanying them to the inn. And Fiona wasn't able to ask him any questions.

Fiona helped her mother set the table. Six places; apparently Mother Kestra wasn't coming to this meeting. Was that good or bad? Fiona had no idea.

After the di Asturiens returned, they had some of Gorsali's good chicken soup along with the bakery bread, some new-made soft cheese, herbal tea and of course her mother's honey-cakes, of which the judge took two. Then, after everyone had eaten, the judge looked at Fiona and winked.

"We need to go get some rest, or I'd start in with the test questions today," the judge told her. "Can you wait one more day, Fiona?"

What was this? She was being asked if she could wait? Well, she could wait forever, if she must—but of course she wanted to take the test as soon as she could. The longer she waited, the more butterflies seemed to creep into her stomach…but all she said was, "Of course, sir. I completely understand."

"She's a well-spoken lass, isn't she?" the judge commented. "You two have raised her well."

"Thank you, I think," Gorsali said dryly. "It's mostly my husband's doing, you know."

The adults laughed, while Fiona exchanged glances with Cassilinde. Would these adults ever get to the point?

"Are you sure you want to do this?" the judge asked Fiona directly. "Even now, you can back out. We can do this another year."

Or never, Fiona thought.

"No, sir," she answered. "I want to take the test. But I can wait until tomorrow, when you've rested and refreshed yourselves."

"Just as I told you, husband," Miranda said, nodding firmly in Fiona's direction. "She's ready for this."

"I know *I'm* not," Cassilinde muttered, but Fiona pretended not to hear.

The day of the test finally arrived. Dominic brought Fiona to the Dew Drop Inn's common room, and left her there with Miranda di Asturien and Cassilinde, who'd apparently be her chaperones for the day. "I'm not allowed to stay, I'm afraid," he said with a sigh. "But if you want, I think I could talk Lorill into allowing your mother to sit with Miranda and Cassilinde."

"No, thank you," Fiona said. She felt quite nervous—would she remember all of those legal terms she'd learned at Nevarsin, that her father had quizzed her on? But she did her best to project calmness and serenity. "I'll be all right, Da."

So he turned her over to the women, and went to get Lorill di Asturien.

"You'll have three hours to answer all the questions my husband puts to you," Miranda said quietly as they waited. "The first part of the test is written. The second part is oral. When my husband starts asking you questions, my daughter and I will sit on the other side of the room. I will bring you water or tea if you need it in between the two halves of the test, and you will be allowed a quick snack if you need it also. Are you ready?"

"Yes, I am." Then Fiona had to ask, "How do you know so much about this?"

"Oh, I have my ways," Miranda said, conceding nothing.

Fine, be that way, Fiona thought.

Then the judge walked in, handed her two scrolls, a thick packet of vellum, a quill and a good supply of black ink, and the test proceeded.

Fiona looked at the first legal term—*jurae noveet curaea*—and her mind went blank. What did that mean again?

C'mon, she told herself. *You know this stuff backward and forward...you can do this!* Then she closed her eyes, put her hands to her temples, and concentrated hard.

Aha! She wrote, "The court knows the law."

The next question asked her to explain what she'd just translated meant. "It means," she wrote, "that the parties to a case do not need to understand how the law applies to them. The court itself is solely responsible for determining what laws apply, and why."

Over the next hour, she was asked a number of other questions. About what an *a fortioriae* argument meant; what *ab inaetio* meant; what any number of other legal terms she might come into contact with meant. Then she was tested on her knowledge of alphabetical and numeric filing—child's play—and her knowledge of written *casta* and *cahuenga*.

She'd just finished her last question when Judge di Asturien said, "Time's up. Pass me the vellum, please." She did so, he checked her answers, and told her, "So far, so good. We'll now take a brief recess."

As he hurried out to Goddess-knew-where, Miranda di Asturien said, "You're doing well, Fiona."

"But he didn't say anything, really," she protested.

"He'd have told you not to worry about the second half of the test if you hadn't passed, cousin," she was told.

"Oh." Then Fiona went to use the garderobe, had some herbal tea and a bit of bread, and readied herself for the second half of the exam.

When Judge di Asturien came back, he wore a fearsome frown. Before he could sit down or say anything at all, Miranda and the silent Cassilinde had relocated to the other side of the room.

Inwardly, Fiona quailed. But she did her best not to show that she was rattled.

"Why do you want to be a court clerk, Fiona macAnndra?" the judge asked in thunderous tones, still standing.

"I love the law, and wish to serve it with all my heart," Fiona told him.

"Not good enough," the judge said in a quieter tone of voice as he seated himself. "Try again, please."

She nerved herself to give him the best answer she could. Avoiding his eyes, she spoke.

"Sir, ever since I was a small child, I have loved the law. I used to go with my father every day to court when he was holding session here in Nevarsin...I'd ask him questions, and he'd answer them. Slowly, I started to learn about what to do when people argued. When two parties came to court and neither had 'clean hands,' my father told them gently to go home, that he could not help them...and I wanted to know why. I learned more and more, but it wasn't enough; I had to get to Nevarsin, to study the records there, and until recently I wasn't allowed to go." She swallowed hard, and finished with, "Those records have taught me there's so much more to learn. And I want to learn it all!"

The judge looked at her gravely, but said nothing.

"I want to help people, just like my father does. He understands the law, far better than I do. Through him, I can see what needs to be done, and I want to help him do that as a court clerk. I know there has never been a female court clerk here in the Hellers, but I want to be the first. I know I can do the job, sir."

"Why do you think you'll do a good job as a court clerk, Fiona macAnndra?"

This seemed to require a thoughtful response also. She sighed, and told him, "Because I've been doing the job now for over a year and a half. I've traveled with my father to Caer Donn, to the Ardais Domain, anywhere he's needed to go. And I don't just go there and fill out the forms he says to fill out; I observe what goes on in the court, and try to help him. My father says I have a talent for noticing body language, and has told me often that my observations help him. I don't know how to explain this any better; I just know that this is the job I want to do right now."

"And ultimately? What is your goal?"

"Sir, I want to be a judge. Just like my father."

Judge di Asturien laughed. "Miranda told me you'd say that...she was right."

"What does Cousin Miranda have to do with anything?" Fiona asked, wondering if she'd missed something. Then she ventured to ask, "Is the test over, sir?"

"Yes, yes. You've passed the test."

"But we still have an hour, and—"

"You don't need it. You've shown me already that you're ready, despite being only thirteen, to be an official court clerk."

"Thank you!" Fiona beamed, wishing her father was here to share her joy. And her mother, too—maybe she'd never have to go to the hives after this. "I'm so pleased!" Then she asked again, "But what does Cousin Miranda have to do with anything?"

Lorill di Asturien waved his wife and daughter over with a smile. Miranda and Cassilinde hurried over; both hugged Fiona fiercely.

"Tell her why you were sure Fiona wanted to become a judge, dear."

"Well, it's simple, Cousin Fiona." Miranda's eyes sparkled. "You see, you never asked my husband who *his* court clerk is...and it's me."

"But—but—you're not a Renunciate, and I thought—"

"No, I'm not. But I would've been, had I known about them before I married Lorill *di catenas*. And he knows it."

I can't wait to tell Mother Kestra and Cassilde about this! Fiona thought. But she only said, "So I'm not the first female court clerk?"

"Oh, no, dear," Miranda assured her. "Though you are the first regular court clerk in the Hellers...and down the line, you may just become our first female judge, too. I'd never bet against you." She winked.

"And I'm happy you passed the test, because that means I don't have to," Cassilinde put in. "My parents wanted me to follow in their footsteps, but I have no interest in the law at all, except not to break it."

Her parents sighed, then nodded their heads. Fiona could see this must've been a huge point of contention in their household

"I think I might take up beekeeping instead. Your mother's so enthusiastic about the bees, and she needs an apprentice…right?" Cassilinde asked hopefully.

Fiona hastened to agree, thinking, *How could this day possibly get any better?*